The assignation . . .

Sebastian softly eased open the door and found himself in a long corridor, sconced candles at intervals throwing a degree of light. At the end of the corridor a pool of bright light spilled from the wide landing from which the main gaming salons opened. Serena's note had said her bedchamber was at the front of the house. He was to look for a red ribbon around the door handle.

His step quickened with his heartbeat as he moved down the corridor, keeping close to the wall. The red ribbon was a splash of color against the cream paint of the door. He untied the ribbon and was inside the chamber before anyone could so much as detect his shadow. The room was in semidarkness, the only illumination a candle on the table beside the bed. Serena rose from the window seat, the soft folds of an ivory nightgown drifting around her, her hair long and loose framing her face.

"You came," she said.

"Did you think I would not?" He could feel the tension, the anticipation, build between them. "Why did you send for me, Serena?"

"Isn't it obvious?" she responded softly.

Turn the page for rave reviews of
Jane Feather's romantic storytelling . . .

"A poignant love story . . . strong characters, political intrigue, secrets and passion . . . it will thrill readers and keep them turning the pages."

—*Romantic Times*

A Wicked Gentleman

"Will enchant readers. . . . Filled with marvelous characters—and just enough suspense to keep the midnight oil burning."

—*Romantic Times*

"Intriguing and satisfying. . . . The captivating romance is buttressed by rich characters and an intense kidnapping subplot, making this a fine beginning for Feather's new series."

—*Publishers Weekly*

All the Queen's Players

"Beautifully moving . . . rich in period detail."

—*Booklist*

"A truly fantastic novel."

—The Romance Readers Connection

"Terrific."

—Genre Go Round Reviews

A Wedding Wager **is also available as an eBook**

Also by Jane Feather

JANE FEATHER

A WEDDING WAGER

POCKET BOOKS

New York   London   Toronto   Sydney

Pocket Books
A Division of Simon & Schuster, Inc.
1230 Avenue of the Americas
New York, NY 10020

This book is a work of fiction. Names, characters, places, and incidents are products of the author's imagination or are used fictitiously. Any resemblance to actual events or locales or persons, living or dead, is entirely coincidental.

This Pocket Books paperback edition July 2011

POCKET and colophon are registered trademarks of Simon & Schuster, Inc.

For information regarding special discounts for bulk purchases, please contact Simon & Schuster Special Sales at 1-866-506-1949 or business@simonandschuster.com.

The Simon & Schuster Speakers Bureau can bring authors to your live event. For more information or to book an event contact the Simon & Schuster Speakers Bureau at 1-866-248-3049 or visit our website at www.simonspeakers.com.

Cover design by Lisa Litwack; photo © Barry Marcus.

Manufactured in the United States of America

10 9 8 7 6 5 4 3 2 1

ISBN 978-1-4391-4525-8
ISBN 978-1-4516-5483-7
ISBN 978-1-4391-5550-9 (ebook)

A Wedding
Wager

Prologue

The young man had a spring in his step as befitted a man in love as he made his way down Charles Street, the raucous music of Covent Garden's Piazza filling the air around him. He was a tall, elegant young man, his tricorne hat edged with the same silver lace as his gloves, his coat and britches of deep gold silk, a fine pair of calves doing justice to silk stockings adorned with golden clocks.

It was a beautiful May morning, well suited to the pursuit of love, the new leaves on the trees still fresh and green, as yet untainted by the polluted atmosphere of the city with its foul-smelling sea-coal smoke mingling with the rotting odors of the open kennels. Windows stood open to the cool, fragrant air, and the throngs in the street seemed to wear a universal smile at the prospect of spring's new start.

Outside a tall, narrow house halfway along Charles Street, the young man paused for a moment, looking up at the building with an expectant smile on his lips. Then he ran lightly up the flight of steps to the front door and banged the knocker with all the confidence of a visitor assured of his welcome.

He had to wait a few minutes before the door opened slowly. "I give you good morning, Flanagan." He doffed his hat, his hair glinting gold in the bright sunshine as he greeted the elderly retainer and stepped swiftly past him, again with all the assurance of a welcome visitor. In the narrow hall, he stopped, his smile giving way to a puzzled frown. Bandboxes, trunks, and portmanteaus littered the floor.

"Is someone going somewhere, Flanagan?" He glanced over his shoulder at the retainer, who still stood at the half-open front door.

Before the man could respond, a harsh voice came from the shadows behind the staircase. "As it happens, Sullivan, yes. My stepdaughter and I are traveling to the Continent." A gentleman of middle years, with a thick crown of iron gray hair and the ramrod posture of a soldier, stepped into the light.

"This is rather sudden, is it not, sir?" The Honorable Sebastian Sullivan regarded General Sir George Heyward with sudden suspicion. "Serena said nothing to me about traveling when I saw her yesterday evening."

"I daresay Serena was unaware of my plans," the gentleman responded carelessly. "But she is aware of them now. I am afraid she's unavailable at present. She has much to do in preparation for our departure this afternoon."

"This afternoon?" The young man looked aghast. "I . . . I don't understand, General Heyward."

The general took a pinch of snuff before responding with a half-smile, "I see no reason why you should, Sullivan. My plans are no concern of yours."

Sudden anger sparked in Sebastian's clear blue eyes. "I consider Serena's plans to be very much my concern, sir."

"Then you are even more impudent than I gave you credit for, young man. You have no claim on my step-daughter now or ever."

Sebastian controlled his anger with a supreme effort. It was true enough. Serena was not her own mistress. She lived under the authority of her stepfather, who had made no secret of the fact that he barely tolerated the Honorable Sebastian's frequent visits to the house unless they concerned play at the tables in the gaming rooms abovestairs. "May I see her, sir?" He kept his tone moderate.

"She's too busy for visitors," Sir George responded with a dismissive gesture.

"I find that I am not, sir." A clear, light voice spoke from the stairs, and both men turned swiftly. The young woman who had stopped halfway down the flight, one hand resting on the banister, regarded them gravely. "Come up, Sebastian." She went back upstairs.

Sebastian didn't wait for the general's permission. He followed her at a run, taking the stairs two at a time. At the top, she turned aside into a small parlor that overlooked the street. The window stood open, and iron carriage wheels clattered on the cobbles below.

"Serena . . . Serena, my love, what is this?" Sebastian tossed his hat onto a chair and took a step forward, his hands outstretched. "What the devil did the general mean? He says you're going away this afternoon."

"Yes, we are." She made no move to take his hands, and after a moment, he let them fall, gazing at her in bewilderment. "To Brussels, I believe."

"Why?"

"Business affairs." She shrugged lightly. "Sir George feels that we can conduct our business better on the Continent. Who am I to disagree?"

"You can't go, Serena . . . you can't mean to go . . . what about us?" He stared at her, his eyes stricken.

She shrugged again. "Apart from the fact that I have no choice, Sebastian, I think I'm ready for a change. London grows tedious, and the play at the tables has lost its excitement here. The gamesters don't play as high as we need them to, and the authorities are becoming unpleasantly watchful. We need to move on."

"What about us?" he repeated, his voice strangely flat.

"What about us?" she responded. Her eyes were a startling violet in a complexion as smooth and pale as clotted cream, but they were without expression as she looked at him steadily. "We had an enjoyable dalliance, my dear, but that was all. All it could possibly be, given our circumstances. My stepfather would never consider an alliance with a penniless aristocrat, even if your family could be brought to contemplate taking one of faro's daughters into their midst."

She laughed without humor.

"Don't tell me, Sebastian, that you ever contemplated anything more than a pleasant but short-lived flirtation. Because I certainly did not. If I gave you that impression, then I am deeply sorry for it." She brushed a stray ringlet, black as a raven's wing, away from her cheek as she spoke.

Sebastian's face was suddenly ashen. "You know that's not true. I love you, Serena. You love me . . . you know you do."

She shook her head impatiently. "You're so young, Sebastian. What do you know of the world? I was afraid you would be upset, which is why I wanted to tell you myself, but believe me, my dear, I have never loved you. I cannot afford to love anyone. You will find the right woman soon enough. But I am not that woman."

Silence greeted her words, then he spoke very quietly. "I don't know you," he said. "I don't know you at all." He turned on his heel, picked up his hat, and left the parlor, closing the door softly behind him.

Serena stood still, staring at the closed door, her face expressionless, her eyes unreadable. The slam of the front door seemed to shake the house, startling her into movement. She went to the window, looking down on the street, watching as Sebastian strode towards the Piazza without a backwards look.

"You did your work well, I trust . . . sent him to

the right-about?" The general's voice behind her made her jump slightly. She didn't turn to face him, but her mouth was set, her shoulders rigid.

"As you ordered, sir." Her voice was cold. "Just as you ordered."

"I would not have imposed that interview upon you, but since you insisted on seeing him, you have only yourself to blame if it distressed you. Hurry now, we leave for Dover in one hour."

Chapter One

Jasper St. John Sullivan, fifth Earl of Blackwater, surveyed his twin brothers with a quizzical smile. "So, my dears, I've done my part, and 'tis up to you now to fulfill the terms of our esteemed uncle's will."

The Honorable Sebastian Sullivan raised a questioning eyebrow at his twin, who was staring blankly at the rich Aubusson carpet at his feet. "Well, Perry, Jasper has his bride. What are we going to do about finding our own?"

"It's insane, worthy of a bedlamite," the Honorable Peregrine declared, raising his eyes at last. Ordinarily serene, those deep blue eyes flickered with derision. "Somehow each of the three of us before the old man's death has to marry a woman in need of spiritual or moral salvation in order to share equally in his fortune. What kind of nonsense is that?"

"But think of that fortune," Jasper said gently, taking a pinch of snuff. "Nine hundred thousand pounds, my dear Perry, is not to be sneezed at." He dropped the enameled snuffbox back into the deep, lace-edged pocket of his coat.

" 'Tis riches almost beyond the dreams of avarice," Sebastian agreed with a short laugh. "But I'll believe it when I see it. 'Tis some trick of the devil, I'll lay odds."

"You could be forgiven for thinking that." Jasper chuckled. "Our esteemed uncle is the devil incarnate, whatever he might prate about repentance and his wholehearted return to the bosom of the church."

"But can we really take him on trust?" Sebastian pressed. "He could rewrite his will at any time, while we're struggling to turn some lost female onto the paths of righteousness."

Jasper shook his head. "No, I doubt that, Seb. Viscount Bradley has a strange sense of honor, and he'll not leave his fortune away from the family if he can help it. He just wants to watch us squirm." He set down his sherry glass on the mantel behind him. "Well, I assume you still have most of the five thousand pounds he gave you to aid you in your quest, so I suggest you get to it. There's no knowing how long the old man will last."

"Oh, he'll probably never give up this mortal coil, just to spite us," Sebastian declared.

His elder brother laughed. "He'll hang on as long as possible, you can count on that." He picked up his bicorne hat and silver cane on his way to the door. "I've a dinner engagement, so you must excuse me."

The door closed behind him, and the twin brothers regarded each other in silence for a moment. "So what now?" Peregrine asked. "I've been putting off even thinking about the whole ludicrous proposal, but Jasper's right. He has *his* bride, so we have to do our bit. But where do *we* start to look for our own fallen women? Not that I think, for one minute, that Clarissa was ever a fallen woman."

At that, Sebastian laughed, thinking of his elder brother's new wife. "No, I suspect you're right there. But London's teeming with the real article, Perry. Just take a stroll through the Piazza."

"I've never found whores appealing," his twin stated. "And I'm damned if I'm going to marry one, a fortune notwithstanding."

Sebastian grinned. "I'm not so nice in my taste, brother. A tasty tidbit from one of the better class of nunnery can provide fine entertainment. At least you know where you are with them." A shadow crossed his face, not missed by the ever-observant, ever-sensitive Peregrine.

Peregrine said nothing, although he knew his brother was thinking of Serena Carmichael, the woman he had loved, the woman who had cast him aside without explanation. In the three years since Serena's betrayal, Sebastian had amused himself as he saw fit but had never allowed a relationship with a woman to go further than superficial dalliance. He had chosen his mistresses from the ranks of the Cyprian corps, opera dancers and orange sellers, and once or twice had dallied with courtesans from the upper echelons of Society, but never anything serious.

Sebastian rose from his chair, stretching luxuriously before heading for the door. "Well, I'm on my way. Harley has a pair of chestnuts he's thinking of selling. I've a mind to look them over. They'd make a fine matched pair for that neat curricle I've been hankering after these last twelve months."

"How's that going to advance your search for the perfect bride?" His brother followed him to the door.

"The appurtenances of wealth, my dear brother, are irresistible to the kind of women we need," Sebastian said airily, stepping out onto Stratton Street. He set his hat on his head at a jaunty angle. "Will you come?"

Peregrine considered the question. "Oh, why not? I've nothing more interesting to do this afternoon."

"Your enthusiasm overwhelms me, brother." Sebastian waved his cane at a passing hackney.

Lord Harley was on the point of going out when the brothers arrived at his house on the Strand. He greeted them with a languid wave as they stepped out of the hackney. "Seb . . . Perry . . . to what do I owe the pleasure?"

"I've a mind to look over those chestnuts of yours, Harley, if you're still interested in selling 'em." Sebastian tossed a coin to the jarvey.

"To the right buyer, for the right price," his lordship said carefully. "Let's stroll over to the mews."

"You sure you haven't another engagement?" Peregrine asked. "Looks like you were going somewhere."

"Oh, nothing that cannot wait," Harley said. "There's a new gaming house just opened on Pickering Place. Thought I'd look it over later. A regular hell, they tell me."

"Who runs it?"

"Don't know exactly. Newcomers, as I understand it. Crawley was playing there last night . . . very high stakes, he tells me." Lord Harley turned into an alley that cut through to the mews at the back of his house.

Sebastian surveyed the match chestnuts with an experienced eye as they were paraded around the yard. "What d'you think, Perry?"

"I don't know. I think Jasper would say they were showy." Peregrine frowned as the animals were brought to a halt in front of them.

"Nonsense," Sebastian scoffed. He bent to examine the horses more closely, running his hand down their hocks, over their smooth, muscular flanks. "They're magnificent creatures, Harley."

"Five hundred guineas," his lordship said promptly.

Sebastian frowned. "I'll think about it," he said with a reluctant shake of his head. "I had it in mind not to spend above three hundred."

"Well, I'm in no hurry to lose 'em." Harley indicated to the groom that he should take the animals back to their stable. "Think it over, and let me know." He walked back down the alley and into the Strand. "Don't know about you both, but I'm devilish sharp set. Dinner at Whites, I think, then a visit to Pickering Place. What d'you think?"

"Not for me," Peregrine said. "I'm engaged to dine with a party at the Royal Society."

"Astronomers or scientists?" Sebastian inquired, not in the least surprised by his brother's engagement.

Peregrine laughed. "Neither. In this case, I am dining with two philosophers and a somewhat mediocre poet."

"Well, enjoy their company." Sebastian patted his brother's shoulder in companionable fashion. "I shall enjoy a good dinner and a visit to the gaming rooms in Pickering Place."

"Don't spend it all at once," Peregrine warned as he strode away.

"What did that mean?" Harley inquired.

Sebastian smiled. "Just a little fraternal teasing. Let's to Whites and dinner."

The coffee house was crowded, and the two men were quickly drawn into a group sitting at a long trestle table in front of the fireplace, where, despite the mellow early-autumn afternoon, a fire burned to heat a cauldron of steaming water suspended just over the flames, ready to refill the coffee pots ranged on a sideboard against one wall. Waiters dodged hither and thither with laden platters of roast mutton and carafes of wine. In one corner, the rattle of a dice cup was accompanied by the shouts of exuberant gamesters. In another, a more solemn group of players stared at the cards in their hands and made their bids in low tones.

Sebastian glanced around the room, acknowledging friends and acquaintances with a wave, before sliding onto the bench at the table and greeting his companions with upraised goblet. He held his own throughout the dinner-table conversation, but his mind was elsewhere. A third share of nine hundred thousand pounds was an almost unimaginable fortune, most particularly to one who had no private funds. Jasper, as head of the family, did his best to keep his brothers solvent from the diminishing revenues of the Blackwater estates, but he himself was, as he often bemoaned, in danger of incarceration in debtors' prison at the Fleet or Marshalsea. He seemed to make light of his predicament, but his younger brothers knew him too well to believe that the threat was not a very real one. And Jasper's situation was exacerbated by the demands made upon him by the extended family, who all seemed to believe that his lack of generosity stemmed from miserliness rather than genuine lack of funds.

In order to realize the fortune dangled in front of them by their eccentric uncle, all three brothers had to fulfill the terms of the will. All three had to convert and marry women who had somehow strayed from the straight and narrow.

Why the devil had the old man come up with such a devious scheme? Jasper had a theory, and it seemed reasonable enough. Viscount Bradley had been the black sheep of the Blackwater family since he was a very young man. No one seemed to know why anymore, but his name was never mentioned within the family. Bradley's response had been to cut all ties with his family himself and take himself off to India, where he'd made his fortune as a nabob, merely adding to the family's disgust. The idea of a Blackwater in trade was anathema to the high sticklers, and the rumors about the young viscount's dissolute life were anathema to the moral arbiters in the family. And, as Jasper had pointed out rather sourly on several occasions, there were more than enough of those showering shocked criticism upon any family member who strayed even an inch from the straight and narrow.

Jasper's theory was that this devious plan of their uncle's was a piece of pure vengeance. By forcing three highly unsuitable and less than upright women on the Blackwater family, Bradley could go chuckling to his grave. Jasper's unsuitable bride would, of course, be the crown jewel in his plot. Jasper was head of the family, and his countess would take precedence over every other woman in the family, however high in the instep. The idea of those women compelled to give precedence to an erstwhile whore was a prime jest. And the cream of it was that the viscount's fortune, earned in the grubby world of trade, would go to rescue the family fortunes. Even the three brothers could enjoy the idea of it. But putting it into practice was a rather different matter.

"Sebastian . . . Sebastian . . . pass up the wine, man. We're dying of thirst up this end of the table."

Sebastian snapped out of his reverie with a muttered

apology and pushed the carafe up the table. He speared a forkful of roast mutton and doused it liberally with onion sauce.

"Sullivan and I are going to try out that new hell on Pickering Place," Lord Harley announced, refilling his goblet. "Anyone care to accompany us?"

"The play will be too rich for my blood. I'm out of funds for the quarter," a young man grumbled from across the table. "I'll be lucky if I can play anything but silver loo for the next two months." He buried his nose in his goblet.

"You're wise to stay away from Pickering Place in that case, Collins," Lord Harley said. "From what I hear, they have tables where the stakes start at a thousand guineas."

Sebastian whistled softly. He had set his own limit for the evening at a hundred guineas. He was tempted to change his mind and avoid Pickering Place, but gambling was not in his blood, and he knew, win or lose, he would not be tempted to play higher than his limit. He'd go, he decided, and if the play was far too high for him, then he'd simply leave.

He and Harley acquired two other curious gamesters at the end of dinner, and the four of them set off for Pickering Place. They strolled down St. James's Street, chatting amiably in the soft evening air, and turned onto Pickering Place. The house was a handsome building, nothing in its discreet outward appearance hinting at the illegal activities behind its grand double frontage.

Lord Harley ran his cane along the highly polished railing leading up to the double doors as he observed, "Nothing to draw unwelcome attention here. The owners obviously know what they're about."

Sebastian nodded agreement. Private gambling clubs restricted to members only were one thing, but gambling houses run for profit and open to anyone who could afford the stakes were illegal, although in the absence of a public disturbance, they were rarely troubled by the law. The more high-toned the establishment, the greater the stakes and the more elevated the clientele, none of whom would readily risk being caught in a raid by the officers of the watch.

"Shall we go in?"

The door was opened by a liveried footman in powdered wig who bowed them into a pillared, marble-floored hall from which an elegant divided staircase rose to a galleried landing and sparkling chandeliers poured light from the frescoed ceiling. Strains of music drifted from above, together with the subdued murmur of voices. Double doors stood open to a large supper room to the right of the hall.

Sebastian and his friends unsheathed their swords and laid them in the long racks set up along one wall. Armed men in a gambling establishment, where tempers could run as high as the stakes, were clearly an unacceptable risk. They strolled up the staircase and through the double doors of a large salon at the head of the stairs. A waiter proffered a tray of rack punch and champagne, and they stood for a moment absorbing the scene.

The salon was set up with gaming tables, groom porters moving among them, calling the odds in hushed tones. A soft murmur of voices rose from the tables, with the click of dice and the snap of cards. Further rooms opened off the main salon, where smaller tables were occupied by pairs playing piquet.

Sebastian's companions wandered away into the depths of the salon, pausing at the various tables, assessing the odds. Sebastian remained at the door, looking around with a knowledgeable eye. The expenses of an establishment such as this one, with waiters, fine wines, elegant suppers, would be more than a thousand guineas a year at the very least, he calculated. The owners would need to run a very successful faro bank to realize any profit. And often enough, the most successful faro banks were rigged in some way in the bank's favor.

He sipped his punch and then took a step into the room. He stopped. A tall young woman in a gown of pale lavender silk, opened over an underdress of violet silk that exactly matched her eyes, was in the act of drawing two cards from the dealer's box at a table at the far end of the salon. Her unpowdered hair, black as a raven's wing, framed her face in a cluster of side curls.

Sebastian stood as if mesmerized, and almost as if drawn by a lodestone, the young woman's gaze moved from the cards on the table in front of her to look across the crowded salon. Her eyes met his, and for a moment, it was as if the intervening three years had never happened, except that she was even more beautiful than before.

He took a step towards her, and she dropped her eyes, turning her attention back to her table of gamblers. At the same moment, General Sir George Heyward stepped in front of Sebastian. "So, Sullivan, are you here to play?"

Sebastian's eyes held naked loathing, but his voice was cool and composed. "So you are returned from the Continent, General."

"As you see," the general agreed. "Are you here to play, sir?"

Sebastian ignored the repeated question. "Your business must have prospered, Sir George, for you to be able to set yourself up in London with such opulence."

"Aye, it did, but that's no business of yours, Sullivan." A smile flickered over the general's thin lips. "Allow me to take you to a table, where I have no doubt you will find some congenial play." He laid a hand on Sebastian's arm and directed him away from Serena's table.

Sebastian made no demur. The moment he had seen her again, the residual anger at her treatment on that last occasion had surged into bright flame once more. He had been a lovesick moon calf then, barely four and twenty, but he was now that much older, wiser, more experienced, and he could laugh at the immaturity of such a passion. Neither Serena nor her stepfather need fear that he would be renewing his attentions. Without casting a further glance in Serena's direction, he allowed his host to seat him at a hazard table. It was not a game he cared for, based as it was on pure chance, but it would keep his mind off a fickle, black-haired beauty.

Serena had prepared herself for the inevitable encounter with Sebastian, or so she had thought. Three years was a long time, she had told herself. Sebastian could be married with a hopeful family by now. She had never mentioned his name to any of the English travelers who had passed through the various salons of Europe where she and her stepfather had played their games, and in turn, she had heard no mention of any of the Sullivan brothers. She looked back on the brief months of their loving idyll as the dream time of a naïve pair of youngsters who had yet to cut their teeth on the real world. The last three years had forced her into adulthood, and she knew she viewed the world now through eyes wide open and cynical, unflinching in their acceptance of the general duplicity of life.

And yet she had felt Sebastian entering the room before she had seen him. Her skin had lifted, prickles running down her spine. In that moment when their eyes had met, the last three years melted away. He was as handsome as ever, with that golden hair and those penetrating blue eyes, the rangy, lean length of him still slender, supple as a willow, and when he had taken that involuntary step towards her, her heart had seemed to jump into her throat. Then it was over. Her stepfather had moved in front of him, blocking her view, and the vision was gone.

Her hands shook a little now as she dealt the cards, and her usually focused mind wandered from calculating the odds as the cards played out in front of her. The worst was over, she told herself. The first encounter was always going to be the most awkward. There was no real need for them even to speak to each other, beyond maybe a bow, a murmured courtesy as between very distant acquaintances. She would not be caught off guard again.

Her loss of concentration caused the bank's loss in the play, something she should not have allowed to happen, but she told herself that once in a while, it was good to show that the bank wasn't unbeatable. Even inveterate gamesters would eventually refuse to play at a table where the faro bank was the inevitable winner.

The clock struck nine, and she looked towards the double doors where the butler now stood, ready to announce the first supper. She smiled around the circle of players. "Gentlemen, may I suggest we go downstairs for supper? A break from the cards will refresh us all."

The men agreed willingly enough, casting down their cards, pushing back chairs. "May I escort you, Lady Serena?" A young viscount bowed eagerly, proffering his arm. His powdered wig crowned a cherubic countenance that belied the heavy-lidded, red-rimmed eyes of a man well into his second bottle of burgundy.

"Thank you, Lord Charles." Serena laid her gloved hand lightly on his brocade sleeve and led the way out of the salon, down the wide staircase, and into the lavishly appointed supper room. She moved among her guests as they nibbled from the dishes arrayed on the long buffets, sipped champagne and the finest Rhenish and burgundy, her eyes everywhere, noting when platters or decanters needed refilling.

General Heyward was everywhere at once, exchanging ribald comments with the gentlemen, offering flowery compliments to the ladies, refilling glasses himself with all the genial bonhomie of the perfect host. Any outsider would assume that this was an elegant, extravagant private party with the most hospitable hosts, instead of a carefully designed entertainment whose single object was to fleece as many guests as possible in the salons abovestairs. They would all pay well for the elegance of their supper.

Sebastian and his friends descended with the rest of the company to the supper room. He lingered for a moment in the doorway, covertly watching Serena as she played her part to perfection under the brilliant light of myriad candles. He found himself trying to find things to criticize. Maybe she was still as beautiful as ever, but something had changed. There was a hardness that hadn't been there before, he thought her laugh had a brittleness, and those wonderful, luminous violet eyes were warier. But her hair was the same deep blue-black, her figure as tall and graceful as ever, and he couldn't tear his gaze away from her.

"Seb . . . Seb . . ." Lord Harley lightly punched his upper arm, hauling him out of his reverie. "Are you staying for supper or not?"

Sebastian dragged his gaze away from the woman across the crowded salon. She was laughing at something, some supposed witticism of the cherubic young viscount downing a large bumper of burgundy, and for a moment, he had to suppress a violent urge to go to her, to drag her out into the street, to force something . . . something, he didn't know what . . . to happen between them. Something real and true, at any rate. Not that last cold, artificial parting that had had no truth to it.

"No," he said abruptly. "No, I'm not staying." He turned on his heel and returned to the hall to retrieve his sword. He sheathed it as he left the house, the door closing firmly behind him.

The cool night air cleared his head a little as he walked briskly down St. James's Street. It was still early by the standards of London's players, not yet midnight, and yet Sebastian could think of nowhere he wished to go, no entertainment among the many on offer that would please him. He was in no mood for company, or at least, not that of his friends. He turned off St. James's Street into an alley. Halfway down, light spilled from the open door of a tavern, and the sounds of raucous voices raised in merriment heavily laced with obscenities filled the narrow lane.

Sebastian pushed his way through the throng blocking the doorway. A heavy-set man, objecting, grabbed him by the arm. Sebastian turned his head and regarded this obstacle to his progress in cold silence. His free hand rested on his sword hilt. There was a moment of wordless confrontation, but something in the younger man's eye, a certain reckless gleam, as if he were inviting the man to provoke him further, caused the heavy-set man to drop his hand, murmur something akin to an apology, and step aside. Sebastian elbowed his way to the rough-hewn bar counter and demanded a pint of porter. It came quickly, and he leaned back against the counter, drinking the rough liquor, looking sightlessly over the rowdy taproom. No one approached him.

The porter did little to alleviate his mood. He drained it with a grimace, tossed a coin onto the counter, and pushed his way back out into the alley. As he started back towards St. James's Street, he felt something, a flicker of sensation at his back.

He spun around and grabbed a skinny child who was about to dive back down the alley. "Just one minute." Sebastian tightened his hold. A grimy-faced urchin looked up at him with wide, frightened eyes.

"Beg pardon, sir." The child suddenly twisted, bent his head, and bit Sebastian's hand. Sebastian let go with a yelp. The lad ducked away and with a sinuous twist was off down the alley. Sebastian realized instantly that the small coin purse he kept in an inside pocket of his coat was missing.

"Fool," he castigated himself, examining his hand. The skin was not broken. He looked back down the alley. As he'd expected, there was no sign of the pickpocket. They were so small and quick, these street children, they could disappear into a hole in a wall barely big enough for a cat. It was an ordinary enough occurrence if one ventured into the back alleys. He should have been more alert. But oddly, the incident had restored some part of his customary equanimity. It had brought him back to earth, anyway.

He walked back up the wider, brighter thoroughfare of St. James's Street towards the lodgings he shared with Peregrine on Stratton Street.

Candlelight shone from the long windows of the sitting room at the front of the narrow house. The front door opened directly on the street, and Sebastian let himself into the narrow hall. "Perry . . . you in?"

"Aye, in here."

Sebastian pushed open the door to the small but comfortably appointed sitting room. Peregrine was reading in a deep armchair beside the grate where a small fire burned to combat the night's chill. The contents of a brandy goblet on a small table beside him glowed amber in the candlelight.

Perry greeted his brother with a smile, closing his book over a finger to keep his place. "Good evening?"

Sebastian shrugged slightly. "So-so." He filled a goblet from the decanter on the sideboard and took the chair opposite his brother. "Harley and I visited the Pickering Place hell."

Peregrine looked a little alarmed. Something was troubling his brother, and he could think of only one thing. "Did you lose too much?"

"No." Sebastian shook his head dismissively. "You know me, Perry. I like the excitement, but I hate to lose more. At the tables, I'm as timid as an infant and as tight-fisted as a miser. The play was far too rich for my blood. More in Jasper's line."

"Jasper don't like to lose, either," Perry pointed out, stretching his feet on the andirons.

"Jasper, my dear, don't lose," his twin retorted smartly, and they both laughed. Their elder brother had a gift for the cards.

Sebastian swirled the brandy in his goblet, watching the light play across the amber surface. Peregrine watched him. Eventually, Peregrine said, "So, what is it?"

His brother didn't raise his eyes, said only, "Serena and that damned stepfather of hers are running the hell."

A shiver of apprehension touched Peregrine's spine. He looked closely at his twin, and the apprehension grew stronger. Sebastian had the same bleak expression that had haunted his face for so many dreadful months three years ago. Neither of his brothers had been able to get close enough to his unhappiness then to help him. His previous happiness, on the other hand, he'd been more than willing to share. For close to a year,

Sebastian had been deliriously happy with the woman he described without embarrassment as the love of his life. Jasper had raised an elder brother's skeptical eyebrow and murmured something about puppy love, but he'd done nothing to quell Sebastian's joyful exuberance. Perry had merely enjoyed his twin's happiness and been delighted for him. They had shared in each other's highs and lows all their lives.

And then something had happened, and Sebastian's world had come crashing down. When pressed, he had said only that Lady Serena and her stepfather had left the country, and neither of his brothers could get anything further from him. They had watched and waited until eventually the pain had eased, the bleakness had left Sebastian's eyes, and he had plunged wholeheartedly back into the whirling social scene. There had been an edge of wildness for a while, but gradually, the Sebastian they both knew and loved had been restored. He was his old amused and amusing self.

And now Peregrine, looking at his brother's expression, feared that the bad times were beginning again, and he was filled with anger at the woman who, having so callously abandoned his twin, should now reappear to break open the old wounds.

"You won't be playing there, then, I assume," Peregrine said neutrally, reaching for his glass.

Sebastian raised his eyes and gave his brother a cool smile. "As I said, Perry, the play on Pickering Place is too rich for my blood."

Chapter Two

"Well, I must say, my dear, that bonnet looks very well on you." Marianne Sutton nodded, her towering and elaborately powdered coiffure swaying precariously, as she regarded her only daughter with complacence. "Such a pretty little thing as you are, 'tis no wonder the general has taken such a fancy to you."

"Mama, I don't believe he has," Miss Sutton protested, blushing to the roots of her fair curls. "Indeed, General Heyward is . . . is far too used to . . . to fashionable women to find anything pleasing in me." What she meant was that the general was old enough to be her grandfather and could have absolutely no appeal for a young girl of barely seventeen hovering on the brink of her first London Season.

"Nonsense, child." Mrs. Sutton snapped her fan at her daughter. "You mark my words, once the general has returned to London, your father will bring him up to scratch before Christmas." She sighed pleasurably, leaning back against the leather squabs of the very fashionable barouche, raising her lorgnette to look around the thronged street as they drove up Piccadilly, her attention piqued to catch an eye of even a nodding acquaintance.

If they were to launch the dear child as they wished, her dear husband, the admirable Mr. Sutton, had told her to miss no opportunity to ingratiate herself with London's fashionable world. He would ensure their enterprise did not lack for funds but, being a bluff and somewhat down-to-earth fellow himself, was more than happy to leave the social side of the business to his wife, who had some pretensions to move, if not in the upper circles, at least in the next tier down.

"Ah, I believe that is Lady Barstow . . ." She bowed, smiling, to a passing landaulet, receiving the merest nod in response. Her smile faded, and her voice took on an acid edge. "What a sorry-looking carriage. You'd think Lord Barstow would set his wife up in a more commodious vehicle. Quite the drab she looks."

Abigail said nothing. It was always better to let her mother's tongue follow its own path. She tucked herself up into a corner of the barouche and was content to observe the passing scene. She had been in London only three weeks, and it was still a city of wonderment. She never tired of gazing into the shop windows with their lavish merchandise or watching the ladies, often followed by little black pages, maneuvering their wide-hooped gowns through narrow doors. The gentlemen were for the most part magnificent creatures, with their powdered wigs and embroidered coats with deep-turned back cuffs, jeweled pins nestling in rich lace cravats.

She yearned to be part of this scene, to move confidently among these glorious butterflies, to acknowledge bows and greetings with her own graceful curtsy and sophisticated tilt of the head, but as yet she had not made her debut. London was still thin of company, as the Season would not officially begin until after the opening of Parliament, and their social life was limited to her parents' friends and those few acquaintances they had made during their two months' sojourn on the Continent.

Abigail had not cared for Paris, and even less for Brussels. The foreign tongue, so fast and strange, made her head ache, and the people were all so supercilious they seemed to look right through her. Except for General Sir George Heyward and his stepdaughter, Lady Serena, without whom Abigail had often thought she would have died of boredom. But Serena had introduced her to the libraries and the musical salons. She had accompanied her shopping, gently teaching her what suited her and what didn't. She was so much more worldly, knew so much more than Mama about prevailing fashion, it had been like having an elder sister. They had promised to be in touch as soon as they had returned to London, and Abigail waited every day for the knock that would bring the visiting card that would open this world to her.

But so far, it had not come. General Heyward knew

where they were lodging—her father had made a point of giving him the address before they left Brussels—but perhaps the general and his stepdaughter had not yet returned to London. They were still in Brussels when the Suttons had left on a packet bound for Dover. It was an infinitely preferable explanation to the thought that once in London, Lady Serena had forgotten all about her protégée.

Or perhaps there was something not right about their London address. Perhaps it was an address that no lady of quality would visit. This thought haunted Abigail. What did her father know of the fashionable residential streets of London's ton? He was a bluff, good-natured merchant from the Midlands, wealthy enough after years of shrewd business practices and careful acquisitions to satisfy his wife's social aspirations. Aspirations that could not be satisfied among Staffordshire's County set. To give Marianne her due, as he had often acknowledged, her aspirations were more for her daughter than for herself. And William Sutton was a very proud father, who doted on his golden-haired angel of a child.

Nothing but the best would do for Abigail, so she had been sent to a school for young ladies, far away in Kent, where she had been wretchedly homesick, but the Midland vowels had been knocked out of her speech, and she had been made to walk with books on her head until her back was ramrod straight and her head beautifully poised on a swanlike neck. A few weeks on the Continent had been intended to round out her education and prepare her for a London debut. Occasionally, Marianne allowed herself to dream of her daughter's presentation at a Drawing Room, if somehow they could move in circles where a patroness could be found to present Abigail. If such a miracle occurred, then so, too, could vouchers for Almack's. It was a far-fetched dream, Marianne had to acknowledge, but London Society encompassed more than the Upper Ten Thousand. There were gentlemen aplenty, minor aristocrats, impoverished for the most part, who would exchange their name and breeding for the fortune that would devolve upon William Sutton's daughter.

General Sir George Heyward, whose late wife had been the widow of an obscure Scottish earl, could be considered a little old for Abigail, but his credentials were impeccable. He got along famously with William, whom he introduced to the military gentlemen littering the salons and clubs of Brussels, and his stepdaughter, Lady Serena, was clearly out of the top drawer, a perfect example and mentor for Abigail. Marianne swallowed what misgivings she had about the general's age and concentrated her mind on the delightful prospect of a well-married daughter who had the entrée into social circles that she herself could only dream of.

"I do hope General Heyward has not misplaced the card your father gave him." Marianne spoke directly to her daughter's thoughts, startling her.

"He did not say when he and Lady Serena would be returning to London, Mama."

"No . . . no, true enough. But it has been three weeks

already." Marianne's voice was fretful, and she began to tap her gloved hands on her knee, warmly covered with a woolen lap rug.

"Perhaps the address on Bruton Street is not one the general would care to visit." Abigail gave voice to her fear, trying to make her tone light and careless, as if, of course, she were in jest.

"Nonsense, my dear. Your father had it on the best authority that Bruton Street is a most select address. And you must agree, the house is very elegant and well furnished."

Abigail nodded. It was true, but she was less confident of her father's *best authority*. She loved him dearly, but from the first weeks at the school in Kent, she had been forced to acknowledge that his manners left much to be desired, and his bluff good humor would come across as rough and countrified in more sophisticated company. It stood to reason that those whose opinions he relied upon would not necessarily move in the elegant circles of high fashion.

The barouche drew up outside the house on Bruton Street, and Abigail was obliged to acknowledge that with its gleaming paintwork and brass, its sparkling windows and flourishing window boxes, it certainly gave the appearance of a gentleman's residence. She followed her mother into the house, the footman in their wake laden with parcels.

At the sound of their steps on the parquet, the door to the library opened, and the jovial figure of William Sutton loomed large, beaming at them, one hand resting on his ample paunch. "Ah, there you both are . . . looking as lovely as ever. What have we here . . . a few trinkets, I daresay. I'll be lucky if you don't bankrupt me between you." He laughed heartily at this witticism. "So, have you had a pleasant outing, my dears?"

"Very, thank you, Papa." Abigail stood on tiptoe to kiss his cheek. "And I promise we won't bankrupt you . . . just a scarf and some new ribbon for an old bonnet and a piece of lace to touch up Mama's blue gown."

"Oh, I spoke in jest, puss, you know that." He chuckled and patted her cheek. "Nothing is too good for you. Indeed, you should be buying new bonnets, not refurbishing old ones. Shame on you, Mrs. Sutton. I said no expense was to be spared."

"And none has been, my dear sir." His wife soothed him with a well-practiced hand. "Go back into the library, and I'll have Morrison set out a light repast. It's been several hours since breakfast, and you know how hungry you get. Dinner will not be served until six o'clock. We live by London hours now, you must remember."

"How could I forget?" William said with a mock grimace. "How a man's to eat his dinner that late and then sleep afterwards, I'll never understand."

"But in general, Papa, people in Society do not sleep immediately after dinner. They rarely seek their beds until two or three in the morning, sometimes not even until the sun is up." Abigail tried to keep a wistful note out of her voice at the thought of such nighttime revelry but failed.

Her father looked at her sharply. Then he shook his head. "Well, I can't be doing with it, I'll tell you that. But you young things . . . another matter . . . quite another matter. But I'll not have you getting all haggard and drawn, my girl, with all these late nights. Just you remember that."

"Oh, I will, Papa." Abigail dropped a curtsy, giving him a dimpling smile that made him laugh again and call her a minx. Then she turned and hurried up to her own chamber.

She untied the ribbons of her bonnet and tossed it onto the bed before going restlessly to the window. The street below was quiet, but she could hear the sounds of London, the iron wheels on cobbles, the raucous calls of barrow boys, chairmen, and piemen, the shouts of jarveys as they drove their hackneys through the unruly traffic.

Abigail didn't want to be in the serenity of her chamber or even on the quiet residential street below her window. She was in London, the world at her feet, and she was cooped up waiting for someone to produce the key to the door. But she could take a walk for herself, surely? Along Piccadilly, which was not very far away, just at the end of the street, really. She took walks alone at home all the time. She would be quite safe.

Abandoning her bonnet, Abigail ran softly downstairs, hoping not to meet a servant. She flew across the hall and pulled open the front door. Miraculously, no one had come into the hall. She stepped outside onto the top step and breathed deeply. Conscience told her she should not be doing this, at least not without an escort. This was London, not the provincial town she was used to. She could have demanded the company of a footman, or even her maid, but a recklessness was in her blood, unusual because, in general, she was not one to stir the waters. She tossed her head, relishing its bonnetless freedom, and set off up the street, walking quickly, looking behind her once or twice, half expecting an arresting shout. But she reached the end of the street undetected and turned down towards Piccadilly.

Already the scene was livelier, the sounds of the city noisier. People glanced curiously at the well-dressed young woman, hatless and coatless and unescorted, but Abigail didn't care; it merely added to the excitement of the adventure.

She walked slowly along Piccadilly, looking in the shop windows, ignoring the stares, until a young buck in a flamboyant gold-and-scarlet-striped waistcoat put up his quizzing glass and ogled her, beckoning to her. She turned away with a toss of her head and increased her pace, aware as she did so that he was following her. Suddenly frightened, she ducked into a narrow opening and found herself in a noisome court, enclosed on four sides by the high brick walls of surrounding buildings.

Her eyes darted from side to side as panic threatened to engulf her. A slatternly woman leaned against a wall at the far side of the court, watching her, a corncob pipe between her lips. Beside her, a man leaned, whittling a piece of wood. They both regarded the new arrival with a speculative air.

Abigail turned to run back the way she had come and found herself confronting the man in the striped waistcoat. "Well, well, what pretty little thing have we here?" he asked. His voice was rather unpleasantly high, with a whining note that set her teeth on edge.

"Let me pass, sir," she demanded as confidently as she could, but she could hear the tremor in her own voice.

"Oh, I don't think I wish to do that," he said, holding her upper arms tightly. "That would be looking the proverbial gift horse in the mouth. Such a tasty tidbit to run into my arms. Let's have a kiss, chuck." He bent his head, the full, glistening mouth descending.

Abigail screamed and kicked at his shins. She could smell the wine on his breath, his sweat overlaid by a heavy perfume. She screamed again just as his mouth engulfed hers, and she thought she would suffocate in the vile, heated stench of him.

And then he was spinning away from her, falling back against the wall, spluttering. A voice said quietly, "Are you hurt, my dear?"

She let her hand drop from her mouth, where she had been desperately rubbing at the imprint of those foul lips, and looked at her savior. A young man, his fair hair tied at his nape with a black velvet ribbon, shining in the gloomy courtyard, bent his concerned blue eyes upon her. And Abigail thought she had never before seen such a beautiful creature.

"No . . . no, I don't think so, thank you, sir," she stammered.

Sebastian blinked at the well-modulated tones of a young woman of breeding. He had assumed the buck's victim had been a servant girl running an errand or even a denizen of a Covent Garden nunnery, but now, as he took in the girl's clothes, the freshness of her complexion, the elegance of her speech, he realized he had been mistaken. Her assailant, still bent double against the wall, coughing and choking as he struggled to get breath back into his lungs after the powerful blow to the pit of his belly, had obviously assumed that a lone young woman, hatless and seemingly fancy-free, was fair game.

"Come." Sebastian took the girl's arm and led her out of the fetid court and back into the sunlit street, where the air immediately smelled fresher, and Abigail's breathing slowed, the panic fading.

"Where is your maid . . . your governess . . . whoever's with you?" Sebastian asked, looking up and down the street.

Abigail shook her head reluctantly. She knew what this man would think of her the minute he realized she was alone. "I . . . I came out alone," she confessed, hanging her head. "I only wanted to be free for a little while."

Sebastian regarded her in silence for a moment. He understood the desire; it had often struck him that women, young women in particular, must find the restrictions on their movements unendurable at times. Even Serena, who had more freedom than most women, obeyed certain social conventions. Or had done, he amended. He didn't know what she did now.

"Where do you live?" he asked finally.

"Bruton Street."

He nodded. As he'd assumed, a most respectable address. "Your family will be beside themselves with worry." He hadn't really considered the comment in the nature of a reproof, but the girl's china-blue eyes welled with tears, and her lip trembled. She was little more than a child, he realized, and presumably had acted as impetuously as any child.

"I don't mean to scold," he said hastily. "'Tis hardly my place to do so, but I will escort you home now." He offered her his arm with a small bow that went a long way towards restoring Abigail's dignity. "Sebastian Sullivan at your service, ma'am."

Abigail managed a small curtsy. "Abigail Sutton, sir. And I am most truly grateful for your assistance."

He laughed, but not in mockery. "'Tis a pleasure, Miss Sutton."

On the short walk to Bruton Street, Sebastian learned a great deal about Abigail Sutton. She had recovered her equanimity with remarkable speed and chattered as if to an old and valued friend. "I did not care for Paris particularly," she confided, "but Mama thought it necessary I should acquire some experience of the Continent and to practice my French. I'm afraid I wasn't very good at foreign languages at school. My French is barely passable, but I do speak a little Italian, and my drawing is quite good, or so Miss Trenton told me at school. She said I had quite a talent. I play the pianoforte a little, and I sing, so I have all the accomplishments, although I am not at all proficient with the harp."

"I cannot imagine why one would wish to become proficient with the harp. It seems to be an instrument purely the province of elderly ladies with very severe coiffures," Sebastian said solemnly, eliciting a delighted chuckle from his companion.

They arrived at the house on Bruton Street, and Sebastian would have been prepared to leave his charge once he had seen her admitted, but the door flew open before he could even raise the knocker, and a distraught lady of ample girth seemed to explode onto the top step.

"Abigail . . . child . . . where have you been? Your father is beside himself with worry. I have been tearing my hair out."

Hands waved in the general direction of her powdered coiffure illustrated the truth of this. Wisps escaped from the tight confines of hidden pins, and straggling locks tumbled around her face. Scarlet rouge stood out dramatically against the white of her powdered cheeks.

"What on earth can you have been thinking of?" she continued, her voice rising. "And who is this? A man . . . you have been alone with a strange man in the public street. What kind of man would take advantage of a young girl . . . oh, your father will have to call him out, and I daresay—"

"Just a minute, ma'am." Sebastian's crisp tones cut through Mrs. Sutton's rising hysteria. "That seems an unnecessarily vigorous response to what was intended only as a courtesy with the best of motives. I merely escorted Miss Sutton home after she ran into some unpleasantness in Piccadilly." He bowed, hat in hand. "The Honorable Sebastian Sullivan at your service, ma'am."

Marianne had been dumbstruck during this masterly speech and looked at her daughter's escort properly for the first time. Everything about him spoke of refinement and breeding. "Oh, my goodness, sir, I didn't mean to imply . . . you have done my daughter a great service, I'm sure. Will you come in? I know my husband would wish to thank you in person."

Abigail was sinking with embarrassment as she saw her mother through Sebastian's eyes. Her mother's less refined vowels had escaped in the passion of the moment, and with her hair adrift and her gown in disarray, she looked a fright. But Sebastian was smiling at Mrs. Sutton, bowing over her hand, as if he didn't notice any of these giveaway indications of the lady's less than genteel origins.

"I should be honored, ma'am. But believe me, it was a mere bagatelle, and I enjoyed Miss Sutton's company." He turned to Abigail, indicating the open front door. "Miss Sutton, allow me to complete my self-appointed task and see you safely within doors."

Abigail blushed and hurried into the house ahead of him. As she had feared her father emerged instantly from the dining salon, a napkin tucked into his collar. His face was flushed. "Eh, what's this, Abigail? Where've you been? Mama's near hysterical with worry." His eye fell on Sebastian, and his flush deepened. "And who might you be, sir? What business d'ye have with my daughter?"

Sebastian, reflecting that it was enough to stop anyone doing a good turn, bowed once again and introduced himself. "The Honorable Sebastian Sullivan, at your service, sir. I escorted your daughter home."

"Eh?" William frowned at the young man. "Home from where?"

"Oh, Papa, indeed, you mustn't," Abigail exclaimed, mortified at this catechism. "Mr. Sullivan rescued me from a most horrid man, and I am so grateful to him. You mustn't speak to him like that."

William cast a glance at his wife, who said, "Indeed, William, we must be most grateful to the gentleman. He has done Abigail a great service."

William snorted. "It wouldn't have been necessary if she hadn't been out where she's not supposed to be in the first place. But I suppose I must thank you . . . Sullivan, did you say?" He extended a hand.

"Yes, sir." Sebastian took the hand and responded to the firm warmth of the handshake in like manner. "And believe me, I did nothing."

"Well, you can say that if you please, but I'll not believe it. Come in and have a bite of nuncheon with us.

'Tis well past noon. You'll be glad of a bite and a draught of ale, I'll be bound." He swept Sebastian ahead of him into the dining parlor, leaving Abigail with her mother.

"Come upstairs at once, child. I wish to hear everything that happened." Marianne had recovered her composure and was already beginning to think that Abigail's unwise adventure could be turned to advantage. "What a personable young man he is." She shooed her daughter ahead of her upstairs. "You must tidy yourself and change your gown, and then you must thank Mr. Sullivan prettily for his kindness."

Abigail did not interrupt as her mother fussed, summoning her maid to help Abigail change her gown and rearrange her hair.

"So what happened, Abigail?" Marianne demanded as she adjusted a fichu in the neck of her daughter's sprigged muslin gown.

"A man accosted me. 'Twas nothing, really, Mama, but I was a little frightened, and Mr. Sullivan offered to escort me home." She concealed the true horror of the attack, reasoning that it would do her mother no good to hear it, and she certainly had no wish to relive it by describing it.

"To be sure, I cannot imagine what he must have thought . . . a young girl walking alone in Piccadilly," her mother scolded. "He must think you a veritable hoyden. You will never catch a suitable husband if you behave in such fashion. You may count yourself fortunate if Mr. Sullivan keeps a still tongue in his head. It will be the finish of all your prospects if the gossip mongerers hear of it. All my efforts wasted, all your father's money wasted." She sighed heavily, and Abigail bit her lip, knowing that her mother would go on like this for several days at least . . . until something else distracted her.

Marianne surveyed her daughter's appearance with a slight frown. The pale green sprigged muslin was made even more demure with the addition of the fichu, and the modest hoop was exactly right for a young girl just out of the schoolroom. Her fair curls were confined simply with pink ribbon, and the pink satin slippers accentuated the smallness of her feet. She looked as dainty as a Dresden doll and every bit as innocent.

She nodded finally. It was almost impossible to imagine this pretty child doing anything immodest or unacceptable. Even the aristocratic Mr. Sullivan would find her irresistible. "It's very well," she declared. "Now you must come downstairs and thank Mr. Sullivan properly."

"Yes, Mama." Abigail curtsied her acceptance and accompanied her mother back downstairs and into the dining parlor. She was rather afraid of what she would find there. Surely, someone as fine as the Honorable Sebastian would find her father impossibly rough and ready in his manners, and he probably would be itching to get away. But when the women entered the parlor, Sebastian was sitting at his ease at the table, his hand curled around a tankard of ale, listening with every appearance of interest to his host's retelling of a thrilling chase during a fox hunt across the Staffordshire countryside.

"Ah, here are the ladies," William declared with obvious pleasure. "Come and join us, my dears. None the worse for your ordeal, I trust, child."

"No, indeed not, Papa." Abigail curtsied, turning her smiling countenance on Sebastian. "I have not yet thanked you properly, sir, for your kindness. I should never have gone out alone. I do hope you will forget the impropriety."

Sebastian laughed and rose to his feet. "My dear Miss Sutton, I know of no impropriety. And if I did, I assure you, I am the soul of discretion." He raised her hand to his lips as he spoke, and Abigail's heart fluttered like a trapped canary.

The sound of the door knocker drew Marianne's attention. "I wonder who could be calling."

The butler's voice could be heard in the hall and then his step across the parquet. The door opened. "Lady Serena Carmichael, madam."

"Oh, my goodness. Show her into the drawing room at once, Morrison. How delightful." Marianne looked distracted, wondering whether to abandon the honorable gentleman in her dining parlor and go to her new and long-awaited guest. She could send Abigail to Serena, but that would mean Abigail would have to abandon the Honorable Sebastian, and that was not something Marianne wanted to happen too soon.

"Lady Serena." Abigail clapped her hands. "Oh, I must go to her at once. Excuse me, Mr. Sullivan . . . an old friend."

Sebastian bowed. "Of course, Miss Sutton. I must make my farewells now, anyway. I have overstayed my welcome." He wondered desperately if he could slip out of the house while Serena was being shown into the drawing room. The falseness of a social introduction in such a circumstance was unendurable. How could they bear to bow, to curtsy, to murmur politely? It didn't bear thinking of. He'd already persuaded himself that as long as he didn't frequent Pickering Place, there would be no need for social encounters. Serena would not be persona grata in the houses that Sebastian visited, for all her aristocratic lineage. Dealers of faro were not received in the best houses. And soon enough, Heyward and his stepdaughter would up sticks and head for pastures new. It was their habit, after all. The bitter reflection rose like acid in his throat.

"Thank you, Mr. Sutton, for the excellent ale. Mrs. Sutton . . ." He bowed, kissed the lady's hand, and was out of the room before anyone could remonstrate.

Serena stood in the hall, reaching into her reticule for a visiting card. She glanced up as a door at the rear of the hall opened and Sebastian emerged. There was a moment that seemed to stretch to eternity when they simply looked at each other. And for a moment, a very brief moment, their eyes locked as they had done so often before, and she could see herself reflected in the penetrating blue depths, as she knew he could see himself in her own violet pools. It was a game they had played, this losing themselves in each other's souls. A dangerous game, and there was no place for it in this reality.

"Mr. Sullivan, what a surprise." Her voice, light and easy, surprised herself. It gave away nothing of her inner turmoil. "I didn't realize you were acquainted with Mr. and Mrs. Sutton."

"No, how should you?" He spoke pleasantly as he bowed, his eyes now hooded, their expression hidden. "As it happens, we are but newly acquainted. But how delightful to run into you like this. I believe it's been several years since our last meeting."

And every minute of those three years a wretched wasteland, Serena thought. She herself had felt every miserable minute of those years in her very skin, bone, and muscle. She couldn't believe it didn't show, drawn deep on her countenance. But Sebastian looked so nonchalant, so utterly unchanged, still the picture of gleaming, golden, masculine perfection. She wondered if she had imagined that visceral moment of connection. Perhaps it had been wishful thinking.

"Has it been that long, sir?" she murmured. "I can hardly believe it. How quickly time flies." A cool smiled touched her lips but came nowhere near the violet eyes.

Lying jade, Sebastian thought. *You know damn well how long it's been.* But he merely smiled.

"Oh, my goodness. You know Mr. Sullivan, Lady Serena?" Abigail exclaimed. "Just fancy, Mama, Mr.

Sullivan and Lady Serena are acquainted. Isn't that amazing?"

"Yes, my dear, so it is." Mrs. Sutton silenced her daughter with a small gesture as she smiled warmly at Serena, offering a small bow of welcome. "My dear Lady Serena, how good of you to call. Do please come into the drawing room. Morrison, will you bring refreshment, please?"

"Thank you." Serena turned to Sebastian. "Good day, Mr. Sullivan." Her bow was as chilly as her smile. She turned to follow her hostess.

Abigail lingered for a moment, hesitating uncomfortably. It seemed wrong somehow to abandon her savior in the middle of the hall and chase after the newcomer as if she were glad to see the back of the former and overeager to welcome the latter.

Sebastian read her dilemma and, despite his grim thoughts, was a little amused. He spent very little time with ingénues. He had several young female cousins, but they had never held much interest for any of the Sullivan brothers. He remembered them as shy children in starched ruffles, always hiding their faces in their mothers' skirts, and these days, they were all simpers and giggles, fussing over dresses and bonnets and potential husbands to the exclusion of all sensible conversation.

He smiled at Abigail, saying, "You must go to your guest, Miss Sutton. You have given me so much of your time already. I would be a bear to expect more of it." He raised her hand to his lips as she curtsied, blushing, murmuring denials. He made a swift departure and had walked halfway up the street before his step slowed.

Damn Serena. He stopped. Had he imagined that moment when their eyes had met? Had she deliberately tried to engage him in their old game, when they would try to lose themselves in each other's eyes? *But of course she hadn't.* He was a fool to think it. Just as he was a fool to imagine it was possible to walk away and leave matters between them like this. Something had to be said. He didn't know what, only that *something* had to clear the air between them. He had been haunted by the memory of their parting for too long.

Serena listened to Abigail's excited chatter with half an ear. *What on earth brought Sebastian to this house?* He could not have met any of the Suttons in the ordinary course of events; they could have no acquaintances in common, except for herself, of course, but that was irrelevant. She was waiting for a suitable break in the chatter to inquire, but Abigail was in full flood about the miserable Channel crossing and the kindness of a young man, "a most respectable young man, Lady Serena, one of the Wedgwood family, would you believe? They live so close to us in the country, but we had never met before. He was kind enough to lend me his boat cloak, it was so cold on deck, but I couldn't stay in the cabin, it made me so wretchedly ill. Were you ill on your crossing?"

"No, I'm never seasick," Serena told her, her tone unintentionally dismissive. She saw Abigail's face fall and was instantly remorseful. "I am fortunate, you know. Some people don't suffer at all, but few people are so lucky."

She was reminded suddenly of an afternoon on Loch Morar, near the Highland home where she had been born and spent her childhood until her father's death. She and Sebastian were in a small boat in the middle of the loch when the wind rose abruptly, as it often did in those parts, and a black squall raced across the previously smooth green waters. Sebastian had sailed the lakes of Cumbria all his life and had seemed unperturbed by the violence of the brief storm. He had handled the little boat with a competence that awed her, instructing her where to move, what to do, in a voice as calm as the waters had been a few minutes earlier. But when he had managed to steer under minimal sail to the shores of one of the islands in the loch, he had knelt on the rocky strand and vomited, cursing vigorously throughout at the weakness of a stomach that could not withstand a boat's violent pitching.

Serena had been drenched but laughing, full of exhilaration at the danger now past, and Sebastian's sickness had astounded her. She liked to think she had hidden her surprise and her slight sense of superiority, but Sebastian had clearly resented her immunity, and it had taken until the evening for him to recover his equanimity. In other circumstances, the memory would have made her smile . . . the memory of the night they had spent later could still fill her with—

Enough. "But tell me how you came to know the Honorable Sebastian Sullivan, Abigail." She turned the subject as she smiled her refusal of a glass of ratafia, repressing a shudder. The sticky sweetness of the drink would make her sick where the roughest seas could not. "No, thank you, ma'am."

"Oh . . . well, it's a little awkward." Abigail glanced uncomfortably at her mother. Could Lady Serena be trusted with the truth of her indiscretion?

"Abigail's maid disappeared for a moment when they were shopping this morning." Mrs. Sutton stepped in smoothly with what would now be the accepted version. "They were shopping, and something in a window caught the eye of the wretched creature, and she disappeared, leaving my poor child alone. An unpleasant encounter with some gentleman ensued, and Mr. Sullivan was good enough to step in and protect Abigail. He brought her home safe and sound. We are most grateful to him. Aren't we, my dear?" She smiled and tapped her daughter's hand with her closed fan. "Such a silly child."

Abigail bridled at this demeaning comment, but common sense told her to run with the fabrication. "I believe it was more Matty's fault than mine, Mama."

"Well, maybe so, but fortunately, no harm was done. May I offer you coffee, Lady Serena?"

"Thank you, but I mustn't stay, ma'am." Serena rose. "I have another engagement this afternoon. But I wished to call upon you as soon as we arrived in town to see how you're going on. Such a pretty house . . . you're most fortunate to have secured such a residence before the Season begins in good earnest. Abigail, perhaps you will ride with me one morning?"

"Oh, but I don't have a pony in town." Abigail looked at her mother.

"Mr. Sutton is still setting up his stable, Lady Serena," Marianne said, directing her response at her visitor. "He will procure a lady's riding horse for Abigail, you may be sure."

"Then I look forward to many pleasant rides together." Serena drew on her gloves.

"Perhaps General Heyward would offer Mr. Sutton his advice on setting up his stable," Marianne suggested rather tentatively. "If he's not too busy, of course. But Mr. Sutton is not familiar with Tattersalls, and I believe that's where one goes for buying horses."

"Indeed, it is, ma'am. I'll mention it to my stepfather. I'm sure he'll be happy to help." She couldn't manage to inject any enthusiasm into her voice.

"We should be most honored to receive a call from General Heyward." Marianne reached for the bellpull.

Not if you know what's good for you. Serena wanted to shout it aloud, but foiling her stepfather required cunning, not brute force. She fixed a smile on her lips and held out her hand. "Abigail, I will leave my card with your butler. Do call on me. We shall have a comfortable chat, and you shall tell me all about the young man on the boat."

Abigail blushed, and Marianne said sharply, "Young Mr. Wedgwood is not in town. I'm sure he has returned to Stoke-on-Trent."

Serena had heard rather a lot in Brussels about the glories of the pottery towns, Stoke-on-Trent in particular. Abigail had compared her hometown very favorably to the capitals of the Continent. She offered her anodyne smile and followed the butler, who had appeared in answer to the bell, out into the hall, where her maid sat patiently awaiting her pleasure on a bench by the door. The fresh, cool air on the street was a welcome relief from the stuffy heat of the drawing room, and she breathed deeply, hoping it would clear her head of the churning turmoil of her thoughts.

Chapter Three

Serena and her maid had walked the short distance to Bruton Street from Pickering Place, and as they turned onto Berkeley Square, Sebastian stepped away from the railings of the garden where he had been waiting, hoping she would be on foot. "Lady Serena." He bowed with a flourish of his hat. "May I escort you?"

"I already have an escort, sir, as you can see." She indicated her maid, standing several paces behind her.

His eyes narrowed. "Nevertheless, it would be my pleasure, ma'am."

"It would not be mine, sir." Her heart was beating ridiculously fast despite the coolness of her tone. She had to keep him at arm's length, had to maintain the coldness that had informed her dismissal of him three years past. Nothing had changed. And yet she could see that Sebastian had changed. The youthful softness, the almost gullible idealism that had allowed her to crush him as she had done, was missing now, and she sensed that he could not be so easily dismissed now. It should have alarmed her, but, perversely, it gave her a tiny thrill of excitement. *To be instantly banished.*

His expression hardened, but he spoke softly so that only she could hear. "Come now, Serena, you know as well as I that we must have this out. We can't live in the same four square miles and never bump into each other. It's not realistic, and I, for one, am not prepared to live every day dreading that I might run into you and have to endure this ridiculous pantomime."

He was right, of course. And in truth, it would be a relief to clear the ground, so that they could meet as civil acquaintances. She answered as softly. "Are you still lodging in Stratton Street?"

"Yes."

"I will write to you. There is somewhere we can meet in private." Then she dropped a curtsy, raising her voice. "Another time, sir. Good day to you."

"Ma'am." He bowed as she swept past him, her maid scurrying in her wake.

Sebastian watched her go, the long, energetic stride he remembered so well. One of the things he had loved most about her was her impatience with feminine conventions. Not for Serena the appearance of frailty, the delicately hinted weaknesses, the inability to totter more than a few yards on dainty little feet in satin slippers. Serena cared not a jot for those who considered women unappealing if they thought for themselves, had political opinions, spoke their minds. Her father, an eccentric Scottish earl, had encouraged an unconventional upbringing for his only child, and his influence on Serena had been more lasting and important than her mother's more orthodox beliefs. Sebastian had loved the vigorous to-and-fro of their discussions, the frequent arguments that had always ended the same way . . . in a passionate tangle between the sheets.

His body stirred as the memories flooded back. But it was over. There was nothing between them now but the arid wasteland of a memory turned sour. They simply had to find a way to coexist as civil but distant acquaintances in the same four square miles of the city. He walked off towards Upper Brook Street, hoping that Jasper would be at home. For some reason, he needed the bracing presence of his elder brother's somewhat caustically humorous view of the world.

Serena walked quickly back to Pickering Place. The butler opened the door to her knock, and she entered the hall, automatically looking around to check that the salons were being prepared for that evening's gaming. In the daytime, the house appeared like any grand gentleman's residence. The transformation came as darkness fell.

The tables were laid in the dining salon; the small, private card room on the opposite side of the hall, which was reserved for the deadly serious games among fierce competitors, was prepared, the baize table brushed so not a hint of lint or dust could impede the fall of the dice, new packs of card waiting to be cut, fresh candles on every surface, the decanters fully charged.

Satisfied, Serena hurried upstairs. The grand salon was still being prepared, but everything looked as it should. She gave a few instructions for the placement of candles and had turned to go to her own bedchamber in the opposite wing when the door to the library opened and her stepfather emerged. "Thought I heard your voice, Serena. Come in here. Burford is here, wants to wish you good afternoon." He rubbed his hands together in genial fashion, but there was an edge to his voice and a hard glitter in the gaze he bent upon his stepdaughter.

Serena loathed the Earl of Burford. But she knew he held the mortgage on the house on Pickering Street; it had been the only way the general had been able to set himself up in such style. The assumption was that the house would pay for itself in no time, and the mortgage could be paid off in no more than two years. Serena had always thought such optimism misplaced, but her opinion had been neither offered nor asked for.

"I'm just going to take off my hat and pelisse, sir." She moved towards the corridor.

"You can do that later. Burford wishes to see you." The general put a restraining hand on her arm, and the grip was firm enough to be painful.

Serena jerked her arm free. "Very well. But I would think I could make his lordship more welcome if I was not in my street clothes." She stalked past her stepfather into the library.

The Earl of Burford was a widower in his late fifties. A thick mane of silver hair crowned a distinguished, leonine head. His eyes were disconcerting; so light as to be almost colorless, they were impenetrable, giving no indication of his thoughts or emotions. His complexion usually bore the roseate bloom of a man well into his burgundy, and this afternoon was no exception.

Serena curtsied from the doorway. "Good day, my lord."

"Ah, the lovely Serena. Come close, my dear." He beckoned her. "Let me look at you. I haven't see you since Brussels."

Serena, aware of her stepfather close behind her, had no choice but to move farther into the library. "When did you arrive in London, my lord?"

"A week ago, but I had matters to attend to in the country." He waved a hand dismissively. "Tiresome business, troublesome tenants, nothing to interest your pretty little head." He put up his quizzing glass and examined Serena with an unmistakably proprietorial leer that made her scalp crawl.

"How tedious for you, my lord," she responded blandly as she stepped aside, out of his immediate line of vision, and moved to the sideboard. "May I refill your glass?"

"Indeed, you may." He watched her closely as she

returned with the decanter. She filled his glass carefully, aware of those strange, lightless eyes fixed upon her.

"Now, if you will excuse me, I must take off my hat and pelisse." Adroitly, she stepped past her stepfather, curtsied briefly to the earl, and slipped from the room, closing the door firmly behind her.

Outside in the hall, she couldn't help a reflexive shudder. Burford disturbed her, but she couldn't put her finger on it. Her stepfather fawned on him, behaved as if they were the best of friends, and yet Serena knew that the general was more than a little afraid of the earl. Of course, the latter held the power of the creditor over him.

She hurried down the corridor to her own apartments. Once there, she closed the door and turned the key in the lock. It was an automatic gesture. She had learned the hard way about leaving her door unlocked under her stepfather's roof.

A fire burned a cheerful welcome in the grate in her boudoir, and, having cast aside her outer garments, she sat down in a low chair beside the fireplace, stretching her feet in their elegant half-boots to the andirons, and contemplated the events of the afternoon.

It was an extraordinary coincidence that Sebastian should have come to Abigail's rescue in such fashion and at such a moment, but she supposed that their own reunion would have happened somewhere at some point, when her stepfather was not around to deflect it. Sebastian was right; they couldn't live in the same few square miles and not run into each other, even if she was generally barred from the drawing rooms that Sebastian would frequent. It struck her now as unutterably stupid of her to have imagined that such a meeting would not occur. She had somehow believed she could live in London, run her faro bank, make her own plans, and cast into outer darkness all memory of that passionate idyll three years earlier.

But of course, she couldn't. The memories lived deep within her, an essential part of her. They framed her every thought for the future, her every expectation of how life should be. And she couldn't endure dwelling on them when compared with the hopeless misery of her present existence.

Restless now, she got up from her chair and paced from window to door and back. Her existence was miserable, but it was *not* hopeless. Soon she would have enough funds of her own to make her escape. Every morning, she did the previous night's accounts, cleverly diverting a little here, a little there. It all mounted up, and General Sir George Heyward, greedy though he was, was more than happy to leave such tedious work to his stepdaughter. He would not acknowledge that she was infinitely better at such intellectual intricacies than he, instead maintaining the useful fiction that women were trained to manage household accounts. Serena did not disabuse him.

He had robbed her of her mother's jointure, a healthy sum that should have come to her when she attained her majority. Instead, it had mysteriously disappeared. At first, she had blamed her mother's gullibility, her inability to see the bad in anyone, but in her heart, she knew that Lady Elinor had lived in terror of her second husband. She would not have confronted him about anything, even if it meant leaving her daughter destitute and at the general's mercy.

Serena ceased her pacing. Dwelling upon such bitter memories achieved nothing. Action was the only way to banish them. She put on her pelisse and hat again and hurried from her room, using the back stairs to avoid coming across her stepfather. The long case clock in the hall struck four as she crossed to the front door. The house would not open for business for another four hours.

Flanagan, the butler whom the general had inherited from Serena's mother, appeared from the kitchen regions or, rather, materialized as he always did whenever Serena was in the vicinity. "Are you going out again, Lady Serena?" Disapproval was apparent in his voice.

"Just to St. James's Place, Flanagan. A mere step."

"Unescorted, my lady?"

"Yes, Flanagan. I will barely be out of sight of the house." She offered him a cajoling smile. "You're a veritable mother hen, Flanagan. I love you for it, but believe me, 'tis not in the least necessary."

"If you say so, my lady." He held the door for her. "And if the general should inquire. . . ?"

"Tell him I am resting in my chamber. I have the

headache." She stepped out onto the top step. "I'll be less than half an hour." The door closed behind her, and she walked quickly in the direction of St. James's Street.

Sebastian arrived at the Blackwater mansion in Upper Brook Street just as his brother was coming down the street from the opposite direction. Sebastian paused at the foot of the steps to the front door, waiting for Jasper.

"Seb, this is a surprise. Was I expecting you?" Jasper greeted his brother with a wave as he approached.

"Not unless you have second sight," Sebastian declared, grinning. "If 'tis a bad time, I'll come back later."

Jasper's quick scrutiny told him more about his brother's frame of mind than Sebastian realized. Jasper had been looking out for his younger siblings since they were toddlers, and very little escaped his notice. They probably would have been surprised at how much of the ins and outs of their lives was known to their brother. Now he clapped his younger brother on the shoulder in companionable greeting, saying, "Not a bit of it. Come in. I'm always delighted to see you, as you well know." He ushered him up the steps to the door. "Where's Perry?"

"We're not joined at the hip, you know, Jasper." Sebastian waited as his brother fitted his key in the lock.

"You were as children," Jasper responded, pushing

the door wide. "One only ever had to look for one of you, the other was sure to be close by."

"I suppose that's true," Sebastian conceded. It was certainly a fact that he and his twin had been inseparable as children. He glanced around the hall. "Is the fair Clarissa at home?"

"No, she's taken that scapegrace of a brother of hers shopping. He's going to Harrow after Christmas, which will do young Francis a power of good." Jasper shook his head, but Sebastian wasn't fooled. Jasper was very fond of his wife's little brother.

"Ah, Crofton." Jasper greeted his butler. "We'll be in the library. Is there claret in there?"

"On the sideboard, my lord."

"Claret? From the Blackwater cellars?" Sebastian followed his brother into the shabby but cozy library. The formal rooms in the house were rarely used despite the advent of Lady Blackwater. Jasper maintained that it was too expensive to open them up and heat them on a daily basis, and Clarissa had made no demur. The main salon was used for formal entertaining, on the rare occasions in which it was necessary, but for the most part, they were content with the library, a small dining parlor, Clarissa's private sitting room, and their adjoining bedchambers. The household staff was also kept to a minimum. Of course, that would all change with Viscount Bradley's inheritance, should the three brothers manage to fulfill the terms of the old man's will.

Jasper shook his head ruefully at his brother's question. "The last person to replenish those cellars, dear boy, was our great-grandfather. But this is passable." He lifted the decanter, holding it to the light. "Who knows, if we can satisfy Uncle Bradley, the Blackwater cellars may see another heyday."

He poured wine and handed a glass to his brother.

"So, Seb, much as I like to think this is a social call. . . ?" He sat down, crossing one leg over the other, swinging his ankle, regarding his brother with a question in his dark eyes.

"It is, and it isn't," Sebastian confessed slowly. He took a sip of his wine, nodded appreciatively, then glanced down at the faded carpet. "Do you remember Lady Serena Carmichael, Jasper?"

Jasper's expression didn't change, although his mind was suddenly alert. "Certainly," he said neutrally. "Why?"

Sebastian pulled at his chin. "You probably remember how things were between us?"

Jasper nodded. "It ended badly, I remember that."

"Well, they're back in town, running a hell on Pickering Street. Very high stakes, in quite another class from the previous one on Charles Street."

Jasper regarded his brother over his wine glass. "I heard a new hell had opened. I was unaware it was run by Heyward and his stepdaughter."

"I went there not knowing it myself," Sebastian said.

"I take it, if you had known it, you would have avoided the place." Jasper's voice was level.

"Like the plague." Sebastian stared into the fire's glow.

Jasper leaned over to refill his wine glass. He waited for a moment or two before prodding gently. "So, what happened?"

Sebastian shook his head briskly as if dispelling cobwebs. "Nothing then, but the devil of it is that I bumped into her again this morning, and I realized that we can't possibly both live in town without meeting accidentally."

Jasper sipped his wine with every appearance of serenity. "I can see that there could be some awkwardness."

"*Awkwardness?*" The word seemed to explode from Sebastian. "That's the least of it, Jasper. The moment I saw her again, it all came back." He ran a distracted hand through his hair, disturbing the neat queue held at his nape with a black velvet ribbon. "Every little thing about her, everything that I had loved, everything that had driven me to distraction. And the bitterness, the anger . . ." He shook his head as if searching for words before continuing, "I thought I was over her. How could it be otherwise after the way she treated me? But now . . . now, I just don't know, and I can't go through that again." He raised his eyes from the fire and looked at his brother, who saw in the blue eyes the dreadful bleakness that Perry had seen.

"No," Jasper agreed, reflecting that he couldn't bear to see Sebastian suffer like that again. And he could easily imagine what it would do to Perry to see his twin revisit that hell. "What can I do to help, Seb?"

Sebastian smiled suddenly. "Just be here, as you always have been. I'm going to see her, try to establish clear ground, so that we can at least nod in a civilized fashion should we have to meet. I'm a little scared that I might succumb again, that's all."

"Would you like me to see her for you?"

Sebastian shook his head. "No, thank you. I can't have you doing my dirty work for me. I know you've done it often enough in the past, but I am all grown up now, big brother."

Jasper laughed a little. "I don't doubt it, Seb. But remember, Perry and I are standing behind you. There's no shame in needing a little support now and then."

" 'Tis backbone I need," Sebastian said ruefully.

They heard the sound of the front door, and a moment later, Lady Blackwater put her titian head around the library door. "Oh, Seb, how lovely to see you."

"Why don't you bring the rest of you in here?" her husband suggested, a smile in his dark eyes as they rested upon his wife's countenance. "Where's the lad?"

"We met the Langston boys on their way to Green Park with their tutor, so he joined them. They'll bring him home before dark." Clarissa went to give her brother-in-law, who had risen to his feet, a kiss on the cheek. "How are you, Seb? Perry's not with you?"

Sebastian shook his head in mock exasperation.

"Why does everyone assume that we walk the world hand in hand?"

"Because mostly you do," Clarissa responded. "Should I leave you two alone again?"

"No, of course not," Sebastian said swiftly. "I'm on my way, anyway."

"Oh, don't let me drive you away."

"You're not, my dear." He kissed her lightly. "I really have to go." He walked to the door. "Thank you for the claret, Jasper . . . and for the brotherly ear."

"You're more than welcome, dear boy, to either or both. Anytime." Jasper walked his brother to the door, then stood thoughtfully in the hall, frowning.

Serena walked quickly to a small, unassuming house on St. James's Place and lifted the brass knocker. The door opened immediately. The maid curtsied.

"Is your mistress in?" Serena walked past the girl into the hall.

"I don't know as she's receiving, ma'am."

"Ah." Serena hesitated. If Margaret was entertaining one of her many gentlemen friends, she would not welcome the intrusion, even of a very good friend. "Is she alone?"

"Oh, yes, m'lady." The girl bobbed a curtsy. "The gentleman left half an hour ago."

"Well, why don't you run up and ask her if she'll

receive me?" Serena suggested gently. "I'll wait here. If she's unable to see me, I'll leave her a note."

The girl curtsied again and scampered upstairs. Serena stood examining a painting she didn't recognize on the far wall. Margaret's house was all her own, paid for, for the most part, by her gentlemen friends, but she had always managed to avoid being under the singular protection of any of them. Serena had long envied her, and one day, she was determined, she, too, would have her own little house and entertain her own friends. Except that somehow the prospect of emulating Margaret's way of life didn't sit well with her, however she looked at it.

"Madam will see you at once, m'lady." The girl bounced down the stairs.

"Thank you . . . no, no need to show me up. I know the way." She went up to the pleasant salon that looked down on the street at the front of the house.

Margaret Standish was a young widow, whose brief marriage to an elderly merchant had left her in possession of a respectable if not lavish settlement, which she had turned to good use, setting herself up in a charming house on St. James's Place, where she entertained her numerous gentlemen friends, some more personally than others, and graciously received their appropriate expressions of gratitude.

She greeted Serena warmly. "My dear, how delightful of you to call." She came towards her, hands outstretched in welcome. "I have been moping for the last hour and am sadly in need of diversion." She took Serena's hands and kissed her on both cheeks. "I can't tell you how happy I was to get your note saying you were back in London. Brussels seems an age ago, doesn't it?" She drew her guest to the fire. "Take off your things, and I'll ring for tea."

"An age," Serena agreed, discarding her hat and pelisse on a chair before sitting down on an upholstered Chippendale sofa before the fire. "We have been so busy setting up the house since we arrived I've had no time to visit anyone."

"But you are established now. The house on Pickering Place is on everyone's lips these days . . . tea, Clara, please." She nodded at the maid who had come in answer to the bell.

"Well, we've only been in business for a week, but the general seems happy enough with progress so far . . . thank heaven," Serena added with a significant sigh.

Margaret gave her a look of sympathetic understanding. She knew that when the general was unhappy, everyone in his vicinity suffered accordingly.

Serena shrugged, effectively dismissing her stepfather from the conversation. "So, why are you moping? 'Tis not like you."

"Oh, I was obliged to give young Lord Peter his congé," Margaret explained, turning a dainty diamond bracelet around on her wrist. "He was becoming rather possessive. But his ardor was always very invigorating . . . I shall miss him."

Serena chuckled. Margaret was a few years older than she, a woman who made the most of her unconventional looks. Her features were sharp in an angular countenance, her nose a very prominent aquiline, her chin pointed and more than decisive. Her pallid complexion was sadly freckled, and her hair was an unmistakable carrot, but she had flair and a mesmerizing pair of green eyes that drew attention away from whatever faults there were in her appearance. Her clothes and lavish jewelry were always at the forefront of fashion; her plunging décolletage made the most of a rather insignificant bosom. Her tongue was sharp, her wit acerbic, and she was the one person with whom Serena felt she could truly be herself, the one person she could confide in.

Apart from Sebastian. But Serena quashed that reflection; it did her no good, but it brought her back to the business in hand. The maid brought in the tea tray, and she accepted a dish with a slightly distracted smile.

Margaret noticed the distraction immediately. Her green eyes narrowed as she stirred her tea with a delicate silver spoon. "So, is this purely a social call, my love, or is there an ulterior motive?"

"Both," Serena said frankly. She sipped her tea, then set the dish back on the side table beside the sofa. "I need a quiet, private place for a rendezvous, Margaret."

"And where better than here in my little love nest?" Margaret swept her arm in an encompassing gesture at their surroundings. "Is this some new liaison?" Her gaze sharpened with curiosity. "I thought you not interested in such *affaires.*"

Serena shook her head vigorously. "I'm not. This is, if anything, the opposite. I need to settle matters once and for all with Sebastian."

Margaret's eyes widened. "Ah," she murmured. "Has he made an appearance, then?"

" 'Tis impossible not to bump into him at every turn," Serena said a little crossly. "First he was at Pickering Place, and then, of all things, he pops up at the Suttons', when I was visiting there this afternoon."

"The Suttons?" Margaret's well-plucked eyebrows rose. "I remember them from Brussels. Decent enough people but hardly the kind of company the Blackwater family would keep."

"He apparently did Abigail some service when she was out shopping . . . some unpleasantness she encountered in the street. Sebastian is, if nothing else, always chivalrous." She heard the acidity in her voice and welcomed it. It gave her much-needed armor against something, she just wasn't sure what.

Margaret was regarding her in thoughtful silence. After a moment, she said, "So is this meeting to be in the nature of a reconciliation?"

"No, how could it be?" Serena shook her head. "You know how things stand with my stepfather, Margaret."

Her friend gave a sober nod of assent. "Has he been up to his tricks again?"

"Not exactly . . . but I think he's cooking something up with that loathsome Lord Burford." Serena twisted her fingers into a knot in her lap. "He won't find it so easy this time." Her voice was barely above a whisper, but Margaret heard every word.

"If you need sanctuary, love, you know you will find it here." She leaned over and grasped Serena's busy fingers, stilling them with her own long, thin hand.

"I know, and believe me, the thought of that is ineffably comforting, Margaret. But I wouldn't want to cramp your style." She laughed a little. "And I believe I can handle the general. Forewarned is forearmed, as they say."

"As they say." Margaret sat back again. "So when would you wish to meet with the Honorable Sebastian? I can be out at any time if you tell me when."

"Oh, I don't want to dispossess you, Margaret. Indeed, there's no need. A few minutes' conversation is all that's necessary, just to clear the air, so to speak. I can meet him in the dining parlor downstairs."

"No, I won't hear of it. You will entertain him in civilized comfort up here." Margaret got to her feet and went to the secretaire. She flipped through the pages of a day book. "On Thursday, I can be out the whole day. Will Thursday do for you?"

"I don't need the whole day," Serena protested. "Just an hour or even half an hour will be sufficient."

"I shall be out all day Thursday," Margaret responded

firmly. "You may set whatever half-hour you wish from eleven in the morning until late evening. In fact," she mused, "I may not even return in the evening."

Serena was intrigued. "A new conquest?"

"Possibly. We will see how he performs on Thursday. He has a small hunting lodge in Windsor Park, and since he is rather beautiful and even more wealthy, I am anxious to try his paces."

Serena laughed, feeling lighthearted for the first time in weeks. "You are incorrigible, Margaret. Very well, I'll write to Sebastian and suggest he meet me here at midday on Thursday."

She rose to her feet as the dainty ormolu clock on the mantel struck five.

"I must go back. We dine at six before the doors open at eight." She set her hat on her head, adjusting the position in the mirror above a console table, then slipped her arms into her pelisse before turning to embrace her friend. "I can't thank you enough, Margaret."

"Nonsense" was the robust response. "I would be of service to you in many more ways if you'd let me, you know that, Serena." Margaret hugged her, then stood back, holding Serena's arms, looking closely at her. "Why don't you just pack your bags and leave, my dear?"

"Not yet." Serena smiled a little mistily. "But soon. There's one particular piece of mischief that I must forestall first."

"Oh?" Margaret raised her eyebrows again.

"He's getting his hooks into an innocent with a very

wealthy papa. I have to stop it, and to do that, I must be there watching the general, ready to step in. If I don't, the poor child will end up like my mother." Her face closed, and shadows crossed her eyes. "I can't stand by and let that happen."

Margaret said nothing. There was nothing to be said. She knew only a very little about Serena's and her mother's life with General Heyward before the latter's death of what Serena had described once as desperation. But what she did know was enough to convince her of Serena's resolution now to prevent anyone else suffering the same fate.

"Well, you know best, of course." She accompanied Serena to the head of the stairs. "But don't forget you have a friend and a roof here whenever you need either or both."

"Thank you." Serena's violet eyes filled with tears for a moment as she fought the temptation to throw everything to the four winds and cast herself upon her friend's bosom. But now was not the time. She would be strong for a while longer.

Chapter Four

Sebastian received Serena's note early that evening. It was brief and to the point: *I will await you at 12 St. James's Place next Thursday at noon. Do not reply to this. S.*

Sebastian's gaze lingered over each pen stroke. He knew her writing so well, and it never failed to set his pulses racing. They had written many letters to each other in the past, ardent pages of lyrical prose, rekindling memories of passionate nights and equally passionate days. Serena had never been shy about expressing her feelings, and how he had relished the frankness of her desire, the naked lust apparent in her sensuous descriptions of their erotic encounters. Now he looked at the bald sentence and felt oddly bereft. Where was she? That woman who had so inflamed him.

When he thought of those dreadful moments of her betrayal three years earlier, he thought he must have imagined the Serena he had loved with such passion. What he had said that morning was true: *"I don't know you . . . I don't know you at all."* The cold cipher who had dismissed him with such hard, emotionless words was a stranger to him. It was as if some malign spirit had occupied Serena's loveliness. And judging by these cold instructions on the smooth vellum, nothing had changed.

He scrunched the paper and threw it into the fire, then poured himself a glass of madeira, staring into the fire, one arm resting along the mantel.

"In the doldrums, Seb?"

He looked up as Perry came into the parlor, buckskin breeches and boots dusty with the fine sand of the riding path in Hyde Park. "No, why should you think so?"

"Because you only ever stare into the fire like that when you're hipped," his twin observed, tossing his riding whip onto a table. "What's amiss?" He poured himself madeira.

"Nothing of any moment. D'you have plans for the evening?"

"Nothing that couldn't be changed." Perry's gaze sharpened. "Serena?" he hazarded.

Sebastian gave a short laugh and left the fireplace. "The very same. I ran into her this afternoon in the strangest circumstances." He described the events of the afternoon to his brother, who listened attentively from deep in an upholstered armchair to the right of the fire. "I assume she came across the family in Brussels; the little Abigail was full of their travels. Not much impressed by them, either, I gather." He smiled rather more cheerfully and brought the decanter over to refill their glasses.

"A lively little innocent but not much to her. Father was a decent man . . . good, honest folk, I think would describe the family."

"In trade?" Perry sipped madeira.

"Indubitably. Not quite sure of the details, but in the Potteries, I gather. Wedgwood was mentioned as a neighbor."

"Doesn't sound as if they'll receive vouchers for Almack's," Perry observed. "I'm not sure the Wedgwoods, for all their fine work, are quite acceptable Society."

"Maybe not, but that doesn't mean they aren't decent people," his twin retorted.

Perry held up a hand in disclaimer. "Did I say they weren't?"

"No, you didn't," Sebastian conceded. "But you're right, brother dear, as so often. I doubt I'll be seeing anything more of Mr. and Mrs. Sutton and the sweetly pretty Abigail." He returned the decanter to the sideboard. "What d'you say to a mutton chop at Whites this evening? Followed by a hand or two of whist. There's always someone there willing to make up a four."

Perry shrugged easily. For all his brother's careless demeanor, he could tell Seb needed company and distraction, and he was more than willing to provide both. "If that's what you have in mind, it'll suit me. I have no firm engagements this evening." He stood up and stretched before going to the door. "I'll go and change."

In the house on Bruton Street, Mrs. Sutton was having one of her earnest conversations with her husband, who, in her opinion, did not fully grasp the vital importance of the right kind of social contacts. "I wonder if we could invite Mr. Sullivan to a small gathering, nothing as formal as a dinner—"

"Good God, woman, is there anything wrong with our table? I'll lay odds that Mr. Sullivan, whatever his breeding, has not eaten any better at any of the noblest tables in the land," her husband expostulated. "My cellars are as good as any, and a great deal better than most, and you, my dear, are a first-rate housekeeper."

"Yes . . . yes, William, of course." His lady made haste to soothe him before the issue became too much of an irritant. "Of course, we can put on as fine a dinner as can be found outside the royal palaces . . . but I wonder only whether we can summon the kind of company the Honorable Sebastian would find congenial."

"A plain-speaking gentleman, he seemed to me. Not high in the instep in the least. Drank his ale like a regular fellow. If you like, I'll invite old Parsons . . . he's got some distant relative with a title knocking around in his family. Would that do?" William looked kindly upon his wife. He sympathized with her ambitions for their daughter but found it hard to understand her social anxieties. They were who they were and, in his opinion, as good as anyone. His money was certainly as good as any duke's.

"Oh, dear . . . I don't know." Marianne adjusted a pin

in her coiffure, shaking her head. "Of course, if Lady Serena is to be one of the party, we'll have to invite the general."

A frown creased her brow. The general had seemed a good prospect for Abigail until the serendipitous encounter with the Honorable Sebastian Sullivan that afternoon. She was such a pretty girl, it would be a shame to waste her on a man so much older. Besides, a mere general could hardly compete with the scion of an earldom when it came to social status.

She decided against expressing this thought to her husband and continued, "But we need younger people . . . people Mr. Sullivan can talk to, be comfortable with. But apart from dear Lady Serena, we don't yet know anyone suitable in London."

"Then ask Lady Serena for help," her husband suggested reasonably. "She will be able to put together a guest list . . . maybe you could ask her to share the hostess duties with you. Then she could invite her own friends. This Sullivan fellow seems to know her, so what could be more natural?" He beamed, pleased with his inspiration.

"Oh, that could be the very thing, Mr. Sutton. Oh, William, how clever you are." Marianne planted a kiss on his cheek and bustled from the room.

William returned to his perusal of the *Gazette* with a fond smile.

❧

Much later that evening, a massive old-fashioned carriage stood outside an impressive double-fronted mansion on the Strand. The coachman in white wig and dark green livery stood by the carriage door, emblazoned with the arms of Viscount Bradley, and glanced impatiently at the firmly closed front door of the mansion. He had been waiting for more than half an hour and wondered if, as on so many other occasions, the steward would come out and tell him that his lordship's health had taken a turn for the worse and he no longer felt up to going out tonight.

He seemed to spend most of his life waiting, he reflected, and the horses in his charge got so little exercise they spent their days eating their heads off in the mews. But just as he'd decided he was going to spend all night standing out in the cold, the double doors were flung open, and an elderly gentleman in a powdered wig, resplendent in a full-skirted blue satin coat adorned with gold frogging, black knee breeches, and white stockings emerged on the arm of a bewigged and liveried footman.

The coachman opened the carriage and bowed as the old man, leaning heavily on a cane, shuffled towards the vehicle. He helped his master up into the dark interior, receiving curses for his pains, while the footman arranged a lap rug over the viscount and set a hot brick at his feet. The coachman put up the footstep and closed the door.

"Where to?" he inquired.

"Pickering Place . . . new gambling hell," the footman said. "He's in a foul mood, so be careful."

"When's he ever in anything else?" The coachman climbed back onto the box and took up the reins. The carriage lumbered down the Strand.

Fifteen minutes later, it drew up outside the house on Pickering Place, where light poured forth from every window, and a doorman stood at attention outside the front door. The coach drew up, and the viscount descended on the arm of the coachman. He looked up at the house for a moment. The doorman flung the door wide, said something rapidly to a servant within, then stood bowing with a murmured, "Good evening, my lord."

The viscount didn't deign a response as he passed the man to enter the well-lit hall, where another footman hurried to offer assistance, taking his lordship's tricorne hat and silver-laced gloves.

"Lord Bradley, this is indeed an honor." General Heyward came rapidly down the stairs, having been alerted by the servant. "I hardly dared hope we would have the honor of entertaining you in our new home." He bowed with a flourish. "Will you play in the salon, my lord, or would you prefer the private room?" He gestured to the door to the small card room. "Several gentlemen are playing dice."

"Faro," the viscount stated, moving slowly to the stairs. "That stepdaughter of yours still holding the bank?"

"Serena, my lord . . . I believe she is playing hazard in the upper salon. She'll be delighted to see you." The general escorted his visitor upstairs.

Serena had yielded the faro bank to an inveterate gambler and was engaged in a lively and not too serious game of hazard with some of the younger players in the smaller salon when the viscount and the general appeared. She was laughing at some quip made by one of the young men at the table as she cast the dice, then she glanced up from the table towards the door and stiffened, the laughter dying on her lips. Her stepfather beckoned imperatively, and she excused herself from the table, making her way over to the two men.

"My lord." She curtsied, her voice without expression, her countenance impassive.

The viscount put up his glass and surveyed her. "You seem none the worse for your travels, my dear. Still the beauty. Who's in your toils these days?"

"I don't know what you mean, sir." She returned his look steadily.

He gave a snort of derisive laughter. "Butter wouldn't melt, eh?" He turned to the general. "Can't say I blame you for keeping her on the market. Good for business, I daresay."

The general cast his stepdaughter a warning look before acceding to this apparent witticism with a smile. "What will you play, general?"

"Oh, this pretty young thing shall engage in a game of piquet with me," he responded, taking a japanned snuffbox from his deep pocket. "Your wrist, my dear, if you would be so kind."

Serena extended her arm and set her teeth, concealing her distaste as he dropped a pinch of snuff on the underside of her wrist. He bent his head and inhaled the scented powder, before dropping her wrist and mopping at his nose with a snuff-stained handkerchief. "Lead me to the cards, my dear. I have an amusing stake in mind. You shall stake a kiss and one dusky curl against my hundred golden guineas. Fair enough?"

"Oh, most amusing and very fair, indeed," the general declared, his eyes gleaming at the prospect of a windfall at no risk to his own funds. "Serena will be delighted to accommodate you, my lord. Indeed, I am sure she's very flattered. Are you not, my dear?"

Serena gave him a look of unutterable contempt. The general would ignore it, she knew, but it relieved her feelings somewhat. She moved towards a small card table in an alcove at the side of the salon and sat down, cutting the pack as the viscount took the chair opposite.

He was a good piquet player, as she had learned in the past, but in the last three years, she had sharpened her own skills and realized quickly with a wash of relief that his lordship was out of practice. She played in a cool, calculating silence as she selected her discards shrewdly, counted the odds against finding a desired card in the pickup almost without error, and took the first two games relatively easily.

She laid down her cards and said, "Two out of three gives me the win, sir."

The viscount did not immediately reply. He took a rouleau of golden guineas from his pocket and placed them on the table, then said, "You have learned a lot since we last played together. But I insist on a consolation prize, my dear." He reached out and took her hand in a surprisingly firm grip. "One kiss."

Serena could barely conceal her revulsion. Three years earlier, the viscount had made her pointed and definitely less than honorable advances, which she had turned down flat. The general had been furious when she had refused to entertain the viscount's protection, but before he could do anything to persuade her, his lordship had for some reason withdrawn his offer. Now, looking at the old man's wizened countenance, in which only the eyes retained any signs of the vigorous, good-looking man of his youth, she felt a flicker of dread that he was going to renew his offer.

"No kiss, my lord," she said firmly, withdrawing her hand with a jerk as she stood up. "But a curl you may have, if you wait here for a moment." She whisked herself away from the table, just as the general, who had been watching them from a faro table across the salon, started towards them.

How long can I keep this up? Serena felt exhausted, drained, as if she'd been playing for her life instead of a degrading kiss. Every day was like this, and she couldn't drop her guard for a moment. There was no knowing what move her stepfather would make next.

In the sanctuary of her bedchamber, she took a moment to herself, examining her reflection in the mirror. The strain of her struggle was there on her face in the tiny lines at the corners of her eyes and mouth, the slight blue shadows beneath her eyes. The signs were not too pronounced yet, but at the present rate, they would be etched as deep as canyons by the end of the year.

She took a pair of tiny gold scissors and snipped a lock of hair from behind her ear. Its loss would not be noticed. She brushed a little rouge on her cheekbones and a touch of paint on her lips. Three years ago, she would have scorned such cosmetic aids, her fresh complexion had no need of them. But things had changed, she reflected grimly.

When she returned to the salon, it was time for the second supper. "I will take you down, Lady Serena," the viscount declared, tucking the dusky curl into an inside pocket of his brocade waistcoat and offering his arm. Unsmiling, Serena laid a hand on his sleeve, and they led the party down to the supper room.

The viscount had little appetite these days and none at all for the richness of crab pâtés, lobster soufflés, scalloped oysters, and the other dishes that made up the lavish hospitality of the general's residence on Pickering Place. Bradley's diet was, through necessity, uniformly bland and tasteless, and he despised it heartily. Looking at the succulent dishes of which he could not partake made him irritable. He rejected champagne, drank two glasses of claret, and stared morosely at Serena, sitting beside him but engaged in a lively conversation with a pair of young men sharing their table.

Abruptly, he pushed back the little gilt chair with a scrape on the wooden floor. "Enough. Summon my coach." He grabbed his cane and levered himself to his feet as Serena, startled, jumped to her feet.

"Is something the matter, my lord?" Heyward came hurrying over. "Should I call for assistance?"

"No, just summon my coach. There's nothing that interests me here." He waved his cane precariously at the assembled company, before glaring at Serena as if she was the architect of all his woes, and shuffled to the door.

"What did you do?" Heyward hissed at his step-daughter before hurrying after the viscount.

"He's always an irascible old bear," Lord Carlton said with a chuckle. "Very rarely goes in company. I heard he was at death's door a few weeks ago. I was surprised to see him here."

"Oh, he came only to play piquet with the fair Serena," declared another young man with a grin. "And who can blame him for that?"

"You don't play piquet with Lady Serena and expect to win," Carlton said. "I was watching your game, Serena. A masterly repique."

"Why, thank you, kind sir." She rose from the table. "I had better go and see if I can pour oil on troubled waters. If you'll excuse me, gentlemen."

She found the general in high dudgeon, having seen his guest into his coach. "What did you say to him?" he demanded.

"Almost nothing at all," Serena said with admirable truth. "I find I have no conversation with the viscount. And he certainly isn't one for small talk. I expect he's annoyed because he lost the game."

"You should have let him win. The man's pride was wounded. One game at least you could have given him."

"It would have merely prolonged the agony for both of us," she returned. "Besides, I gave him a lock of hair."

The general's eyes narrowed. "He wanted a kiss. What harm is there in that?"

"A great deal to my reputation, sir."

He gave a short laugh. "Reputation, indeed. You're one of faro's daughters, and the law could have you whipped at the cart's arse for it if it wished. Face facts, girl. You're no more respectable than any Covent Garden whore or madam." He stalked back to the supper room.

Serena stood still for a long time, hearing the buzz of conversation as a distant hum. The general had spoken only the truth, but he had made her into this. And until she had amassed sufficient funds to be independent, she had no choice but to stay as she was. One of faro's daughters.

Viscount Bradley sat slumped in the carriage as it bore him back to the Strand. He was more than put out now. He was angry. Who the hell did the girl think she was? She was little better than a whore; the most she could hope for in life was a rich and respectable protector, and that only while she was young and for as long as her looks lasted. She had turned him down once, three years ago, and he had given up the pursuit, not for her sake but because against all the inclinations of character, he had a·certain fondness for his nephews.

Bradley closed his eyes as the carriage swayed around a corner. He had assumed Sebastian wanted Serena for his mistress, and he'd yielded the field with relatively good grace. His own sexual prowess had been waning then, although he could still manage a few bouts with the right woman. But then, the next thing he knew, the general and his stepdaughter had closed their house on Charles Street and gone abroad. So neither he nor Sebastian had managed to snare the woman.

The carriage halted, and he clambered out, cursing at the ache in his joints, the clumsiness of the servant, the chill in the air. Once upstairs, ensconced in his own bedchamber, where a fire blazed and curtains were drawn tight at the windows and around the great four-poster bed to keep out any flicker of a draft, he sank into a deep armchair by the fire and found he was not in the least ready for bed. His ill humor had to be assuaged before he could sleep. Vigorously, he rang the little handbell on the table beside him.

"Yes, my lord." Louis, his manservant, who waited

in the antechamber until his master was finally abed, appeared immediately.

"Send that black crow, Cosgrove, to me. I'm in the mood to write," Bradley mumbled from the depths of his armchair. "And bring me the cognac."

"At once, my lord." Louis placed the decanter and a goblet on the table beside the viscount and went to summon the luckless Father Cosgrove, whose unhappy task it was to perform as the viscount's personal priest, confessor, and amanuensis. The latter task involved transcribing his lordship's memoirs, which ranged freely over his romantic and sexual encounters. The young priest could rarely hide his horror at the lascivious exploits he was obliged to set down, and the more shocked and horrified he was, the greater pleasure the viscount took in the compilation of his memoirs.

Father Cosgrove, woken abruptly from a deep sleep in his monastic little room under the eaves, wearily donned his black cassock and went to his employer, who greeted him with the instruction, "Pen and paper, crow. I've another installment burning to be told."

The young priest sat at the secretaire, sharpened a quill, dipped it into the inkwell, and waited, stifling a yawn. Bradley decided to recount his fantasies about the lovely Lady Serena, the fantasies he had had when he had first seen her, and because he was in the mood to make mischief, he indulged those fantasies, embellishing them as the mood took him, peopling them with beautiful women entwined together for his delectation, describing the sinuous smoothness of Serena's skin, the firm breasts and backside, the supple limbs, just as he had imagined them. And Father Cosgrove squirmed and suffered as he faithfully wrote down every dictated word.

It took two hours for the viscount's ill temper to dissipate, and by that time, he had imagined himself into his own fantasy world so successfully he was as lustful as a satyr. He knew, alas, that his erection was a feeble thing and wouldn't last, but for a few minutes, he could indulge in the memory of himself as the virile, lusty man of his youth and middle age.

"Go to your bed, crow." He dismissed the priest with a weary wave. "And send Louis to me. I'm ready for my own bed now."

The young priest disappeared as swiftly and silently as he'd arrived, and Louis came in to help his master to bed.

Sleep didn't come to the viscount immediately. He lay wakeful, his mind, for the moment purged of venom, slipping back into memories of the young man he had been, full of ambition, certainly, but also open to love. And how he had loved Aurora. Such a fanciful name for a lady's maid, but she had been in every way the epitome of the rosy dawn, or so he had thought, lost in the sickly realms of calf love. At least, that was what they had said. *Calf love.* They had told him he'd get over it quickly enough, told him to look for a wife among his own people, told him he would be bringing disgrace on the name of Blackwater. And for some idiotic reason, he had believed them. He had been willing to sacrifice his love for the family, until he discovered what they had done to Aurora. Thrown onto the street in the dark hour before dawn, penniless, without references, to fend for herself. She could have been with child; he didn't know, but he did know it was very possible. And although he had hunted high and low for her, the family had managed to dismiss her from the face of the earth. There were no signs that she had ever walked upon it, except for the imprint she had left in his heart.

The family had to pay. He had visited as much disgrace upon them as he could while making his fortune and, indeed, in the manner in which he had made that fortune. But his final revenge was sweet indeed. The stiff-necked moralists of the Blackwater clan would be obliged to take to their collective bosom the disreputable brides of the Blackwater sons. And on his death, his little literary masterpiece would be published, a scandalous pamphlet that would shock and titillate the polite world. Bradley's only regret was that he would not be there to see it. His chances of watching from a roseate cloud in heaven were fairly minimal, he reflected with a twisted grin. And he wasn't sure how clear a view of the world he had left would be possible from the fiery depths of Lucifer's domain.

⁓∞⁓

The following morning, Serena was discussing the supper menus with the cook in the small parlor she had appropriated as her own sitting room when Flanagan came in.

"A Mrs. Sutton and Miss Sutton wish to know if you are at home, my lady."

"Oh . . ." Serena frowned. She hadn't expected them to call so soon. "Yes, of course, Flanagan. Show them up . . . I think we've covered everything for this evening, Mrs. Drake."

"Aye, reckon so, Lady Serena. Them cold roast partridges always go down a treat."

Serena smiled a vague acknowledgment, reflecting that it was always the most expensive delicacies that disappeared first from the supper tables. She got up from the secretaire and went to poke the fire into a more vigorous burn. The day was cloudy, with a chill breeze that needled its way into the room through an ill-fitting window frame. She made a mental note to tell Flanagan. The caretaker ought to be able to plug the gap with something before winter set in.

She straightened, setting aside the poker, as the door opened and Flanagan announced her visitors. "Mrs. Sutton . . . Abigail, my dear . . . how good of you to call. Flanagan, would you bring coffee?"

"Right away, my lady." He backed out as the two ladies came in, Mrs. Sutton's curious gaze already sweeping the room.

"My dear Lady Serena, what a charming room . . . a charming house altogether," she declared. "Much grander than our little lodging on Bruton Street."

"Your house is delightful, Mrs. Sutton, and a very good address. Please, sit down." She indicated a sofa and took a seat opposite. "You've had no more unpleasant adventures, I trust, Abigail."

Abigail shook her head. "Oh, no, not at all. Indeed, it was not very serious, I was foolishly alarmed, I think. Mama and I went shopping this morning in Piccadilly, and it all seemed so busy and ordinary I couldn't imagine why I had been so frightened. But Mr. Sullivan was so very gallant. I shall always be grateful to him." She sighed a little. "I think, and Mama thinks so, too, that I should write him a note to thank him for his kindness. Do you think I should, Lady Serena?"

"If you and your mama feel it would be the right thing to do, then of course, you should . . . thank you, Flanagan . . . there's no need to serve it, I'll pour." Serena nodded to the butler as he set the coffee tray on the table in front of her.

"Unfortunately, he didn't leave his card, so I don't have an address to write to," Abigail said. "Would you know how to get in touch with him?"

"I'm sure I have his card somewhere," Serena said vaguely. It would look strange for a single woman to know by heart the address of a single man who was not related to her. "I'll look for it." She poured coffee, passed the cups. "What plans do you have for the rest of the day?"

"Well, that's why we came to call," Abigail said excitedly. "We wanted to ask you something very important."

"Now, Abigail, let me explain . . . there's no need to rattle on like that, whatever will Lady Serena think." Her mother tapped her knee with her closed fan, and Abigail subsided.

Serena smiled. "Indeed, ma'am, I think nothing of it. 'Tis no wonder Abigail is excited, being in London for the first time. There is so much to see. The lions in the Exchange, the Tower of London, Vauxhall, and Ranelagh Gardens, just as a start."

"Yes, and we shall do all of those things in due course," Mrs. Sutton declared. "But I really wished to ask you, Lady Serena, if you would help me give a dinner party, a small entertainment, very select."

Serena looked surprised. "Help you, ma'am. How?"

"With the guests," Abigail burst in. "You see, we don't really know any of the right kind of people, except you and the general, of course. And I suppose it could be said that we are acquainted with Mr. Sullivan now. He drank ale with Papa . . . but that is the difficulty, because we don't know how to invite him if we don't know where he lives, and we must have some proper guests for him. Papa says he should come and take his mutton with us at any time and not stand on ceremony, but I don't think that's the way people in London do things." She paused for breath.

"Well, that is the long and the short of it, Lady Serena," her mother said, looking reprovingly at her daughter. "For all that the child rattles on so, it is our errand in a nutshell. If you would invite your own friends to dinner at our house, we would start the social ball rolling for Abigail's come-out."

"I see." Serena sipped her coffee. It was a most unusual request, quite extraordinary, in fact, but she could see the sense in it. In fact, it rather amused her. It would be a pleasant distraction from the kind of entertaining she was accustomed to doing in Pickering Place.

"Your friends will find nothing to complain of in my hospitality," Mrs. Sutton said, seeing Serena's hesitation. "I set as fine a table as anyone, though I say it myself. And Mr. Sutton knows his wine, even though he's a plain man, with no nonsense about him. He knows what's what, and he'll do anything to launch his daughter . . . no expense will be spared, I can promise you."

"Indeed, ma'am, I wouldn't give such a consideration a second thought," Serena protested. "And I'm sure I could think of some friends of mine who would be delighted to attend such a party. I need a little time to consider." While Serena herself would never be accepted in the drawing rooms of London's ton, the young men and women who frequented the gaming salons at Pickering Place would probably be willing to accept a social invitation from her, even if their parents would not.

"Well, I'm sure you can find some congenial company for Mr. Sullivan," Marianne said with a little affirming nod. "And I'm just as sure we can't. And we would like to thank him for the service he did Abigail. So tell me when you'd like to invite your friends, and I'll set everything in train. We should have a little music . . . or maybe dancing?" Her eyes gleamed at the thought. "Just a few couples . . . nothing big. What d'you think of that, Lady Serena? Will that be a fine party for you young people?"

"None finer," Serena agreed, somewhat breathless at the speed with which Mrs. Sutton had moved from a small, intimate dinner to a full-scale dance. "I think, though, that it might be wise to have just a few couples for dinner to start with, just as a means of getting established, you understand."

Abigail looked disappointed, but her mother immediately nodded. "Well, you would know best, Lady Serena. You know best how matters are conducted in Society. I'll leave it all to you. You just tell me when and whom to invite, and I'll make it happen." She set down her coffee cup. "Now, we mustn't intrude on your time any longer. Come, Abigail. We have an appointment with the dressmaker for a fitting. Do you know Madame Betty, Lady Serena? I have it on the best authority that she is the most notable dressmaker to the quality."

"I'm sure she is," Serena murmured, never having heard of the seamstress before. Her own clothes were made by the same woman who had made her mother's before her. A quiet Frenchwoman of impeccable taste, who kept her clientele to a select few.

The door to the parlor suddenly opened with undue vigor. "How delightful . . . Mrs. Sutton and the entrancing Miss Sutton." The general entered, all smiles, rubbing his hands with pleasure. "I could hardly credit it when Flanagan told me of your arrival. You do us too much honor, ma'am, indeed you do, to call upon us so quickly after your return to England."

"Lady Serena was kind enough to call upon us just yesterday, General." Marianne gave the general her hand with a bobbed curtsy. He bowed deeply, lifting her hand to his lips, before turning to Abigail. "So, Miss Sutton, how are you enjoying town? Comes up to expectations, I trust. You do look most charming this morning. Fresh as a daisy."

Abigail blushed to the roots of her hair and curtsied low. "You are too kind, sir . . . too kind," she murmured.

"I speak only truth, my dear. Only truth. And is Mr. Sutton not with you?" Heyward looked around as if expecting to see the ebullient corpulence of the redoubtable William popping up from behind the sofa.

"Mr. Sutton had business this morning, but I am charged with a most particular request, General." Marianne fluttered her fan.

"Anything, my dear, ma'am. Any service I can render any of you, I should be honored. Pray, won't you be seated again?" He moved a chair forward for her, and Marianne sat down with another flutter of her fan.

Serena took a seat on the sofa and gestured to Abigail that she should sit beside her, effectively ensuring that the general would have to take a chair on his own. Abigail gave her a grateful smile and accepted the invitation. The general had a disconcerting habit of patting her knee, her hand, even her upper arm if he was sitting close beside her. It was a familiarity not practiced in Stoke-on-Trent Society; indeed, ladies and gentlemen in her experience hitherto did not usually sit beside each other in the confined space of a sofa, unless they were betrothed or related in some way.

"So, how can I be of service, dear ma'am?" The general leaned forward with flattering attention.

"It is not so much for me, sir," Marianne protested. "But for Mr. Sutton. He is in some difficulty about setting up his stable . . . unfamiliar with the way matters go on at Tattersalls, for instance."

"Oh, I should be delighted to assist Mr. Sutton," the general assured her. "Indeed, I am known to be a very fair judge of horseflesh. I'm sure I can advise your husband to good purpose."

"Oh, I don't believe my husband needs advice on the horses themselves," Marianne made haste to assure him. "Indeed, sir, he prides himself on his stables at home. His stud is known the length and breadth of the County, and farmers and gentry alike bring their mares to stud at Bellingham Grove. I doubt there's another man in the country who could best his judgment on horseflesh."

Serena hid a smile at this masterly but unintentional

snub. She could see that her stepfather was distinctly put out, but he could only swallow his chagrin.

He rose rather abruptly to his feet, saying gruffly, "Well, as to that, ma'am, who's to say? I should be happy to be of service to Mr. Sutton in any way he wishes. He should call upon me. I am generally at home in the mornings. Now, I bid you good day, ma'am . . . Miss Sutton." He bowed and marched in soldierly fashion from the parlor.

Marianne and Abigail took their leave almost immediately, leaving Serena to savor the memory of her stepfather for once put out of countenance. And to wonder at the extraordinary request made of herself. To invite her own friends to be guests of someone else was most peculiar.

She was, however, perfectly happy to help with Abigail's social debut, at least as far as she was able. The highest echelons of Society were as much beyond her as they were beyond the Suttons, although the Suttons didn't know that. As far as they were concerned, General Heyward and Lady Serena were impeccable members of Society, and that was how it must remain until Abigail was safe from the general's clutches. She could expose herself and the general for the charlatans they were, of course, but from what she'd seen of Mr. Sutton, his reaction to that would be to sweep his wife and daughter back to the Midlands without ado. And Serena could see no reason Abigail should be deprived of her debut and the opportunity to make a good marriage just because Heyward was on the prowl. Serena would forestall him somehow, and it would give her enormous pleasure to do so.

Of course, once the highest echelons of Society would not have been beyond her. But there was no point dwelling on the happy times before her mother's remarriage.

Resolutely, Serena put memories of the past behind her. They only depressed her and made her present existence even harder to endure. At least, her mother had been spared the worst. Life with her second husband had been bad enough, but she had not experienced the worst degradations. Serena could take some measure of comfort in that.

She turned her thoughts down another rather interesting path. Both Mrs. Sutton and Abigail seemed very keen on advancing their acquaintance with the Honorable Sebastian Sullivan. Could they have set their sights there? It was an intriguing idea but surely impossible. Sebastian would never consider such a misalliance. He was by no means a high stickler for convention, but there were some things a man of his lineage just did not do.

Chapter Five

"No, this won't do. Help me take this off, Bridget." Serena regarded her image in the glass with a frown of distaste. She had liked the lavender silk sacque gown when she had first put it on, it still flowed in graceful folds around her tall, slender figure, but now the color didn't seem right. It seemed to make her look sallow, and where it ordinarily accentuated the color of her eyes, it seemed this morning to make them appear dull.

Her maid helped her out of the gown, hanging it up again in the armoire. "Which will you wear, then, my lady?"

Serena leaned over Bridget's shoulder to flick through the contents of the armoire. Even when the general had less than two pennies to rub together, Serena's wardrobe was always at the forefront of fashion. It was considered a necessary business expense.

"The green and white muslin over the green satin petticoat," she decided at last, casting a glance at the clock on the mantel. It was already eleven o'clock, and her rendezvous with Sebastian was at noon.

It was quite a simple gown as prevailing fashion went, the sleeves banded in dark green velvet at the elbow, delicate falls of lace ending just above her wrists. The pale muslin overskirt opened over a dramatic dark green silk underskirt. The décolletage was edged with a deep lace collar, and a dainty white fichu tied just above her breasts gave the impression of modesty.

She surveyed her reflection anew, eyes narrowed, head tilted slightly. It would have to do.

"Will you wear the dark green cloth mantle, my lady? It's quite chilly out, and it would look very well with the gown," Bridget suggested rather tentatively.

Serena turned and smiled. "Oh, forgive me, Bridget. I'm being a miserable, irritable cat this morning. I didn't sleep well. Yes, the green mantle will be perfect." She hadn't slept well, but then, she often didn't these days. It had nothing to do with the upcoming meeting with Sebastian, or so she told herself.

The maid draped the short, hooded cloak over her shoulders, fastened the jet button at the throat, and handed Serena her dark green kidskin gloves, a perfect match for her heeled shoes. "You look beautiful, Lady Serena." Her eyes widened with admiration.

"And you're very sweet to say so." Serena gave the young girl a kiss. "If General Heyward asks for me, tell him I will be back later this afternoon."

"Should I tell him where you're going, ma'am?"

"How could you, my dear? You don't know," Serena said with a smile. "Would you have a bath prepared for me this evening, before dinner? And I will wear the ivory silk."

"Yes, my lady." Bridget curtsied as Serena hurried from the room.

She walked quickly to St. James's Place, where Margaret's footman opened the door at her knock. "Mrs. Standish told us to expect you, Lady Serena. Refreshments will be served to you and your guest when you wish for it." He took Serena's mantle and gloves as he spoke, then walked ahead of her upstairs to Margaret's parlor.

The room was immediately welcoming. A fire burned in the grate; decanters of sherry, madeira, and claret were arrayed on the sideboard; fresh flowers bloomed on windowsills and side tables; fresh candles only awaited flint and tinder.

Serena looked around appreciatively but couldn't help the wry thought that it was a veritable love nest, exactly as Margaret intended it to be. In Margaret's eyes, a rendezvous was a rendezvous, after all, and anything could happen. But then, she didn't know the history behind this meeting.

Serena wondered for a moment if Sebastian would get the wrong idea but quickly dismissed the thought. He was still far too hurt and angry for that. Her cruel-to-be-kind strategy had certainly worked, she reflected, thinking of the coldness in his voice, the flicker of contempt in his eye. He had requested this meeting to clear the ground sufficiently for them to meet with a convincing semblance of civility in public if and when it happened. And she was perfectly happy with that.

"Should I bring up your guest as soon as he arrives, Lady Serena, or announce him first?" Margaret Standish's butler knew his job well.

"You may bring up the Honorable Sebastian Sullivan as soon as he arrives, Horace. Thank you."

She went to the window as the door closed on the man and looked down at the street. From here, she would see Sebastian as he turned the corner of the square. She felt unaccountably nervous and found herself twitching at the curtains, moving around the room, straightening perfectly aligned cushions, adjusting the arrangements of the flowers in the vases. It was close to noon, ten more minutes. Sebastian would be punctual. He was nothing if not courteous.

Precisely at two minutes to noon, Sebastian rounded the corner exactly as she'd predicted. He was on horseback, in buckskin breeches and a dark wool coat, a brilliant scarlet plume in his silver-laced bicorne hat. Her heart turned over. How many times in the old days had he come to her like this, while she waited in the little room above the taproom of the inn on King Street, all impatient anticipation for his arrival? For a moment, as she watched him dismount beneath the window, she could almost imagine she was back in that halcyon past . . . that in a moment, she would hear his feet on the stairs, racing to be with her. He would fling open the door as he had so often done and be beside her with two long, quick strides, catching her up into his arms, his mouth on hers in a long kiss that would seem to draw her very soul from her body.

She lost sight of him as he stepped to the front door, but she heard his firm, decisive knock. She seemed to be having trouble breathing, and her face felt flushed as she waited for his step in the corridor outside. She heard his voice, so achingly familiar, speaking to the butler, and then the door opened. "Mr. Sullivan, my lady." Horace stepped back as Sebastian entered the parlor. The door closed, and they were alone.

Sebastian stood with the door at his back. He tucked his whip under his arm while he drew off his gloves. "So, Serena" was all he said as he looked at her, a strange light in his blue eyes.

"So, Sebastian," she responded, trying for a light tone but failing miserably. Just speaking his name seemed weighted with significance, with so many memories now flooding back in a tidal wave of emotion and loss.

She turned away hastily, afraid that he would see the sheen of incipient tears.

"Thank you for coming." It sounded absurdly stiff, laughably incongruous in the circumstances.

"Not at all," he responded politely, tossing whip, hat, and gloves onto a console table.

He was waiting for her to make the first move, Serena realized, which was unfair, considering that he had insisted on this meeting. Annoyance banished tears, and she said rather sharply, "So, what did you wish to talk about?"

He laughed, a short crack of mirthless amusement. "Don't be ridiculous, Serena."

She spun around, her eyes now snapping with anger. "You call *me* ridiculous? You're the one who insisted on this ground-clearing meeting. So let's get on with it. Start clearing the ground, Sebastian."

He sighed and glanced around the cozy room. "This is a pleasant house," he observed. "Whom does it belong to?"

She should have remembered Sebastian's adroit way of changing the subject to small talk when tempers were inclined to get heated, Serena reflected. She responded in like manner. "An old friend. She happens to be out of town for the day."

"I see. 'Tis certainly a discreet rendezvous." His eye fell on the decanters on the sideboard. He suggested gently, "A glass of wine would not come amiss?"

Serena fought the well-remembered urge to throw something at him. Now he was trying to put her out of countenance by pointing out her lack of courteous hospitality. It was another of his infuriating habits that she remembered all too well. Of course, in the old days, it tended to make her laugh. But that was then. She produced a calm smile and gestured to the sideboard. "Please. Help yourself."

He turned to do so, saying over his shoulder, "Will

you drink sherry, as usual . . . or have your tastes changed?"

For a moment, she wished she could say that they had, but it would be a childish act that would hurt no one but herself. "Thank you."

Sebastian poured wine and brought the glasses across the room. He handed her one and raised his own in a mock toast. "To clear ground, then."

She shook her head and took a sip, before saying, "So, how are things with you, Sebastian?" She didn't tell him how she had scoured the English papers whenever she could lay hands on them, dreading to see a notice of his engagement or even marriage.

"Well enough. And you, Serena? How is it with you?"

She wanted to give him a bold answer, tell him that everything was wonderful, but the words would not form themselves. Instead, she shrugged with an assumption of carelessness, saying only, "Business is good. The general is pleased enough."

He regarded her over the lip of his glass in silence for a moment. He didn't believe her. Something of the essential Serena was missing, the sensual energy, the spirit, the liveliness that he had loved so much. It was as if a flame had been extinguished. But then, he reflected, that flame had been extinguished three years ago when she had denied any feelings for him.

"And *you*?" he pressed. "How is it with you? I care nothing for the gambling hell you run."

How should you? she thought bitterly. *What could you*

possibly know of my life? "My well-being and the success of the business are inextricable," she told him with a chilly smile, setting down her glass.

He was silent again, before saying quietly, "Why did you betray me, Serena? Did you fall out of love with me overnight? Because it's no good telling me that you were never in love with me. We were both deeply in love with each other, and nothing you can say will ever convince me otherwise."

She shook her head. "We felt something for each other, Sebastian, I won't deny that. But it was a youthful frolic, a summer temptation. It couldn't last . . . of course, it couldn't. You were not being realistic if you thought it might become something lasting, established in some way. I'm one of faro's daughters, and you're a younger son of a noble and proud family with no prospects. What would we live on, air?"

Scorn laced her voice, and Sebastian's face became very pale, a telltale muscle twitching in his cheek. "We could have managed," he stated. "If you'd had the courage to tell the truth and face the truth, we could have managed. You were a coward, Serena." He drained his glass and set it aside. "That is all I have to say."

He picked up his hat, whip, and gloves, turning to the door.

The monstrous injustice of the accusation overwhelmed her. She struggled with herself for a moment before saying with credible mockery, "And that's cleared the air, I suppose. We can now exchange civilized bows should we happen to have the misfortune to bump into each other again."

Sebastian spun around sharply, lips thinned. He stood tapping his gloves against his palm, his nostrils flaring as he fought to control the surge of fury at her insulting, dismissive tone of voice. It was just as she had spoken to him that afternoon three years ago, and whereas then it had devastated him, seemed to cut him off at the knees, now it just made him angrier than he could ever remember being.

She had turned away from him and stood at the window, her back rigid, shoulders set, staring out at the houses opposite.

There was something about the way she was standing that penetrated his anger. She seemed suddenly so vulnerable, the slender white column of her long neck looking too fragile to bear the weight of her head. For a moment, he had to fight the urge to go to her, to press his lips to the hollow of her neck. It had always been one of his favorite spots to kiss. The memory was so vivid he thought he could smell the fresh rosewater scent of her skin and hair.

He hesitated, then said more moderately, "I shouldn't have called you a coward. I beg your pardon. You had your reasons, I'm sure. And if I mistook a fleeting attraction for a deeper love, then that was my error." He gave a short laugh. "I was something of a moon calf, after all."

His voice was low and strong, and Serena slowly turned back from the window. His mouth was set in a decisive line, his blue eyes clear and unflinching, fixed upon her countenance. And she realized with a start that the tender, loving, carefree young man of that wonderful, long, passionate idyll had matured, grown into this broad-shouldered man radiating strength, confidence, determination. His features were somehow more defined, and his eyes, luminous as always, held a gravity that had not been there before. Distractedly, she found herself wondering if they would still light up with laughter as they once had done so readily. It would be a pity if experience had vanquished that capacity for merriment.

But at the moment, despite his apparently conciliatory words, their chief expression was one of controlled anger, and she knew he was entitled to it. She had been trying to provoke anger rather than sentiment and had certainly succeeded.

"Think nothing of it," she said with a light shrug. "Can we call a truce?"

"A truce," he agreed, extending his hand.

She stepped forward and placed her own hand in his. His fingers closed tightly over hers, and for a moment, their eyes met, and once again, they both had the sensation of losing themselves in each other. Sebastian dropped her hand quickly, averted his eyes for a moment, breaking the connection.

"Goodbye, Serena." He walked quickly to the door.

"Goodbye, Sebastian. Horace will show you out."

"Thank you." And he was gone.

She listened to his retreating step on the stairs, his

voice exchanging pleasantries with Horace, the snap of the front door as it closed behind him. She went to the window, standing slightly to one side, shielded from the street by the velvet curtain as she looked down to watch him untether his horse and mount. For an instant, he glanced up at the window, and she stepped back swiftly, even though she knew he couldn't see her. Then he turned his mount's head in the direction of St. James's Street.

Suddenly exhausted, drained as if she had run a marathon, Serena sank down into the low armchair beside the fire and rested her head against its cushioned back, closing her eyes. The first time she had seen Sebastian Sullivan had been at a small party given by one of the regular patrons of General Heyward's gambling house on Charles Street. The young host had professed undying love for Lady Serena Carmichael and followed her around like a lost puppy. Left to herself, she would have let him down gently and moved on, but her stepfather had decreed that she keep the young man on a leading rein. He stood to inherit a large fortune and was kept in ample funds, and it suited the general to see most of those funds absorbed by the Charles Street faro bank.

Serena had obeyed, as she usually did. Young Lord Fairfax would not be hurt overmuch, certainly not enough for her to risk her stepfather's wrath. And then into that intimate gathering had walked the Honorable Sebastian Sullivan. A golden-haired Adonis, with the most startling blue eyes and a smile that filled her with sunshine. He had seemed only to glance once at her before moving into the room, losing himself among his friends, but it hadn't been many minutes before he'd materialized at her side, handing her a glass of champagne with the careless comment, "I have a feeling this will be welcome." She had laughed, asked how he could tell, and he'd responded, "Oh, I have a feeling that I'm always going to know exactly what you would like and when you would like it."

The audacity of it had taken her breath away, and even now, bruised though she was, Serena smiled, remembering the overpowering thrill those words had given her. And Sebastian had fulfilled that promise in every detail.

Until . . . until she'd done what had to be done. And now he couldn't forgive her. How could he? She couldn't forgive herself.

Chapter Six

The young man who stood outside the house on Bruton Street self-consciously adjusting his cravat was clearly nervous. He was dressed with impeccable taste in coat and breeches of dark brown silk with a waistcoat of old gold striped with green. His black leather shoes were highly polished, their red heels showing not a hint of scuff, his silver-knobbed cane carried at exactly the right angle, his black tricorne hat nicely edged with gold. Twice he stepped up to the door to lift the brass knocker, and twice he stepped back. After a moment, he turned and walked away to the corner of the street, where again he stopped, looked back, seemed to make up his mind, and turned to walk back to the house.

Abigail had been watching the pantomime from the parlor window. "Oh, Mama, only see, Mr. Wedgwood's coming back again. D'you think he's afraid he has the address wrong?"

"I'm sure I don't know, Abigail. Now, come away from the window. It's not in the least ladylike to be hanging out into the street like that. Whatever will the neighbors think?" Marianne was not looking best pleased as she plied her needle to her tambour frame.

"I don't believe the neighbors so much as glance from their windows, Mama." Abigail withdrew her head with a little pout. "No one is the least curious here, haven't you noticed? At home, everyone knows what's happening on the street. Who's visiting whom . . . who's not talking to whom. It's so much friendlier."

"That kind of nosiness is not appropriate in good society," her mother informed her with a sniff. "Now, pick up your work. If we're to have a visitor, he can't find you with idle hands."

Abigail picked up her embroidery, her ears pricked for the sound of the door knocker. She jumped when she heard it, and a slight flush enlivened the perfect peaches-and-cream complexion. Resolutely, she kept her eyes on her work, not looking up when the butler appeared in the doorway.

"Mr. Jonas Wedgwood, ma'am, wishes to know if you are at home."

Marianne glanced up. It was a nuisance that Abigail had come to the attention of the young man. For all his family's prominence in their local Society, he was not the husband Marianne had in mind for her daughter. But good manners forbade her denying hospitality to the son of such a family, whose social consequence in Stoke-on-Trent was of the highest. "I believe we are, Morrison. Desire Mr. Wedgwood to step up, please."

Morrison bowed and retreated, and a few minutes

later, the young man appeared in the doorway, sweeping off his hat in a deep bow. "Mrs. Sutton, ma'am . . . Miss Sutton . . . how good of you to receive me. I had hoped to leave my card . . . had not dared to hope to find you at home." His eyes darted to Abigail, who remained head down at her embroidery.

Marianne set aside her tambour frame and smiled graciously. "Do sit down, Mr. Wedgwood. We had not expected a call from you so early. I had thought you to be on some business for your uncle."

"I am, ma'am, but it does not occupy all my time, and my uncle has encouraged me to take some time to become familiar with London." He glanced at Abigail, who finally raised her head and bestowed a shy smile on the visitor. "I was hoping you and Miss Ab . . . Miss Sutton would accept an invitation to the theatre one evening, followed by supper. I have a box at the Drury Lane Theatre. They are playing *The Tempest,* I believe, and if you would not think it an impertinence, ma'am, I would be most honored . . ." The speech faded. He twisted his hat between his hands, and his cane fell to the floor with a clatter. Blushing, he bent to pick it up.

Abigail clapped her hands. "Oh, Mama, that would be wonderful . . . to visit the theatre . . . oh, how I have longed to go. Who is playing Miranda, Mr. Wedgwood? Do you know?"

His blush deepened as he straightened, his cane firmly held across his lap. "I'm afraid not, Miss Sutton. I . . . I fear I neglected to discover that." In truth, he had no idea what the play was about, only that it was respectably classical. He looked appealingly at Marianne, who was frowning at her tambour frame.

Mrs. Sutton looked up with a chilly smile. "I will have to consult Mr. Sutton. He may not consider the theatre a suitable place for a young girl, Mr. Wedgwood. Abigail has a reputation to consider."

Crestfallen, the young man stammered that he hoped he had not offended with his invitation. He had merely wished to give Miss Sutton pleasure . . . and her mother, of course. Marianne responded with another chilly nod, and silence fell.

"I do so hope Papa will let us come, Mr. Wedgwood," Abigail said after a moment's awkwardness. "I would dearly love to go, and you must not think for an instant that such an invitation could offend . . . oh, no, quite the opposite." She cast a defiant glance at her mother. "In fact, I will ask him at once." She darted to the bell and, before Marianne could expostulate, had given it a vigorous tug. Morrison appeared immediately.

"Please ask Papa if he would come up to us and decide something, Morrison." Abigail spoke in a rush, trying to forestall her mother. "It's a matter of the utmost importance, tell him."

Marianne would not countermand her daughter's instructions in front of a servant. She set her lips tightly and returned to her embroidery as the butler left.

Mr. Sutton bustled into the parlor in a very few minutes. "Now, what is all this about, my sweet? What do

you want from your old papa now? Oh, it's Jonas Wedgwood, isn't it? Welcome, young man . . . welcome, indeed." He pumped Jonas's hand heartily. "So how has
your business fared . . . tell me all. I'm fair starved of
good business talk these days." He looked as if he was
about to bear the young man away, down to the library,
there to discuss the pennies and guineas that so interested him.

"No, Papa," Abigail stated, jumping to her feet. "You
cannot take Mr. Wedgwood away until you have ruled
on his invitation. He has invited Mama and me to the
theatre one evening. It would be the best thing of anything, and I so long to go, but Mama says you must give
your permission."

"Oh, does she, indeed?" William looked at his wife
and had no difficulty understanding the situation. Marianne expected him to veto the outing, although he could
not for the life of him see why. In general, he followed
his wife's wishes when it came to their daughter, telling
himself that women understood these things better than
men, but this morning, a little devil stirred. Abigail was
looking with those great, pleading eyes fixed upon him,
her soft little hand was on his arm, and he liked young
Jonas Wedgwood, had known his uncle for years.

"I see no harm in it," he pronounced. "It will be good
for you, puss, to see a little town life, have a little excitement, don't you agree, my love?" He offered his wife a
cajoling smile, which she did not return.

"If you approve, sir, then that is all there is to say

on the matter," she declared, setting her needle with a vigorous jab that caused her husband a stab of vicarious pain.

"Well, now that's settled, I must take Jonas here down to the library for a tankard of ale and a good talk about the markets. Come . . . come, my friend. Say farewell to the ladies. You'll be seeing enough of them, I don't doubt." He tucked a hand under the younger man's arm and bore him off after Jonas had managed a hasty bow to the ladies.

"Oh, Mama, what should I wear?" Abigail was jumping with excitement. "I shall go and choose straight away. Becky shall help me. Do you think the blue velvet with the overskirt of sky-blue gauze? 'Tis exactly the color of my eyes, the seamstress said so. And I could wear the blue straw hat with the gauze veil . . . or perhaps the jonquil muslin . . . or d'you think that will be too light for the evening?"

"Do stop rattling on, child." Marianne attempted to repress this exuberance. "'Tis only a visit to the theatre on some evening. No one will see you, you're not going into Society."

Abigail stopped bouncing. "People *will* see me, Mama. Everyone is on show at the theatre. I know 'tis not like going to a ball, but it is my first real outing, and I know people will notice me. People always notice me," she added with a slightly complacent smile.

"You're a pretty enough child, I grant you," her mother said, "but 'tis most unbecoming in a girl to draw attention to her beauty. Now, sit down and get on with your work."

Abigail hesitated, then obeyed. She had won one victory, the most important one. It would be politic now to rest on her laurels.

"So, have you talked to the girl yet?" The Earl of Burford stood, hands behind his back, in front of the fire in the library at Pickering Place.

General Heyward poured claret into two glasses before answering. He brought one over to the earl. "Not as yet." He raised his glass in a silent toast that was not returned.

"When d'you propose telling her, then?" His lordship took a sip of wine. "I tell you, Heyward, I'm not prepared to wait forever. I want the girl now, not when she's lost all her freshness. I thought she was looking peaky the other night at the tables."

"I assure you that Serena is perfectly well, Lord Burford." The general's tone was a little haughty. "I will talk to her when I have the mortgages in hand."

The earl gave a sharp bark of laughter. "Indeed? And you think I'm fool enough to pay up before I've sampled the goods?"

"You will not sample them else, my lord." General Heyward was a gambler through and through. He watched his visitor carefully through hooded eyes, judging how far he could go before the earl called his bluff.

"And what if the girl's not willing?" Burford changed tack, sipping his wine with a critical frown. "Not bad, this . . . not bad at all. One thing I'll say for you, Heyward, you keep a good cellar."

The general looked gratified but answered the question with a vague gesture. "Serena will do as she's told, Lord Burford. You may rest assured."

His lordship merely grunted. "Let's to business."

"By all means." The general waved to a chair. "Shall we be comfortable?"

The earl sat down, stretching his rather stubby legs clad in fashionably striped stockings to the fire, twisting the stem of his glass between his fingers. "So the terms of our agreement . . . I have exclusive rights to your step-daughter for as long as it pleases me. In exchange, I will return to you the mortgages that I hold on this property, giving you free and clear title."

"Exactly, my lord." The general's eyes gleamed. He leaned forward a little in his chair. "I suggest as earnest money that you burn in my presence the smaller of the two mortgages, for nine hundred guineas, I believe, and then I make Serena available to you. Once you have . . . uh . . . consummated your liaison, shall we say, then you will destroy the larger of the two . . . that for ten thousand guineas. After that, Serena will be yours for as long as she pleases you."

The earl considered this, still twirling his now empty

glass between his fingers. The general reached for the decanter on the table beside him, leaned forward, and refilled his guest's glass.

"Talk to her first," Burford stated finally. "When you can assure me that she understands the situation . . . the bargain . . . then I will destroy the first mortgage. After one week, if she remains cooperative, I will destroy the second."

General Heyward closed his eyes as he rested his head against the chair back. There were ways to compel Serena initially to the earl's bed, but whether she cooperated afterwards was a rather different proposition. After a moment, he opened his eyes. The earl was watching his deliberations with a cynical curl of his lip.

"I believe, Burford, that ensuring my stepdaughter's cooperation once I have delivered her to you should be your responsibility," the general said. "I will not be present, after all."

"Do you doubt her willing cooperation?" the earl asked sharply.

"That depends very much on you, my lord," the general returned deliberately. "As I have said, I will guarantee her cooperation as far as the bedchamber door. The rest will be up to you."

The earl set down his glass and stood up. "I will send word when I am ready to make a decision." He moved to the door. "Good day to you, Heyward."

The general was on his feet now, ready to usher his visitor from the house. He was fairly certain he had won the concessions he wanted but not positive. However, he must play the cards to the end. "I will await your word, sir." He bowed the earl from the room.

Serena was approaching the house with her maid as the earl emerged from the front door, half turned to complete his farewells to the general who stood just inside. Her skin crawled as she saw him, and she wondered if she could turn tail and duck into a side street before he saw her, but it was too late. He had turned from the door before she could decide which way to go.

"Why, Lady Serena, well met, indeed." He came down the steps and waited for her to reach him.

He bowed, and she curtsied in return with a murmured, "My lord," hoping to move quickly past him and into the house. But he blocked the steps up to the door, one foot on the bottom step, one hand resting on the iron railing, smiling at her with an appraising air that made her feel slightly sick. It was as if he were assessing the qualities of a filly at Tattersalls.

"So where have you been this fine morning?" he inquired with an attempt at a genial smile. "A pleasant stroll, I trust." He saw the parcels her maid was carrying. "Ah, shopping, I see. Something delectable to enhance your exquisite figure."

It was an offensive comment, something no gentleman would say to a lady, and it conveyed exactly what he thought of Serena's position in his world. With supreme effort, she held her tongue and stared at him in haughty silence before she turned to her maid as if the general were not standing there, leering at her. "Take the parcels to my bedchamber, Bridget. You may go before me."

His lordship was obliged to step aside for the maid, who hurried up the steps to the door. Without a word, Serena swept past him in her wake and vanished into the hall, leaving him standing on the pavement.

She realized she was shaking a little as she attained the calm safety of the house and was ill prepared to face her stepfather, who was about to reenter the library. He turned as she came in. "Ah, Serena, did you meet Lord Burford on the street?"

"Briefly, sir." She hurried to the staircase.

"I trust you were courteous," he demanded curtly. "Need I remind you that his lordship holds the mortgages on this property?"

"No, sir. You have no need to remind me of that fact. His lordship makes it clear on every occasion how much we are his debtors. Now, if you'll excuse me, I have work to do abovestairs." She hurried up the stairs without waiting for a response.

Heyward watched her go, a speculative frown on his brow. She was so unlike her mother, made of much stronger material, but that was what made her such a good partner in the business. She was competent, a clever gambler, good with figures, careful with household expenditures. He really did not wish to antagonize her. She must understand how her cooperation in this rather distasteful business was absolutely necessary if they were to carry this enterprise off. If necessary, he would compel her obedience. Burford wanted her, and Burford must have her. But he couldn't help hoping that compulsion would not be necessary.

Sebastian heard the front door bang, heralding his brother's return from whatever scintillating dinner at the Royal Society he had been attending. He put aside the book he had been reading with rather less than wholehearted concentration and waited for Perry to enter the parlor.

"What ho, Seb." Perry greeted him cheerfully as he came in, his cheeks reddened by the cold wind blasting the streets. "You having a quiet evening? Not like you." He threw his cloak and gloves onto a chair and came to the fire, rubbing his hands. "Nippy out there."

"Warm in here, though," his twin pointed out. "Have you supped? There's an excellent pheasant pie if you fancy it." He waved towards the sideboard, where covered dishes stood. "Jasper brought back four braces of pheasants from Blackwater after his visit there last week, and Mrs. Hogarth made these excellent pies. Our considerate brother sent one over for us to enjoy."

"Did he have good shooting?" Perry lifted the lids on the dishes, deciding he'd postpone supper for a while, although the pie did look toothsome. He poured wine and sat down opposite his brother.

"Apparently. But he's concerned about maintaining

the coverts in the North Wood. They need money spent on 'em, and the revenues from the timber are lower than usual."

"Mm." Peregrine kicked a fallen log back into the hearth. "No getting away from the fact that Blackwater is in need of a sizable injection of capital. I wonder if Jasper's getting impatient with us. After all, he's done his bit to satisfy the terms of Bradley's will."

"If he is, he said nothing . . . gave no indication of it." Sebastian cocked his head at his brother. "Any progress on your bride hunt?"

Peregrine shrugged. "I don't know yet . . . maybe . . . but 'tis early days. How about you?"

Sebastian frowned, looking for words to express a feeling that he hadn't quite identified even to himself. But his brother was always a reliable sounding board. "To tell the truth, Perry, I can't seem to summon much enthusiasm for the quest anymore."

"Oh? Any particular reason?" Perry's eyes sharpened. He'd lay odds Lady Serena Carmichael's reappearance had something to do with it.

Sebastian didn't answer at once. He leaned forward to add another log to the fire, poking the wood to create a bright burst of flame. That morning's confrontation with Serena had thrown him off balance in a way that he had not expected. It had brought all the old feelings to the fore again, his hurt, his anger, but stronger than either were the sweeter memories of their long-ago passion. Just seeing her had stirred into a wave-tossed tempest the calm waters into which he had finally steered himself.

His head was too full of Serena to allow room for another woman. And yet he knew family obligations meant that he must play his part in the bargain with his brothers. The family as a whole was more important than any individual's inclinations. But how could he pursue a bride who would answer Viscount Bradley's criteria if he couldn't get Serena out of his head? But of course, he couldn't renege on the bargain. His brothers were depending upon him.

He became aware that his twin was regarding him quizzically but with a slightly anxious air. "Serena's reappearance, as I'm sure you've guessed, is complicating matters," he said, hoping the vagueness would satisfy Perry.

"How so?" Perry repeated.

Sebastian shook his head in frustration. "I don't know, Perry. I can't forgive her, and yet when I see her, she just . . . oh, I don't know how to put it." He shook his head again. "She just seems to fill me up."

Peregrine absorbed this in silence for a moment, then uncurled his long lean frame from the chair. "I think I shall sample the pheasant pie now." He cut himself a hearty slice and returned to his fireside chair. "So, is the Lady Serena as beautiful as ever?" he mumbled through a mouthful of flaky pastry and succulent bird.

"Yes, but in a different way," Sebastian responded, still feeling for words. "She's older, of course, but there's something else I can't put my finger on. Something about her eyes. A sadness, I think it is. As if something's been extinguished." He sighed deeply. "When I see it, Perry, I forget to be angry with her. I can't help wondering what happened in the last three years to cause that."

Perry swallowed his mouthful. "Why don't you ask her?"

"Because I do not want to get entangled again," his twin declared vehemently. "I can't afford to, Perry. I thought I was over her, over the whole business, and now I don't know if I am. But I do know that she's not good for me. And," he added grimly, "she's certainly not good for this bride quest we're on."

"I can see the problem," Perry said through another mouthful of pie. "But not the solution, I'm afraid."

"No, well, I'll think of something." Sebastian sipped his wine, feeling a little better. It was always a relief to confide in Perry, who never failed to respond in exactly the right way, even if he had no answer to his twin's dilemma.

Perry accepted the subject as closed, at least for the present. "This pie is vintage Mrs. Hogarth, isn't it? I do miss her cooking. Mrs. Croft does not have the same touch somehow."

Sebastian smiled. "We can always wangle a dinner invitation to Upper Brook Street. Clarissa's always pleased to see us."

"True enough. Will you tell Jasper about your bind?"

Perry raised an eyebrow and was not surprised when his twin shook his head. "Wise of you," he agreed.

"No point stirring the waters unnecessarily," Sebastian responded. "And I'm sure it'll resolve itself soon enough."

Peregrine was not as sanguine as his brother, but he kept his own counsel. It was the devil's own work that had brought Serena Carmichael back into Seb's life, and the devil worked his own mischief.

Sebastian lay wakeful that night, unable to find a comfortable position in the deep feather bed. The chamber grew colder as the fire died down, and wind gusted against the panes, making them rattle. He was not accustomed to insomnia, ordinarily falling asleep within moments of putting his head on the pillow, and he found himself growing increasingly irritable as the hours crept past, and he lay listening to the rattling windows and the creaks and groans of the house.

He knew what the problem was, of course. Wretched Serena. He couldn't get her out of his head. Those huge violet eyes, shadowed with some hidden distress, the tiny lines of tension around her eyes and mouth. The Serena he had known three years ago had seemed so much more carefree, even impulsive on occasion, but he couldn't imagine the Serena of this morning giving in to impulse. She had struck him as constantly on the watch for something, alert to the possibility of danger like a rabbit in the middle of an exposed field. Why? What had happened in the last three years?

Why don't you ask her?

He had dismissed Perry's suggestion out of hand, but Sebastian recognized that cowardice had been behind his reflexive response. He was afraid to be drawn in again. Afraid of being hurt . . . or, rather, of opening himself to hurt.

And yet, as he threw himself onto his other side, flinging his legs wide in an effort to find a cool space, he knew that he had no choice. He would never find peace if he didn't somehow understand what had happened to change Serena. And maybe if he discovered that, he might finally understand why she had betrayed their love in the first place.

Chapter Seven

General Heyward found Serena sitting at her secretaire in her parlor. "Ah, I'm glad to find you in, my dear." He beamed at her, closing the door behind him. "How fetching you look, as always. That particular shade of dark red suits you very well. But then, you have always known how to dress, to be at the forefront of fashion . . . just like your poor dear mother."

Serena made no comment, merely set aside her quill, rose to her feet with a small curtsy, then resumed her seat. "You wished to see me, sir."

"Yes . . . yes, indeed." He rubbed his hands together as if about to announce a wonderful treat. "In truth, my dear, we have some urgent business to discuss."

"Oh?" She raised her eyebrows. "Something to do with the accounts? Is something wrong?"

"No . . . no, nothing like that. You have them right as always, my dear. Such a clever puss . . . such a head for figures." His beam grew even brighter, if that was possible.

Serena thought it made him look like a gargoyle, it was such an unlikely expression on the pouchy cheeks and doughy features, and it came nowhere near his eyes, which remained as small, hard, and suspiciously calculating as ever. It was a beam that made her very uneasy.

He sat down on the chaise, then stood up again, pacing from fire to window, hands behind his back. "The fact is, my dear, the business is rather unpleasant."

That came as no surprise to Serena. She remained seated, her hands clasped lightly in her lap, and waited.

"Lord Burford, you see," he said, sounding almost apologetic, which astonished her. "He holds the mortgages on this house, as you know."

"Yes." She was determined to give him no encouragement for whatever was to come next.

"Yes . . . two of them."

She inclined her head in silent acknowledgment.

"Well, I'll come straight to the point. Burford is prepared to cancel them both."

"In exchange for what?" Serena asked coldly, a little shard of ice behind her ribs. "Or is his lordship perhaps suffering from an attack of generosity?"

"Don't be absurd, Serena." The old Heyward broke through the congenial and conciliatory surface. "Burford wouldn't give anyone the parings of his nails."

"So what does he want?" she demanded bluntly, even though she knew. That little shard of ice was digging deeper.

"You, daughter. He wants you." The general took out

his handkerchief and mopped his brow as if he found the parlor unusually warm.

Serena, on the other hand, was chilled to the bone. "No," she said flatly. "I won't do it."

"Daughter, you *will*." All pretense of amity left his expression. "You will do your filial duty."

"You are not my father, General Heyward." With a supreme effort, Serena remained in her chair as he strode towards her, his fists clenched, his face scarlet with choler.

"You will do as I say. You have not a penny to your name. If I throw you out on the streets, which I promise you I will not hesitate to do, how will you live? You'll be selling yourself behind the columns of the Piazza before the year is out."

His spittle showered her face, and with a disdainful movement, she wiped the back of her hand across her face, rising gracefully from her chair as she did so. "If I must prostitute myself, I will do it on my own terms," she declared. "I will not be sold to Burford. And believe me, General, if you make the slightest attempt to touch me, I will kill you." Her voice was deadly quiet, her violet eyes glacial.

She moved sideways suddenly, unlocking a drawer in the secretaire. When she turned back to him, she held a small silver-mounted pistol in her hand. He could be in no doubt about the seriousness of the threat.

Heyward stared at the weapon. "Where did you get that?"

"That is no concern of yours, sir. What is your concern is the certainty that I will use it if you ever so much as attempt to do to me again what you did in Brussels."

His nostrils flared, and shock filled his eyes. He stared at her, then down at the pistol. "I don't know what you're talking about."

She lifted the pistol and relished the moment when he drew back involuntarily, a flicker of fear crossing his face. "You lie . . . but I, sir, do not. I *will* kill you."

"You'd hang?" He almost spat the question.

"For that . . . willingly," she answered. "Believe me."

And he did. For the moment stymied, General Heyward glared at his stepdaughter, then stalked from the room, slamming the door behind with such vigor a picture fell off the wall.

Serena bent to pick it up. She returned it to its hook, straightening it, every movement consciously deliberate, almost in slow motion as if she were inhabiting a dream, except that it was a nightmare.

Last year in Brussels . . . one bitterly cold winter night . . .

She could still taste the food on the dinner table that night, still taste the wine on her tongue, the strangely bitter aftertaste that had puzzled her. She had said nothing, because she and the general were the guests of one of their most regular gaming clients, a Spanish grandee, with a neat spade beard and piercing black eyes that never left Serena. For three days, he had flirted with her, and she had returned the compliment automatically; it was part of the business. It brought the gamesters back to the faro tables, as much for her violet eyes as for the cards she dealt.

His gaze that night had made her unusually uncomfortable, but she had shaken it off. Their fellow guests were congenial, if rather rowdy, as the levels in the wine bottles got lower. If they noticed the strange aftertaste, they gave no sign of it, and after a while, Serena decided she must be imagining it. She drank more than usual that night; it helped her to ignore her discomfort at the Spaniard's hungry gaze.

She vaguely remembered being bundled into the coach to take her back to the rented house the general had taken, where the gaming hell for the moment thrived. She still vaguely remembered her maid helping her to bed, playfully chiding her for being the worse for wear, something that had never happened before. She didn't remember falling asleep. But she did remember waking up.

It had been as terrifying as it had been strange, that feeling of living in a fog, of being unable to move or react but aware of every sensation. The memory still filled her with a bone-deep horror. At first, she had only been aware of something pulling her, stretching her, moving her legs apart, stretching her arms above her head. There had been no voices. But the Spaniard's face hung over hers; she could smell the wine on his breath, taste it when he smothered her mouth with his own. She had wanted to fight, to move her head sideways, to kick out, but she was immobilized, paralyzed by something. He had entered her, she had felt every movement, every short, quick stab, and then he had left her body.

It was the general who had pulled the sheet back over her, keeping his eyes averted. The bed curtains had fallen back into place, and she had been alone again, and the red mists of oblivion had taken her once more.

She had awoken late in the morning, her head splitting, nausea heavy in her belly, bile in her throat, the nightmare as vivid as if she had lived it, not dreamt it. And then the full horror swamped her as her body told her she had indeed lived every moment of it.

She had not left her room for three days. Her stepfather had sent messages, had knocked on her locked door, had pleaded, and had demanded entrance. She had ignored him. When she had emerged on the fourth day, she had said nothing about that night. He had at first been puzzled, uneasy as her silence continued, and then had become visibly relieved, as if he could believe that she had truly not been aware of the violation. The drug that had paralyzed her body had also made her insensible. And Serena was prepared to let him believe that, until the time she decided to tell him.

That time had just come. And now, as she returned to the hard, metallic reality of the present, she wondered if she had wasted the perfect card, but in her heart, she knew she had not. He would not have drugged her so easily this time, but there were other ways to render her insensible, to give Burford what he hungered for. And that must never happen again.

And it mustn't happen to Abigail, either. If the general made Abigail his wife, he could as easily sell her to the highest bidder as he had done his stepdaughter, and Abigail was not equipped to look after herself. Serena was fairly certain the girl was unlikely to succumb to the general's attentions. Indeed, how should she; the man was old enough to be her grandfather. But, encouraged by her mother, she could be flattered by them and find it difficult to hold her own in his company. She needed protection, and there was only Serena to provide it. She could not walk away until she knew the young woman was safely out of the general's clutches.

There had to be a way to do that without alerting Mr. Sutton. For a start, he'd find it almost impossible to believe in the general's motives as described by Serena. After all, Serena had seemed openly to encourage her stepfather's interest in Abigail. Why would she suddenly turn against him? And if she did manage to persuade him of the truth, his reaction was all too easy to foretell. Abigail's dream of a London Season and a good marriage would be dust and ashes.

Another suitor was the answer. If Abigail fell in love with an impeccable parti who would satisfy even Mrs. Sutton's high aspirations, then the general would be left out in the cold, and he need never know of his stepdaughter's part in the business. But how to find the perfect suitor?

Sebastian's image came unbidden to her mind. Abigail and her mother had already expressed an interest in him. They were having a dinner party for the express purpose of entertaining him. Was there a way to use that? If Sebastian could be persuaded at least to show some interest in the ingénue, it would give Serena some much-needed breathing space to find an alternative. But quite apart from the difficulty in finding a convincing reason for asking it, how could she possibly expect any kind of a favor from Sebastian after the farce of their last meeting? It had cleared neither ground nor air, merely accentuated the vast chasm between them.

It seemed obvious that Sebastian's life in the last three years had followed the inevitable path of a young aristocrat. Once he'd recovered from the hurt and anger at her betrayal, he had picked up the threads of his life with barely a pause. She could see that just by looking at him. The diffidence of a green young man in his early twenties had been replaced with the poise and self-assurance of a man sure of who and what he was in his own world. As for herself, she had been barely twenty during those months of love, and now, although she was barely twenty-three, she felt as if the last three years had sucked all the promise out of life, leaving her only a barren future. She had nothing to offer Sebastian now. And why should he even consider offering *her* anything?

She put the pistol back into the drawer of the secretaire, locking it with the key she kept on a fob tucked into a hidden pocket in her skirt.

A knock at the door brought Flanagan with a sealed letter on a silver tray. "A messenger brought this, Lady Serena." He presented the tray with a bow.

"Thank you, Flanagan." She took it, staring down at the handwriting. It was as if her thoughts had somehow materialized in this folded sheet of vellum.

"The messenger awaits an answer, my lady."

"Yes," she said vaguely, still looking at the sheet. Only Sebastian enlivened his bold, plain script with little curlicues when the mood took him. It had always made her smile. But what was he doing writing to her now? Well, she wouldn't find out by staring at a sealed paper. "Ask him to wait."

"Very well, ma'am." Flanagan left, and Serena slit the wafer with her paper knife. She unfolded the single sheet.

Will you come to Stratton Street at three o'clock this afternoon? Take a closed carriage and no one on the street will notice you. S.S.

Sebastian had never been reckless with her reputation, Serena reflected. Indeed, he'd been more careful of it than she herself. Nothing had changed, it seemed. Why did he want to see her? Hadn't they said everything that could possibly be said between them?

But almost without volition, she took a sheet of vellum and wrote simply: *At three o'clock, then.* She folded and sealed it, then rang for Flanagan.

He took the note, and Serena went into her bedchamber. Regardless of why Sebastian needed to see her, pride—and vanity, she had to admit—insisted that she show herself at her best. The dark red silk was all very well, it suited her coloring as her stepfather had pointed out, but she had a sudden loathing for the gown. If he had complimented her on it, then she would never wear it again. She rang for Bridget as she tugged impatiently at the laces.

"Lord love us, Lady Serena, whatever's the matter with the gown. Is it stained?" Bridget in consternation hurried across to her. "You'll break the laces going at them like that."

"Oh, I want it off, Bridget, 'tis uncomfortable." Serena walked to the armoire as Bridget struggled with the laces.

"Oh, hold still, my lady, do," Bridget pleaded, following her at the end of a lace.

"I wish for something lighter, more frivolous." Serena riffled through the rich ranks of silks, muslins, velvets, damasks. "Ah, this, I think." She drew out a heather-colored silk, embroidered with delicate garlands of red roses, each with a tiny amethyst embedded in its center. "Is this not pretty, Bridget?"

"Very, my lady." Bridget was smothered in the folds of dark red silk as she divested Serena of the gown. She laid it over a chair and turned her full attention to her mistress. "Are you going visiting, m'lady?"

"As it happens," Serena said, smoothing the folds of her cambric petticoat. "Just a small hoop, Bridget."

Bridget tied the small hoop at Serena's waist and then helped her into the gown, arranging the silk skirt over the pannier so that it swayed elegantly but not with extravagant width around her hips.

Serena examined her reflection in the cheval glass. Sebastian had always liked simplicity. He dressed himself without frills, and while he admired fashion, he had preferred to see Serena dressed in its less extravagant extremes. Since that suited her own tastes, she had been more than happy to accede to his wishes. The soft heather of the gown was a perfect contrast with her dark hair and a wonderful complement to her eyes. The décolletage was edged with a lace ruff that, while it did nothing to conceal the swell of her breasts, kept her nipples hidden. Something she preferred in the afternoon, although she generally acceded to prevailing fashion at the tables.

Not, of course, that she was in the least interested in dressing to please Sebastian, only to please herself.

"That'll do, Bridget," she pronounced finally. "The black felt hat and black woolen cloak, if you please."

Bridget brought the garments over, and Serena adjusted the hat; it had a wide brim that covered much of her face. The cloak was voluminous and could be drawn up at the neck.

"Lord love us, m'lady, you looks a bit like a highwayman," Bridget declared as her mistress swathed herself in the cloak. "All you needs is the mask."

Serena smiled. "'Tis cold out, Bridget. I've no wish to catch a chill. Run downstairs and ask Flanagan to summon a hackney for me."

Bridget bobbed a curtsy and hurried away. Serena followed her more slowly, and by the time she reached the hall, the hackney was waiting in the street.

She gave the jarvey the address as she climbed into the sour-smelling interior and sat forward on the edge of the seat, unwilling to touch the greasy leather squabs lining the bench any more than was absolutely necessary. It was too cold, the wind too sharp and brisk, to lift the leather curtain at the window aperture, so she took shallow breaths and prayed that the air was not infected with the breath of previous riders. Fortunately, it was not far to Stratton Street, and within ten minutes, the carriage drew up outside the narrow row house where Sebastian and his brother lived.

She opened the door and stepped down to the street, twitching her skirts aside so that they didn't drag in the filthy water of the kennel. She paid the jarvey and raised her hand to the door knocker. But the door opened before she could even touch it, and she found herself whisked inside, the door firmly closed at her back.

"No one will have seen you," Sebastian said. "Let me have your cloak." He was standing behind her, reaching over her shoulders to unfasten the clasp at her throat even as she tried to take in her surroundings.

Serena almost laughed. It was so typical of Sebastian; he never wasted energy, never used two words where one would do, and never hesitated when it came to action. She needed to remove her cloak, and he was doing just that with well-remembered efficiency. She let him take it from her and hang it on a hook while she drew off her gloves. He took those and laid them on the bench below the hook and then stood back and looked at her, a question in his blue eyes.

"Will you take off your hat? I'd like to feel you were going to stay awhile."

"Why?" She frowned at him. "Why do you want to see me, Sebastian?"

He reached out a hand and gently placed a finger over her lips. "Let's agree to say nothing that's provocative or aggressive, Serena. I don't wish to quarrel with you again."

She took a breath, conscious of the warmth of his finger on her lips, and suddenly had the absurd urge to suck his finger into her mouth, to stroke it with her tongue, graze it with her teeth, as she had so often done in their lovemaking. She caught a surprised flash in his eye and understood that the shared memory was as vivid for him at that moment as it was for her.

She turned her head a little so that his finger fell away, and she untied the ribbons of her hat. Sebastian took it from her, setting it down with her gloves. Then he took her hands in his, regarding her with his head to one side, a quizzical gleam in his blue eyes.

"Thank you for coming."

"I couldn't seem to help myself," she responded with

a tiny shrug. "Will you not tell me why you wanted to see me?"

His fingers enclosed her hand in a warm, firm clasp, and time fell away. They were back where they once had been, and Serena felt herself slipping into a strange trance. She wanted nothing more than this, even though the rational part of her mind screamed that it was madness, would only plunge them into more grief and heartache than they'd already endured.

"Come to the fire. Your hands are cold." He put an arm around her shoulders, easing her through a door into a warm, firelit, candle-bright parlor. "We will be more comfortable here."

Serena looked around, trying to recapture her sense of control. She had never visited the house before. In their past, she and Sebastian had rented a small room in an inn on King Street for their rendezvous. For all that it was spotlessly clean, the parlor was clearly a room inhabited by bachelors. No embroidered cushions, curtains that were a little short for the windows, no flowers, dried or fresh, no little ornaments or feminine trinkets around. There was a faint musky smell, a hint of leather and sweat in the air mingling with wood smoke and candle wax. Nothing unpleasant, but it smelled as she imagined a gentlemen's club would smell.

"Where's your brother? I thought you shared the house with him." Her voice sounded amazingly normal, perfectly matter-of-fact.

"Oh, Perry's out and about," he said easily, following

her lead. "He has his own circle of friends. Strange birds they are, scientists and philosophers, poets and men who write pamphlets for the edification of the ignorant." He shook his head with a faint self-deprecating smile. "I'm certain Perry puts me firmly in the latter category."

"I only met him a few times," Serena said. "You're so startlingly alike; once or twice, when I saw him without you, I was convinced he was you."

Sebastian inclined his head with a smile. "Most people, apart from our older brother, have that problem. But there are little differences. Perry has a widow's peak." He touched his brow.

"So do you," Serena pointed out.

"His is more pronounced. And my nose is longer."

Serena laughed. "Is that all that distinguishes you from each other?"

"Physically, yes. But in every other respect, we're chalk and cheese." Sebastian patted a cushion on a sofa. "Won't you sit down?"

"Thank you." Serena sat down. The cushion at her back was hard and scratchy, pieces of horsehair protruding through the fabric.

"Tea?" Sebastian asked. "Or coffee, if you'd prefer." He yanked on the bellpull by the mantelpiece.

"Tea, thank you." Serena looked up at him as he stood hovering over her, a puzzled frown in his eye. "Why am I here, Sebastian?"

"Devil take it, why is this so difficult?" he exclaimed abruptly. "I need to be alone with you like this, with no fear of interruption. I know exactly what I want to say, but now I feel like a schoolboy, all big red hands and huge feet that won't go where they're supposed to."

Serena made a move to stand up, but the door opened, and the boy who helped the housekeeper stuck his head around. "Yes, sir?"

"Fetch tea, Bart." Sebastian welcomed the interruption. It gave him a moment to compose himself. He hadn't expected this sudden yearning, but he probably should have done. All rational thought was blocked by the overwhelming need to feel her against him again, to explore that glorious body, find again the little nooks and crannies that had once been so familiar to him. It had been so long, so many bad feelings had soured the loving memories, that he had thought he would be impervious to the old longings. He should have known better.

"'Tis unusual to find tea in a bachelors' establishment," Serena remarked, searching for a neutral topic. The tension was like a high wire stretched taut between them, thrumming with unspoken memories and the need to speak them.

"Perry drinks tea on occasion." Sebastian bent to poke the fire. "I confess I find it an insipid drink, not worth the trouble."

"I enjoy it on occasion," she returned, wondering how long they could keep up the inanity of small talk before Sebastian finally got to the point.

The lad returned with a tray with a small casket of

tea, two shallow dishes, a porcelain teapot, and a copper pot of hot water. Without instruction, he set it down on a table beside Serena. "Water's just boiled, ma'am."

"Thank you." She smiled at him and opened the casket. "So you won't drink tea, Sebastian?"

He shook his head with a grimace. "No . . . no, thank you. I prefer claret."

Serena measured tea into the teapot and poured on hot water. She let it rest while Sebastian poured himself claret, then she poured the pale liquid into the shallow cup. She raised the cup to her lips and sipped, aware of his searching gaze.

"I have ached for you, Serena," he said in a low voice.

And slowly, Serena felt the tension loosen, felt herself slide into peaceful acceptance of what had to be, of what she had known had to be from the moment she'd received his summons. They were not done with each other yet.

"When you came to Pickering Place, you gave me such a look of contempt, I thought you could never forgive . . . never understand," she responded as softly as he. "I had no choice, Sebastian. I thought . . ." Her voice faded.

"You thought what?" His voice had sharpened a little, his eyes still searching her face.

She shrugged. "That I had hurt you so deeply three years ago that there could be no going back." She sipped her tea, then set the dish back in the saucer. "It was what I had tried to make happen, so I should have been glad . . . instead, I was even more miserable than I had been on that dreadful afternoon."

"I was angry," he admitted. "Furiously angry, dreadfully hurt, because I didn't understand. I still don't, Serena. I know you weren't speaking the truth, so why . . . *why*?"

She hesitated, her little finger tracing the embroidered pattern in the silk of her skirt. How much could she safely tell him? The degradation of the full truth was more than she could ever confide to anyone. But she owed him some part of it. Something genuine.

She took a deep breath and spoke slowly, picking her way through the tellable and the untellable. "When the general married my mother, what she did not know . . . indeed, neither of us knew . . . was that he was a mere heartbeat away from debtors' prison. He needed my mother's fortune, and as soon as he had it, he took us both off to Paris, where he lost nearly every last penny at the tables. He dragged us to Brussels, and with the small sum he had managed not to lose, he set up his own gambling hell. When he fell afoul of some players who didn't like the odds at his tables, he dragged us to Vienna, to Salzburg, anywhere where the play was high. And in each place, we were obliged eventually to flee in the middle of the night a step ahead of those he had cheated.

"My mother could not endure such a life. She faded day by day, and the weaker she became, the more demanding he was, until finally she just faded into nothing."

Serena turned slowly from the fire to face Sebastian. "There you have it. The whole sordid story."

"But I don't have *your* story," Sebastian said. "I understand you could not leave your mother while she was alive, but after her death. . . ? Surely there was someone you could turn to for help . . ."

"An obvious solution, of course." She sounded bitter, and Sebastian winced a little. "But not as easy as it sounds. I had no confidantes of my own by that time; the general made sure of that. He had also spent my own fortune, my mother's jointure, so I was, and am, penniless and utterly dependent upon him. When he decreed that our London venture on Charles Street was failing and we had to run again, I had no choice but to follow him. I didn't feel able to tell you the truth." She blinked away inconvenient tears. Now was not the moment to show her vulnerability. She didn't want Sebastian's pity.

Sebastian was standing by the fireplace, one arm resting along the mantel. He looked down into the fire's glow. "I wonder why you didn't feel you could tell me the truth. Why was it impossible to confide in me? I can't say I would have known what to do to help you then . . ." He gave a small, reluctant laugh. "I was so young, so naïve in so many ways, I probably would have protested and exclaimed in a positive flurry of sound and fury, but I would have achieved nothing. I understand that now. But at least, if you had told me, I would have known that you had not suddenly become another person. I would have known that the love we had shared was true, that I had not imagined the feelings we had for each other."

"Oh, Sebastian, I thought that if I gave you a disgust for me, you would be less hurt," she said with a helpless smile. "We may have had all sorts of superficial sophistication, but we were each other's first love. We didn't have a chance when a fantasy of perfect love came face-to-face with the harshness of the real world."

"I disagree," he said quietly, raising his eyes from the fire. "We knew how to love. That was no fantasy."

And Serena bowed her head in acknowledgment. "Yes," she agreed as softly as he. "We knew how to love."

Sebastian set aside his glass. "And we still know, Serena." He came towards her, hands outstretched. "Could we try this again?" A tiny smile touched his mouth.

Silently, she put her hands in his and let him draw her to her feet. There was a sense of inevitability now, but more than that, an overwhelming need for him, for his touch, for his body, for the power of his desire that shone bright and dazzling as a desert sun as his blue eyes seemed to devour her. He would make her whole again. Only Sebastian's love, his passion, could do that, and her own would rise to meet his, and she would find her true self again, the violations vanquished.

He kissed her, gently at first, a kiss of rediscovery, his tongue exploring her mouth, sliding along her lips, dipping into the corners of her mouth. She inhaled his scent, tasted his mouth, remembered with a piercing sweetness how it had been, and with a surge of joy realized that it was still as wonderful, as sensual, as lustful as it had ever been.

His hands moved to her hips, cupped her buttocks, pulling her against the hard jut of his loins, and Serena reveled in the full flood of desire, sliding a hand between them to caress the wonderful bulge of his penis pressing against his breeches. He moved her sideways without taking his mouth from hers, easing her back onto the chaise, coming down with her. His mouth moved from hers to kiss the fast-beating pulse in the hollow of her throat as his hand slid upwards beneath her skirt, caressing her silk-clad thigh. She moved against him, her own hand pressing into the hard-muscled backside. She shifted slightly, putting one leg over his hips, pulling him closer as he pushed down the neck of her gown, lifting her nipples for his lips. She murmured with delight as he flicked her nipples with his tongue, suckled, grazed the sensitive crowns with his teeth, and she was lost for the first time in an eternity in the glorious swirl of lust.

She lifted her hips as he pushed her skirts up to her waist. She felt for the laces of his breeches, tugging impatiently as his hand found her core, a finger rubbing urgently against the little nub of flesh, sliding within her moist cleft. His penis sprang free, as hard and muscular as she remembered, and a laugh of delight escaped her as she ran her closed fist up and down the corded, pulsing shaft.

For a moment, he drew back, looking into her face with a slightly startled expression, as if he'd discovered something he hadn't expected. She stroked his cheek, reading his thoughts correctly because they were so much like her own. "*Plus ça change, plus c'est la même chose,* my love. 'Tis always reassuring to discover that the more things change, the more they stay the same."

That made him laugh, too. He slid down her body, burying his head between her thighs. "How right you are," he murmured, his voice muffled, his teeth nibbling, his tongue stroking, his breath hot and then cool on her inflamed center. "How wonderful it is to find that the memories were not the fantasies of inexperienced passion."

He parted her thighs, moving up her body, holding her hips on the shelf of his palms. As he entered her, he gazed into her eyes in the way she remembered so well. It was as if he would connect with her very soul, engage every part of her in this passionate union. And her own spirit rose to meet his as the joyous waves of pleasure peaked and broke, and it was as if the past three years had never existed.

They lay together for long minutes, before Sebastian moved indolently, kissed her mouth, and knelt up, fumbling with the laces of his breeches. He smiled down at her as she lay sprawled on the chaise. "I love you. I have always loved you. Since before I was born, I have loved you."

Serena smiled, reached up a hand to run her fingers over his mouth. "You are absurdly extravagant, but I love that in you." She struggled onto her elbows. "Let me up, now."

Sebastian slid off the chaise, standing up, adjusting his clothes. He held out his hands to her, pulling her to her feet and then drawing her against him. He held her tightly for a moment, then, as she drew back a little, released her but still held her hands, looking her up and down.

"What shall we do now? Are you hungry? Making love always used to make you hungry."

Serena considered as she straightened her skirts. "I could drink a glass of that claret and nibble on a little bread and cheese, but first I would like to refresh myself. A bowl of water and a towel." She passed a descriptive hand down her body.

"Of course." Sebastian hurried to the door. "Come to my bedchamber." He led the way up a flight of stairs to a narrow landing with two doors on either side. He opened one and with an exaggerated bow ushered Serena inside. "I'll fetch water and a towel."

He disappeared, leaving Serena to look around the square bedchamber. It contained a canopied bed, a dresser, a basin and ewer, and an armoire. A small fire burned in the grate. Again, it was a room that, while adequate, had no personality to it. A rather grimy window looked down onto a back garden, where a few desultory chickens pecked at the dirt below.

Sebastian reappeared with a jug of steaming hot

water and a towel over his arm. "Madam, allow me . . ." He poured water into the basin and turned back to her with an unmistakably lascivious grin. "Where would you wish me to start?"

"Nowhere," Serena stated definitely. "Leave me alone, Sebastian, and find bread and cheese and claret. I will not be above ten minutes."

He looked disappointed but acceded with good grace. "One kiss before I go?"

"One kiss," she agreed. She resisted his attempt to kiss her on the mouth, turning her cheek so that his lips brushed her cheek.

He took her face between his hands, holding her head steady, and made to kiss her full on the lips, but she pulled violently away from him, rubbing her mouth with the back of her hand. "No . . . *never* do that. If I don't wish to kiss you, I will not."

He looked at her, distress and confusion in his eyes. "I didn't mean . . . we've just made love, Serena. I . . . what did I do wrong?"

She took a deep breath. In the old days, she would have responded playfully. But she could no longer do that. "Nothing. You did nothing wrong. I just don't like anyone to hold my head." She tried for a smile, a light laugh. "It's been so long, Sebastian, I have to get used to you again."

He inclined his head in acknowledgment. "As you wish . . . always as you wish, Serena. I'll do something about refreshments." He left her, closing the door quietly behind him.

Serena closed her eyes. She had to learn to forget that night, and she thought for the most part she had done so. That violent reaction had shocked and surprised her as much as it had shocked and surprised Sebastian. But he was not to blame. And she could never explain it to him.

Chapter Eight

"Mrs. Croft, have you been baking? What have you in the pantry?" Sebastian entered the kitchen, sniffing appreciatively at the wholesome aroma of fresh-baked bread.

The housekeeper straightened from the kitchen range as she withdrew a golden loaf from the bread oven, balancing the paddle as she slid it onto the kitchen table. "Why, 'tis hardly time for your dinner, sir. 'Tis barely five o'clock."

"I know, but I have a guest who is sharp set. That bread looks wonderful and smells even better." He picked off a piece of hot crust and popped it into his mouth. "Delicious. This will do very well. All that remains is to find something toothsome to accompany it." He went into the pantry, peering at the offerings on the cold marble shelf. He selected a round of cheddar, half a cold chicken, and a pat of butter. "This will do very well. Where will I find a tray?"

"Lord love us, Mr. Sebastian, you go on back to the parlor. I'll send Bart through with this." Rather distractedly, Mrs. Croft tucked a strand of gray hair back into the pins that held the fat bun at the nape of her neck. She was unaccustomed to seeing either of her employers in her kitchen and wasn't at all sure that she cared for the visitation. She fetched plates from the Welsh dresser.

"No, I can carry it," Sebastian protested. "Knives, we need knives." He looked around vaguely.

"I'll send Bart with the tray." The housekeeper shooed Sebastian as if he were a buzzing fly. "You go back to your guest now, sir."

Sebastian, somewhat surprised at how his presence in the kitchen discommoded the housekeeper, yielded with good grace. "Very well, Mrs. Croft. I'll just fetch up a bottle of claret from the cellar." He headed for the cellar door before she could object to that, too.

"You'll need the lantern, Mr. Sebastian." She shook her head. "'Tis black as pitch down there."

"Oh, yes, I suppose it is." He looked around. "Where d'you keep the lantern?"

"On the wall, sir. By the back door. And there's flint and tinder on the dresser." It would have been a lot quicker to have done it herself, she reflected, assembling food, knives, and plates on a wooden tray.

Sebastian carried the lantern high and made his way down the steep steps to the cellar. He examined the wine racks by the light of the lamp, frowning. Why had Serena reacted to his kiss like that? It seemed such an extreme response, particularly in light of the previous half-hour. If he hadn't known better, he would have said her response to him at that moment was revulsion.

Still frowning, he selected a bottle from the rack, dusting off cobwebs as he returned to the kitchen.

"Bart's taken the tray through," the housekeeper informed him. "I'll pull the cork on that bottle."

"No . . . no . . . I'm quite capable of uncorking a bottle, Mrs. Croft." He looked around. "Just point me in the direction of the corkscrew."

Mrs. Croft sighed and pulled open a drawer in the kitchen table. "Here you are, sir."

"Thank you." Sebastian bestowed his most dazzling smile upon her and left the kitchen with bottle and corkscrew.

Bart was arranging the contents of the tray on the small table at the window when Sebastian returned to the parlor. "Will that be all, sir?"

Sebastian cast a quick glance at the table and nodded. "Just put some more logs on the fire, if you would." He drew the cork on the bottle, sniffed it, then poured a small measure into one of the glasses.

"Will it do?" Serena's light tones came from the door.

"'Tis one of your favorites," he said. He was smiling as he turned to look at her, but the smile was shadowed with a question. "*Un bon* Bordeaux from Nuit St. Georges." He poured a glass and handed it to her.

She took its scent with an appreciative nod, sipped, and smiled. "Fancy you remembering."

His eyes took on a smoky hue as he said quietly, "I remember everything about you."

She glanced with quick warning at the boy making up the fire, and Sebastian turned aside to the laden table. "What may I offer you, ma'am? A little cold chicken, perhaps?"

Bart finished with the fire and scurried from the room. Sebastian cut a thick slice of still-warm bread, buttered it lavishly, and put it with a slice of chicken breast on Serena's plate. He looked the question at her again, and she gave a rather tentative smile.

"Forgive me, Sebastian. I don't know what came over me. I suppose it's because men are always pawing me at the tables. 'Tis as if I am as much an attraction as the cards, and they have as much right to me as they do to play."

He paled, a white shade around his mouth. "Heyward lets them do that?"

If you only knew, she thought. She said with a careless shrug, "He sees nothing wrong in it, as long as it brings them to the tables. I just find it annoying." She picked up the plate and took it to a fireside chair, sniffing hungrily. "Why is it that the simplest food always tastes the best?" She piled chicken on the bread and took a hearty bite. "This is so good."

Sebastian accepted that the subject was closed, at least as far as Serena was concerned this afternoon, but he determined to revisit it soon. He smiled, nibbling on a cold leg of fowl. "Anything tastes good when you're hungry."

"Oh, that reminds me . . . have you received a dinner invitation from Mrs. Sutton?"

Sebastian looked astonished. "Good God, no. Why should I?"

"Oh, you will," she assured him. "Mrs. Sutton has set her heart on giving a dinner party to introduce Abigail to a wider society. But since she doesn't know anyone from a wider society, she has co-opted me to make up a guest list from my own acquaintances." Her eyes danced merrily as she saw his dumbfounded expression. "You are to be the guest of honor, sir. The people I invite are all to be those who will make you feel comfortable."

Sebastian flopped into an armchair, still holding the chicken leg. "Is this some kind of jest?"

She shook her head. "Not as far as the Suttons are concerned. They wish to thank you for the service you did Abigail but were unsure how to go about it. They asked for my help." She shrugged easily, took a sip of her wine and another mouthful of bread and chicken.

Sebastian shook his head in confusion. "But I don't wish to be a guest of honor. I don't know them at all."

"A situation they wish to remedy," Serena informed him with a tranquil smile. "Come now, it won't be so bad. I will be there, and I'll make sure some congenial folk make up the guest list. They won't be high sticklers, you can be confident of that."

"What of the general? If he's to be included, Serena, I

will not accept. I could not break bread at the same table as that . . ." Words failed him. He drained his wine glass.

She nodded. "I understand that. Indeed, I will do everything in my power to exclude him. The less he sees of Abigail, the better. And the fewer opportunities he has to ingratiate himself with her parents, very much the better."

Sebastian's gaze sharpened. "Oh? Why is that?"

Serena hesitated, once again caught between the whole unpalatable truth and the need to give Sebastian a good enough reason. "I believe he's making a play for Abigail, and he's too old for her, for a start. And then . . ."

"And then?" he prompted, his gaze still sharp.

She set aside her plate and leaned forward. "After seeing the way he treated my mother, I'm not prepared to see Abigail become another victim. Besides," she added, an edge to her voice, "it would be the sweetest revenge to deny him a new bride."

Sebastian absorbed this for a moment. It made perfect sense, and in a way, it was reassuring to hear Serena bent on vengeance. She had lost none of her spirit after all. "Fair enough," he said easily.

"I'm glad you think so," she said with a sudden smile that illuminated her countenance, set her eyes dancing, and warmed him to his core. "Because I have a kind of a play . . . one that makes it very difficult for my stepfather to pursue Abigail . . . and it involves you, Sebastian."

This made him frown, and a wary look came into his eyes. "How?"

Serena picked her words carefully. "Abigail is drawn to you already—her knight in shining armor. And I have formed the impression that as far as her mother is concerned, you are a much better catch than the general."

"*Me?*"

"Yes, my dear, *you*." She couldn't help laughing at the horror on his face. "I'm not asking you to offer for her. She could solve your financial problems once and for all, but in truth, I don't think I would like it one little bit."

"Believe me, that's not going to happen." He shook his head vigorously. "Utter nonsense, Serena."

"Only listen, Sebastian." She reached forward, putting her hand on his thigh. "All I'm asking is that you just show a little interest in her, just enough to give them cause to hold the general at arm's length. I'm convinced that the parents are entertaining the possibility of my stepfather's suit simply because he's the best offer at the moment. If there's a rival and a much more suitable suitor on the horizon, they'll drop the general like a hot brick."

"And where will that leave me?" He took her hand and put it firmly back in her lap. "You'll not get around me that way, Serena. I ask again, where will that leave me?"

"Well, there, I admit, is the one small flaw in my otherwise flawless plan." She frowned into her glass, wondering how best to approach the ticklish issue.

"Go on," Sebastian prompted in a rather direful tone.

"Well, obviously, you cannot offer for Abigail, you can only lead her on, and—"

"What?" Sebastian exploded. "What kind of coxcomb will that make me? Serena, I give you fair warning, you say another word in this vein at your peril."

She shook her head, half laughing. "No . . . no, Sebastian, only hear me out. Of course, I wouldn't want you to behave badly. But if you could just allow Mrs. Sutton at least to have hopes that you might come up to the mark, then she won't be in a hurry to encourage my stepfather's suit. Abigail is a simple soul. She'll enjoy a harmless flirtation, and in the meantime, we'll hope she falls desperately in love with someone utterly suitable and everyone will live happily ever after." She regarded him with a cajoling smile.

It was a wasted smile. Sebastian looked both horrified and wrathful. "No."

She wrinkled her nose, an unconscious gesture that Sebastian had seen in his dreams every night of the last three years. "I will undertake to find her a suitable match if you'll just buy me some time," she pleaded. "And just think . . . it is the perfect scheme. Her parents think of me as a kind of respectable elder sister for Abigail, and they'll be delighted to have me act as her chaperone if you take her driving, or riding, or walking. Think how much time that would give us together."

Sebastian stared at her in wonderment for a long moment, then he threw back his head and laughed, great gusts of pure enjoyment. "Oh, Serena . . . Serena . . ."

he managed to gasp at last. "I had completely forgotten your predilection for concocting the most harebrained schemes. But I have to tell you, my sweet, this one takes the cocked hat."

"Well, I'm glad you approve." Serena was not in the least discomposed by his laughter. "And we should begin first thing tomorrow. You will pay a call in Bruton Street, ostensibly to inquire after the health of Miss Sutton after her ordeal, and I shall just happen to bump into you on the doorstep. We will go in together, and I'll protect you from any predation from Mama Sutton, I promise."

Sebastian shook his head. "I will go along with this crackpot scheme just until I decide it's getting out of hand. And you may be sure, sweetheart, that I will decide that long before Miss Abigail feels the slightest serious *tendre* for me."

That was probably as good as she was going to get, Serena reflected. The long case clock in the hall struck six, and she sighed. "I must go. I need to make sure the rooms are ready for tonight and there are no kitchen dramas to sort out."

"Do you ever take a night off from the tables?" Sebastian asked as he rose with her.

"Sometimes . . . if the general thinks that accepting another invitation will improve business in the long run, he'll open only the small private salon. He can manage that alone, while I go and play my part at some dinner table . . . ballroom . . . rout party." She shrugged. "I play many roles, Sebastian."

He said nothing. He could feel the anger curling tight in his belly. It wasn't fair to direct it at Serena, and yet her acceptance of the situation, so easy and unquestioning, it seemed to him, made him want to shake her. He felt as if she were moving through the travesty of her life as if through a dream, as if it didn't, *couldn't,* touch her. As if she could preserve a purity of spirit, of intention, even as she obeyed the dictates of a dissolute. But she couldn't. If she continued like this, she would end up as devoid of a moral compass as her damnable stepfather.

"Why don't you just leave him?" he demanded, his voice harsh. "For God's sake, Serena, walk away. You're not a minor child; he has no legal authority over you. Any other life has to be better than the one you live now."

She looked at him with a flash of scorn in her violet eyes. "Are you really such a child, Sebastian? A naïve, dreaming child who truly believes the world is a decent place?" She moved past him to the door. "When you've seen as much of it as I have, you'll understand why what for you is a simple solution for me is an impossible one at the moment." She reached for her cloak in the hall.

Sebastian came up behind her, snatching it off the hook. Resentment mingled with his anger now, resentment that she should dismiss him so lightly, in such patronizing terms. "Maybe you're right about one thing," he said, his mouth taut. "Maybe I don't understand what you understand, but it's not because I have not seen what you have seen. It's because I don't understand your passive acceptance of an intolerable situation. But I won't presume to argue the toss with you." He draped the cloak around her shoulders before calling for Bart.

"Fetch a hackney," he instructed the boy curtly as he handed Serena her hat and gloves.

Her expression was closed as she asked without expression, "So, will I see you tomorrow?"

He wanted to say no. He wanted to say, *I don't want to see you again until you understand my point of view.* But he knew absolutely that if he said that, she would go, and he would never see her again. And he couldn't face that, not after finding her again.

"Very well," he said coldly. "I will pay a call in Bruton Street tomorrow. What time will suit you, ma'am?"

"Eleven o'clock." She drew on her gloves, awash with unhappy frustration. She didn't want to part like this, this angry chasm between them, but she didn't know how to bridge it. Not now, at least. She felt too raw. She looked at him, hesitating, trying to find words.

Sebastian suddenly took her hands, enclosed them tightly in his own. "Come now, Serena, we can do better than this. We *must* do better than this."

Her attempt at a smile was tentative, but she leaned into him, kissing the corner of his mouth. "I am so sorry, Sebastian. I feel so . . . so jangly, as if no part of me is in harmony with another, when we have these conversations."

"I would hardly dignify them as such," he said with a dry smile. "But I would not have you *jangly* for all the world." He drew her against him, pushing up her chin with his palm. "Would it restore a degree of harmony if I kissed you?"

She smiled, and this time, there was nothing tentative about it. "Yes, please."

He kissed her for a long time, ignoring Bart, who stood in the open doorway, his eyes wide as saucers, the words stopped on his lips. When Sebastian raised his head and brushed a kiss on Serena's brow, Bart blurted, "If you please, sir, the carriage is outside. As you ordered, sir."

Sebastian exchanged a startled glance with Serena. They had both forgotten the lad. Then he said hastily, "Thank you, Bart. Ma'am, may I escort you to your carriage?" He offered his arm.

Serena was suddenly taken by an irresistible fit of the giggles. Struggling with her laughter, she tucked her hand in the crook of Sebastian's elbow with a mock-dignified "Thank you, sir," and allowed him to usher her to the street and into the dark confines of the coach.

"Oh, the poor child," she said with a smothered chuckle. "Perhaps you should sit him down and tell him the facts of life."

"What a revolting idea," Sebastian declared. "I daresay he could teach me one or two. I'll see you in Bruton Street at eleven tomorrow." He closed the carriage door firmly and stood back as the vehicle creaked off down the street.

A cold wind gusted sharply from around the corner, and he returned to the house, heading for the drawing-room fire and the claret bottle. He heard the front door open and Peregrine's cheery "Halloo, anyone at home?"

"In here," Sebastian called back.

Perry came in, glancing quickly around, taking in the two glasses, the plates, and the remnants of the feast. "Visitors?" he inquired.

"Of a kind," his twin said.

Peregrine looked at him closely. "Now, that sounds intriguing." He picked up the half-empty wine bottle and whistled softly. "A visitor worthy of the Nuit St. Georges, no less. Who could that be, I wonder?"

Sebastian chose for the moment to ignore both the question and his twin's significant glance. He gestured with his glass to the bottle in Perry's hands. "It's a fine Bordeaux. I'm wondering how it got into our cellar. I certainly don't remember acquiring it."

Peregrine set the bottle down. "Jasper sent us a case from the Blackwater cellars, don't you remember? He said it was time it was drunk, and he wasn't going to leave it at the manor for our greedy uncles to gorge upon."

"Oh, yes, I remember now." Sebastian nodded. "So, what have you been up to?"

"Why do I get the impression you're trying to distract me from your activities this afternoon?" Peregrine mused. He picked up Serena's empty glass, holding it to the light. "At least, assure me that whoever was drinking from this glass was in the peak of health. I've a mind to borrow it."

"You'll be quite safe," Sebastian said with a careless wave of his hand.

"Well, I, for one, had a very pleasant afternoon." Peregrine filled Serena's empty glass and sat down at his ease in front of the fire: "I take it you did, too." He sipped wine, eyebrows raised in question.

Sebastian gave in. "As it happens, Serena was here."

"Oh? Really?" Peregrine's amused expression died. "By invitation, Seb?"

"How else?" Sebastian leaned forward to refill his glass. "I needed to clarify matters. There's too much water under the bridge, Perry, to be ignored."

Peregrine nodded slowly. He was uneasy and couldn't quite explain why. Every rational part of his brain screamed that for Sebastian to entangle himself anew with Lady Serena Carmichael was a very bad idea, but he didn't know how to say that without offense. "And did you manage to drain the water under the bridge?"

"In a manner of speaking," his brother said, his eyes on the fire. "She gave me an explanation of sorts. I'm just unconvinced that it was the whole truth and nothing but."

"Is it wise to rekindle things, Seb?" Perry decided not

to beat about the bush. "She hurt you so badly before. How can you be certain it won't happen again?"

"I can't," his twin said baldly. "But 'tis the damnedest thing . . . I don't think I ever fell out of love with her, Perry."

"And Lady Serena? Did she fall out of love with you?"

Sebastian shook his head. "I don't think so."

"But you're not certain?"

"No, damn it, I'm not. Why d'you have to probe so deep, Perry?"

Peregrine's shrug was self-deprecating. "I don't mean to pry, Seb. But it matters to me . . . how you feel . . . what's going on with you."

Sebastian had no response. He knew how Perry felt because that was exactly the way he felt about his twin. They had always shared each other's innermost thoughts, felt each other's sorrows, reveled in each other's joys. Of course, Perry needed to know.

After a moment, he said, "I need some time, Perry. And so does Serena. We have to see where this is leading. Her life is complicated . . . to say the least," he added with a grim smile. "Mine is complicated by the need to fulfill the terms of Uncle Bradley's will." He picked up his wine glass. "Let's agree to let the subject rest for the moment. I can't see my way clearly, so until I can, it seems there's little to discuss."

"Agreed." His brother raised his own glass in salute, and they both drank. "So, on the subject of Uncle Bradley, perhaps we should pay court a little more assiduously. 'Tis good manners, not to mention good business, to visit the ailing relative whose heir you happen to be."

"Practical as ever, Perry. We'll visit as soon as may be."

Peregrine accepted the original subject as closed. He set down his glass and got to his feet. "Are you dining in?"

"I've invited Sefton, Carlton, and Ripley to dinner and cards. You're welcome to join us."

Perry shook his head, heading for the door. "Thank you, but no. I have another engagement."

"Anyone interesting?"

Perry laughed. "Probably no one you would find so, Seb." His laughter hung in the air as he went upstairs to change for the evening.

Sebastian followed him after a minute. Perry was hiding something, or at least not being totally forthcoming. Peregrine could claim the right to know what was going on in Sebastian's life, and by the same token, Sebastian could certainly sense when Perry had things he was keeping to himself. He wondered if it had anything to do with the quest for an inheritance-worthy bride. Perry would tell him when he was ready, of course, but his twin claimed the right to probe deeply in his turn if he felt it necessary. At the moment, he was too wrapped up in his own concerns to feel sufficient curiosity about Perry's to go on the attack, but his brother couldn't count on being left to his own devices for too long. The reflection brought a reluctant smile to his lips.

He was halfway up the stairs when the front door knocker sounded from the hall below. He frowned. It was too early for his guests, too late for visitors, and tradesmen would have gone to the kitchen door. He paused on the stairs as Bart hastened from the kitchen, racing to the door to pull back the locks. He hauled it open.

Sebastian listened from the stairs, waiting to see if it was something that would concern him. The disembodied voice outside declared, "Message for the Honorable Sebastian Sullivan."

Bart's muttered reply was inaudible, but the door closed as the lad backed into the hall again. He set the message on the console table beside the door and scampered back to his supper going cold on the kitchen table.

Sebastian retraced his steps to the hall. He picked up the wafer-sealed letter. The writing was unfamiliar but definitely feminine, too fancy for his tastes. He would indulge in the odd curlicue himself if he was in a festive mood, but this script was adorned with a positive garden of flourishes. The paper was also scented. Gingerly, he slit the wafer with his thumbnail and opened the sheet.

Mr. and Mrs. William Sutton request the pleasure of the company of the Honorable Sebastian Sullivan at dinner on Wednesday, October 31, at their residence in Bruton Street, at the hour of eight o'clock.

Sebastian raised his eyebrows. Serena, it seemed, had alerted him just in time. Of course, if she hadn't cajoled him, he would have returned a courteous but absolute refusal and put the whole matter out of his mind. Now, of course, he was honor-bound to accept. He cast the sheet aside on the console table and went back upstairs. He was committed to a return to Bruton Street in the morning, anyway. Not for the first time, he wondered what it was about Serena that addled his thinking, drove him to impetuous acts that held no conceivable benefit for himself—in fact, quite the opposite. In this case, he was gravely at risk of emerging from the tangle labeled a dastard, a coward, a coxcomb, and any number of disparaging epithets.

Chapter Nine

Serena retired to bed in the dawn hours as usual. It had been a successful night. The house bank had won consistently at faro. Lord Burford had, as usual, been in attendance, but for once, he had made no attempt to engage Serena in conversation. She had felt his eyes on her for most of the evening, but not even at supper had he approached her. Her stepfather had barely spoken to her, but he, too, had watched her closely throughout. The business of Burford's proposition was not over, Serena knew that. It made her on edge, *jangly,* as she had described it to Sebastian, and it took all her self-discipline to concentrate on the play, to ensure that the faro bank ended the evening as the winner.

She had long since given up on moral scruples about the ways in which she ensured that the cards she dealt came out in a certain pattern. On one level, she quite enjoyed the dexterity of mind necessary to achieve the right outcome for the bank. There was no room for scruples in the life she led. She flirted, flattered both young men and old, treated the ladies, of whom there were far fewer, with friendly and disarming deference.

Every now and again, a very young lady would appear at the tables, accompanied by a youthful cicisbeo. She would be an elderly peer's new bride, giddy with her sudden independence, a seemingly enormous quarterly allowance, and the flattering attentions of a wide circle of young men.

Only then did Serena allow her conscience to dictate to her. Smiling, she would befriend the child in question, steer her to a table where the play was not quite so deep, try to keep her from deep basset or the faro tables, and intervene occasionally when it looked as if a family heirloom was about to be cast upon the table as a stake when the hapless bride's purse had run dry.

Occasionally, she had earned the undying enmity of a young woman she had forced to leave the house on the arm of a reluctant cicisbeo, whom, in turn, she had roundly chastised for exposing such a naïve child to the dangers of the tables.

Not once did it occur to Serena that she was barely older than these youngsters whom she felt such a need to protect.

She fell into bed just before daybreak, told her maid to awaken her at nine o'clock, and for once found sleep quickly. The afternoon's lovemaking with Sebastian replaced the tumble of yearning dreams that ordinarily interlaced her sleep, and she awoke, when Bridget drew aside the curtains, feeling wonderfully refreshed, as if she had slept twelve hours instead of four.

"Here's your hot chocolate, Lady Serena." Bridget set the silver tray on the bed. "'Tis a beautiful day. A bit chilly, but it's such a pleasure to see the sun." She bustled around, gathering up Serena's discarded clothes from the previous evening. "What will you wear this morning?"

Serena nibbled a piece of bread and butter as she considered the question. "I'm visiting a friend, so the gray velvet gown with the silver fox pelisse, I think, Bridget."

Bridget nodded her approval as she drew the gown out of the armoire, examining it for creases. "A quick touch-up with the flat iron, ma'am . . . I'll be back in a moment." She hurried from the room, leaving Serena with her hot chocolate and a small pile of billets-doux that regularly accompanied her early-morning tray.

Among them she discovered an invitation to the Suttons' for dinner on the 31st of the month. Had Sebastian received his at the same time? It seemed likely. She cast aside the bedcovers and went to the secretaire to pen her acceptance. She wanted it to arrive before she and Sebastian paid their morning visit.

Bridget returned with the freshly pressed gown, accompanied by a kitchen maid with a jug of steaming hot water. "I'll need you to accompany me this morning, Bridget." Serena poured hot water into the basin on the washstand.

"Yes, m'lady. Will you take breakfast in the dining room, or shall I bring it up to your parlor?"

Serena had no desire to run into her stepfather, and

she was bound to find him at breakfast downstairs. She wrung out a washcloth in the basin of hot water, pressing it to her face. "In the parlor, please. Just a coddled egg and some more bread and butter."

She sat on the bench at the end of the bed to draw on silk stockings, fastening the garters above the knee, while Bridget shook out the folds of the stiffened cambric petticoats before lacing Serena's corset. "Is that tight enough, m'lady?"

"Yes, quite tight enough," Serena declared, taking a deep breath. She stood still as Bridget tied the small hoop at her waist and dropped the stiffened petticoats over her head. The gray velvet gown was one of her favorites. It opened over an underskirt of turquoise velvet, and the elbow-length sleeves ended in delicate lace ruffles banded with ribbon in the same turquoise velvet. Lace edged the décolletage, and she fastened a turquoise pendant at her throat.

"How would you like to wear your hair, ma'am?" Bridget knew that her mistress disdained powder except on the most formal of evening occasions, and she could understand why. Why would anyone want to cover that glorious blue-black mass with sticky white powder?

Serena considered the question, tilting her head as she examined herself in the cheval glass. "Curl the side ringlets, Bridget, and fasten the rest in a braided coronet. If it's windy outside, it won't blow about." It was a simple style all her own, one that suited her small, neat head and somehow accentuated the size of her eyes. And

Serena was under no illusions that she wanted to look her most appealing for Sebastian. It was such a familiar feeling, so well remembered now, and now, as in the old days, it was accompanied by a little surge of excitement in the pit of her stomach.

She sat down to her breakfast with enthusiasm, noticing how buttery sunlight poured through the bay window of her parlor, how the brightness of the fire in the grate was dimmed by the sun's light, noticing how good the egg tasted, how rich the butter on her bread, the delicious aroma of the coffee when she poured it into her cup. For the first time in an age, Serena felt truly alive. And she gloried in the sensation.

It lasted until she was crossing the hall, Bridget just behind her, to the hackney that Flanagan had summoned for her, and her stepfather came out of the library. "Where are you going, Serena?"

At the sound of his voice, her skin seemed to feel thin and raw, and a tiny pulse started to beat behind her eyes. She stopped, drawing on her gloves. "To Bruton Street, sir, to visit the Suttons." Her voice was soft and level, and she met his gaze with stony eyes.

"Ah, good," he said. His eyes slid away from hers. "I intend to visit Mr. Sutton myself later this morning. He wanted some advice on setting up his stables. Inform him that I will do myself the honor of calling upon him a little before noon. And mention in passing how much I am looking forward to seeing the enchanting Miss Sutton again." He retreated to the library.

Damn, thought Serena. Sebastian and her stepfather could not run into each other, so somehow she would have to get Sebastian out of Bruton Street after only half an hour. Perhaps she could contrive to get Abigail out of the house as well before the general paid his promised visit.

She and her maid climbed into the hackney. Bridget leaned out to pull the door shut, calling the address up to the driver as she did so.

Serena frowned in thought for the duration of the short journey. Bridget was accompanying her for form's sake and could usefully provide an extra chaperone if Serena could persuade Abigail's mama to allow her daughter to take a walk with herself and Sebastian, making their escape before General Heyward arrived. That would effectively kill the two birds with one stone.

The hackney drew up at precisely eleven o'clock, and as Serena and Bridget stepped down, Sebastian appeared, strolling nonchalantly along the street. He arrived at the doorstep a few seconds after Serena.

"Well met, Lady Serena." He bowed with a flourish of his hat. "Is it not a beautiful morning?" His blue eyes gleamed with a conspiratorial amusement, as if all their shared memories were at the forefront of his mind. He stepped back, gesturing that she should precede him to the front door, then reached over her shoulder and lifted the knocker.

The butler opened the door, and Serena greeted him.

"Good morning, Morrison. Is Mrs. Sutton at home?"

"I believe so, my lady." His gaze glanced off Sebastian. "Who shall I say is calling, sir?"

"The Honorable Sebastian Sullivan," Serena said swiftly. "He is known to Mrs. Sutton."

"Of course, my lady." Morrison bowed and progressed in stately fashion upstairs to the drawing room. The ladies were at their embroidery, Abigail, at least, bored to tears. When Morrison announced their visitors, she jumped up.

"Oh, Mama, how lovely. 'Tis Serena and that kind Mr. Sullivan. Do show them up, Morrison."

Morrison looked to his mistress for confirmation. Marianne set aside her needlework. "Indeed, Morrison, show our guests in. And bring refreshment. I daresay Mr. Sullivan would enjoy a glass of madeira . . . or sherry, perhaps."

"Yes, ma'am." Morrison bowed himself out and within a few minutes announced, "Lady Serena Carmichael and the Honorable Sebastian Sullivan, ma'am."

"Mrs. Sutton, I hope I find you well . . . and Abigail, my dear, you are looking positively radiant. London suits you." Serena moved into the room, talking as she did so, sketching a curtsy to Mrs. Sutton and embracing Abigail. "See who I found on your doorstep." She gestured lightly to Sebastian, who made his bows, kissed hands, and murmured all the correct platitudes.

"I do hope we shall see you at our little dinner next week, Mr. Sullivan," Mrs. Sutton said with a winning smile. "Lady Serena has already been good enough to accept."

Sebastian bowed his head. "Indeed, ma'am, I shall be honored."

"Well, I do think you might enjoy it," Marianne declared with a complacent smile. "Mr. Sutton keeps a fine cellar, you should know, and my cook is as good as any outside one of the royal palaces." She nodded in emphasis.

"Indeed, Mama, I'm sure Mr. Sullivan is not concerned with such things," Abigail protested, blushing a little.

Sebastian smiled. "Oh, you are mistaken, Miss Sutton. I am most concerned with such things. But I must say, even without those inducements, I would find it impossible to refuse such an invitation." His smile seemed painted on his lips, and he struggled not to glance at Serena. He could well imagine her expression, a wicked mix of amusement and satisfaction.

"Indeed, sir." Mrs. Sutton nodded, as if it was only to be expected. "Will you take madeira or sherry . . . Lady Serena, what may I offer you?"

"Sherry, if you please, ma'am."

"Sherry, thank you," Sebastian murmured in his turn.

Their hostess gestured to the hovering Morrison, who filled glasses and brought them over. The sound of the door knocker made Serena's heart jump. She glanced at the clock. It was barely eleven-fifteen. The general could not be this early. But she waited apprehensively until the butler returned to announce, "Mr. Jonas Wedgwood, ma'am."

Marianne stiffened, her mouth tightening, and Abigail flushed. Serena noticed both reactions and regarded the newcomer with interest. The young man bowing in the doorway was impeccably dressed, handsome enough, and his expression was a mixture of eagerness to please and the self-confidence of one who had always been assured of his own value.

Marianne offered a chilly smile. Abigail's greeting was a curtsy and a flustered "Good morning, Mr. Wedgwood."

"I see you have visitors already," Jonas Wedgwood said, having made his bows. "I trust I'm not intruding?"

"Not at all, sir," Serena said readily.

"Allow me to introduce Lady Serena Carmichael and the Honorable Sebastian Sullivan, Mr. Wedgwood." Marianne managed to emphasize the titles of one set of guests, whilst murmuring the name of the lowly new arrival.

"How d'you do." Sebastian stepped forward, hand outstretched in ready welcome. He despised snobbery, as did most of those secure in the knowledge of their own immutable place in Society's hierarchy. "Wedgwood . . . anything to do with the china family?"

"Everything to do with it, sir." Jonas took the hand with a relieved smile.

"The Wedgwood family is very prominent in Society

in Stoke-on-Trent, Mr. Sullivan," Abigail put in with a timid smile.

"A long way from here, my dear," Marianne declared. "We need not bore Lady Serena and Mr. Sullivan with tittle-tattle from the provinces."

"Indeed, ma'am, I find such conversations most interesting," Serena said. Her mind was dancing along. Here lay the perfect answer. Abigail and Jonas Wedgwood. Abigail clearly felt an attraction, judging by her wide-eyed look and blushes, and it was as clear as day that Mr. Wedgwood had no interest in Bruton Street but the sweetly pretty Abigail. Foster this, she thought, and they would be home and dry. The general would be left to find some other prey, and she . . . oh, sweet fortune . . . she would be free.

"We were hoping, ma'am, that you would permit Abigail to accompany Mr. Sullivan and myself on a short walk in Green Park. 'Tis such a beautiful day, far too lovely to be cooped up inside. My maid will accompany us if you think it necessary."

"Oh, no, my dear Lady Serena, I consider you a perfectly adequate chaperone," declared Mrs. Sutton. "You are like an elder sister to dear Abigail."

"I am flattered you consider me as such." Serena studiously avoided looking at Sebastian.

Abigail jumped eagerly to her feet. "I'll fetch my hat and pelisse." She whirled out of the room in a flurry of muslin skirts.

Jonas looked dismayed, but there was little he could do. He hadn't been invited to sit and stood awkwardly twisting his hat in his lap, until Serena said, "If your way takes you in the direction of the park, perhaps you'd care to walk with us that far, Mr. Wedgwood."

"Oh, I should be delighted," he said with alacrity. Mrs. Sutton set her lips but said nothing.

Sebastian drew the young man aside and began a conversation on a pamphlet he had read about ceramics, and Serena listed with admiration. Sebastian's manners were always faultless, but she was greatly surprised that at some point in his carefree existence, he had taken the time to read about such an esoteric subject. He was certainly putting Jonas at his ease.

Abigail returned, wearing a most fetching straw bonnet adorned with brown velvet roses and a brown velvet pelisse lined and trimmed with gray fur. She looked enchanting, Serena thought, glancing at the two men, both of whom were regarding Abigail with open approval.

"Miss Sutton . . ." Sebastian offered his arm with a smile. Mrs. Sutton looked a little less tight-lipped and even managed a small, complacent smile at the sight of her daughter.

"A short walk will do you good, my dear. But no more than an hour. I don't wish you to catch cold."

"Indeed, no, ma'am," Sebastian said solemnly. "That would never do, but have no fear, at the very first shiver, I will escort Miss Sutton home without delay."

Serena glanced at the clock. It was almost a quarter

to noon, high time they were gone. She smiled at young Mr. Wedgwood. "Shall we, sir?"

"Oh, yes . . . forgive me, ma'am. Will you take my arm?" He proffered his crooked arm with a bow.

Serena curtsied a farewell to Marianne, and the four of them departed. Only when they had turned the corner of Bruton Street did Serena take a relieved breath. For the moment, they were safe. Abigail was chattering away to Sebastian, who listened with head bent towards her, offering an occasional comment.

"Are you to stay long in London, Mr. Wedgwood?" Serena addressed her companion cheerfully, seeing the longing looks he cast upon the couple walking a little way in front of them.

Jonas was too well brought up not to give his companion his full attention. "I have been on business for my uncle, ma'am, and have his leave to prolong my stay in town for a little pleasure. I am putting up at the Queen's Head in Henrietta Place."

"And what is it about London that gives you pleasure?" she inquired with a smile.

It proved to be a happy inquiry, and the young man launched into an enthusiastic description of the lions at the Exchange, the delights of Vauxhall, and a ridotto he had attended at the pleasure gardens at Ranelagh.

When they reached the entrance to Green Park, Jonas seemed not to notice and accompanied them through the gates. A herd of cows tended by a trio of milkmaids grazed on the grassy expanse, and Abigail exclaimed with delight, "Cows in the middle of London. How amazing . . . it's just like in the fields at home."

"Would you care to drink a cup of milk, Miss Sutton?" Jonas asked, stepping up quickly beside her. "The milkmaids will draw you a cup, fresh from the cow. If you'd like."

"Oh, yes, of all things." Abigail started off towards the cows, and Jonas followed quickly.

Sebastian glanced at Serena and grinned. "Shall we leave them to it for a moment?"

"Absolutely. Don't you think that would be a perfect match?"

"I doubt Mrs. Sutton would agree," he commented. "She seems ill disposed to one of their own."

Serena shrugged. "We'll see. Mr. Sutton is much more practical, and he adores Abigail; she's the apple of his eye. I don't think he would stop her marrying a man she loved, even if he didn't come up to her mama's standards."

Sebastian nodded. They stood a little apart, conscious of the public arena, but they were both acutely aware of the current of excitement, of anticipation, running between them. "When will I see you again?" he asked softly.

Serena understood that he was not talking about a social call. "I wish we had somewhere of our own," she murmured. "I don't like the idea of dodging around your brother, and while I'm sure Margaret will let me borrow her house occasionally, it makes everything seem so hole-in-the-corner, sordid almost."

"There is nothing in the least sordid about what I feel for you," Sebastian stated, his tone almost harsh. "The only sordid aspect of any of this is the loathsome influence of your stepfather. If you would agree to leave him, we would find a way out of this morass."

Serena sighed. "Don't start that again, Sebastian. I've told you, 'tis impossible at the moment. I'm the only person who can protect Abigail from him, and until I know she's safe, I'll not leave her in the lurch."

"So, you'd martyr yourself for the sake of a chit whose mother is determined to use her to advance her social pretensions?" He sounded harsher than he had intended and saw too late the quick anger flash in her eyes, the sudden tautness of her mouth.

"I've no interest in having this conversation." Serena walked away from him, over to the herd of cows, where a milkmaid was dipping a cup into the pail of milk she had just drawn from the cow.

"This is delicious, Lady Serena," Abigail called. "You should have some."

"Yes, allow me, Lady Serena." Jonas was in the act of paying the milkmaid for Abigail's cup and opened his purse readily again as Serena approached.

"No . . . no, thank you, Mr. Wedgwood. I'm not overly fond of milk." Serena forced a smile. "I think we should be getting back, Abigail. I've just remembered a pressing engagement with my dressmaker." She ignored

Sebastian, who had come up behind her. "Perhaps Mr. Wedgwood would be good enough to escort us back to Bruton Street. Mr. Sullivan has also recollected a previous engagement."

Sebastian glared but restrained himself from the swift rejoinder that came so readily to his lips. He bowed to Abigail. "I will do myself the honor of calling upon you again, Miss Sutton, if you will receive me."

Abigail's enormous eyes widened, and she fluttered her eyelashes. "Oh, yes, indeed, sir. Please, I do wish you would."

Sebastian nodded a farewell to Jonas. "Mr. Wedgwood . . . a pleasure. Lady Serena." He bowed formally, then turned and strolled away across the park.

Jonas, left in possession of the field, beamed delightedly. "Ladies, may I . . ." He offered his right arm to Serena and his left to Abigail, and the three of them returned to Bruton Street.

"I believe that's General Heyward's horse," Abigail observed as they turned onto Bruton Street. The general's black gelding was tethered to the railings outside the house, and Serena swore to herself. She had intended to stay out for at least another half-hour, but Sebastian had put a stop to that.

"Yes, I forgot . . . my stepfather said he had business with Mr. Sutton," she said vaguely. "I believe we must leave you here, Mr. Wedgwood." She offered her hand to their escort as they reached the front door.

He kissed her hand, paid Abigail the same courtesy, and then waited until they were inside the house before going on his way with a jaunty step.

"Ah, there you are, dearest." Marianne came out of the library at the sound of the front door. "General Heyward is here, with your father in the library. He was asking after you. Go into the library and make your curtsy, child." She glanced at Serena. "Won't you come through, too, Lady Serena?"

"No, I thank you. I have an engagement with my dressmaker," Serena said. "If Morrison would be kind enough to fetch my maid."

The butler bowed and disappeared into the back regions to summon Bridget, who was enjoying a comfortable chat with the upstairs maid in the laundry room. Adjusting her bonnet, she hurried back to Serena and received the information that they were to walk back to Pickering Place with an inner grimace. But she was accustomed to Lady Serena's passion for exercise and merely bobbed a curtsy in acknowledgment.

Marianne waited until the front door had closed on her visitor before reentering the library. Abigail was standing beside her father's desk. General Heyward, cradling a wine goblet, was standing in front of the fire, beaming at her. He held her hand in his, having just kissed her fingers. "You are to be congratulated, Mrs. Sutton. Your daughter is a vision of perfection. I was telling Mr. Sutton the same thing. What a joy it must be to have that lovely countenance and lively spirit around the house."

In Brussels, Abigail had found the general's fulsome compliments quite pleasant. But now they struck her as rather tasteless. She couldn't imagine the Honorable Sebastian making such a forward comment. Or even the less exalted Jonas Wedgwood. She extracted her hand from his grip and looked askance at her mother, who was smiling and nodding, accepting the compliments as her due.

"So kind, General. So very kind," Marianne murmured.

"Oh, yes, we're very proud of our pretty puss," William declared with his hearty boom. He chucked his daughter under the chin. "You've been walking with Lady Serena, have you?"

"Yes, Papa. We went to Green Park. Mr. Wedgwood bought me a cup of milk from the milkmaid . . . only fancy, sir, a herd of cows in a park in the middle of the city." Abigail was more than happy to relate the events of her morning, and her father listened with a benign smile, while his wife, at the mention of Mr. Wedgwood, pursed her lips.

"Well, now, Sutton, if you've a mind to visit Tattersalls, we'll go this afternoon." The general was not interested in Abigail's adventures in Green Park. He presumed Mr. Wedgwood was a member of the Wedgwood family and thus a friend from their hometown and easily dismissed as a significant character.

"Splendid . . . splendid. No time like the present. You'll take a bite of nuncheon with us first, General. Just pot luck, you know, but Mrs. Sutton can set a more than decent table."

The general accepted the invitation and offered his arm to Abigail as they went into the dining room. He took a seat beside her and set out to be charming. "Have you been to any balls yet, Miss Sutton?"

"Oh, no. I'm not really out yet, sir. I have to meet a wider circle of Society first, Mama says." It was on the tip of her tongue to mention the upcoming dinner party, and she swallowed the words in the nick of time. Serena had discreetly implied that the general would not wish to be included in a party of young people, and Abigail could see the sense in this. He was a fine figure of a man, certainly, but he was definitely of her parents' generation. She prayed that her mother would not mention it, either, but she needn't have worried. Marianne was prepared to keep the general in reserve, but she had set her sights on a younger, more eligible candidate for her daughter.

"Oh, we must arrange a visit to the theatre, then," the general said. "Show you off in your finery there. Mark my words, the minute you appear in my box, the questions will be flying, and I'm sure we shall receive any number of visitors in the interval."

Abigail glanced at her mother. Marianne had finally persuaded her husband that a visit to the theatre as a guest of Mr. Wedgwood would do nothing to advance their daughter's cause. William, good-natured as always, had demurred but finally yielded to his wife's greater knowledge of such matters, and Mr. Wedgwood's invitation had been declined in a stiff letter from Marianne.

"Why, General, that would be delightful," Marianne said. "But only a classical play would be suitable for a young debutante. Or perhaps a concert . . . something of the first style of elegance."

"Of course, dear lady. Of course. You mustn't forget, I have a daughter of my own. I should certainly know what's correct entertainment for young ladies." He drank deep of the wine in his glass and took a hearty forkful of the splendid veal and ham pie on his plate.

Mrs. Sutton seemed to find nothing strange in this comment. Lady Serena was a credit to her stepfather, she had often thought, although she seemed rather older than her years. But losing a mother would certainly force a child to grow up too fast.

"I wonder that Lady Serena is still unwed," William declared. "I'd have thought you'd have found her a husband by now, Heyward. If she were mine, I'd have had her wedded and bedded long since. As beautiful and accomplished as she is."

Abigail blushed furiously at her father's lack of delicacy, but she could say nothing in front of their guest, who did indeed look rather put out.

"Well, as to that," the general said after a moment, "Serena knows her own mind. She'll find her own husband when she's ready, but for the moment, she has enough to do looking after me." He laughed heartily and gestured to the footman to refill his glass.

"Well, Abigail won't be hanging out for a husband for long," William said with a proud smile at his daughter. "Such a pretty puss. I've been turning lovesick swains from the door since her fifteenth birthday. And unless I'm much mistaken, there's another one or two in the offing. Isn't that so, puss?" He refilled his tankard from the ale jug at his elbow.

Abigail's blush deepened, and she murmured, "For shame, Papa. I don't know what you mean."

"No, that's no way to talk, Mr. Sutton." Marianne came to her rescue. "You're putting the poor child to the blush."

"Oh, she's not embarrassed by her foolish old papa," William declared with a dismissive gesture. "A proud father is allowed to be just that, don't you agree, Heyward?"

"Certainly." The general's smile was a mere flicker of his lips. "Might one ask, Miss Sutton, who has been lucky enough to find favor in your eye?"

"My father is mistaken, sir." Abigail found strength in indignation. "And even if he were not, I would not be so indelicate as to enter such a discussion." She glanced at her mother, who nodded her approval.

"Abigail is quite correct, Mr. Sutton. Such matters are hardly subjects for the table."

"Oh, we are among friends, Mrs. Sutton," her husband remonstrated with a chuckle. "Isn't that so,

Heyward?" He waved at the butler. "Brandy, Morrison."

"I would certainly hope so," the general concurred.

Marianne pushed back her chair. "Come, Abigail, we will leave the gentlemen to their brandy."

Abigail, greatly relieved, followed her mother from the room and up to the drawing room, where Morrison was setting down a tray of coffee. "I can't like it when Papa talks with the general like that, Mama."

"No, well, that's just your papa's way." Marianne poured coffee. "He wants only the best for you, child." Privately, she resolved to keep her husband as much away from Society as she could during Abigail's debut. She was fond enough of William, but he lacked refinement, and while his generosity was wonderful where his daughter was concerned, his manners could be offputting in the more genteel circles where she hoped to find Abigail's husband.

Abigail sipped coffee and quickly dismissed the general as she dreamily contemplated the prospect of two suitors, both handsome, charming gentlemen, one with whom she felt instantly familiar—she and Jonas Wedgwood shared too many experiences for them to be anything but instantly comfortable with each other—and the other an exotic aristocrat with the most beautiful manners and the entrée into the most rarefied circles of Society.

She resolved to ask Serena about him the next time they were alone. He and Serena seemed like old friends, or at least acquaintances.

"The Blackwater earldom is one of the oldest in the country," her mother said suddenly, uncannily tuning in to her daughter's thoughts. "If the present earl does not have an heir, his brother will inherit." She sipped her coffee. "There are two younger brothers, as I understand it. Twins, but the Honorable Sebastian is the older of the two by some three minutes."

"How d'you know that?" Abigail was always amazed at her mother's ability to glean trifles of information from thin air.

"Oh, just something Morrison told me. Apparently, Lady Serena's maid was very talkative in the kitchen and seemed to know a great deal about the family. It's often the case that the servants know more than most about Society families."

"What's his brother's name?" Abigail was fascinated.

"The earl is Jasper Sullivan; the youngest brother is the Honorable Peregrine Sullivan."

"Oh . . . I wonder if they're identical twins." Two blue-eyed, golden-haired Sebastians wandering the London streets struck Abigail as too much good fortune.

"As to that, I cannot say," her mother replied. "But I wonder that Lady Serena didn't suggest we invite the Honorable Peregrine to join our dinner party with his brother."

"Perhaps she doesn't know him very well," Abigail suggested.

Marianne nodded and took a sweet biscuit from the tray, dipping it into her coffee. "Maybe so. It will be a great success, anyway. I do wonder, though, if we shouldn't have invited the general. He could always decline."

"But why oblige him to go to the trouble, Mama?" Abigail asked, taking up the *Lady's Gazette.* "'Tis a young people's party. You said so yourself."

"Perhaps you're right." Marianne settled back in her chair and closed her eyes, preparing to take an afternoon nap.

Chapter Ten

Sebastian returned home, kicking himself for provoking that acid exchange and yet convinced that he could not hold his tongue about something as vital as Serena's well-being, let alone her happiness. How could she possibly expect him to stand aside wringing his hands while she persisted in this grim and dangerous charade with her stepfather? If she had any true feelings for him, she would surely acknowledge his right to speak up. He may have spoken immoderately, but he had been provoked in his turn. Perhaps he needed to accept that Serena's feelings for him did not run as deep as his for her. And if that was the case, then, based on past experience, he needed to run as fast as possible in the opposite direction. It was a grim thought that he wanted to resist, but it sat like a persistent shadow over the sun-filled meadow of his earlier contentment.

Peregrine was coming down the stairs as his twin let himself into the house. "You look as if you lost a guinea and found a farthing, Seb," he observed, adjusting the set of his hat in the small mirror.

"I wish it were that simple," Sebastian responded with a twisted smile. "Where are you going?"

"I thought it was time to pay a duty visit to the old man. I haven't seen our esteemed Uncle Bradley since last month. D'you feel like keeping me company?"

"Why not?" Sebastian sighed. "It couldn't make this day any worse."

"Care to talk about it?" Perry turned his full attention on his brother. "I'm in no hurry."

Sebastian shook his head. "Not at present, Perry, but thank you for the offer. I'm too confused to know where to start."

Peregrine had little difficulty guessing the source of his twin's dour expression. He had seen it all too often three years earlier, and he wished Lady Serena Carmichael at the devil. She had never been anything but trouble for Sebastian. But there was a line even the closest brother couldn't cross. So he said nothing further, following his brother out to the street.

"Shall we walk?"

"If you wish. 'Tis a nice enough day." Perry acquiesced easily, and the two of them set off towards Piccadilly and the Strand. They walked in silence, dodging the foot traffic along Piccadilly. Conversation would have been difficult, anyway, with the strident yells of street vendors, carters and chairmen bellowing for custom, the clatter of iron wheels on the cobbles, the barking of mangy dogs, and the occasional high-pitched squeal of a horse, rearing to an abrupt halt at some obstacle in the stream of traffic.

Sebastian seemed sunk in a morose reverie, failing to notice even the painted and powdered Cyprians in their dramatic décolletage, strolling with their maids through the crowd, their exposed bosoms an indication of the wares on offer. This seeming blindness was out of character, Peregrine reflected, and yet further evidence of his troubled mind. Sebastian would usually be ogling the passing ladies with his quizzing glass, offering a cheerfully obscene running commentary on their attributes. He wondered what the hell it was about the woman that enabled her to hold such sway over Sebastian.

Outside Viscount Bradley's stately mansion on the Strand, they both paused, automatically and without consultation preparing themselves for whatever might await them within. There was no knowing in what mood they'd find their uncle, although sharp-tongued was a certainty, whether he was in a good frame of mind or bad. It depended to a large extent these days on his physical well-being.

Louis, their uncle's general factotum, opened the door at their knock. He was resplendent in green livery and white wig. "Mr. Sebastian . . . Mr. Peregrine. I'll see if his lordship will see you. Lord Blackwater is with him at the moment."

"Oh." Sebastian raised an eyebrow. "Well, shall we go up?" He moved to the staircase.

"I suggest you wait in the antechamber, sirs, until Lord Blackwater leaves. I will then ascertain if his lordship is willing to entertain further visitors today."

It was couched as a suggestion but, coming from Louis, had the full force of a commandment. The brothers nodded their agreement and made their way up the ornately carved horseshoe staircase to a set of double doors to the right of the galleried landing. The doors opened onto a thickly carpeted antechamber. The brothers were so accustomed to the rich furnishings in Indian and Oriental style, the profusion of gold and silver ornaments, the delicate porcelain figures, and the heavy gilt-framed paintings, that they barely noticed them. Viscount Bradley had made his considerable fortune in India and the Orient, and his house and possessions reflected a life spent in the Far East.

"Wonder what brings Jasper to the old man's bedside?" Sebastian made straight for the decanters ranged on the sideboard, examining them with his quizzing glass. "Lord, you'd think the old man could run to a decent port or cognac once in a while, wouldn't you? Nothing here but sherry."

"I suspect he keeps the decent stuff for himself." Perry frowned. "I haven't seen Jasper for a couple of weeks. He's probably just making a duty visit, as are we."

At this opportune moment, the door to the viscount's bedchamber opened, and Jasper emerged. He looked at his brothers without undue surprise. "Seb, Perry, how are you? You've timed a visit to the old man rather poorly, I'm afraid. He's in one of his worst moods, irascible and ready to insult anything that moves."

"You didn't bring Clarissa, then." Peregrine glanced mischievously towards a screen painted with a most voluptuous odalisque. "She's not hiding behind the odalisque today."

Jasper smiled and shook his head. Peregrine was remembering the first occasion he and Sebastian had met Mistress Clarissa Astley, now Countess of Blackwater. "No, I shield her from the old devil as much as I can." He poured himself sherry. "Be careful in there." He gestured with his head to the bedchamber behind him.

As he did so, the violent clanging of a large handbell came from the bedchamber, and before the last discordant note had died down, a lean, black-robed figure appeared from a side door and slid into the bedchamber without acknowledging the occupants of the antechamber.

Jasper grimaced. "Poor devil. Take a look at the old man's memoirs if you get the chance. He's tormenting that innocent Benedictine priest he has acting as amanuensis with the most obscene confession you could imagine."

"What d'you mean, Jasper?"

"Just that our revered uncle is composing his memoirs as a sort of final confession, using Father Cosgrove as his confessor, so that he will meet his maker properly shriven. And by paying us to save a lost soul apiece, he has formed the twisted idea that he will achieve his own redemption." He gave a short laugh, drained his glass, and set it down.

"You didn't exactly find a lost soul," Peregrine pointed out, sipping his sherry. "Clarissa was never really in need of redemption."

"True enough," Jasper agreed. "But that little fact we keep to ourselves. The viscount had to accept her, whatever he believed." He regarded the twins over his glass, his eyes sharp and shrewd. "So tell me, how are your quests going?"

Sebastian shrugged. "Not as well as yours." Now was not the moment to share his dilemma with either of his brothers. In fact, he wasn't sure there ever would be a right moment.

Peregrine blurted suddenly, "To tell the truth, Jasper, I don't like it. We're playing a game of our uncle's. He's baited the hook, and he's playing us like trout."

"So you've said before," Jasper responded, his voice harsh. "And as I've said before, Peregrine, you will *not* neglect your family duty. If we don't meet the terms of Bradley's will, the estates will be gone. They're already mortgaged to the hilt, and the Blackwater name will be dishonored. I understand it doesn't seem fair, but little in life is. We were not responsible for the burden of debt, but *I* am responsible for dragging the family out of the River Tick. And I need your help. So find yourself a wife to fit Bradley's specifications. I don't give a damn how you do it, but do it you will. Is that understood?"

Perry, ashen-faced, nodded. "Understood."

The earl nodded. "Come for dinner next week, both of you."

The door closed behind him, and the brothers looked at each other. "I don't think I have the stomach for Uncle Bradley anymore," Perry said after a moment.

"I don't blame you." Sebastian shook his head. "I can't remember the last time Jasper went off at one of us like that."

"He's carrying the full burden of the family's demands and running the estates," Perry said. "It must be a constant anxiety. But damn it, Seb, I didn't mean I wouldn't play my part. I was just expressing my reservations. Don't tell me you don't have any."

Sebastian thought of Serena. Adhering in love and loyalty to Serena, if indeed that was what he intended to do, meant he could not fulfill his part of the bargain. But after Jasper's castigation, he couldn't imagine confessing that. "Of course I do," he conceded.

Perry nodded. "We'll find a way through the maze, I'm sure, but I definitely can't face an irascible Uncle Bradley now; one tongue lashing a day is my limit. Are you staying?"

"Having got here, I might as well," his twin said. "Besides, I'm curious to get a peek at the scandalous memoir."

Louis came into the antechamber, having seen the earl and his companion out. "I'll see if his lordship is receiving, sirs."

"Oh, just me, Louis," Sebastian said. "My brother has recollected a pressing engagement."

"Very well, sir." Louis knocked on the double doors to the bedchamber and entered at a muffled command.

Peregrine raised a hand in farewell to his brother and hurried from the antechamber. Sebastian couldn't blame him for needing to lick his wounds. Jasper was rarely angry with his younger brothers, but when he was, they crumbled beneath his tongue.

"His lordship will see you, Mr. Sebastian," Louis announced from the door to the bedchamber.

Sebastian nodded and stepped past him into an overheated chamber, where a fire blazed in the massive hearth. Heavy velvet curtains were drawn across the windows, blocking out the crisp autumn sunlight, and the room was illuminated with the glow of wax candles. There was a faint odor of sickness in the stuffy air.

Sebastian bowed to the figure ensconced in an armchair beside the fire. The old man was wrapped in a fur-trimmed robe, with a fur rug nestled across his lap. He held a wine glass between his fingers and regarded his nephew with surprisingly sharp eyes in a rather waxen countenance.

"Two nephews in one day. I'm honored. Where's the other one? You don't normally come singly."

"Perry had another engagement, sir." Sebastian stepped further into the room, and Louis closed the door gently behind him. "How are you, sir? Feeling better, I trust."

His uncle laughed. "Don't give me platitudes, boy. I've no time for 'em. Sit." He pointed imperatively at a straight-backed chair opposite. "Cosgrove, you black crow, fetch a glass of wine for m'nephew."

Sebastian, glancing towards the shadowy far corner of the room, made out a darker shadow than the rest. A shadow that moved forward into the light and became truly visible as the tall, gaunt, black-robed priest with a heavy cross around his neck and rosary beads at the waist of his cassock.

"Good day, Father Cosgrove." Sebastian greeted the priest with a polite smile.

"Good day, sir." The priest filled a wine glass from the decanter and brought it over to the visitor. His angular face was expressionless, except for his eyes, which held a rather haunted look, much like a fugitive with the hounds baying at his heels. Sebastian felt only compassion. He took the glass with another smile, and the priest melted back into the shadows.

"So, I wonder if you can imagine who I saw the other night?" the viscount challenged, his eyes gleaming with malicious amusement.

"I didn't realize you went out at night, sir." Sebastian sipped his wine. It was certainly superior to the sherry on offer in the anteroom.

"Oh, when the mood takes me." The old man settled

back in his armchair, looking very pleased with himself. "I'd heard tell of a new hell just opened on Pickering Place." He regarded his nephew with the same amused malice. "Thought I'd pay it a visit."

"Indeed, sir." Sebastian wondered uneasily what was coming next. "I trust you enjoyed your evening."

Bradley sipped his wine before saying, "I did enjoy myself. Played piquet with the ever lovely Lady Serena. I must say, she's improved over the last three years. A few years on the continental circuit always does wonders for the demimonde . . . teaches them a few tricks of the trade, gives them a touch of varnish, smooths over the rough edges."

Sebastian maintained an impassive expression. His uncle watched him through lowered lids. "I've a mind to renew my suit there. What d'ye think, boy? D'ye think she'll have me?"

"I wouldn't know, sir." Sebastian leaned forward and kicked a falling log back into the hearth. The movement gave him time to compose himself. "How should I? I am no longer particularly acquainted with the lady."

"Ah, is that so?" The viscount set down his glass with a snap. The light from the candle on the table beside him caught a massive ruby carbuncle, which glowed against a strangely youthful, slender, and elegant white hand. "Cosgrove?"

Instantly, Father Cosgrove stepped forward with the decanter. In silence, he filled the viscount's glass and retreated once more.

"Well, if you've not visited Pickering Place, nephew, I suggest you do. Quite a tasty morsel she's turned out to be. I hear that Burford is interested in having her under his protection. Can't make up m'mind whether to enter the lists against him. That old fool Heyward is only interested in the highest bidder for the girl, of course, so I could probably outbid Burford. Just can't make up m'mind whether 'tis worth the effort."

Burford. Highest bidder? Sebastian felt suddenly nauseated. The wine became acid on his tongue. Was this just the old man's malice, or was Heyward genuinely intent on prostituting his stepdaughter? She had said nothing of the kind when she'd talked of the miseries of her life. She'd referred to degradation, in terms of running a gambling hell, of debts unpaid, of running always a step ahead of creditors. But nothing of prostitution.

He managed to say with icy calm, "Well, I certainly can't help you to make it up, sir." His eye fell on a stack of closely written sheets on a table on the far side of the earl's chair.

The earl followed his eyes, and he chuckled suddenly. It was a chuckle that merely increased Sebastian apprehension. "My memoirs, m'boy. I was showing 'em to Blackwater just now. Perhaps you'd like to take a look . . . Cosgrove, you crow, fetch me the pages from the chapter about Charles Street." He clicked his fingers imperatively.

Sebastian steeled himself. Charles Street had been General Heyward's first gaming house, the house where

Sebastian had first met Serena. His uncle had been a frequent player there and, like the majority of the players, had enjoyed Serena's company. He couldn't possibly have been aware of the nature of the relationship between his nephew and Lady Serena, they had been scrupulously careful, but now Sebastian wondered if that had been a pipe dream. In such a small, close-knit society, utter secrecy was almost impossible to achieve.

"I hardly think . . ." he began, but then stopped as the priest brought a slim sheaf of papers to his employer. Curiosity had the best of him now. However unpleasant it was going to be, he needed to see what his uncle had written.

"Take 'em into the antechamber, boy. I'm tired." Viscount Bradley abruptly brought the visit to an end, waving away the papers. "Crow, ring for Louis. I want him to put me to bed."

Silently, Father Cosgrove handed Sebastian the sheaf of papers, then rang the handbell.

Sebastian rose from his chair and bowed to his uncle. "Good afternoon, sir. I hope you'll feel better s—"

"Spare me the platitudes," his lordship repeated irritably. "Get out, and leave me alone."

Sebastian took his leave without a further word. In the antechamber, he sat down beside a lascivious sculpture of Indian origin, where a scene of multiple and improbable copulations was taking place, and took up the first sheet of paper.

It began: *An afternoon with the lovely Serena . . . how*

delicious to bring that proud beauty to her knees, to teach her how to please—"

Sebastian felt a renewed wave of nausea and raised his eyes from the priest's spidery script. The viscount seemed to be implying that he had had Serena in his bed, and yet Sebastian was confident that that had never happened. Or was he so confident? There was so much about Serena that she kept to herself. And now this talk of Burford's protection . . . what did that mean? Did Heyward force her to sell herself? And if he did, how often had it happened?

But he couldn't believe Serena had ever been in Bradley's bed . . . *wouldn't* believe it. The old man was out to make mischief as he always did. He had the irresistible urge to hurt, to maim, whenever he had the power to do so, and if he knew or guessed at his nephew's long-ago liaison with Serena, he would know how sickened Sebastian would be by these debauched ramblings.

Resolutely, Sebastian began to read again, and as he did so, he suddenly began to see clearly through the fog of revulsion. His uncle was painting a lecherous picture of Serena as he imagined in his twisted mind how she would be, how she would respond sexually to his demands. And vile demands they were, for the most part. Sebastian wondered how many of the other incidents laboriously recorded by the pious Father Cosgrove had actually taken place. Were they all like this? The obscene but unrequited dreams of a pathetic old man?

He read through to the end, even though just entering the viscount's dark imagination made him feel soiled. When he had finished, he stacked the pages neatly, set them down on an ornately carved table, and quietly left the house.

He walked briskly, letting the chill air of late afternoon blow the murky residue of his uncle's filthy dreams out of his mind. He realized suddenly that he was in Covent Garden. He had been so absorbed in his reverie he hadn't noticed where he was going. The Piazza was thronged at this time of day, the courtesans and common whores all plying their trade in their own fashion, the drinkers stumbling from the taverns in various stages of inebriation, and the sellers of pornographic prints doing a roaring trade under the colonnades.

Sebastian turned aside into the Shakespeare's Head Tavern and called for a bumper of ale. He took it to the fireside, where he found a seat in the inglenook, and idly watched the noisy scene around him. And as he did so, letting his mind wander where it would, the answer to his dilemma became crystal clear. How could he possibly have failed to see the obvious? And if he hadn't read the viscount's disgusting memoirs, it would probably still have eluded him. It was the perfect answer to the dilemma, the perfect answer to Lord Burford, to General Heyward, and to Viscount Bradley.

Except . . . and it was a significant *except*. Would Serena see it as he did? Was she still the same woman he had loved? He really didn't know. She had become an enigma. What if she *had* been selling herself across Europe? Even if her prostitution was coerced, could he live with that?

Some days later, Serena was reading in her parlor when Flanagan informed her that Lord Burford was below and wished to see her.

"Tell him I'm not available," she said, barely looking up from her book. Her skin crawled at the thought of an interview with his lordship. The general was not at home, so she could safely deny the earl without fear of being countermanded.

"Yes, m'lady." Flanagan bowed and retreated, making his stately way back down to the library, where the earl was waiting.

"Lady Serena is not at home this afternoon, my lord."

The earl looked with irritation at the impassive butler, who stood holding the door, ready to escort the visitor from the house.

"Tell your mistress that my mission is of considerable urgency, and I must see her without delay."

Flanagan hesitated. He couldn't bodily throw the earl from the house, but his loyalty was always first and foremost to Lady Serena. "I will convey your message, my lord, but Lady Serena was very firm in her desire not to be disturbed."

"Go and tell her what I say." The earl waved an imperative hand in dismissal.

Flanagan retraced his steps. "Your pardon, my lady,

but Lord Burford insists that the matter is of great urgency and he must see you without delay."

Serena felt the familiar sense of futility that she forced herself to fight every day of her life. It was as if she had no free will, and yet she *did* have, she told herself. She could tell Flanagan to repeat her denial, and eventually Burford would have to leave. He couldn't force himself into her private parlor. But she knew that that was only delaying the inevitable. At some point, she had to see him and confront the issue. For as long as the general let the earl go on thinking that her capitulation was eventually inevitable, Burford would continue to pester her. Now was a good moment, when her stepfather was out of the house and couldn't interfere or attempt to coerce her.

"Very well, Flanagan. I'll see him in the small parlor downstairs." She set aside her book and went to check her reflection in the mirror above the mantel. She looked absurdly radiant and glowing, she thought with a flicker of gallows humor. Her eyes were bright, her complexion like thick cream, and her hair gleamed with blue-black lights. The picture should have pleased her, but she found herself wishing she could look a little less enticing. A drab appearance, with lank hair and dull complexion, preferably with a few carefully situated spots—a big red one on the end of her nose would do beautifully—might serve to put off the earl.

Well, there was nothing to be done about it. She was as she was. A morning's spat with Sebastian in the fresh air of Green Park could do wonders, it seemed. She made her way down to the small parlor, where the earl was already waiting.

"My lord." She curtsied. "Your message was rather importunate. I trust nothing grave has occurred."

"No . . . no, indeed not, Lady Serena." He bowed low, but his eyes devoured her. "Forgive me if I sounded importunate, but I have been wishing for a private word for several weeks now, and it seems that whenever I call, you are already engaged. And, of course, in the evening, you are so occupied at the tables 'tis impossible to catch you alone."

"I rather think, sir, that *catching me alone,* as you put it, is hardly a gentlemanly objective." A chilly smile hovered on her lips, but her violet eyes had taken on a glacial hue.

A faint flush darkened his lordship's already florid complexion, and he made a visible effort to control his temper. "I'm sorry you should think that, ma'am. But the proposition I have to put to you can only be made in private, and I am most anxious to make it."

"I see. Did it occur to you, my lord, that perhaps I may not be anxious to receive it?" She remained standing by the door and did not invite her visitor to take a seat.

His flush deepened. "Your stepfather desires that you hear me, ma'am."

She inclined her head in acknowledgment. There was no point in denying the truth. "Maybe so, and in courtesy, I will hear you out. But no one can compel me to accept your proposition. And I tell you now, my lord, that I will not."

He sighed, took a turn about the room, then faced her. "Let us leave your stepfather out of this. This matter is between just us, Lady Serena. In a word, I wish you to become my mistress. I will make handsome provision for you; you will want for nothing. And when our liaison is over, as inevitably will happen, I will make provision for your future." He held out his hands. "I am a wealthy man. What could be fairer than that?"

"I find your proposition insulting, my lord."

"Oh, come now, girl. There's nothing insulting about such an arrangement. Women of every situation enter into such arrangements every day. What makes you too good for such offers? You are one of faro's daughters. Oh, I accept that your father was a nobleman, but your situation has changed since then, my dear girl. You need to face realities."

It could have been her stepfather speaking. Serena regarded the earl with open distaste. "I believe there is nothing further to say, my lord." She turned back to the door, but he moved quickly, catching her arm.

She whirled on him, pure anger now ablaze in her eyes. "Take your hand off me, sir." She raised her free hand, prepared to strike him if he didn't instantly comply. He looked at first startled, then laughed, dropping her arm.

"Oh, you do look particularly ravishing when your

eyes flash, my dear." He was standing very close to her still. "Now, listen to me for a little while longer. I hold the mortgages on this house, and if I call them in, you and your stepfather will be ruined. Do you fancy a sojourn in the Marshalsea or the Fleet? Life in a debtors' prison is not overly pleasant, I should warn you."

"Blackmail, my lord?" Her eyebrows rose as her voice took on a tone of derisive amusement.

For a moment, she thought he was going to strike her, but he mastered himself with an effort. "Merely a plain and simple truth, my dear. Now, your stepfather has promised you to me in exchange for those mortgages."

"I am not my stepfather's to promise," she responded coldly.

"No, I begin to see that." He made his tone reasonable, conversational, all confrontation banished, but his small, pale eyes held a calculating look. "But what would you say if I were to give you the mortgages . . . make them over to you as part of our arrangement? You would hold your stepfather's future in the palm of that pretty little hand." He made a move to take her hand, but she jerked it behind her. "What d'you say?" he pressed.

Serena was momentarily at a loss, as the prospect of such a gift, or payment, to be exact, grew in dazzling glory. What a glorious prospect that would be. To have the upper hand over the general, after the years of dancing to his tune. To own the gaming house herself. The profits would be hers. Her future would be secure. Oh, not a reputable future, indubitably, but so what? She didn't exactly lead a reputable existence now. But she would be her own mistress. The decisions would be hers and hers alone.

And then she thought of Sebastian.

"What say you?" Burford repeated, a greedy look in his eyes as he saw her hesitation for what it was. She was tempted.

"Good day, Lord Burford." Serena turned on her heel and had slipped through the door before he could recover from his surprise.

"You will think about it?" he called after her as she flitted across the hall to the stairs.

"Good day, sir," she repeated, flying up the stairs to the sanctuary of her own parlor.

Had she been a fool? Was she just utterly unrealistic about her prospects? She went to the window, looking down on the street as the Earl of Burford emerged from the house. He stood for a moment, looking up at the house, and she stepped sideways into the shadow of the curtains. He had a puzzled, uncertain air, and Serena realized that he still thought she had not refused him outright. And of course, she had not. *Not outright.*

Chapter Eleven

Lord Burford did not appear at the gaming tables in Pickering Place for several nights, and Serena's stepfather gave no indication that he had heard of her refusal from the earl. He certainly would have confronted her if Burford had told him. She knew her relief would be short-lived, but she guessed that the earl was giving her time to think about his offer. When the general remarked on his lordship's continued absence she said lightly, "Perhaps he is playing somewhere else for a few evenings." He had frowned at the thought of the competition but knew it was a fact of life so made no argument.

Serena played her part as the perfect hostess, and no one looking at her would imagine how night after night, she longed for Sebastian to walk into the salon with that languid grace, the long stride, the easy smile, those brilliant blue eyes alight when they saw her. He would not come, not when it would mean a confrontation with Heyward, but her heart yearned for the sight of him. She bitterly regretted walking away from him in the park, wanted more than anything to curl up in his embrace, the abrasiveness of their last encounter forgotten. In his arms, somehow the rest of the world seemed to retreat. But he would not come, and she heard nothing from him, not so much as a note.

On the third night after their argument, as she was leaving the supper room after checking arrangements for the second supper, the door knocker sounded, and Flanagan, ever present, moved to open it. "Message for Lady Serena Carmichael," a very young voice piped.

Serena's heart jumped. She knew that voice. It belonged to the lad who worked for Sebastian and his brother in Stratton Street. She hurried forward, anxious to take it before her stepfather could appear and wonder who was delivering messages in the early hours of the morning.

"Is that for me, Flanagan?"

"Yes, Lady Serena." He handed it to her, eschewing the regulation silver tray delivery.

She took it, glancing only once at the handwriting on the folded sheet, and hurried to the stairs. "If anyone asks for me, Flanagan, I'm making a minor repair to my gown." She flew up the stairs, her wide panniers swinging with the speed of her ascent. She went into her parlor and closed the door with a sigh of relief, leaning against it as she slit the wafer with her thumbnail, too impatient to fetch the paper knife from the secretaire.

It was one sheet with Sebastian's distinctive script: *Come to Stratton Street as early as you can tomorrow. I will be waiting for you. It is imperative that you ensure you can be away at least until the evening. My love. S.S.*

Serena frowned a little. Except for the valediction, the tone of the note was distinctly peremptory. She re-read the sheet. Why was it imperative that she be away all day? It seemed he had some kind of plan, a scheme of some sort. After their last parting, she'd wondered when, or even whether, he would get in touch. A slow smile lit up her eyes. It didn't matter what he had in mind, what mattered was that they would be together for a while. At this point, she would trust Sebastian to make whatever plans he deemed necessary to make that happen. So much of her life was spent finding solutions, dodging pitfalls, anticipating traps and dangers, negotiating her way through the obstacle course that was her present existence, that the idea of letting Sebastian find a way out of their own maze was a cool balm smoothing away all the accumulated aggravations of her daily life.

She slipped the note into a drawer in her secretaire and went back to her duty in the gaming rooms.

The rest of the night seemed interminable, but they finally closed the doors at four o'clock. She undressed and sent Bridget to her bed, then knelt on the window seat in her bedchamber, opening the window onto the cold night air. It helped to clear her head after the stuffiness of the candles, the heat from the well-stoked fires, the odor of hot, overdressed bodies mingling with the heavy perfumes that failed to disguise the smell of un-washed flesh.

The moon was low in the sky now, and the city sounds were muted, although an occasional shout or the iron wheels of a dray on an early-morning delivery could still be heard from the streets. A clock chimed the half-hour. Goose bumps lifted on her arms, and she reluctantly pulled the window closed. Suddenly, she was no longer tired. A new energy coursed through her veins. She and Sebastian would be together again in a few short hours. She couldn't imagine that he would send such a note if he intended to continue their quarrel, and if it was passion he had in mind, then she was determined that this time, nothing would disturb the loving interlude.

Finally, Serena climbed into bed, sinking into the deep hollows of the feather mattress with a luxurious stretch. She would sleep for a few hours and then go straight to Stratton Street. She wouldn't need to leave an explanation for her absence as long as she was back in plenty of time for the evening's entertainment.

She awoke at eight and rang the bell for Bridget, who came in with a tray of hot chocolate and bread and butter, looking surprised. "You're up early, m'lady. You don't usually stir till nine at least." She set the tray down on the coverlet. "Oh, you slept with the curtains open . . . no wonder you woke early. I made sure I closed them last night."

"You did, Bridget. But I opened them when I came

to bed. It was a lovely night, and the moon was very pretty." Serena poured chocolate into the cup.

Bridget looked doubtful. "Maybe it was, ma'am, but 'tis bad to let the night humors in. You didn't open the windows?"

"Only a little," Serena confessed with a smile. "And believe me, Bridget, the air was too cold and clear for any malign humors."

Bridget looked as if she didn't understood a word her mistress had said. "I dunno, m'lady. Mam says the air's too bad t'breathe at night."

Serena chuckled. "If you didn't breathe, Bridget, you'd not be alive in the morning."

"I suppose so, m'lady. But I still covers my nose an' mouth with a blanket and keeps the windows tight shut." Bridget went to the armoire. "What'll you wear this mornin', ma'am?"

Serena sat back against the pillows for a moment and gave the question due consideration. Without knowing what Sebastian had in mind for the day, it was a difficult question. Were they to be riding? Walking? Lounging in sybaritic nakedness in some secluded paradise? Typical male, she thought. They never considered such issues.

"The rose velvet with the pink-striped underskirt," she decided. "And a very small hoop." She couldn't ride in such an outfit, but she could do anything else, and if her last scenario was the right one, it wouldn't matter a damn what she wore. That same smile, again without volition, found its way to her lips.

Serena was ready by nine o'clock. It was very early for visiting, but Sebastian's note had said as early as possible. She toyed with the prospect of a proper breakfast but dismissed the idea. The last thing that interested her was food. "Ask Flanagan to summon a chair, Bridget. I won't need you to accompany me this morning."

Bridget looked surprised but curtsied and went off to instruct the butler. A quarter of an hour later, Serena, a dark velvet hooded cloak over her shoulders, came downstairs.

A sedan chair waited at the door, and she stepped in, murmuring the address to the chairmen, anxious that no one in Pickering Place should overhear her destination. The chairmen picked up the poles and trotted off in the direction of Stratton Street.

They set her down at Sebastian's door, but she had barely raised a hand to the knocker before the door was opened. Sebastian pulled her in, wrapping her in a tight embrace. "I was watching for you from the window." He gave a self-deprecating chuckle. "Would you believe I've been standing there since seven?"

Serena smiled as he cupped her chin in the palm of his hand, lifting her face for his kiss.

"I've missed you so . . . I didn't think it was possible to miss someone so much," he murmured against her mouth.

"I know," she agreed. "I was afraid I had angered you so much you had given up on me."

"Never." He drew her into the parlor, where the fire

burned brightly. "You could never anger me that much, although . . ." He grinned. "I will say you've come close to it on more than one occasion." He unclasped her cloak and dropped it onto a chair, taking her hands and pulling off her gloves one at a time, dropping them beside the cloak.

Serena laughed. "I can do this for myself."

He shook his head. "You're not going to do anything for yourself that I can do for you. For the rest of today, that's how it's going to be. Understood?" He caressed the line of her cheek with a long forefinger.

Serena felt a little shiver of excited anticipation, and a surge of desire jolted her belly, moistened her loins. She touched the tip of her tongue to her lips but said nothing.

"Understood?" he repeated softly, running his fingertip over her mouth.

She nodded. "If that's what you wish."

"Oh, yes, that is exactly what I wish." He bent his head and kissed her, gently at first but then with increasing pressure. His tongue demanded entrance, and her lips parted for him, her own tongue dancing with his in a delicious fencing match that made her remember anew the glory days of their early liaison, before the world had intruded. She moved against him, her loins pressing into the hard bulge of his penis, and his hands went to her buttocks, pulling her yet closer to him, kneading the rich curves beneath her gown.

He finally raised his head, his breathing rather ragged

as he smiled. "Oh, my sweet, how I have missed you."

"And I have missed you," she murmured, stroking his face just as the door opened behind her.

"Oh, I beg your pardon. I didn't realize Lady Serena had arrived already." Peregrine bowed to Serena. "Forgive the intrusion, ma'am."

She could sense immediately that Sebastian's brother did not approve of her presence. There was something stiff, almost cold, in his manner, despite the impeccable courtesy of his greeting. She smiled as warmly as she could as she curtsied. "No, 'tis I who must ask forgiveness, sir. 'Tis brutally uncivilized to disturb a man before he has breakfasted."

"Nonsense," Sebastian declared heartily, giving his twin something akin to a scowl. "Perry knew you would be here early and is perfectly happy to share the breakfast table with you."

"Indeed, ma'am." Peregrine bowed again. He moved in front of the fire to the table set with breakfast dishes. "Allow me." He pulled back a chair.

Serena glanced uncertainly at Sebastian, who said calmly, "Sit down, Serena. Even if you have already breakfasted, I'm sure you'll be glad of coffee."

Serena hesitated, then, with a tiny lift of her chin, took the chair Peregrine still held for her. "Thank you," she murmured. "I own some coffee would be welcome."

Sebastian nodded and pulled the bell rope. When Bart appeared, his interested gaze flicking between Serena and the brothers, Sebastian told him to bring breakfast and coffee for the lady. He took his seat opposite Serena and wondered how to defuse the tension. The previous evening, Peregrine had made no overt objections to Serena's visit when Sebastian told him to expect her the following morning, but neither had he seemed overjoyed. Sebastian knew his brother's hesitation was out of concern for himself, but he was beginning to find it annoying. Perry ought to know by now that Sebastian could in general manage his own affairs. And he was damned if he would allow Perry to make Serena uncomfortable.

Bart brought in a covered dish of veal cutlets and another of eggs. He set the coffee pot on a trivet in the hearth and put a jug of ale for the gentlemen on the table. "That be all, sirs?" He still couldn't take his eyes off Serena.

"For the moment." Sebastian waved him away, saying as the door closed on the boy, "I can't blame him for making cow's eyes at you, Serena, but it is a little irksome."

"He's but a child," Serena observed. "And I'm sure he's just intrigued at what is, after all, a rather uncommon situation."

"That's true enough," Perry agreed. "May I serve you some eggs, Lady Serena?"

Serena considered the offer, regarding Peregrine thoughtfully. "I would hate to put you off your own breakfast, sir."

Peregrine looked at her, startled, and then a touch

of color bloomed on his cheekbones. Lady Serena had effectively tossed the ball into his court, challenging him to candor. And so be it. "As you said, Lady Serena, 'tis a rather uncommon situation. I would be more than happy for your presence at the breakfast table to be a regular occurrence, if that pleases both you and my brother. If, on the other hand, this is simply a case of ships that pass in the night, I would like a little advance warning of any impending shipwreck."

"Perry, you have no right . . ." Sebastian half rose from his chair, indignation throbbing in his voice.

But Serena raised a hand. "No, Sebastian, wait. Your brother *does* have a right. You and he share a roof, and a deal more than that, I'll wager. He's entitled to fair warning if there's thunder on the horizon."

Sebastian looked at his brother and was astonished to see that Peregrine was now smiling. Perry reached a hand across the table. "Well said, Lady Serena. And I thank you. 'Tis always better, I believe, to speak out to avoid any misunderstanding. Now, may I serve you some eggs?"

Sebastian shook his head, saying drily, "I'm glad you're both in agreement." He took the plate from Peregrine, ladled eggs, forked a cutlet to go beside them, and placed the plate in front of Serena. "Coffee?" He reached for the coffee pot.

"Thank you," she said with a placid smile.

For the next half-hour, it seemed to her that they were existing in a suspended bubble, or at least she and Sebastian were. They ate and talked over a range of unimportant subjects, Peregrine playing his part as congenial fellow diner admirably, but Serena was ever conscious of what was to come, even as she found herself enjoying the postponement that merely enhanced anticipation. *And just what is to come?* Serena knew Sebastian had some plan, but he gave no indication of it, seemed so relaxed, so completely comfortable, as if nothing could spoil his pleasure in the moment, that she allowed herself to be lulled into a most unusual feeling of careless enjoyment. What would be would be.

Peregrine, if he was conscious of the current of suppressed anticipation in the room, didn't show it. He had clearly decided to let matters run their course and made amiable small talk and discreetly failed to notice the covert glances, the half-smiles, that flew between his table companions.

Finally, Sebastian sat back, replete, and drummed his fingers rhythmically on the table, watching Serena. She put down her fork. "Are you in a hurry to do something, go somewhere, Sebastian?"

"When you're ready," he said. "Take your time." His tone completely lacked conviction, and she laughed.

"I am ready now . . . for whatever it is."

He sprang to his feet. "I ordered the coach for ten. It should be outside now."

"Coach?" Peregrine raised his eyebrows. "Where did that come from?"

"Blackwater House," his brother informed him succinctly. "Jasper was perfectly happy to lend me Baker and the coach for the day. You know how little he uses it himself."

Peregrine nodded. "Yes, he much prefers that curricle of his . . . can't say I blame him."

"No," Sebastian agreed. "And unfortunately, our esteemed brother, generous to a fault though he is in most things, is adamant that he won't lend anyone his horses. So Baker and the coach it has to be."

"Where are you going?"

"Yes," Serena said. "Where *are* we going?"

"Oh, you'll find out when you get there." He seemed immensely pleased with himself. "Come along now." He urged her into the hall, where he draped her cloak around her shoulders, fastening the clasp, then took up her gloves, carefully easing them over her fingers.

"Oh, let me do it," she said with a laugh, trying to take her hands back. "I've been putting on my own gloves since I was three years old."

"Keep still," he commanded, tightening his grip on her hands. "There now. All done." He opened the front door and stood impatiently holding it. "Hurry, Serena. We have quite a drive."

More than ever intrigued, she went past him to the street, where a rather old-fashioned coach and four stood, the Blackwater arms on the panels, a groom at the horses' heads, a liveried coachman at the door.

"Morning, Baker." Sebastian greeted the coachman, whom he had known most of his life.

"Morning, Mr. Sebastian." The coachman touched his forelock, with a bow. "Morning, ma'am." He let down the footstep and held open the door.

Serena smiled her own good morning as Sebastian handed her up into the carriage. She settled into a corner, arranging her skirts becomingly on the rather faded, rather worn velvet squabs, while Sebastian had a low-voiced conference with the coachman before climbing in to sit opposite her. The coachman closed the door, enclosing them in the dimly lit space.

Sebastian leaned back, stretching his legs across the narrow aisle between the seats, and regarded Serena with the same possessively complacent smile.

"I shall expire of curiosity, Sebastian, if you don't tell me at once what's going on." Serena found the smile both unnerving and strangely thrilling. It made her feel as if Sebastian somehow possessed her. She couldn't understand why she found the sensation thrilling, when ordinarily she would have fought tooth and nail for control of the situation. It was her own extraordinary response that unnerved her.

"No, you won't," he said matter-of-factly. "I don't want to spoil the surprise."

"A good surprise?" she asked cautiously.

"Oh, Serena, for shame," he chided. "Would I ever have an unpleasant surprise for you? That's more your style than mine."

"You know why that happened," she protested softly. "I explained it to you. Must it still lie between us?"

Sebastian realized that he was in danger of losing everything he had worked so hard to achieve. And it was entirely his fault. He should never have alluded to the past. It was just that the hurt was still never far from the surface, even when they were as close as they were now. Or maybe especially then.

He leaned across the aisle, taking her hands, pulling her onto his lap as the carriage slowed, the groom's horn blowing up for a toll gate. Fleetingly, Serena wondered where on earth they were, but the question slid from her mind without a trace.

"Mea culpa, sweetheart." Sebastian tilted her sideways so that she lay across him, looking up as he gazed down into her face. He ran his tongue over her eyelids in a moist caress that banished all bad feelings. She reached her arms around his neck, lifting her head to kiss the corner of his hovering mouth.

"It is over," she murmured. "It is behind us now. We have to go forward. Somehow we have to let the past go."

"We are," he promised. The coach lurched into motion again, the horses lengthening their stride. He slipped a hand beneath her head and kissed her, his free hand sliding beneath her cloak to cup the swell of her breasts, to trace the line of her rib cage, the curve of her hip. "I can't wait to get this wretched gown off you," he grumbled. He moved his hand down, sliding it up her leg beneath her skirt and petticoat, over the silk-stockinged calf, and up, smoothing over her thigh, reaching higher. She shuddered with pleasure as his fingers probed in a wicked, knowing caress. She shifted, her body lifting to his touch, which increased in pressure as she responded, until she gave a cry, muffled instantly by his mouth, as her body became taut on the verge of orgasmic delight. When the wave broke, it engulfed her, finally washing her to shore, limp and spent.

Sebastian gathered her against him, holding her steady as the carriage rocked around a corner. He smiled down into her flushed and glowing countenance, and after a moment, her eyes opened and she smiled back.

"You always were a wicked lover," she said, running a finger over his lips. "But that, I have to tell you, was particularly wicked. I wasn't expecting it."

"Did you wish to expect it?" He raised an eyebrow.

"No . . . no, that wasn't what I meant. You know what I meant," she protested.

"Well, I'll tell *you* something, my adorable Serena. I have decided that treating you to the unexpected shall be my mission from now on. You're tight as a coiled spring, my dear, and for today at the very least, I shall make it my business to unravel you. I promise you will never know what surprises I have in store until I spring them upon you."

This time, she made no mention of good or bad surprises.

Sebastian helped her up and back onto the opposite seat. Then he sat back, resting his head against the squabs, smiling as she straightened her skirts and tried to put herself to rights in the confines of the carriage. Her hair had escaped in wisps from the knot on top of her head, and her side curls were in disarray. She tugged her fingers through them, but it was fairly futile.

"What do I look like?" she groaned. "What will people think when I step out?"

"There won't be any people to think anything at all," he said with a lazy smile. "You look entrancingly disheveled, which is a completely new sight. I like it, so do me a favor and leave everything as it is."

She gave up. "Oh, well, if you say so." She rested her head against the back of the bench and regarded him through half-closed eyes, reflecting that he was very different these days, and she found the difference only exciting.

After a few moments, she sat up and drew aside the leather curtain at the window aperture. As she had assumed from the toll, they had left the busy London streets behind and were now driving through a rather pretty village of thatched cottages lining the rutted lane on both sides. Green fields stretched behind them, cows grazing peaceably under the trees.

"Where is this?"

Sebastian sat up and looked out. "Oh, good, we're nearly there. 'Tis the village of Knightsbridge. Very quiet, very sleepy."

"So that must have been the Knightsbridge toll we passed. I didn't realize we were going into the country." She sounded as surprised as she felt. Sebastian had always struck her as the quintessential London denizen.

"You weren't supposed to realize anything," he said with another complacent smile. He leaned out of the window, calling up to the box, "The last cottage on the right, just before the Bear and Ragged Staff, Baker."

"Right y'are, sir." The coachman drew rein outside the cottage, and the groom hurried to open the door and let down the footstep.

Sebastian jumped down, disdaining the step, and reached in for Serena's hand, helping her down to the lane. She stood looking around. The cottage sat in a pretty garden, ablaze with chrysanthemums and dahlias. A small gate opened onto a narrow path that wound its way between two small patches of lawn to the front door, which had bay windows on either side.

"How pretty," she observed, fascinated by this bucolic retreat. What on earth did Sebastian have in mind?

"Take the horses to the inn, Baker. They're expecting you. We'll be ready to leave again at four o'clock."

The coachman nodded, touched his forelock, and drove the coach the few hundred yards to the inn.

"Does it please you?" Sebastian asked softly, watching Serena's face.

She smiled. "Yes, indeed, but what is it for?"

"Oh, Serena, can't you guess?" he exclaimed. "I had really thought you sharp-witted. How could I have been so mistaken?"

She pulled a face. "I am sharp-witted, more than you'll ever know. But how could I possibly know what you have in mind?"

He merely looked at her in silence, and slowly she realized that she was, indeed, being dim-witted. "Oh," she said.

"Precisely. You expressed a wish for somewhere private of our own. Well, here it is." He made an expansive gesture to the cottage. "I have taken a lease for six months. That should be long enough to settle Miss Abigail's future."

Serena shook her head in wonder. "How could you afford it, Sebastian?"

He shook his head in mock reproof. "That, my dear girl, is no concern of yours." He unlatched the gate. "'Tis a most indelicate question. Now, let us go in." He put a hand at the small of her back and propelled her unceremoniously ahead of him up the path to the door, where he banged the shining brass knocker.

It was opened by a plump, smiling lady of middle years. She curtsied, smoothing down her apron. "Ah, there you are, sir. And this is the young lady you mentioned." She looked Serena up and down, a searching but not unfriendly scrutiny. "I trust you'll be comfortable, ma'am."

Serena, still slightly bemused, looked around the small hall. Everything gleamed, and the air was scented with beeswax and dried lavender. "I'm sure I shall, Mistress. . . ?"

"This is Mistress Greene, Serena. She is our landlady and will look after us when we're here," Sebastian explained.

"I daresay you'll be glad of a little refreshment after your journey." The landlady opened a door onto a parlor whose bay window looked onto the garden. "I'll fetch you up some of my cowslip wine and a few little cakes. Just baked 'em, I have."

Serena could smell the aromas of baking mingling with the beeswax and lavender. She went to the fire, pulling off her gloves. The fender was polished to an impossible shine.

Sebastian came up behind her, reaching over her shoulders to unclasp her cloak. He slipped it away from her, dropping it onto a wooden settle. "We have all day to ourselves," he told her. "No one will disturb us. No one apart from Baker knows where we are."

"'Tis perfect, love." She turned into his embrace, smiling up at him. "How clever of you to find it."

"Oh, 'tis only one of several things I have found," he declared with a chuckle, stroking the curve of her cheek as he loved to do. But he was not yet ready to reveal his pièce de résistance. Not until he was sure of Serena's response. This time, he was taking nothing for granted.

Mistress Greene knocked discreetly on the door and then came in with a tray. She set it down on a gate-legged table in the bay window. "When you've refreshed yourself, ma'am, I'll show you around."

"Oh, no need for that, Mistress Greene," Sebastian said swiftly. "I know my way around. I will show Lady Serena myself."

"Very well, sir." The landlady curtsied and left them alone.

"How did you find this place?" Serena took a sip of cowslip wine and broke a little sweet cake in half. Suddenly, it seemed important to prolong this moment, to let the suspense build between them, the longing, soon to be satisfied, to grow until they could bear it no longer.

Sebastian regarded her with his head to one side. "Small talk, my sweet?"

"Polite discourse," she amended with a wicked smile.

Sebastian set his glass down with a definitive click. "Enough. My patience is done. 'Tis time for business."

Chapter Twelve

Serena set down her own glass. Sebastian's blue gaze seemed to hold her, pull her to him, as if they were connected by an invisible chain. She stepped forward slowly until she stood close enough to feel his breath on her cheek, the warmth of his body. She lifted her face and saw that he was looking at her with a grave intensity that had banished his usual lighthearted, smiling gaze.

"What is it?" she whispered.

"I love you," he responded. "I love you so much it hurts. I do not know what I would do if you were not here."

She bowed her head, feeling suddenly the weight of an enormous responsibility. She had failed him, failed the power of their love once, she must not, *could* not do so again. But she could not, not yet, give him the unconditional declaration of an undying love. She could only give him what was safe and in her hands to give. She raised her eyes again. "I love you, too, Sebastian, more than I can say."

If he was disappointed, he gave no indication. "Come." He surprised her by swiftly lifting her off her feet, holding her against him.

"I'm too heavy," she murmured in faint protest as he carried her to the door.

"You weigh nothing," he responded, and his voice was once again light and amused.

"I know that's not true." But she put her arms around his neck, resting her cheek against his shoulder, and allowed herself the indulgence of feeling delightfully helpless in the face of this masculine show of power. What was love play, after all, but an arena for games of make-believe?

Sebastian carried her up the short flight of stairs to a door on a small landing. "Lift the latch, love, my arms are full."

Serena raised the latch on the door, and Sebastian pushed it open with his foot, carrying her in and dropping her on the quilted bed cover with a barely concealed sigh of relief.

"I told you I was too heavy," she said, laughing up at him as he caught his breath. "You could probably carry Abigail with one hand, but you forget I come from the blood and bone of a Scottish clansman. We're made tall and broad."

"I'll give you tall," he said, "but I dispute broad. However, I've a mind to have a proper look." He bent over her, deftly removing her shoes, before taking her hands and hauling her upright. "You have to stand up. I can't undress you lying down."

Serena obliged, sliding to her feet beside the bed. Sebastian unbuttoned her gown, slipping it off her shoulders to fall in a rose velvet puddle at her feet. He untied the tapes of the hoop, tossing it aside, and turned his attention to the laces of her corset, unthreading them with experienced ease.

"You have the touch of a lady's maid," Serena murmured with a soft chuckle. "It seems you've put the three years of our separation to good use, my dear."

"That is a thoroughly indelicate comment," he chided, tossing the corset to the floor. He unfastened the tiny pearl buttons of her chemise and lifted it over her head, so that she stood naked, except for her gartered stockings.

He stepped back, looking her over, an appreciative smile on his lips. "Magnificent. I always forget between times how glorious your body is." He moved his hands over her sloping shoulders in a leisurely caress, flattening his palms along her ribcage, smoothing over the curve of her hips, before caressing her belly, pressing his thumbs into the sharp points of her hip bones, moving up to cup her breasts, flicking lightly at her nipples with his forefingers.

Serena stood very still, only her skin rippling with sensation, the little pulse at the base of her throat beating faster than usual. He turned her wrists and pressed his lips against the soft, blue-veined skin, where the same pulse beat rapidly against his mouth. Then, with a soft chuckle, he pushed her lightly so that she fell back on the bed.

He bent over her, unfastening her garters before carefully unrolling her silk stockings, easing them over her long legs. He lifted her feet in turn, kissing her toes, watching her face as she lay on the bed.

"Hurry," she whispered as he ran his tongue over her arched instep. Her body lifted on the coverlet as lust, urgent and imperative, swept through her.

Sebastian dropped her foot to the bed, stepped back, and began to take off his clothes, each movement tantalizingly slow and deliberate. Serena rolled onto her side, resting her cheek on her elbow-propped palm as she drank in every inch of his body so slowly revealed.

When he pushed off his underdrawers and stood naked beside her, she reached for his engorged penis, enclosing it between her fingers, feeling the corded veins pulsing against her palm.

Sebastian knelt on the bed, straddling her as she continued to hold him. He caressed her nipples, making small circles with a fingertip until she groaned in need. Only then did he slide his hands beneath her bottom, lift her on the shelf of his palms, and enter her welcoming body one minute fraction at a time, until she thought she could bear it no longer, as the exquisite sensation filled her pulsing body, every sensitized nerve ending throbbing with delight as he sheathed himself within her.

Much later, when pale afternoon sunshine shone through the bedroom window under the eaves, Sebastian disentangled himself from Serena, gently sliding his legs out from beneath hers, flung warm and heavy across his hips. He shivered a little. The fire in the hearth was burning low. He threw on kindling and watched as the fire caught again, before he threw on several larger logs.

"What time is it? Must we go now?" Serena struggled onto an elbow, aware of a deep sense of impending loss. The prospect of leaving this sanctuary, going back to the life she had to live, filled her with desolation.

"Not yet. I thought you were still sleeping." Sebastian turned from the fire as the logs crackled. He came over to the bed, drawing back the covers, drinking in the sight of her body, naked, supple, glowing in the firelight. "Are you hungry?"

"Ravenous." She stretched, smiling up at him, determined that he should not see her unhappiness. "Something smells wonderful."

"Mistress Greene will be preparing something for us. I'll go in search." He pulled on his breeches and shirt and went barefoot to the kitchen, where the landlady was busy with pots and cauldrons over the black-leaded range.

She turned, flourishing a ladle, as he entered the room. "Oh, sir, you startled me."

"I beg your pardon, Mistress Greene. Something smells delicious, and we find ourselves famished."

The landlady beamed. "Well, not knowing quite what you and the lady might feel like, I've artichoke soup, a nice roast duckling with juniper sauce to follow, and a good blackberry and apple pie. Apples from our own orchard, and I preserved the blackberries straight from the bush a month or so past. Will that suit?"

"Admirably, Mistress Greene."

"Will I lay the table in the parlor, or will you dine abovestairs?"

Sebastian thought of Serena, naked and languid in the feather bed, and said swiftly that they would eat abovestairs, but he would carry the tray himself.

The landlady made no demur, piling cutlery, plates, and a soup tureen on a tray, which Sebastian carried with some difficulty upstairs. He'd left the door un-latched and was able to elbow it wide enough to give him entrance. Serena was sitting, still naked, on the rug in front of the fire, one elbow propped on a crossed knee, gazing into the crackling flames.

"Shameless," he chided with a chuckle. "Supposing Mistress Greene had brought up the tray." He set his burdens on a table beside the fire.

"She would have knocked," Serena said, rising to her feet. She came over to the table and sniffed hungrily.

"There's a second course," he said, momentarily dis-tracted by the long, graceful curve of her naked body leaning over the table. He smoothed a hand over her backside. "For God's sake, sit down, before you give me other ideas."

She chuckled and sat down, shaking out a square linen napkin, saying with a wicked smile, "I wouldn't want to spill soup at the moment."

"No," he agreed, ladling soup into a bowl and placing it in front of her. "That could be a little uncomfortable."

She smiled but said only, "How long do we have, Sebastian?"

He took a mouthful of soup, covertly watching her expression as he said deliberately, "As long as you wish, Serena."

She looked at him, startled. "You know I must be back by seven at the latest."

"Today, yes," he agreed. He passed her a piece of bread on the tip of a knife, his eyes still on her expression. "You should try Mistress Greene's bread. 'Tis excellent."

Serena took the bread, saying thoughtfully, "I wonder if I can come up with a convincing excuse for spending the night away from Pickering Place one day." She smiled, savoring the possibility. "Wouldn't that be wonderful, a whole night here to ourselves?"

Sebastian merely smiled, hiding his disappointment. He'd hoped . . . well, he didn't really know what he'd hoped for. That she'd give him an opening, perhaps, to test her reaction to his grand plan? But it was early days yet. Better to take things one step at a time. "It would be," he agreed. "Hurry with your soup, and then I'll fetch the roast duck."

She ate her soup, pondering the question of how to escape Pickering Place for a night. There had to be a way.

Sebastian went down for the second course. He brought up a bottle of burgundy and filled their glasses before carving the duckling, which came with crispy roast potatoes and a compote of mushrooms. They ate in a companionable silence, occupied with their own thoughts. Finally, Sebastian set aside his knife and fork, refilled their wine glasses, and asked, trying for nonchalance, "Is Burford one of those who paws you at the tables?"

Serena looked at him sharply. It seemed such a non sequitur after the afternoon they'd spent. Of course, she remembered now that when she had turned from his kiss that time, she'd offered as excuse the overly free hands of the clients in Pickering Place. But why would he bring up Burford in particular? What could he know of how matters stood in that quarter? "That's an odd question," she said with a careless shrug. "Are you well acquainted with the earl?"

Sebastian shook his head. "Not really, but I heard something . . . just a word here and there that seemed to imply he was particularly interested in you."

"Maybe he is," she responded with a light laugh. "But he's not alone. I seem to have that effect on a lot of men."

Sebastian felt a bitter anger suddenly. She seemed so nonchalant about the business, as if being the object of lust for a host of men was somehow perfectly normal.

"I suppose," he said, "in your line of work, it goes with the territory."

Serena frowned, a chill running up her spine. The warmth seemed to have vanished from the room, although the fire was burning fiercely. "I don't understand what you mean, Sebastian."

"I mean, my dear, that as one of faro's daughters, being propositioned by your clients must come as no surprise. Has Burford propositioned you?" He realized even as he spoke that he didn't want to be saying these things. It was as if his uncle's vile imaginings had worked their serpentine way into his brain and were infecting his thoughts and, by extension, his words.

Serena shivered. Sebastian had changed; a stranger inhabited the familiar figure. There was a look in his eyes she had never seen before. "I'm cold," she said. "I have to get dressed."

Sebastian got to his feet and went to the armoire, returning with a heavy brocade night robe. He draped it around her shoulders, then stood for a moment behind her, his hands resting on her shoulders. "*Has* he propositioned you, Serena?"

"What difference does it make to us whether he has or he hasn't, Sebastian?"

"How could you ask such a question?" he exclaimed. "If he did, would you accept the offer?"

Serena felt sick. "If you can think that of me, Sebastian, why are we here?"

"I need to know," he said simply.

She reached behind her and pushed his hands from her shoulders, rising to her feet in one fluid movement. "As it happens, he *has* made me a proposition, one that's actually quite difficult to turn down. He holds the mortgages on Pickering Place and has offered them to me if I become his mistress. I'm sure you can imagine the pleasure it would give me to hold my stepfather's life in my hands."

"So you accepted him?"

"I didn't say that."

But you didn't say you haven't . . . or wouldn't.

Serena wrapped the folds of the robe securely around her as she looked at him, her lovely violet eyes ablaze with anger and something else, something he would swear was uncertainty in their depths. "I see no virtue in this discussion, or interrogation, rather. I need to get dressed and get back."

What the hell was he doing? he thought abruptly. It had seemed for a moment as if someone else was inhabiting his body. Serena was right, this interrogation was getting them nowhere. He knew what he wanted from her, and this was no way to get it. His anger melted like butter in the sun. "Oh, Serena, my dear, forgive me. I don't know what came over me. I should never have doubted, 'tis just sometimes so . . . so difficult to see you in that place, to imagine the life you lead there. *Please.*" He reached for her, drawing her against him, burying his mouth in her hair. "Forgive me, love."

Serena made no move to draw away, but neither did she cling to him as he so wanted her to. She said almost wearily, "Of course, I forgive you. I can't really blame you in the circumstances. But they are what they are, Sebastian. And until I can leave him, they won't change."

"Then leave him *now*. This evening," he pressed.

"Not yet. I will not stand aside while he traps Abigail. He's charmed Mrs. Sutton, and even Mr. Sutton finds his company congenial. If I'm not careful, he'll have slipped under their guard, and Abigail will be Lady Heyward in the blink of an eye."

"How could any sane woman be charmed by that brute?" Sebastian stroked her hair.

"Oh, you have no idea how charming he can be if it suits his purpose." She gave a short, mirthless laugh and moved away from him, back to her seat at the table. She traced a pattern in the linen cloth with her fork as she spoke so that he could no longer see her expression.

"I watched him insinuate himself inch by inch into my mother's affections. It started just after my father died. Mama was distraught. She'd always relied on my father to take care of everything, and suddenly she was alone. She'd loved my father and was absolutely bereft. There was nothing I could do. I was still really a child, but I think . . ."

She shook her head with a sad little smile. "I think I was more grown up than my mother even then. But Mama couldn't imagine not having a man to manage her life for her. I would not do, even though I was fairly competent with accounts and household management. My father had encouraged me to take an interest in such affairs. I think perhaps he had a premonition that he would not be around to take care of us forever.

"The long and the short of it was that the general stepped into the void. He was all charm and consideration, and my mother fell into the trap. She ceded all her property to him on their marriage, even though I begged her to keep some in trust." She shrugged. "Perhaps I was trying to protect myself at that point, but it didn't work. My inheritance went to the general, too."

Sebastian had resumed his own seat at the table and watched her closely, wishing he could see her eyes. When she fell silent, he leaned back in his chair, stretching his legs under the table, crossing his ankles. Now was the moment for his own proposal, and yet something held him back. If Serena wasn't prepared to leave her stepfather and her present existence of her own accord, perhaps there was something about it that did please her, maybe something she enjoyed.

He was doing it again, he realized, allowing the venom of his uncle's imagination to infiltrate his own. And yet . . . and yet, did he really know her? He didn't . . . not enough to be sure that he could read her aright, to trust his own judgments. She'd betrayed him once before without warning and without discussion. What was to prevent her doing so again if *she* felt it necessary?

"So let us turn our attention to young Abigail," he said, his voice once more brisk. "I take it young Mr. Wedgwood is not invited to this dinner party at the Suttons'."

"I doubt it." She looked across the table at him then, as if it was no longer dangerous to make eye contact.

"In the face of Mrs. Sutton's opposition, how do we go about promoting this marriage?"

She considered, relieved to be able to turn her thoughts to something that could eventually be solved. "Jonas Wedgwood is putting up at the Queen's Head in Henrietta Place. I think you should pay him a visit as soon as possible. Find out what his intentions are, and be as encouraging about his prospects as you can. I will gently work upon Abigail and will try to plant the seed in her mother's mind . . . maybe suggest that she invite him to the dinner. He's such a personable young man, after all."

"What if Abigail does not have a *tendre* for Jonas?"

Serena smiled a little. "Oh, trust me, Sebastian, I know she does. It's as clear as day, just looking at her."

"Maybe to a woman," he conceded. "Men find it quite difficult, you know, to gain a correct reading of women they wish to court. With every attempt, one entrusts one's pride and self-esteem to the fickle humor of the female."

"Is that so?" Serena queried, her eyes suddenly lively and amused. Teasing was safe ground, a gift horse she was not prepared to look in the mouth.

"In my experience," he said with a lofty gesture. "But still, my question remains. How to overcome Mrs. Sutton's opposition?"

"Simple enough. By removing all other suitors from the arena. Once Abigail's mama realizes that Jonas Wedgwood is not only her daughter's choice but also her only one, she will capitulate. The Wedgwoods are a respectable, highly regarded family in the Potteries. I'll lay any odds Mr. Sutton will be overjoyed at the prospect of such a match. It would keep his beloved daughter close to him, apart from anything else."

Sebastian nodded. "I see your point."

"But you have to appear to find Abigail of some interest," Serena pressed. "Just so that her mama won't press the general's suit."

"If he's capable of being as charming as you say, can you be certain he won't overwhelm Mrs. Sutton with his attentions?"

"No, I can't," Serena said somberly. "Which is why I have to be on the alert and on the spot."

He nodded slowly. "Arguing that point with you is futile, I understand that now." He stood up, came around the table, and pulled her to her feet. "But we have a short time before we must leave. Can we try to put the bad moments behind us?"

"Yes, please," she said, her voice rather small.

He pushed up her chin, kissing her before sliding his hands beneath the brocade robe and pushing it away from her.

They left their hideaway an hour later, aware in their hearts that their lovemaking had merely papered over the cracks that the earlier quarrel had opened, but neither was willing to express such a thought or reopen the old wounds. They sat close in the warm darkness of the carriage, and Serena allowed the swaying motion to act as a lullaby, sending her into a trancelike doze until they were once more rattling over the city cobbles.

Sebastian sat up to draw aside the leather curtain, letting the flickering lights of link boys and candlelit windows illuminate the carriage. The carriage slowed as they turned onto the Strand and then drew up alongside a stand of chairmen, waiting for custom. The groom opened the door and let down the footstep.

"I told Baker to leave us here," Sebastian explained as he stepped down to the street. "I could hardly leave you at your door."

"No," Serena agreed, taking his hand to step beside him. Two chairmen trotted up to them, setting down the sedan chair.

"Take the lady to Pickering Place," Sebastian instructed.

Serena gave her hand to Sebastian. He held on to it for a moment, then raised it to his lips.

"Until soon, Serena." He stood aside as she stepped into the chair.

She smiled up at him as he leaned forward into the chair. "I'll try to bide my time in patience."

He blew her a kiss, then stepped back, waiting until

the chairmen had hoisted the sedan chair and were trotting down the Strand. Then he climbed back into the coach.

Serena felt increasing dread as the chair approached Pickering Place. The prospect of the evening ahead now seemed unendurable. Whenever she escaped from the house and the man who kept her there, she found it harder and harder to return.

The chairmen stopped outside the house, letting the chair to the ground. Serena stepped out, paid the men, and walked up the stairs.

Flanagan opened the door for her. She stepped into the hall and found herself face-to-face with her stepfather. He was incandescent with rage, his face scarlet, a vein beating in his temple, and he seemed for once to be having difficulty finding the words to express himself.

"Is something wrong, sir?" she inquired, her bland tone disguising her flicker of alarm. She unclasped her cloak, glad to find that her fingers were quite steady.

"*Wrong?*" He seemed to gobble for air. "I want you in the library."

He made a move towards her, as if to grab her arm, but she sidestepped neatly and went ahead of him into the library. Her heart was beating rather fast, but she would not show him any fear.

"Where the hell have you been all day?" The door crashed shut behind him.

Serena was slowly taking off her gloves, desperately

trying to think what could have provoked the general's fury. She thought of saying she had been with the Suttons, something that should placate him, but decided it was too easily proved a lie.

She said instead, "I had some errands to run, a fitting at my dressmaker, and I ran into an old friend of my mother's. She pressed me to visit her, and I thought it only courteous to do so." That was a lie he would never disprove, since he had no contact with any member of her mother's previous life and, indeed, had obliged her to sever such contacts herself as soon as they were married.

He stared at her, as if trying to decide whether she was telling the truth, then shook his head as if dismissing the matter. "How dare you refuse Burford's proposition against my direct orders?"

"I have already told you, sir. I am not to be bought and sold." She spoke evenly, anxious to keep all indication of fear from her voice or demeanor. "Now, if you'll excuse me, I need to change my dress before dinner."

She made to move past him, but he grabbed her arm, swinging her back towards him. "No, I will not excuse you, girl. I promised you to Burford, and you will do as I bid you."

She thought she could detect a note of desperation beneath the fury, and it gave her courage. She repeated quietly, "I will not be bought and sold, sir."

He struck her across the face, his flat palm moving so fast she didn't see it coming. She reeled, her hand pressed to her cheek, staring at him in shock through a sudden veil of tears.

"You will do as I bid you, *daughter*. Make no mistake." His voice was almost a hiss as he stepped so close to her that she could feel his breath on her cheek now, smell its sourness. "You will give the earl what he wants, and you will give it with all the appearance of willingness. And he will give me the mortgages. Is that understood?"

She tried to move away, but he still held her arm and jerked her hard towards him. "I broke your mother, and I will break you. And when I am wed, you will be out on your ear. I'll have no further need of you, and you can get your bread on the streets. It'll be all you'll be good for, by the time I've finished with you."

She thought of her pistol, no use to her now, locked away as it was in a drawer abovestairs. He took her wrist between both hands and twisted it so that she cried out in pain. This was new, this overt violence. It had always been there, beneath the surface, but she had never really believed it would be directed at her. And she suddenly had a vivid memory of hearing anguished cries from her mother's bedchamber.

It was soon after the wedding, just after they had reached Paris, ostensibly on a wedding trip. It had become clear soon enough that this was no pleasure jaunt but the beginning of the general's elaborate schemes to make his fortune using his wife's money to open a gaming house. One afternoon, her mother had de-

murred at taking her place in the gaming salon, had
objected to the kind of social intercourse that was required of her there. Her husband had said nothing
then, in front of Serena, but that night, she had heard
her mother scream. And from then on, the general's
wife had been all compliance, and she kept her daughter at arm's length.

"Do you understand, *daughter*?" He twisted again,
and she bit her lip hard to keep from crying out.

"Oh, I understand perfectly," she said. "But you
should understand, sir, that I am not my mother. I cannot be coerced into doing your dirty work. Now, if you
wish me to appear in the salons this evening, you had
better release me."

He seemed to deflate, completely at a loss when his
tried and true methods failed to work. "You *will* do as I
bid you," was his final shot, and she shook her arm free,
conscious of the stinging burn in her wrist.

Deliberately, she touched the place on her cheek where
he had struck her, then walked to the door. There she
turned with her hand on the latch and delivered what she
hoped would be the coup de grace. She didn't stop at this
point to wonder if it was wise to provoke him further; she
was far too angry to weigh the consequences.

"You should know, sir, that Lord Burford has been
playing his own cards in this matter. He has promised
to make the mortgages over to me if I agree to become
his mistress. If I do decide to sell myself to him, it will be

in exchange for the mortgages. I'm sure you can understand how that is an infinitely more appealing prospect than the one you have in mind. I should tell you that I'm quite tempted. To own this house and all that's in it would be an interesting enterprise. But you might wish to reconsider your insistence that I become Lord Burford's mistress. Your position might be less than comfortable in such a situation."

She thought for a moment that he would succumb to an apoplexy. His face was an alarming crimson, bulging veins pulsed in his temples, and he was deprived of speech. Serena walked out then, closing the door with a firm click. She had no idea whether it had been wise to reveal the earl's offer at that point, but the satisfaction was worth anything.

She hurried to her bedchamber and locked the door. She didn't think he would come after her, but there was no point risking it. He was a bully, and bullies could be faced down, but she didn't relish another such encounter so soon. The incident made it clear that she couldn't wait much longer to put a stop to her stepfather's courtship of Abigail. Balked in his plan with Burford, the general would inevitably step up his pursuit. Abigail was still a child in many ways, easily influenced, and she had none of Serena's strength.

She examined her reflection in the glass. The slap had left an imprint, but, touching it gingerly, she didn't think the mark would last. Her wrist, on the other hand, was scarlet and showed the beginnings of bruising. She would have to wear long sleeves and long gloves at the tables that evening.

Except that she was not going downstairs again. The decision seemed to make itself. She had the perfect excuse. His violence had marked her. She could not possibly show herself in public until the bruises had faded. He wouldn't be able to dispute that. He knew what he had done. The fact that she could disguise them if she chose was one she would keep to herself. No, the general would have to manage the salons himself.

A tap at the door made her jump, but she relaxed when she heard Bridget's voice. "Is everything all right, Lady Serena? Should I help you dress?"

Serena unlocked the door. "Come in, Bridget. I would like you to bring up a bath for me. I won't be going downstairs for dinner tonight. Could you ask Flanagan to have it brought upstairs to my parlor, please, after my bath?"

Bridget regarded her in surprise. Lady Serena never dined alone abovestairs, not when the house was to open for the night. Her jaw dropped as she took in Serena's appearance. "Lor'! What happened to your face, ma'am? Oh, and your poor wrist."

"An accident while I was out. I tripped and stumbled against some railings. 'Tis nothing serious . . . nothing that arnica and witch hazel can't put right. But it has given me the headache, and I would remain quiet tonight. Ask Flanagan to inform Sir George."

"Yes, ma'am . . . I'll fetch up that bath straightway,

ma'am, and bring the arnica and witch hazel from the stillroom."

Bridget hurried from the room, and Serena sat at her dressing table, leaning in to look more closely at the mark on her face. It had been a hard slap. She would make the most of it. This evening would be all hers.

Chapter Thirteen

"Nice young man, that Jonas Wedgwood," Mr. Sutton announced at dinner, nodding benignly at his wife and daughter. "I've a mind to invite him to dinner the day after tomorrow. 'Tis a Wednesday, and we usually dine rather well on Wednesdays. Will that suit, Mrs. Sutton?"

"Oh, Mr. Sutton, you've quite forgotten, haven't you?" his lady exclaimed. "I have told you I don't know how many times that we are to have our own dinner party that evening. All the guests have been invited, and Lady Serena has been most helpful. That charming Mr. Sullivan has accepted, and six other couples, all carefully selected by Lady Serena."

"Oh, then we can make room for one more. Invite young Wedgwood, madam. I like him." Mr. Sutton helped himself liberally to the roast sirloin, beaming in his usual fashion.

"But it will throw the numbers out, Mr. Sutton," his lady protested. "I cannot have an odd man at the table."

"Oh, there must be plenty of single ladies about who would be glad of a good dinner. What about that relative of mine, the one who was companion to some querulous lady in Kensington? I'm sure she'd be glad of an invitation."

His wife closed her lips tightly, knowing that if she hinted to her husband that the relative in question was not in a position to advance Abigail's social position, he would become even more stubborn. For all his wish to see his daughter respectably established, he had a most unfortunate disinclination towards understanding the realities of his wife's mission.

"I believe 'tis too late to issue invitations, Mr. Sutton. It would be apparent they were an afterthought and considered most discourteous."

He looked puzzled. "That so? In my experience, no one's ever offended by an invitation to a good dinner and a convivial evening." He looked at Abigail. "What d'you say, puss, should we invite Mr. Wedgwood? 'Tis your party, after all."

Abigail was torn. There was something about Jonas that made her instantly comfortable, happy to chatter away about whatever popped into her head. On the other hand, she knew that all her attention during the evening should be devoted to the handsome Mr. Sullivan. She knew he was her mother's choice, and she couldn't deny that she felt strangely tingly in his presence, a little hot and giggly, but despite that, she had to admit he also made her feel tongue-tied and awkward, and that was not in the least comfortable. It would be comforting to have someone at the party with whom she felt so at ease.

She temporized, anxious not to annoy her mother. "I think it would be nice to invite him, Papa. But I wonder if it wouldn't be pleasanter to invite him to a family dinner one evening. Then you and he can have a comfortable time over the port."

He chuckled. "Well, let us do both. You send him an invitation for this dinner, and I'll invite him myself to take his pot luck with us one other evening. How would that be, Mrs. Sutton?"

Marianne looked less than pleased, but her husband had spoken. "As you wish, Mr. Sutton." She dabbed at her lips with her handkerchief and took a genteel sip of her watered wine before saying, "Abigail, we will repair to the drawing room now."

Abigail rose obediently, curtsied to her father, and followed her mother out of the dining salon to the drawing room, where the parlor maid was just setting down the tea tray.

She sat down and took up her embroidery while her mother fussed with the tea, handing a cup to the parlor maid to deliver to Abigail. When the maid had left, Marianne said, "Abigail, my dear, I think it is not advisable to invite Mr. Wedgwood, but if your father wishes it, then it must be so. But after that, while he will no doubt come to call upon your father, there is no need for him to be received abovestairs."

"He seems a pleasant gentleman, Mama," Abigail murmured.

"Yes, indeed, he does . . . I'm sure he is. Perfectly

pleasant, perfectly respectable, and he will find himself a suitable wife among the better families in the Potteries."

"I was always under the impression that *we* were among the better families in the Potteries, Mama," Abigail said, her demure tone masking the wicked gleam in her eye. "Are we not suitable for the Wedgwoods?"

Marianne regarded her daughter with displeasure. "The Wedgwoods, daughter, are not suitable for us. You are a beautiful girl, although I shouldn't say so, I don't wish you to become puffed up, and you are a considerable heiress. You can look higher than the Wedgwoods."

"As high as an earl's family?" Abigail questioned, gazing at her mother with wide-eyed innocence. "You mean Mr. Sullivan, do you not?"

"You know perfectly well what I mean," her mother said crossly. "Don't play the simpleton, child. Your father and I want only the best for you. Just think what it would mean. A Society wedding in St. George's, Hanover Square, I expect, and a presentation at court. You will be invited everywhere. And I intend to see that happen. Your father must be . . ."

She paused, looking for words. "Sidestepped. He is not fully aware of the nuances of social standards among the aristocracy. Oh, make no mistake, he is a good man, a wonderful man. But . . ." She looked over at her daughter. "A little too set in his ways. He cannot fully see that what is right for him is not necessarily right for his only daughter."

Abigail set her needle and held her tongue. And her

mother, after waiting a few moments for a response, leaned over and patted Abigail's knee. "Now, my dear, you have to understand that gentlemen don't see matters the way we do. And we have to learn how to achieve our objects while letting the gentlemen believe that everything is just as they wish it to be. 'Tis a lesson you would do well to learn before your marriage, my dear. All husbands are the same. And clever women learn how to manage them."

She sat back with the smile of one who considered she had done her duty and took up her teacup. "Will you not play a little, my dear?"

"Of course, Mama." Abigail set aside her embroidery and went to the harp that Marianne had insisted be provided in their London house. Every gentleman's family must have a musical instrument, and every gentleman's daughter must be proficient. Abigail had been taught both pianoforte and the harp, and she was an adequate performer on the pianoforte, with a pretty voice. Unfortunately, the same could not be said for her proficiency on the harp, and she detested the instrument. However, she could play to her mother, who would not hear the false notes, while she allowed her own thoughts to roam.

She felt annoyed, resentful at her mother's dismissal of Jonas Wedgwood. He was a charming young man, beautifully dressed, well spoken, self-assured. What was the great difference between him and Sebastian Sullivan? Jonas was probably a year or two younger, but if you saw the two together on the street, you wouldn't think a social chasm existed between them. It did, of course. Abigail was not sufficiently naïve to ignore that reality, but her mother's opposition to him made her more partisan in his favor than she might otherwise have been.

And there was no denying that she felt a deal more comfortable in Mr. Wedgwood's company than in that of Mr. Sullivan. What would Lady Serena think? She always had something sensible to say, even to questions that Abigail had been afraid were silly. Lady Serena had never given the least sign that she also thought them silly. Abigail resolved to ask Serena. She would have to evade her mother, though.

She plucked a string a little too vigorously, and the twang was quite painful. She looked anxiously at her mother. But Marianne was nodding quietly on the sofa in a postprandial doze.

Sebastian watched the chair bearing Serena out of sight around the corner of the Strand and debated his next move. He was restless, anxious to be doing something. The situation would not resolve itself, and if Serena was adamant that she would not leave her stepfather until Abigail was safely away from the web of his spinning, then he had best do something to make that happen. It was time to pay a visit to Mr. Wedgwood.

He found Jonas sitting over a pile of papers in a

private parlor at the Queen's Head. The young man jumped up when Sebastian entered, sending his chair skittering across the wooden floor.

"Mr. Sullivan . . . an honor, sir." Jonas bowed, clearly flustered by this unexpected visit. "Won't you sit down . . . will you take a glass of wine . . . please . . ." He gestured to a chair by the fire. "I think that's the most comfortable."

"Thank you. A glass of wine would be most welcome." Sebastian took the assigned seat, crossed his legs at the ankle, and smiled warmly at his host. "I hope you'll forgive the intrusion. I was passing and thought I'd see if you were at home."

"Well, as you see, sir, I am. And more than happy to have a visitor. It gets deuced dull of an evening with nothing to occupy one," Jonas confided, bringing a glass of claret to Sebastian. "I trust you'll approve of this . . . 'tis a particular favorite of my uncle's. He is supplied by Randall and Cox, so I ordered a case for myself while I'm here."

Sebastian held his glass to the light, solemnly took the scent, and took a judicious sip before pronouncing, "Very fine, indeed." He regarded the younger man with a quizzical smile. "I must say I'm surprised to find you have nothing to do in town, Mr. Wedgwood. Most young men find they have no time to sleep with all the dissipations and temptations on offer, particularly on their first visit."

Jonas shook his head. "To tell the truth, sir, I have no idea where to go of an evening if I have not an invitation from one of my uncle's business associates. My family has no memberships in any of the gentlemen's clubs, and . . ." He blushed a little. "I find I have not the inclination to look for female companionship in . . ." His blush deepened. "In the places where such can be found."

"Well, that is probably fortunate," Sebastian said cheerfully. "If you go out trawling the streets of Covent Garden, you'll find plenty of female companionship, but there's no knowing what else you'll come back with unless you know exactly where to go." He sipped his wine. "And the very best houses usually require an introduction. I could provide you with one, should you wish it."

Jonas shook his head with vigor. "Oh, no . . . no, indeed not . . . I thank you, but I don't think . . . that's to say, I haven't been in the habit . . . where I come from, 'tis not . . . I mean, customs are very different."

"That I can believe. Well, if you change your mind, you have only to apply to me." It occurred somewhat belatedly to Sebastian that encouraging Abigail's suitor to frequent the brothels of Covent Garden was probably not the best way to fulfill Serena's instructions. He cleared his throat and sought a change of subject. "You seem fully occupied at present," he observed, gesturing to the paper-covered table.

"Oh, just business affairs," Jonas said with a touch of gloom. "There is always that to occupy me."

Sebastian saw a way into the subject that had brought him hither. "Your family is a prominent one in the Potteries, I understand."

"Oh, yes, very much so. My grandfather had a successful pottery, and his sons took over the business. My father died two years ago, and Uncle Josiah recently started his own pottery. I work for him."

"Not as a potter?"

"No . . . no, I have no talent for design. But I have a good head for figures, and I find myself able to gain commissions for my uncle's designs." Jonas looked a little embarrassed. "That is not to say that I have any special talents or such, but I seem to find it easy to persuade people of the beauty of my uncle's designs and their execution."

"I suspect you have a great deal of special talent," Sebastian declared, deciding there was much to like about this modest young man. "I daresay your family is well acquainted, then, with the Sutton family . . . both so prominent in your neighborhood."

"Well, yes, at least, my uncles and Mr. Sutton are acquainted in the matter of civic duties and such. Mr. Sutton is a merchant, with no direct connections to the manufacture of pottery, but like my uncles, he is active in the affairs of the city of Stoke-on-Trent and the neighboring towns."

Sebastian nodded and said lightly with a teasing smile, "So I daresay you and Miss Sutton played together as children."

Jonas blushed anew. "Well . . . no . . . that is to say, I had seen her shopping, and once at a local Assembly ball put on at Christmas for the children of prominent citizens, I attempted to dance with her, but I trod on her flounce, and she burst into tears and ran to her mother." He laughed. "I was left on the dance floor, scarlet with embarrassment, and I don't think I've danced again since that day."

Sebastian chuckled. "That would put off the strongest man. Does she remember?"

Jonas shook his head. "I don't know, to tell you the truth. But I doubt it. I was an insignificant, gawky, clumsy boy. If I can summon the courage, one of these days, I will ask her if she remembers."

Sebastian twirled the stem of his glass between his fingers. "So, when did you renew this early acquaintance?"

"On the packet from Calais." Jonas jumped up to fetch the wine bottle. "Poor Miss Sutton was feeling very unwell and was obliged to sit up on deck. Her mama was prostrate in her cabin, and so was their maid. Only Mr. Sutton seemed unaffected by the swell, and he was playing whist in the salon. I offered Abi . . . Miss Sutton, that is . . . my boat cloak and kept her company on deck during the night." His smile was soft. "I think she was grateful. Anyway, she gave me her direction in London, and I promised to leave my card."

"As you were doing when you and I met," Sebastian concluded. "Mrs. Sutton seems anxious that her

daughter should make her debut in London Society."
He watched Jonas covertly over the rim of his glass.

"Yes, she does," Jonas agreed, and Sebastian was both
pleased and interested to see the young man's expression
harden and to hear a clipped note in his voice.

"A worthy ambition, don't you think?" Sebastian
said, still watching his host's expression.

Jonas looked disgusted. "A ridiculous one, if you ask
me. Abigail is a daughter of the Potteries. She's lovely,
she's talented, she's adorable, but London Society will
eat her alive." His voice throbbed with anger, and Sebastian noticed that he had completely lost his earlier
self-effacing manner. "She's still a child. How could she
hold her own with the old cats looking down their noses
at her, whispering behind their hands because her manners are somewhat countrified?"

Sebastian was amused but also impressed by Jonas's protective attitude towards Abigail. It boded well.
"You've come across these ladies yourself?"

Jonas shook his head. "No, thank heavens. I've more
sense than to seek 'em out. But I can imagine 'em."

"You probably have the right of it," Sebastian agreed,
glancing at the clock on the mantel. "If you've nothing
better to do for the evening, Jonas, why don't you come
with me? I'm engaged to dine with a few friends at the
Swan tavern, nothing special, and we'd all be delighted
if you'd join us."

Jonas looked doubtful. "You can speak for your
friends?"

"Oh, devil a bit, of course I can." Sebastian shrugged off the question and got to his feet. "Come, I promise you a congenial evening, and furthermore, if there's any possibility of visiting a Covent Garden nunnery, I promise I will give you plenty of warning and you may take your leave of us beforehand . . . or not, as the case may be."

Jonas looked as if he was unsure whether Sebastian was in jest, but when he saw the other man's broad grin, he decided he probably was. "I should like it of all things," he said, a touch shyly. "I hope I won't be a bore."

"Nonsense. Fetch your hat and cloak."

Serena would be pleased with his evening's work, Sebastian reflected as he accompanied Jonas Wedgwood to the Swan, introduced him around, and then watched as he quickly found his feet. He would make young Abigail an excellent husband, Sebastian concluded. The difficulty was the mother. But that was Serena's problem, he decided. He would bring the young man up to scratch. Serena would have to take care of the rest.

Serena bathed at luxurious leisure. The general had sent no reply to her message, and she decided he had obviously seen the wisdom of leaving her alone for the time being. Bridget washed her hair, rinsing it in orange flower water, and afterwards helped her into a velvet dressing gown. Flanagan had brought up roast capon with a lemon and tarragon sauce, a dish of buttered artichokes, and a Rhenish cream. She sipped burgundy and ate slowly, savoring every mouthful, surprised that after the roast duckling that afternoon, she could still find an appetite. Lovemaking was an energetic sport, she thought with an involuntary smile, curling her bare toes against the fender as she stretched her feet to the andirons.

But fighting afterwards was the very devil. Serena was suddenly no longer relaxed or languid and sat up in a surge of bathwater. She could understand Sebastian's frustrations, but why did he have such difficulty grasping the complexities of her situation? Surely, if he loved her as he said he did, then he would find it easy to understand her. But perhaps he didn't love her as deeply as he thought. Why else would he have questioned her so harshly about Burford? Maybe he was beginning to doubt the wisdom of loving a member of the demi-monde, one of faro's daughters who could cheat at the tables with the best of them. Maybe he was thinking it was absurd to trust such a woman. And she could hardly blame him. Hadn't she, just for a second, considered accepting Burford's proposal? Just acknowledging that fact made her feel soiled, unworthy in some way.

But she wasn't either of those things. Serena knew her own integrity. Knew who she was, what she had to accept, and what she was able to change. It had been a long and painful road to realize those facts. Was Sebastian able to acknowledge her truly for the person she was, the person circumstances had made her? Could he see beneath the public façade to the eager, passionate, young lover she had been three years ago? And still was.

To do that, he would have to enter her world, acknowledge its realities, and reconcile the Serena imprisoned in this debased existence with the young love of before. Their liaison had always been conducted in neutral chambers, in buildings far from the debauched, polluted world created by Sir George Heyward, but if Sebastian could see that the purity of their feeling, indeed, of their passion, was in no way compromised by her environment, then the muddle of his uncertainty, the untrusting uncertainty he had made so clear that afternoon, would surely resolve itself. She rang the bell for Bridget.

"Can I get you summat, m'lady?" Bridget had been in the middle of her own supper in the kitchen and was still finishing a mouthful.

"Oh, I interrupted your supper, I'm sorry." Serena was instantly remorseful. She should have known that most evenings, Bridget would be free at this time because her mistress would be dining with Sir George.

"That's all right, ma'am. We was almost finished."

"Do you think that a little later, you could arrange to have a message sent for me?"

"Don't see why not, ma'am. Where to?"

"Stratton Street." Sebastian was about to get the surprise of his life. " 'Tis not very far."

"Oh, young Timmy could take it, ma'am. Before he does the boots."

"Good." Serena abandoned her Rhenish cream and went to the secretaire. She scribbled a few lines on a sheet of vellum, folded it, held the stick of wax in the candle flame, and dropped a seal on the fold. She wrote the direction on the front and took a shilling from her coin box. "Give this to Timmy, and tell him the shilling is for a chair if he'd like to take one; otherwise, it's for whatever he wishes."

"Yes, ma'am. Seems a lot for such a little journey," Bridget added with clear disapproval. She didn't believe in overindulging the youngsters who worked beneath her.

" 'Tis late and cold," Serena pointed out.

Bridget shrugged. "If'n you says so, m'lady." She went off with the letter.

Serena sat down at the table again, but she'd lost interest in food, so after a minute, she took her wine glass to the window seat and drew back the curtains far enough to give her a view of the street below. Of course, if Sebastian was not at home or was out with the intention of not going home until dawn, her testing little adventure would not come to fruition.

The sounds from the salons drifted up to her. Voices raised in laughter and greeting, a babble of conversation on the stairs as the guests went down to the first supper, the chink of glasses, the clink of silverware. At least one of the general's faro banks would not come out the winner tonight. He couldn't handle both of them and would have to give the bank to one of the gamesters. She found the reflection immensely satisfying.

A footman came in to clear away her dinner dishes and left her with the decanter and a dish of candied fruits. Bridget came in a few minutes later to say that Timmy had left the note but that the boy at the house who'd taken it had said that neither of the gentlemen was at home.

Serena was a little disappointed but not surprised. Sebastian and his brother had numerous friends; there was no reason to expect them to be kicking their heels by their own fireside in the middle of the autumn season. *Even if one of them had just spent the better part of a day making love.* She squashed the reflection, it didn't suit her mood, and considered her next move.

If Sebastian did not get her message until late, he would not be able to gain admittance to the house as she'd intended. There would be no one around to answer a knock on the side door. That meant she would have to unlock it herself and leave it like that. The trick would be to find the right moment. Too soon, and one of the servants might discover it before they went to bed and lock it again. Too late, and Sebastian could have been standing in the frigid cold in the side alley for goodness knows how long before she got there. And why should he trouble to wait?

So, when?

The servants in the salons would not seek their beds until the last gamester had left, but the regular household staff retired soon after the first supper dishes had been cleared. They would arise early to deal with the second supper's debris while their fellows slept a little longer. The time between the two suppers would be the best, Serena decided. The side door was little used, and the servants taking care of the salons and the second supper would not think to check it. If Sebastian followed her instructions to the letter, he could be in her bedchamber, unseen and unheard.

Peregrine called an early close to his own evening. He'd joined a party of friends at the theatre but the play didn't hold his interest, and, unusually, he found his companions' conversation insipid. His mind was occupied elsewhere.

He excused himself with the hint of an important tryst and strolled home to Stratton Street. His twin, unsurprisingly, was not at home, but a message addressed to Sebastian waited on a table in the foyer. Perry picked it up, idly glancing at the writing, wondering if he could recognize it. It was instantly recognizable as a feminine hand, although he didn't know whose it was. He could guess, though. He stood in the hall, thinking as he tapped the message on the palm of his hand. Was it important?

Still holding the message, he made his way to the kitchen, where Bart was dozing by the fire. The lad jumped up as Peregrine stuck his head around the door. "You want summat, sir?"

"No, I just wanted to know what time this message for my brother was delivered."

Bart rubbed sleep from his eyes. "Dunno exactly, sir. An hour ago, mebbe."

"All right, thank you. We won't need you again tonight, if you wish to seek your bed." Peregrine went back to the hall. He examined the message again, frowning. There had to be some urgency about sending a message so late in the evening. He made up his mind, took up his hat again, and left the house.

Sebastian had not returned to the house since he had left with Lady Serena that morning. If he was still with her, why would she be sending him messages? So it was safe to assume that he had continued with his original plans for the evening. Peregrine remembered he had said something about dinner at the Swan tavern behind St. Paul's church. It was worth seeing if he was still there.

He took a hackney to St. Paul's and went into the tavern, peering through the fog of tobacco smoke and billowing clouds of foul-smelling smoke from the sea-coal burning in the fireplace. The taproom was crowded, but Sebastian would have dined in one of the private rooms upstairs. Perry pushed his way to the counter, where the landlord was filling ale tankards from the keg behind him.

"Did you have a private party dining abovestairs this evening?"

The man straightened, wiping his hands on a stained apron. "Aye, they're still there. 'Aven't paid their reckonin' at all events."

Peregrine nodded his thanks and pushed his way to the narrow wooden staircase at the end of the taproom. Upstairs, he heard voices raised in laughter coming from a room to the left. He pushed open the door. Six men were sprawled around a table laden with dirty dishes and glasses. One of them was shaking a dice cup, the rest chanting encouragement, banging glasses on the table.

Sebastian looked up as the door opened. "Perry . . . come and join us, man. You know everyone . . . oh, except for Mr. Jonas Wedgwood." He indicated a rather flushed young man, whose slightly crossed eyes indicated a well-spent evening. "Jonas, my brother, the Honorable Peregrine Sullivan."

Jonas struggled to his feet, swayed, and sat down again with a thump. "An honor, sir . . . beg pardon," he mumbled.

Peregrine regarded him with an understanding smile, before saying to his twin, "This came for you an hour or so ago. I thought it might be important."

Sebastian took the message, and his expression changed instantly. He stepped away from the table and went to the window, standing with his back to the room as he slit the wafer. The message was short and simple: *I find myself alone for the evening. The side door will be unlocked after midnight. Use the backstairs. My chamber is at the front of the house. A red ribbon on the doorknob will tell you which one. I'll be waiting. S.*

For a moment, he was bewildered. And then slowly, the sense of the message came through. Serena was inviting him to an assignation, in the lion's den, no less. It was so unlike her normally cautious self that his first thought was that she must be in trouble. But there was nothing in the tone of the note to suggest such a thing.

He tucked the message into his inside pocket and turned back to the room, aware of the eyes of his friends on him in question and concern.

"Is everything all right, Seb?" Perry asked for the group. He looked closely at his twin. He could usually read him quite well, but now he wasn't sure. Sebastian had been pent up with whatever complex feelings he had about Lady Serena ever since he'd first seen her again in Pickering Place, and after their joint breakfast that morning, Peregrine had no idea where they'd spent the day, although he could make a guess as to *how* they'd spent it. But Sebastian seemed neither euphoric, as he would have expected after a glorious day of lovemaking, nor as tense as he had been before.

Sebastian nodded. "Oh, yes . . . everything's fine. But I'm afraid I must love you and leave you." His gaze fell on young Jonas, who was leaning heavily on an elbow-propped hand and looked as if he was about to fall asleep. He couldn't leave him to make his own way to Henrietta Place in this condition.

"Perry . . . I don't wish to impose, but could you possibly . . . ?" He gestured to the young man. "Henrietta Place, the Queen's Head."

Peregrine regarded the young man and shook his head. "Shame on you, Seb. Allowing him to get into this state. Clearly, he's not used to his drink."

" 'Tis better to have his first such experience among friends," Sebastian pointed out. Then he said with a rueful smile, "Although I own I was not watching closely enough. I should have reined him in earlier. But could you get him to his bed?"

Peregrine shrugged, saying agreeably, "Of course. But I think we'd best start now, before he falls completely asleep." He put his hands under Jonas's arms and hauled him to his feet. "Come on, then. Time you were in bed, my friend."

Jonas struggled to keep his feet, and one of the men at the table jumped up. "It'll take two of us to get him down the stairs, Perry." He took Jonas's other arm. "We'll get a hackney outside."

Sebastian put a handful of sovereigns on the table. "My share of the reckoning, gentlemen. I beg pardon for leaving in such haste, but something urgent has occurred."

They waved him away with good-natured farewells, and he bounded down the stairs and out into the street, where he saw Perry and his friend hoist the near-comatose Jonas into the interior of a hackney.

He set off at a brisk walk. The clock of St. Paul's church had struck midnight almost an hour since. He must hurry. Whatever the reason for the summons, it was clearly urgent, and he didn't want Serena giving up on him if he took overlong to make the rendezvous. A pair of chairmen were standing idly on the street corner, smoking corncob pipes, leaning against the body of their chair. He raised a hand, and they seized the poles and trotted over to him.

"Where to, guv?"

"Pickering Place. As fast as you can." He climbed in, and the chairmen started off at a brisk trot. It wasn't very far to his destination, but he couldn't run through the streets himself without drawing unwelcome attention, whereas the chairmen could cover the distance at this pace without notice.

Chapter Fourteen

The chairmen set Sebastian down as instructed on the corner of Pickering Place. He didn't wish to draw attention from anyone entering or leaving the house, which he assumed at half past one in the morning would still be in the midst of its entertainment. He kept to the shadows as he walked down the street, looking for the alley that would give access to the side door Serena had mentioned. He couldn't remember having noticed such an alley before, but then, he wouldn't have been looking for it. In general, arrivals at the house would see only the lighted front door.

He found it quickly enough, running alongside the house and leading to the mews that served the houses on Pickering Place. The house itself still blazed with light, but the alley was dimly lit, a flickering sconce at the far end offering the only illumination. But the door was there, towards the rear of the alley, close to the kitchen regions. He tried the latch, half afraid it would be locked, but it lifted easily, and the door swung open onto a dark, cramped space. He slipped inside quickly, pulling the door closed behind him, and stood for a moment getting his bearings while his eyes accustomed themselves to the gloom.

He was in a small hallway, with a narrow staircase leading up from the far wall. The backstairs, presumably. He went up, treading as softly as he could, afraid that each creak of the old floorboards would alert someone to a trespasser. He could hear voices as he reached a branch in the staircase, coming, he assumed, from the kitchen regions. To the right, the staircase led down to what he assumed was the kitchen, where the door was closed but light showed around the edges. To the left, it curved straight up, leading to the upper regions of the house. Serena's instructions had been clear enough. He went up and very softly eased open the door at the very head of the staircase.

He peered around it and found himself in a long corridor, sconced candles at intervals throwing a degree of light. At the end of the corridor, a pool of bright light spilled from what he knew to be the wide landing from which the main gaming salons opened.

The bedchambers were presumably along this corridor. He slid out into the corridor, closing the door gently behind him, barely breathing as he heard bursts of noise from the salons. Serena's note had said her bedchamber was at the front of the house. He was to look for a red ribbon around the door handle.

He turned right, because that was in the direction of the street, although it was also taking him towards the salons. He wondered why Serena was not at the gaming tables tonight. Judging by the noise, they were in full swing. What could be keeping her from her work? It had to be something exceptional. His step quickened with his heartbeat as he moved down the corridor, keeping close to the wall. The red ribbon was a splash of color against the cream paint of the door. He untied the ribbon and set his hand to the doorknob.

A burst of laughter and the general's unmistakable voice coming from the landing stopped his hand. He shrank back against the wall, waiting.

"God damn it, Heyward, I swear you have the devil's own luck," a somewhat slurred voice declared. The general offered some remark that Sebastian couldn't hear properly, and the voices faded as the two men went downstairs.

Sebastian waited a moment, then turned the handle and was inside the chamber before anyone could so much as detect his shadow. He turned the key in the lock instantly, and the click sounded unnaturally loud. The room was in semidarkness, the only illumination a candle on the table beside the bed and one on the mantel. He peered into the dimness, and then he saw her as she rose from the window seat, the soft folds of an ivory nightgown drifting around her, her hair long and loose framing her face.

"You came," Serena said.

"Did you think I would not?" He remained where he was, his back to the door, feeling the tension, the anticipation, build between them. "Why did you send for me, Serena?"

"Isn't it obvious?" she responded softly.   .

"I don't know. You've never done such a thing before. I thought maybe you were in some trouble."

She stepped across the floor, coming to stand close to him, putting her hands on his shoulders. "No trouble," she said. "'Tis wickedly reckless, I know, but . . ." Her shoulders lifted in a little shrug. "I couldn't help myself. I was filled with longing for you." She reached a hand to touch his mouth. "Do you mind coming to me here?"

Sebastian considered the question, aware that somehow his answer was important. He could still hear faint sounds from the gaming rooms, where men pawed her and she flirted and played whatever game they wished. He was flooded with a disconcerting sense of unreality. It was as if two quite different worlds had collided. His love for Serena and his loathing for everything about her situation. How could he separate the two?

Her great violet eyes were on his face, glowing in the dim light of the chamber, and he knew the answer . . . the *right* answer. Slowly, he shook his head. "No . . . no, I'd come to you at the gates of hell, if you asked me to." He put his hands at her waist, feeling the warmth of her skin beneath the silk of her gown.

Serena had kept the lights low to conceal the mark on her face. She had hoped it would fade quickly, but there was still a faint shadow on her cheek. Her long-sleeved nightgown was closed at the wrists with little pearl buttons, finished with lace ruffles that fell over her hands. She was confident that Sebastian would notice nothing amiss, particularly in the even deeper dimness of the bed curtains.

He kissed the corner of her mouth, touched her nose playfully with the tip of his tongue, before moving his mouth to hers, his hands molding the thin ivory silk against her body so that he could feel its contours, the indentation of her waist, the swell of breasts and hips. He cupped her bottom, lifting her slightly off the ground. She put her arms around his neck and pressed her loins against the jut of his penis with sudden urgency. It was as if the afternoon's passion had merely been an appetizer, one that stimulated appetite rather than sating it. She wanted to become a part of him, every inch of his body imprinted upon her own.

Still holding her off the ground, he stepped to the bed, letting her slide down his body before bending his head to kiss the hollow of her shoulder, to trail his tongue up the side of her neck, tasting the sweet fragrance of her skin, inhaling the heady scent of her hair as he lifted it away from the path of his kisses.

Serena's head fell back as he kissed the fast-beating pulse in her throat, and she gripped his hips with her own surge of need. *"Now,"* she whispered. "I need you to be a part of me now, love." Her fingers moved urgently over the fastening of his breeches, and she gave a soft moan of pleasure and satisfaction as his penis sprang forth, pulsing with an urgency to match her own.

Sebastian seized handfuls of her gown, roughly pulling it up to her waist. He gripped her backside again and lifted her against him as she curled her legs around his hips, feeling him slide into her moist and open body. They stood joined, not moving, simply feeling the wonder of this union, the presence of the other as part of themselves.

Serena felt his penis throbbing deep within her, and slowly she tightened her inner muscles around him, heard his sharp intake of breath, saw his eyes open wide. With a soft chuckle of delight, she squeezed him again, feeling her own climax drawing closer even without a single visible movement from either of them. Just the feel of him pulsing inside her was enough, and she reveled in the knowledge that she could bring him to climax with this simple little movement.

"If you do that again, we'll both be lost," he whispered, his fingers curling into the soft flesh of her buttocks.

"I know," she murmured with a mischievous little chuckle, and did it again.

They clung to each other, barely breathing, as the pleasure ripped through them, until the waves of delight finally diminished and with a groan of defeat Sebastian fell forward onto the bed, holding her tightly against him, twisting sideways as he fell so that she did not take his full weight.

They lay intertwined face-to-face amid the tumble of their disordered clothing, waiting for the blood to slow in their veins, their racing pulses to calm. Sebastian could see the pulse in Serena's throat, and he watched it as the violent rapidity of its beating finally took on a more normal rhythm. Lazily, he stroked damp strands of blue-black hair away from her cheek and circled the delicate whorls of her ear with the tip of his little finger. She smiled but had no energy for a more active response. His hand moved down to the smooth, silken flare of her hip revealed by her raised skirt and down the length of her thigh, cupping the rounded kneecap, before moving upwards again.

"Don't," she begged feebly, reaching down to stop the progress of his hand. " 'Tis too soon to do it again."

He laughed and disentangled his legs from hers, hitching himself onto an elbow. "I thought you had a better understanding of male anatomy, dear girl. It'll take me at least half an hour before I'm ready again."

"Oh, you know what I mean," she protested, half laughing. "You were going to arouse me again, tease me, and I'm too weak."

He reached around and patted her bottom. "There, there. No more just yet, I promise."

Serena rolled onto her back, and he was forced to slide his hand out from under her. "There's wine on the table. Maybe you'd be more comfortable if you undressed properly." She reached out a hand and stroked his flaccid penis as it lay limp against his thigh. "Poor little mouse."

"Oh, give it time, and it'll be as rampant a cock as ever crowed in a barnyard," he declared, sliding off the bed. He sat on the edge to pull off his boots, observing conversationally, "Making love in my boots is an unusual occurrence." He shrugged off his rumpled coat and waistcoat, tossed aside his shirt, unfastened his breeches properly, pushing them with his underdrawers down to his feet, where he kicked them away with a flourish. "That is better. But if you don't mind, I'd like to even the playing field." Naked, he bent over her, taking one wrist to unbutton the little pearl studs.

"I'll do it," she said hastily. "Why do you not pour a glass of wine?"

A slight frown crossed his countenance, but he let her hand drop to the coverlet. "As you wish, ma'am."

She had managed to keep the bruised side of her face averted and thought that the dim illumination would conceal the mark from all but the closest scrutiny. Her wrist was still red, though. She had a story to explain it if it became necessary, but it would be better if he didn't notice. She could probably contrive to use only her good hand without it seeming obvious and keep the other one close to her side.

She pulled the gown over her head, tossing it to the floor, and lay back against the pillows, watching as he bent to throw more logs on the fire. The sounds of the house, more an amorphous buzz than distinct speech, continued to drift down the corridor from the salons. "I wonder what the general would say if he could guess what was going on a few paces from the salons," she murmured.

Sebastian straightened slowly. "Was it necessary to remind me of where we are?"

"At the gates of hell?" she questioned lightly, trying to make it seem as if her comment had been in jest.

"As good as. How did you manage to avoid the salons this evening?"

"I told him I was unwell."

"I see. A reasonable excuse." He lit a taper in the fire and brought it to light the branch of candles on the night table.

"Oh, don't, please," Serena said. "I like the shadows for some reason. It makes everything seem like a dream, a wonderful dream from which I don't have to wake up. If you shine light on it, I will wake up."

He shook his head in amusement, his momentary irritation banished, and blew out the taper. "What a strange notion, but it shall be as you wish." He tossed the taper into the fire and poured two glasses of canary wine, bringing them to the bed. He sat on the end beside her and filled his mouth with wine, before leaning in and kissing her. Her mouth opened for him, and the wine flowed between them in a seductive swirl on her tongue.

She laughed. It was the most delicious sensation, liquid and sensual, almost like making love. "Again."

He took another swig, then kissed her again. "What a novel way of sharing a glass," Serena declared, licking a drop of vinous moisture from her lips. "Where did you learn to do that?"

"Ah, wouldn't you like to know?" he teased, taking her own glass away from her. "Lie back. I have another idea."

Serena obliged, sliding down until she was lying flat. She felt a cold trickle in her navel and gave an involuntary start.

"Be still," he chided. "You'll spill it."

Silent laughter shook her, but she kept as still as she could as he bent over her and lapped the wine from the small cup. His tongue teased her belly, and she squirmed a little under the warm, tickling sensation.

He rested his head on her belly and looked up her body, a finger languidly circling her nipples. He loved her breasts, standing full and firm against the slenderness of her torso. Their fullness had surprised him the first time he had seen her naked. Dressed, she was as tall and slender as a willow; even with décolletage, the rich swell of her breasts was masked by her height, and it was a delightful surprise to discover the lush plenitude beneath.

Serena stretched beneath his traveling gaze, offering her body, taut and straight, for his appraisal, lifting her hips in an enticing little movement that sent a surge of lust to his loins. He moved his head down, his tongue parting the swollen lips of her sex, his teeth grazing the hard little nub of flesh. He slid a hand beneath her again, lifting her a little as her thighs fell apart so that her sex lay open, waiting for his touch. He used his tongue, lapping at her honeyed center, and Serena was lost, her body already so exquisitely sensitized that the first moist stroke was enough to send her once more into a luxuriously slow tumble from the peaks into the still waters of release.

Sebastian raised his head slowly, savoring the taste of her on his lips and tongue, breathing deep of the lingering scent of her. He stroked up her belly with his tongue, licking the tiny beads of sweat gathered in the deep cleft of her breasts.

She reached down and ran her fingers through his fair hair, smiling at the little curls gathered on the nape of his neck. Cherubic curls, she thought, reflecting with another smile that there was actually very little of the cherub about her lover. "Are you ready for another bout?" she inquired with one of her mischievous chuckles.

"If you are," he murmured, moving his mouth to hers. She could taste herself on his lips and tongue.

"Always." She moved her thighs apart to accommodate him, but he took her hips and flipped her onto her belly. "Ah," she said into the pillow. "A change of scene."

She heard his chuckle, felt his breath warm on the back of her neck. He reached for a pillow and pushed it beneath her belly, lifting her hips. She drew up her knees a little to make it easier for him and felt him slide within her. The angle was so different it was as if it was the first time they had made love that evening. She pushed back against him, feeling his belly hard against her bottom, his penis deep inside her, moving rapidly, filling her as his hand beneath her rubbed the erect nub of flesh.

When it was over, he lay heavily along her back, his legs following the line of hers, his feet twining with hers. His breath stirred her hair, his hands covered hers, which were raised above her head, limp and still beside her head. After a long time, Sebastian rolled away from her, turned on his side, and pulled her body into him, drawing her backwards into the curve of his body. And they slept while the house continued its business, heedless of the sleeping lovers, and finally just before dawn closed its doors to the last of the revelers.

Sebastian awoke with a start, almost as if he had heard the sound of the shooting bolts in the great front door in the hall below. He lay for a moment, wondering where he was, but the warm, breathing flesh against his own brought awareness soon enough. He slipped away from her, trying not to disturb her, and slid off the bed, padding to look at the clock on the mantel. It was too dark to see the time, and he stuck a taper into the embers of the dying fire and lit the branch of candles that Serena had wanted unlit. He took the light to the mantel to look at the clock. It told him it was past four in the morning. They still had a little time before the house awoke.

He poked the fire into life and added more wood, then approached the bed, holding the branch of candles, hoping to wake her slowly. She still lay on her side, her cheek pillowed on one hand, the other rested along her flank. He frowned, leaned closer. There was a mark on her cheek that he had not seen before. The shadow of an emerging bruise. He held the candles higher and saw her wrist, red and bruised against the pale skin of her hip. Quietly, he set the branched candles down on the night table so that they threw light on the sleeper's face and sat down in a chair by the window, waiting for the light to do its work.

It did soon enough. Serena swam slowly up through the mists of sleep, aware of a flickering light against her eyelids. She lay still, luxuriating for a few more moments in the trance of half-sleep. Something was missing. Her back felt cold and alone. She reached behind her and encountered only emptiness. Startled into full awareness, she rolled over towards the light and blinked in sleepy protest as it hit her eyes. Slowly, her vision cleared, and she hitched herself onto an elbow, blinking blearily into the room. Sebastian was sitting naked in a chair by the window, the fire was once more ablaze, and the room was bright with candlelight.

"Is it time for you to go?" she mumbled.

"Soon enough, but we have time yet." His voice was very quiet, but something in it alarmed her. He stood up and came over to the bed. He reached down and touched her cheek, then lifted her wrist. "How did these happen?"

Serena thought rapidly. It was her own fault for initiating this night. She should have known that in such close quarters, she couldn't hide the marks. There was absolutely no point attempting to lie. Not to Sebastian.

"My stepfather," she said. "When I came in this afternoon, he was livid because I had not done something
he wanted me to do." She was not going to bring up
Burford again. "He lost his temper." She tried to take
her hand away, to smile and touch his cheek, but he still
held her wrist, and his expression was a mask of cold
fury. "'Tis nothing, really, Sebastian."

"What d'you mean, 'tis nothing?" he demanded, his
face as pale as death. "How often has he hurt you?"

She shook her head. "This was the first time . . . oh,
he hurt my mother, I know he did, but he's never done
more than threaten me before. He just lost his temper
this time and forgot himself. If I had had my pistol with
me, he would not have had the opportunity. I promise
from now on, I will have it on my person at all times."

Sebastian's expression changed to one of stunned dis-
belief. "Your *pistol?*"

"Yes," she said simply. "I acquired it from a good
friend in Brussels who felt that I needed protection, living as we did." She tried a reassuring smile. "There's no
need for concern, Sebastian, he taught me how to shoot,
too. I know how to use it, and believe me, if I have to,
I will."

"I'm not interested in your pistol or your skill as a good
shot," he said, sounding harsher than he intended. "I will
not permit you to stay under this roof another instant.
Get up and put together the things you cannot leave behind. From now on, you are under my protection."

Serena's sudden pallor was a mirror image of his own. She swung off the bed, facing him. "Hear this, Sebastian. I have no need of your protection or that of anyone else. I can take care of myself. I will not move from one male roof to another at anyone's bidding. Understand that."

"Do you seriously think, Serena, that I am going to walk away leaving you to the abuse of that bastard? Now, do as I ask. Pack what you cannot leave behind."

"No, Sebastian." She shook her head. "I will not leave until I have ensured Abigail's safety."

"Oh, for God's sake. Leave the girl to her own future. If her parents are fool enough to hand her over to the general, then so be it. She and her future happiness are their responsibility, not yours. You have no right to meddle, Serena."

"*Meddle,*" she exclaimed. "How dare you, Sebastian? And how could you consign that poor child to such a future? You're as bad as my stepfather." She swung away from him with a gesture of disgust.

"What did you say?" His voice was so soft she could barely hear it. "Serena, repeat what you said."

And she realized how anger had led her to say something unjust, something that put her in the wrong, leaving her at a disadvantage when she knew how right she was. She had known Sebastian would react like this if he saw what Heyward had done, and she'd tried to keep him from seeing it. But she'd given in to a self-indulgent whim, and this was where it had landed her.

She took a deep, steadying breath. "I should not have

said that. I beg your pardon. But you should not have accused me of meddling. I am not meddling, I am attempting to save some innocent from what happened to my mother, not to mention from the fate I've been dodging for myself for the last three years. Abigail does not have my strength. He will sell her to the highest bidder once he has run through her dowry."

Sebastian took his own deep breath. "Let me get this straight. Heyward is coercing you into whoredom?"

"Crude but correct," she said, face and voice expressionless. "But I can take care of myself. I've been doing so for many years now." *And only failed once.* But that she kept to herself. It would do Sebastian no good to be told of the Spaniard's rape.

"It makes no difference. I will not leave you here. You must come with me," he stated.

"You have no right of command, Sebastian." Her voice was strangely detached as she gathered up the coverlet, wrapping herself in its folds.

"Marry me," he said suddenly, knowing that it was the wrong moment, that emotions were running too high for the proposal he'd been waiting to make for days now, but utterly unable to keep silent.

"Marry you?" She stared at him. "What are you talking about?"

"Marry me, Serena. Let me look after you."

It felt to Serena as if her head had been dipped in a bucket of icy water. She stared at him. "Look after me? *Assert* a right of command, you mean?"

"That's not what I said."

"No, you didn't have to. You've been stamping around stating what you will and will not tolerate, as if I somehow belonged to you." She waved a hand in abrupt dismissal. "You are in my bedchamber and not welcome here. Please leave. You may leave the side door unlocked. I'll lock it again when you're safely away."

"*Serena . . .*" He took a step forward, his hands reaching for her, intent only on compelling her to see reason, and then he read the revulsion on her face as she held out a hand to ward him off.

"Don't come near me. Don't touch me."

Without a word, he turned away from her and dressed rapidly. "Good night." He bowed to her averted back, heard her own low-voiced "Good night," and went to the door. He let himself out of the house without incident and walked through the cool air of the predawn to Stratton Street, cursing himself for overplaying his hand and Serena for being a stubborn, willful, impossible woman and consigning General Sir George Heyward to the sharpest pitchforks in the deepest depths of Lucifer's inferno.

Serena waited five minutes, then slipped out of her chamber and down the backstairs to lock the side door. She didn't realize that she was weeping until a tear splashed on her hand as she lifted it to the bolt.

She stood for a moment, her forehead resting wearily against her hand still pressed to the door. Why did such a glorious night have to end in such a bitter debacle?

She and Sebastian were and always had been so perfect together, such a wonderfully interlocking fit . . . at least physically, in the ways of love. Maybe that was all they had. And yet she knew in her heart that it was not all. But she would never . . . no, *could* never give up her independence of thought, of action, never give up the right to act as she considered right for herself.

Marriage to Sebastian? She had never even considered it; their situations were so wildly different. Such a union could ruin Sebastian. He had spoken without thought, of course, out of anger, even, because she would not do as he wished. Out of frustration, he had simply fallen back upon the traditional attitudes about the way men and women should behave together. Marriage would give him rights he could not have otherwise. Husbands had the right of command, wives the obligation to obey.

How could she possibly have imagined they were a perfect fit?

Chapter Fifteen

"May I borrow the barouche this morning, Mama?" Abigail slipped into her seat at the breakfast table, fixing her mother with a cajoling smile.

"Good heavens, whatever for?" Marianne demanded, dipping a finger of toast into her teacup.

"I wish to visit Lady Serena before our dinner this evening." Abigail had come up with what she thought was the perfect excuse for such a visit. "She said she would ask her maid to show Matty how to dress my hair in a particularly fashionable way, so I thought Matty could accompany me to Pickering Place. You will be so busy with preparations for this evening, I know you don't have time, and it might be quite a long visit."

Marianne looked doubtful, but her husband, delicately deboning one of a pair of kippers on his plate, said, "Oh, you may be sure Lady Serena knows what's what when it comes to high fashion. I've never seen her looking anything but a perfect picture. You run along, puss, and take all the advice she'll give you. Don't want to look a country dowd at your first party, does she, Mrs. Sutton?"

"I hardly think Abigail would look like a dowd when I have had the dressing of her," Marianne declared with a sniff that told her husband he would have done better to phrase himself more diplomatically.

"No, no . . . of course not, my dear. Heaven forbid," he blustered. "Meant no such thing, I assure you. But Lady Serena knows what young ladies in London are doing with their hair. Stands to reason a word of advice from her can't come amiss, although your opinion is always the final one, my dear ma'am."

Marianne looked a trifle mollified. "Well, I suppose it can do no harm, and there's no knowing whom you may meet in Lady Serena's drawing room. As it happens, I have no need of the carriage myself this morning, so you may have it for an hour, but I shall need you to rest upon your bed this afternoon. You must be in best looks for the evening."

"Yes, Mama." Abigail concealed her jubilation at the ease of her victory with downcast eyes.

She set off an hour later in the barouche, feeling pleased with her appearance. The dark blue pelisse lined and tipped with white fur was of the first style of elegance, and her blue silk cap beneath her fur-tipped hood was adorned with the most fetching velvet ribbons. As she had dressed, she had wondered if perhaps Mr. Sullivan might be visiting Lady Serena. And if not that gentleman, then there could be others. Lady Serena had to have a large circle of acquaintances and gallants dancing attendance.

The Suttons had never been invited to any evening gatherings at General Heyward's residence in Brussels, but Abigail knew they frequently held large parties. Her mother had once or twice expressed a degree of resentment at the lack of evening invitations, but her father had reminded his wife that as Abigail was not yet out, it would not be appropriate to receive or accept invitations to the kind of large gatherings held by the general and his stepdaughter. As for himself, he detested going out in the evening; a quiet time by his own fireside after a good dinner was all he required.

Serena would have been wryly amused at Abigail's assumptions about her social life had she been in a different frame of mind. She had slept badly after Sebastian's departure and gazed at her wan reflection in the mirror with less than approbation. Her eyes were heavy, slightly red-rimmed from the tears she had shed, and her head ached. To cap it all, the Suttons' dinner party was that evening, when she would have to be at her sparkling best, as most of the guests were her own acquaintances. Sebastian would be among them, unless he decided after the previous night's debacle to send his regrets.

Serena could not imagine what kind of meeting she and Sebastian could have. What could they say to each other in public? Indeed, what was there left for them to say? Sebastian, for all his gentle courtesy, quick humor, sensitivity, and tenderness, was also stubborn, as she knew from experience. He would not lightly give up cherished opinions or change an attitude that he believed to be correct. And she had seen no inkling that he was persuadable in his conviction regarding the proper way matters should be conducted between man and wife.

She sighed and picked up the rouge pot. A touch on her cheekbones and a dusting of powder would hide the now faint shadow of her stepfather's hand. Long sleeves were not exactly conventional wear for an evening party, but if she was to hide her bruised wrist, she had little choice. Unless she could come up with a satisfactory explanation.

She turned as the door opened, and Bridget came in. "There's a young lady come to visit you, m'lady. A Miss Sutton, Flanagan says. He wants to know if you're at home."

Abigail here? Serena frowned. "Is she alone?" Abigail on her own she could manage, but Mrs. Sutton was more than she could face at this moment.

"Just with her maid, ma'am."

"Show her into my parlor. I'll be with her directly."

"Yes, ma'am." Bridget curtsied and disappeared.

Serena checked her reflection once more, satisfying herself that she looked as much like herself as was possible in the circumstances. She teased out her dusky side curls with her fingers, making them fall loosely around her face, which she decided had a softening effect. Satisfied, she rose from the dressing stool, draped a paisley shawl around her shoulders, and went to her parlor.

Abigail was standing by the window, nervously pulling at the fingertips of her gloves. She was unaccustomed to paying social calls on her own. But Serena instantly put her at ease as she entered.

"What a lovely surprise, Abigail." She came forward, hands outstretched in greeting. "Let me ring for coffee." She turned to the bell rope beside the fireplace.

"Oh, the maid said she would bring some at once." Abigail looked around admiringly. "What a pretty room. It must be lovely to have a parlor of one's own."

"Yes, my sanctuary," Serena said lightly. "Won't you take off your pelisse and sit down?" She gestured to a sofa by the fire.

Abigail dropped her outer garment over the arm of another chair and sat down, drawing off her gloves. "I have a most particular question to ask you, Lady Serena." She stopped, wondering how to phrase the question without sounding conceited.

"Go on," Serena said with an encouraging smile. Abigail's puzzles would be a welcome change from her own convoluted situation.

"Well . . . it's rather awkward." Abigail played with her gloves in her lap. She looked up and said resolutely, "Do you remember Mr. Wedgwood?"

"Jonas, the young man who accompanied us to Green Park? Yes, of course I do." Serena nodded with the same encouraging smile.

"Well, Papa has made Mama invite him to dinner tonight. He says we must be courteous and welcoming to a member of the Wedgwood family, because he and old Mr. Wedgwood belong to the same business set in Stoke-on-Trent."

"Yes, I quite understand that." Serena nodded again, turning slightly to the door as Bridget came in with the coffee tray. "Thank you, Bridget. Set it down there. You needn't serve it." She poured coffee and leaned over to hand a cup to her guest.

"Of course, Mama is cross because it means she has to invite old Miss Bentley to make up the numbers," Abigail confided. "She's some kind of a distant cousin who's a companion to an old lady in Kensington. Mama doesn't think she's suitable company, but Papa says she'll do very well in a pinch." She sipped her coffee.

Serena concealed her amusement at this artless speech. She said neutrally, "It will be nice to see Mr. Wedgwood again this evening."

"Yes," Abigail said.

Serena frowned. She couldn't tell whether Abigail agreed with her. "Is there some difficulty, my dear?"

Abigail blushed. "Mr. Sullivan will be there, too."

"Ah. I begin to understand." Serena smiled. "Two suitors at the same table."

Abigail's blush deepened. "Oh, please, I don't mean to sound forward or . . . or . . ."

"You're not, Abigail. 'Tis a fact, and you must admit it has its pleasing side." She raised a teasing eyebrow.

"But . . . but Lady Serena, do you think it's possible that Mr. Sullivan might consider an alliance with my family?" It came out in a rush, as if she were afraid that if she stopped to think, she would lose the courage.

Serena considered the question. On the one hand, she didn't want to give Abigail false encouragement, but on the other, she didn't want to create a vacuum for her stepfather to step into.

After a moment, she said delicately, "Would you consider Mr. Sullivan as a suitor, Abigail?"

The girl's blush turned fiery, and her eyes dropped to her lap. "It would be most flattering. I would feel so . . . so fortunate."

Serena pursed her lips. Abigail sounded a lot less than enthusiastic.

"He's . . . he's such a perfect gentleman," Abigail rushed on. "So handsome and so courteous . . . any girl would be immensely flattered, don't you think, Lady Serena?"

"I do," Serena agreed drily. "Mr. Sullivan is everything you say. But tell me, do you have reason to think he might make you an offer?"

Abigail shook her head. "He has never given me cause to think it, although he is always so gallant. But Mama . . . Mama, you see . . . she has set her sights on a great marriage for me, and she thinks that Mr. Sullivan . . ." Her voice faded, and her great blue eyes were fixed pleadingly upon Serena.

"Well, Mrs. Sutton is like all mothers, Abigail. She wants only the best for her daughter." Serena spoke briskly. "But I think, if you have a dislike of Mr. Sullivan, you have only to—"

"Oh, no, please don't misunderstand me, Lady Serena. I do not hold him in dislike, not in the least, 'tis only that . . . that . . ."

"That what?" Serena offered another encouraging smile.

"That I can't be quite comfortable with him," Abigail finally confessed with a great sigh. "And . . . and I am so very comfortable with Jonas . . . Mr. Wedgwood."

"Ah." Serena leaned back in her chair. "And 'tis very clear to anyone with eyes that Mr. Wedgwood is very comfortable with you."

"Yes . . . yes, I think he is." Abigail picked up her cup, but the coffee was now cold, and she set it down again. "But Mama . . ."

"Mama will not favor such a match," Serena finished for her.

Abigail nodded. "And I wouldn't wish any discourtesy to Mr. Sullivan."

"Oh, don't let that worry you," Serena said with a touch of acid. "Mr. Sullivan's heart recovers quite quickly, I can promise you. He will take no offense." She regarded her young visitor with a half-smile. "The issue, it seems, then, is how we persuade Mama that Mr. Wedgwood is the only man for you . . . if one might permit oneself the vulgarity."

Abigail gave her a watery smile. "Papa will not present any objections, that at least I know."

"Then we must recruit Mr. Sutton to our cause." Serena's nod was decisive. "I suggest you cajole him a little before this evening, mention how much you like Mr. Wedgwood, and then at dinner tonight, I will do all I can to encourage Jonas to shine at the dinner table. If your mother sees what a charming, educated, and assured young man he is, one who can hold his own in any company, she might prove easier to persuade."

Abigail's smile was now radiant. "Oh, you are so wise, Lady Serena. I knew you were just the person to ask. Of course, I must be polite to Mr. Sullivan, but—"

"Of course, you must be as polite to him as to all your guests, but you may leave it with me to ensure that he has no inflated hopes."

Abigail rose to her feet. "I am so grateful, Lady Serena. I have often wished for an older sister," she added shyly. " 'Tis as if my wish has been granted."

Serena kissed her cheek. "I am happy to play that part." She pulled the bell rope for Flanagan. "Go home and rest, so that you will be at your best this evening."

Abigail went into a peal of laughter. "Oh, you sound just like Mama, but you are not in the least like Mama."

"For which I am profoundly grateful," Serena murmured, turning as the butler entered the parlor. "Flanagan, Miss Sutton is leaving."

"Very good, my lady. Miss Sutton's barouche is still at the door, and her maid is waiting in the hall." Flanagan held the door wide for Abigail, who went past him with a jaunty farewell wave for Serena.

She followed Flanagan to the hall and was crossing to the door when General Heyward came into the house from the street, slapping his riding crop against his boot. He was frowning, his face a mask of sullen anger, but it cleared miraculously as he saw Abigail.

"Why, my dear Miss Sutton." He bowed over her hand. "What a delight for the eyes. Such rare beauty. Such an honor to welcome you under my roof. Tell me what brings you here." He held on to her hand, his fingers closing more tightly as she made a tentative effort to free it.

"I have been calling on Lady Serena, sir," she said, dropping a quick curtsy. "But Mama will be expecting me any minute. I cannot stay." She managed to get her hand back. "I give you good day, sir." She sketched another hasty curtsy and hurried to the door, her maid following.

Heyward stared at the closed door for several minutes, his expression unreadable, his eyes unfocused. Then he turned on his heel and went into the library. He rarely found himself nonplussed, but he felt the edge of desperation more sharply now than he had ever felt it before. He had run into Lord Burford that morning, and his lordship had been unpleasantly pointed about the mortgages. His lordship had informed the general that the loan had always been a temporary one, and since Heyward didn't seem able to put up the price to buy them back, then he was left with little choice but to call them in.

General Heyward could think only of what Serena had told him, that Burford had offered to give her the mortgages if she agreed to his protection. It seemed that the earl had been intending to double-cross him all along. The conversation had filled him with a deep and terrible rage, fueled by the knowledge of impending disaster, and he had barely managed two words in response. To make matters worse, the earl had gone on his way smiling benignly, as if it had been a perfectly ordinary conversation.

Heyward now poured himself a brandy, staring into the fire. Serena was a lost cause. He knew that now. By resorting to violence, he had burned his boats. Even if he could manage to deliver her to Burford drugged and trussed like a hen ready for the pot, the earl would have none of it. He wanted a mistress who was conscious and willing, at least on the surface. Serena would never be that. He could throw her out to find her own way on the streets, and there would be some satisfaction in that, but he needed her at the tables. They could pack up and flee his debts at dead of night, as they'd done so many times before, but he was getting too old for that game.

No, he had to fall back on his only other option, marriage to the Sutton heiress. He didn't think the girl would fall readily into his hand, but her mother would do his wooing for him, and he was fairly confident that he could win over the father, who already treated him like a familiar friend and seemed flattered by the general's attentions. Serena was in the girl's confidence; at least there, she'd obeyed him without question. It was time to mend fences with his stepdaughter, he decided. He needed to keep her sweet while he pursued the little Sutton.

He set down his brandy goblet and made his way up to Serena's parlor.

After Abigail had left, Serena sank back onto her chair, resting her head against the back. It seemed likely that with a little more maneuvering, Abigail might soon be safely wed to Jonas Wedgwood. For some reason, it didn't fill her with expected elation. Such a marriage would ensure her own freedom, but now she wasn't sure what that freedom meant or why she wanted it. What was she to do with it, all alone?

She felt like throwing something, and at the tap on her door, she turned her head irritably against the chair and demanded, "Who is it?"

"Your father." The general spoke as he opened the door. "May I come in, my dear?"

"Would you stay out if I said no?" She made no attempt to rise as he came in and shut the door.

"This is my house. I have the right to go where I please," he informed her, keeping his voice level with a supreme effort.

Serena merely closed her eyes with an infinitesimal shrug. She felt him come close to her chair and barely concealed her shudder. But she was determined not to speak first.

He looked down at her for a moment before saying,

"Come now, my dear, let us call a truce. I forgive you for your ingratitude and disobedience, so let us speak of it no more."

Serena felt the urge to laugh hysterically. *He* forgave *her?* "Indeed, sir, I am sure I'm suitable grateful. And I daresay the bruises will fade in time." She kept her eyes closed, her head averted.

"It was unfortunate that it came to that," he said with some difficulty. "I exercised a father's right to a daughter's obedience. I did no more than was called for."

"Really?" Her tone was one of indifference.

Her continued silence made him uncharacteristically nervous. What if she refused to take her part at the tables, refused to continue cultivating the Suttons? He couldn't batter her into submission, not when she needed to be in public to play those parts.

"I understand there's to be a dinner party at the Suttons' this evening," he said with an encouraging smile.

"So I believe, sir."

"You will be present."

"If you can manage without me in the salons."

"Of course . . . of course. No difficulty at all, my dear. I shall dine quietly beforehand and close the main salon." He rubbed his hands together in an effort to impart perfect comfort with the solution. "And you must enjoy yourself, Serena. Play the Society lady . . . nothing to concern you tonight except to have a pleasant evening among charming company."

"You are too kind, sir." Her tone was flat, uninviting,

and he stood for a moment, still rubbing his hands until they fell to his sides as the silence continued.

"Well, I'll leave you, then. I'm sure you have things to do."

"I must consult with Cook about the menu for supper this evening." She still kept her eyes closed, her head resting against the back of the chair, and after a few seconds, she heard the door close on his departure.

There was some satisfaction to be gleaned from that encounter, and she felt for the first time that she just might have gained the upper hand. He had overreached himself the previous evening and had put himself at a disadvantage, and Serena had every intention of making the most of that disadvantage. In any other circumstances, she would have viewed her position with unholy glee, but now it was like salt and ashes on her tongue.

Downstairs, General Heyward called for his horse again. The animal had barely reached the mews before the footman brought the message. The groom, who'd been looking forward to a pint of porter and a meat pasty for his midday meal, cursed an inconsiderate master and led the weary horse back to the front door. Heyward had attempted to assuage his rage and frustration with Lord Burford that morning by riding the horse into the ground in Windsor Park, and the groom was muttering that for two pins, he'd give the general a piece of his mind and tell him to ride shank's pony instead. The general was spared the caustic advice, as unfortunately, the groom didn't have two pins, or perhaps fortunately. He'd be out on his ear telling General Sir George Heyward to use his own legs for once.

"You'll be wantin' me, sir?" he inquired as the general emerged from the house.

"No." Heyward took the reins and mounted heavily. He was not wearing spurs, but he kicked the beast into movement with unnecessary force. The groom sent a copious gobbet of spittle to splat onto the cobbles in the general's wake.

Heyward rode to Bruton Street, rearranging his expression into one of benign and gentlemanly friendship. He tethered the animal to the railing at the front door of the Suttons' house and banged the knocker. It was answered instantly by the butler, who offered an impassive bow as he stood aside to admit the visitor. "I'll ascertain whether Mr. Sutton is at home, sir."

"Do so, and hurry up about it." The general stood tapping his whip against his boots while the butler walked in stately fashion to the door at the rear of the hall. He knocked once and opened the door, stepping softly within.

A minute later, he reappeared. "Mr. Sutton will be pleased to see you, General. Will you step this way . . ." He held the library door open.

Heyward marched past him, a smile fixed to his lips. "Ah, Sutton, happy to find you home." His voice had a jovial boom to it, and his hand was outstretched in greeting.

"Welcome . . . welcome, m'dear fellow." William rose from behind a heavy mahogany desk and greeted his visitor warmly. "I'm always to be found at home in the morning . . . like to take care of business first thing. Time enough for pleasure once the books are settled and m'mind's at ease, don't you know."

"Ah, you are a man after my own heart," the general stated, giving his host's shoulder a hearty buffet. "Get the business out of the way . . . tedious though it may be."

"Ah, well, I must confess I don't find it in the least tedious," William confided. "'Tis meat and drink, m'dear fellow. Meat and drink."

Heyward smiled. "Each to his own, dear sir, each to his own."

"Well, I've never been a gentleman of leisure . . . can't see the point of it somehow . . . wine, General, or ale? I'm partial to a drop of strong ale myself at this time of day."

The general concealed a well-bred shudder. "Wine, sir, if you please. I never developed a taste for ale."

William looked a little dubious at this confession. It was his opinion that every right-thinking man understood the pleasures to be had in a morning tankard of golden ale. He poured claret for the general and filled a pewter tankard from a jug for himself. He passed the glass to his guest. "So, sit down, sir . . . be at your ease. To what do I owe the pleasure this morning?"

Heyward sat down, raised his glass in a silent toast,

sipped, and then said, "I'll come straight to the point, Sutton. I would like to offer for your daughter. I like to think that my affection for her must be no secret?" He tilted his head in question, a smile of deep sincerity hovering on his lips.

William did not instantly reply. He sipped his ale, seeming to stare off into the middle distance. The general felt his hackles rise. He had expected instant pleasure. General Sir George Heyward was offering to marry a tradesman's daughter. How could the man hesitate for so much as a second?

"Well, sir," William said finally. "I'm sure Abigail will be honored. But 'tis not for me to give an answer for her."

"Oh, come, sir, you jest, surely." Heyward could hardly believe his ears. "I have every hope of securing Miss Sutton's affections . . . indeed, if I may say so without sounding like a coxcomb, I do believe I may already have done so."

"Then, if that is the case, sir, we may consider the matter settled," William said before adding, "Once, of course, we have settled the small matters of business that need not trouble the dear child."

"Of course, sir, that goes without saying."

This was tricky ground. Somehow, Heyward had to prove his solvency to this astute man of business, while at the same time extricating a large dowry to be paid to him the instant the marriage took place. He hoped that William Sutton understood that he would be selling his daughter in exchange for her advanced social position. He must surely be aware that no aristocrat or gentleman of breeding would consider taking a wife from trade circles, unless there was more than adequate compensation. But now was not the time to point this out.

"I am most deeply fond of your daughter, sir." He smiled again. "Such a lovely girl, so beautiful, so accomplished in her conversation, and her harp playing is truly talented."

William cleared his throat. He was a very fond papa, but even he couldn't quite believe in this catalogue of his daughter's fine qualities. When it came to her conversation, he had to admit he sometimes found it hard to stay awake, and as for her performance on the harp, he had serious reservations about whether he hadn't wasted his money on her teacher. But Marianne had insisted, so he assumed it had been necessary. But who was he to quibble with a suitor's idealized view of the child?

"Well, as to that, sir, Abigail is a darling girl, the apple of my eye . . . never met a girl to hold a candle to her," he declared. "Tell you what, I'll talk it over with her mother, and then we'll see."

This was not quite what the general had hoped to hear. He took a sip of claret. "I had hoped for a moment with Miss Sutton, sir . . . and Mrs. Sutton, of course."

"Of course. My daughter would not see a gentleman unchaperoned." William sounded surprised that his visitor had felt the addendum necessary. He pushed back his chair. "No time like the present, eh? Let us go upstairs and visit the ladies. I heard Abigail come in half an hour past. She was visiting Lady Serena, I'm told."

"I had the good fortune to meet her in the hall just as she was leaving," the general said, rising with his host.

"Her mama wishes her to rest this afternoon to prepare for her first dinner party this evening," William said with another fond smile. "Can't think why 'tis so important the child should be in best looks for mere dinner-table talk, but when m'lady wife decrees it, then it must happen." He chuckled and led the way upstairs to the ladies' parlor.

He entered without ceremony, speaking as he did so. "My dear, I have brought Sir George Heyward to visit. Most anxious he is to see Abigail." He looked around. "Where is the dear child?"

"She's changing her dress, Mr. Sutton." Marianne extended her hand to the general and nodded a seated bow as befitted a matron receiving a gentleman. "General, 'tis a pleasure, I'm sure."

He bowed over her hand, raising it to his lips for a kiss in the air above her knuckles. "You look charming, ma'am, if I may be so bold."

Marianne patted the elegant scrap of a lace cap on her graying hair. "Why, thank you, sir. You are too kind."

"'Tis not hard to see where your daughter gets her looks," Heyward said.

Marianne tittered a little. "You flatter me, dear sir. Pray, sit down." She cast a glance at her husband, who was watching the proceedings with a somewhat sardonic glimmer in his eye. "Mr. Sutton, will you call for wine for our guest?"

"Of course, my dear." William pulled the bell rope.

Abigail was coming from her bedchamber as Morrison was carrying the decanter and glasses to her mother's parlor. "Oh, do we have visitors, Morrison?"

"General Sir George Heyward, Miss Sutton. He is with Mr. Sutton and your mother."

"Oh." Abigail's nose wrinkled. There had been a time in Brussels when she had quite liked the general's flattering attentions, but her views had changed since her arrival in London. She didn't feel like listening to his fulsome compliments this morning and turned back to her bedchamber. "Will you tell my mother I have some letters to write, Morrison? I will come down for luncheon."

"Yes, Miss Sutton." Morrison raised an eyebrow and continued to the parlor. He had met many a General Heyward in his career as butler and had smelled the rat in this one from the first meeting in Brussels. He was more than happy to assist his young mistress's attempts to keep out of the man's way.

He set the tray on the sideboard and spoke softly to Mrs. Sutton. "Miss Sutton, ma'am, begs to be excused. She had some letters to write."

Marianne nodded. "Thank you, Morrison." She waved him away. "I'm afraid Abigail won't be joining us, General. She has some correspondence to take care of."

Heyward looked disappointed but accepted the glass

of wine and began to talk of the projected visit to the theatre, which had still not materialized. In truth, he was finding it hard to lay hands on a suitable box at Covent Garden. He had hoped that one of his friends or clients who played at his tables would lend him a box for one night, but it was proving difficult to pin down any of the gentlemen so endowed. "I haven't found a play that you would consider suitable, ma'am," he now said. "Miss Sutton's delicate sensibilities must be taken into account. And of course, the entertainment must be of a classical nature, as you yourself said." He dabbed his lips with a scented handkerchief. "I wouldn't suggest anything else."

"Of course not, sir." Marianne placidly set her needle into her tambour frame. "We shall wait for the perfect play."

After a decent interval, Heyward made his farewells and departed Bruton Street, more annoyed than satisfied with his progress so far. He had failed to see Abigail, he had not met the kind of overwhelming acceptance he had expected from William, and, while he thought that Marianne could be persuaded to support his suit, he was under no illusions that William, in this matter, was the one to convince.

Chapter Sixteen

Sebastian parried, feinted, and his blade slipped beneath his opponent's guard, pressing into the soft unprotected flesh beneath his armpit.

"*Touché.*" Lord Harley stepped back, wiping his brow with his shirt sleeve. "That felt like you had an axe to grind, Seb. What did I do?"

Sebastian lowered his point to the floor. He had let his emotions get the better of him, an unforgivable sin on a fencing piste. "A bad night, Harley. But unforgivable. I apologize."

His friend regarded him with a degree of concern. "We all have bad nights, Seb."

"No excuses. I beg your pardon." Sebastian held out his hand. "Forgive the unforgivable, Charles. And if you refuse to fence with me again, I'll understand."

Lord Harley laughed, clasping Sebastian's hand tightly. "Don't be ridiculous, dear boy. We all have our megrims." He clapped a hand over Sebastian's shoulders. "Why are you blue-deviled, my friend?"

"Women," Sebastian told him, knowing the one

word would satisfy Harley. No gentleman would tread on that territory unless invited, and the explanation had the added satisfaction of being true.

"Wine," Harley declared. "'Tis the cure for all such ills."

Sebastian shook his head. "Not in this case, Charles." He laid his épée in the rack along the wall. "Let me buy you dinner in recompense. At the Swan tonight . . . oh, no, not tonight, damn it. I have another engagement." He grimaced. He'd forgotten the Suttons' dinner party, and in present circumstances, it was the last place he wanted to be . . . certainly the last place where he wanted to meet Serena for the first time after the previous night's debacle. But he couldn't cry off at this late date.

Lord Harley shrugged as he shelved his own sword. "Whenever you wish, Seb. It'll be my pleasure, if you really feel the need."

Sebastian managed a laugh. "No, 'tis not need, merely the pleasure I take in your company. Let us make it tomorrow evening." He slung his cloak around his shoulders.

Lord Harley laughed. "The Swan it is. I intend to be expensive, take warning." He swept up his own cloak.

Sebastian shook his head. "Nine, then."

"Nine." They parted on the street, and Sebastian, after a moment, headed for home, reflecting that if he could savage one of his best friends on the piste, he was clearly not good company at the moment.

He let himself into the house. "Perry, you home?"

Bart popped his head around the door to the kitchen regions. "Mr. Peregrine ain't 'ere, sir. He went out about an hour ago."

Sebastian nodded. He hadn't expected to find his brother at home in the middle of the afternoon. "Bring me some bread and cheese, will you, Bart?" He went into the parlor.

Bart followed him. "This come for you, sir." He held out a sealed packet.

Sebastian took it, turning it over in his hand. It was addressed to him in a sharp black script and sealed with the great seal of the Archbishop of Canterbury. With a rather grim smile, he slit the wafer with his thumbnail and unfolded the sheet of heavy vellum. It was, indeed, the marriage license he had applied for. A special license that could be issued only by the Archbishop of Canterbury.

When he'd had his epiphany, as he had thought of it at the time, he had spent a long time working on the logistics. He'd spent rather less, he thought wryly, on the issue of gaining Serena's consent. For some hubristic reason, he'd assumed it would be willingly forthcoming. There were three ways to be married. They could have the banns published on three successive Sundays in the church where the ceremony would be performed, but he doubted Serena would be willing to risk the publicity, not until she was safely away from Pickering Place.

The alternative would be to obtain a license. This could be issued by Sebastian's parish priest. Except that he didn't have one. He and his brothers had given up all semblance of church connections long since. They all shared Jasper's caustic opinion that there was more than enough piety, most of it false and self-serving, in the Blackwater family as it was. Failing the parish priest, the same license could be procured from Doctors' Commons for a trifle, and that would allow them to marry in a parish church in the parish where one of them had been resident for more than fifteen days. He had lived at Stratton Street for more than three years, so that proviso was taken care of. Doctors' Commons, situated just behind St. Paul's, was a college of advocates, loosely affiliated with one or other of the bishops. For a small fee, the advocate would apply to their bishop for the license. It was a simple enough process, but it would mean the ceremony had to be performed in a place where he was well known. And again, that didn't suit the need he felt for secrecy until the marriage was a fait accompli.

The final alternative was what he now held. A special license that could only be obtained from the Archbishop of Canterbury. The cost was huge, more than twenty guineas, but it would enable them to marry at any place and any time they chose. It was really the only solution. Sebastian stood looking down at it in his hand for a long moment. Now he didn't know what to do with it.

He became aware of Bart still standing in the doorway, looking at him with unconcealed curiosity. "Bread and cheese, Bart," he reminded him, and the lad scampered off.

Sebastian put the document in an inner drawer of the secretaire and locked it. He could think of nothing else to do with it at this point. He had no idea whether his relationship with Serena could be salvaged, and he was still too hurt and too confused to attempt it. How could she refuse his protection? *Why* would she refuse it? She walked a tight rope with her stepfather every minute of every day, so why wouldn't she seize the chance to jump off it? She was the most damnably obstinate, impossible woman any man could ever have had the misfortune to love.

He sawed savagely at the loaf of bread Bart had set on the table and stabbed his knife point into the wheel of cheese. Maybe he could force a duel on Heyward, offer some public insult that would compel the general to call him out. For a moment, he allowed his imagination full rein. A misty autumn morning at Barn Elms, six men, the two principals and their seconds. Would he choose pistols or swords? Pistols were quicker, but there was something a lot more satisfying about swordplay, the elegance and speed of steel on steel. And he was known for his skill on the piste. Even Jasper admitted that his younger brother was a fine swordsman.

Jasper and Perry would act for him. Of course, killing a man in a duel had awkward consequences. It usually necessitated a hasty trip to the Continent until it was forgotten. But he and Serena could have an extended honeymoon in Paris or Venice or perhaps Rome. Definitely not Brussels. Serena and her unsavory past would be too well known there.

Of course, this flight of fancy depended on Serena's consent, and after last night, he was a long way from achieving that. He chewed meditatively on bread and cheese, poured himself a glass of claret, and sat down by the fire. If he couldn't take Serena away from her stepfather, maybe the answer was, indeed, to take the stepfather away from Serena. Maybe when she was free, her resistance would crumble. It had been a stupid argument, really. He had no intention of wanting to rule her, of expecting that marriage would give him that right. Maybe with some women it would, but not with Serena. That fierce independence was one of the things he loved most about her. But one thing was now quite clear to him: the sooner he had this out with the infuriating love of his life, the better.

Some time before eight o'clock, he was in position on Pickering Place, watching the front door from the concealment of a shadowy alley opposite. Precisely at eight, the door opened, and a footman came out and ran off in the direction of St. James's Street, presumably to fetch a hackney or a chair for Lady Serena. Soon enough, he reappeared, trotting beside a sedan chair. The chairmen set the chair down at the front door, and the footman disappeared inside. A few minutes later, the door opened again, and Serena appeared.

Sebastian couldn't help a sharply indrawn breath when he saw her. She looked magnificent in flame-colored damask with wide panniers opened over a dramatic black silk underskirt stiff with silver embroidery. Ruffles of silver lace fell over her wrists. As usual, her black hair was unpowdered, and tonight she wore it in the fashion made popular by Madame de Pompadour, dressed high over pads. The chairmen's pitch torches caught the glint of silver among the dusky curls, and he guessed she was wearing the silver fillet left her by her mother. She stepped into the chair, and as the chairmen hoisted their burden, Sebastian stepped up beside the chair, keeping pace with the chairmen.

Oddly, Serena found that she was not surprised by Sebastian's sudden appearance. Of course, things were not over between them. How could they be? She said simply, "Good evening, Sebastian."

"Good evening, Serena." There was a moment of silence, and then he said, "Have you nothing to say to me?"

She sighed. "I don't know what there is to say anymore. Apart from the absurdity of the idea of us marrying, I cannot bear to be ruled by anyone, don't you understand that? For the last ten years, I have been in servitude, and once I'm free, I will not voluntarily put myself under the control of anyone, most definitely not a husband. If that's something you cannot accept, Sebastian, then we have nothing further to say to each other."

He sucked in his lower lip, deciding to postpone

arguing about the absurdity of a marriage itself. "I don't wish to control you . . . rule you, Serena. But surely you can understand the need to protect and care for someone you love."

"Sometimes," she said slowly, "loving someone means letting them go, or at least respecting their wish for freedom, even if you have to stand by and watch them being hurt."

He groaned. "How can I accept that, Serena? I can't stand aside and watch while that brute bullies you."

"He won't do it again," she assured him quietly. "I can promise you that."

"I was thinking that I would challenge him to a duel," Sebastian said, slyly watching her expression through the chair window.

"Challenge him to a . . ." She went into a peal of laughter, and the sound warmed him to the marrow. "Oh, Sebastian, my darling, would you really?"

"If you asked me to," he said, grinning now. "In truth, there is nothing I would like better than to cross swords with that bastard at Barn Elms."

"Mmm." She seemed to consider. "You would certainly do better with swords. The general's counted a first-class shot."

"You doubt my prowess with a pistol?" he demanded with mock indignation.

"No, sir. I do not doubt your prowess in anything," she said with the faintest stress on the last word and one of her mischievous smiles that made his heart sing.

"Oh, God, Serena, how can you do this? You twist me in knots, you turn me inside out, and then you smile like that, and I love you so much I think I'll split apart at the seams."

Her smile faded, and her huge velvety eyes glowed like purple pansies under moonlight. "My dear, I don't understand, either, how we can disagree so powerfully on such vitally important matters and yet still have this . . . this connection. I'm only happy when I'm with you, and yet I'm sometimes more unhappy with you than at any other time."

"We'll find a way through this, Serena. We *have* to," Sebastian said quietly.

The chairmen stopped abruptly, and Sebastian realized they were outside the Suttons' front door on Bruton Street. He offered his hand as Serena stepped out of the chair. He held her hand tightly for a moment, looking into her face, his own eyes speaking volumes. Then he released her hand, paid the chairmen, and gestured to the front door.

"Shall we? 'Tis time to put on our other hats."

Serena nodded and slipped her hand into his arm, murmuring, "Do everything you can to bring out the best in Jonas."

"He's to be there? He told me last night he wouldn't receive an invitation."

"I gather from Abigail that Mr. Sutton had something to say about it."

"Good . . . and unless I much mistake the matter, here comes our friend now."

Serena looked to the corner of the street, where a dark-clad figure was striding energetically towards them. "So it is. And he looks most elegant. Not even Marianne could find anything to object to in his appearance."

"No, indeed. Should we wait for him?" Sebastian had already raised an alerting hand to Jonas.

"You go and meet him. I'll go in. It might look better."

"As you say." Sebastian reached over her shoulder to lift the door knocker, then strode off down the street towards Jonas Wedgwood. "Well met, Wedgwood. Do you come to the Suttons?"

"I received a most unexpected invitation this morning, Mr. Sullivan." Jonas extended his hand and bowed as he reached Sebastian. He was blushing fiercely. "I must beg your pardon for the spectacle I made of myself last evening, sir. I do not know what you must think of me."

"Good God, man, think of you? Why, nothing at all. 'Tis no great matter to dip a little deep into the claret. We've all done it on occasion, and I'm sure we'll all do it again." He shook the young man's hand. "Don't give it another thought. I daresay you had a rough morning," he added sympathetically.

"Not too pleasant," Jonas admitted with a rueful smile. "But I find it passes off quite quickly. I feel perfectly well now."

"Good, then let us go in, and you shall lay delicate siege to the exquisite Miss Sutton."

"I doubt Mrs. Sutton will permit that," Jonas replied.

"I said *delicate,* my friend." Sebastian raised the door knocker. "If you play your cards right, the redoubtable Mrs. Sutton will not see what you're doing . . . ah, Morrison, isn't it? Good evening."

"Good evening, sir. Mr. Wedgwood." The butler bowed and held the door wide. They went past him into the hall, where a footman took their cloaks. "The guests are assembled in the drawing room, gentlemen." Morrison proceeded to the stairs, and they followed him up.

The double doors to the salon stood open, and Morrison announced in ringing tones, "The Honorable Sebastian Sullivan and Mr. Jonas Wedgwood."

Marianne's expression was a picture as she stepped away from a circle of guests and came across to greet the new arrivals. Clearly, she was struggling with the dilemma of how to greet one guest with unequivocal pleasure while acknowledging the other with modified rapture.

"Mr. Sullivan, I'm delighted to see you." She curtsied, extending her hand with an inviting smile.

Sebastian bowed over the hand. "And I'm delighted to be here, ma'am."

Marianne turned to Jonas, who bowed. She had not offered him her hand and merely bobbed her head in place of a curtsy. "Mr. Wedgwood."

"Mrs. Sutton." Jonas cast a comical look of dismay in Sebastian's direction as the lady moved off, but his discomfort was short-lived, as William came barreling across the room towards them.

"Jonas, m'dear boy . . . Mr. Sullivan . . . welcome . . . welcome. Come and take a glass of wine. Champagne tonight . . . nothing else would satisfy m'lady wife. Nothing but the best. I daresay you know most of these people better than I do, eh, Mr. Sullivan . . . and there's Lady Serena . . . looking radiant . . . isn't she a picture? But I say as shouldn't, my little Abigail is showing at her best this evening, don't you think?" He gazed fondly across the room to where Abigail was standing beside Serena in a small group in front of the fire.

Abigail did look enchanting, Sebastian reflected. Her mother, for all her shortcomings, certainly knew how to turn out her daughter. Her gown of ivory crepe opened over an underskirt of anemone blue. She wore a very modest hoop as befitted a debutante and her fair hair, confined at her brow with a pearl-encrusted blue ribbon, clustered around her face in soft ringlets. Her appearance was in perfect taste and set off the girl's pale prettiness to perfection. Although Sebastian's tastes ran to the more dramatic, flame and silver and black, for instance, he could appreciate Abigail's appeal.

Jonas couldn't take his eyes off her. He murmured something in agreement with William, who for all his bonhomie had a shrewd look in his eye as he regarded the young man. A footman brought a tray of champagne, and Jonas took a glass with a murmur of thanks, then moved off dreamily towards Abigail.

William glanced at Sebastian. His wife had confided her hopes that Mr. Sullivan might be brought up to scratch, but he rather doubted it. The Honorable Sebastian had barely glanced at Abigail, but William had not missed his quick, covert glance at Lady Serena. That he could understand. Lady Serena was in a different class altogether from his little Abigail. A grown woman, and for all her unmarried status, William reckoned he knew a woman of experience when he met one. He wouldn't call her an adventuress by any means, but Lady Serena Carmichael was no ingénue. And she and the Honorable Sebastian seemed to him to be two of a kind in some fashion. Not, of course, that it was any of his business.

"I reckon you don't need any introductions, Mr. Sullivan, so I'll leave you to plunge in." He strolled away, wishing he could exchange the insipid champagne for a large bumper of porter.

Sebastian went to join the group around Serena. He bowed to the company in general before offering Abigail a most particular bow, taking her hand and kissing it lightly. "May I congratulate you on your debut, Miss Sutton?"

She laughed a little nervously. "'Tis only a very small debut, Mr. Sullivan."

"True enough," he agreed. "But there's never anything wrong with small. Why be in a hurry?"

"Yes, indeed, Miss Sutton. Why be in a hurry?" Jonas repeated eagerly. "Large things grow from small, you know."

"Oh, I know." Abigail gave a little laugh. "I had the tiniest rabbit once, and before I knew it, she had sixteen babies. And she was still a little thing."

Serena didn't dare look at Sebastian. The group around them were staring in astonishment, and Abigail suddenly became aware that she had said something shocking. She paled, looked around in panic, and Jonas said heartily, "Indeed, Miss Sutton, rabbits are a law unto themselves. I remember a black and white I once had . . ." Still talking, he slipped a hand beneath her elbow and bore her off towards another group of guests across the room.

"Well done," Serena murmured sotto voce. She turned her own attention to distracting the group around her with a particularly scandalous *on dit* about the Duchess of Devonshire that she had been told in the strictest confidence by a drunken player at the hazard table.

Sebastian joined in, encouraging the gossipy laughter, and they were both confident that Abigail's indiscretion would soon be forgotten.

Morrison appeared in the doorway to announce, "Dinner is served, madam."

Marianne surreptitiously consulted the paper Serena had drawn up for her, decreeing who was to take whom down to dinner. "Mr. Sutton, you will take down Lady Mountjoy . . . Mr. Amesworth, will you escort Lady Serena, Mr. Sullivan, will you take down Abigail, Mr. Wedgwood, pray escort Miss Bentley . . ."

Jonas stepped up gallantly to offer his arm to the elderly cousin from Kensington. He had expected nothing else. The rest of the party fell into couples, and the procession made its way to the dining salon.

Serena found that Jonas was seated opposite her. Her own neighbor, Freddy Amesworth, was an easygoing gentleman who wouldn't object if his table mate engaged in a cross-table conversation, so after the first course had been removed, she leaned over the table and said, "Mr. Wedgwood, is there good hunting in your county?" Hunting was Freddy's passion, almost more so than hazard.

Jonas looked up in surprise and with a degree of relief. He had been laboring dutifully with the cousin from Kensington, forcing himself to keep his attention on that lady and his eye from wandering along the table to where Abigail, recovered from her embarrassment, was engaged in lively conversation with Sebastian.

"Excellent, Lady Serena," he said. "We hunt over Hanbury Hill, where Mary Queen of Scots used to hunt, when she was imprisoned at Tutbury Castle and also when Lord Shrewsbury was her guardian. 'Tis magnificent country."

"Ever hunted Rutland country, Wedgwood?" Freddy asked, instantly diverted.

"No, but I have been out with the Beaufort on several occasions."

Serena sat back, exchanging a look with Sebastian. Jonas was now the center of the conversation among the people closest to him, and he was holding his own well. Marianne was looking surprised but also gratified. Her dinner party could be counted a success. Abigail's head moved from side to side, her eyes wide as she followed the conversation, looking entrancingly pretty, with her blue eyes a bright contrast to her dewy complexion. William sat at the head of the table, nodding slightly over his wine glass. Every now and again, he'd jerk awake, look rather guiltily around to see if anyone had noticed his absence, join the conversation for a few moments, and then discreetly nod off again.

Marianne finally rose from the table, and the ladies rose with her. The gentlemen stood courteously as the ladies left the dining room, then settled in with the port. William, at this point, awoke fully. He beckoned to Jonas. "Come sit by me, Jonas. I've wanted to ask you something about your uncle's manufacturing process."

Jonas took the place vacated by Lady Mountjoy, more than happy to conduct such a conversation with his host. Impressing the rest of the dinner company didn't interest him particularly, except as a way of gaining favor with Marianne, but if he had Mr. Sutton as his ally, he would be well up on the totem pole.

In the drawing room, Abigail at her mother's bidding took her place at the harp as teacups were passed around. Serena winced a little at the number of wrong notes but acknowledged that the girl looked pretty as a picture, plucking the strings, her fair curls caressing her rounded cheek, a dreamy smile on her lips. Serena was fairly certain the dreamy smile had little to do with the Welsh folk song she was attempting and guessed that Abigail's thoughts were with Jonas.

Jonas was among the first of the gentlemen to enter the drawing room. He had been very circumspect with the port, remembering the previous night's excesses, and, having collected tea from his frozen-faced hostess, went to stand at Abigail's shoulder as she played. She gave him a quick, shy smile, then, conscious of her mother's eyes upon her, bent her head to her instrument again.

Sebastian had followed on Jonas's heels. He took his tea to where Serena was sitting on a gilt-edged sofa and perched on the scrolled arm beside her. "She looks a picture," he murmured. "Jonas can't take his eyes off her."

"I don't think he has much of an ear for music," Serena said with a soft chuckle. "I think it would be good if Jonas declared himself to Mr. Sutton without delay, don't you?"

"Definitely. Should I prod him?"

Serena shrugged a little. "It can do no harm. The fair lady's heart is well and truly won."

Sebastian nodded and sipped his tea.

The party broke up soon after the rest of the gentlemen entered the drawing room. Sebastian drew Jonas to one side as farewells were being made and Marianne was occupied. "Do you think you've fixed your interest with Miss Sutton, Jonas?"

Jonas looked over at Abigail, who had given up her playing with obvious relief and was standing with her mother at the entrance to the drawing room, curtsying her farewells as the guests moved past them. "I believe so . . . she's such a darling. She looks at me in a way that . . . oh, I must sound like a coxcomb . . . but I do think she looks at me in a special way. Don't you, Sebastian? Just a little particular attention."

Sebastian laughed. "Without doubt, and if you'll take a word of advice, Jonas, don't waste any time in talking with her father. The sooner you've made your interest clear to Mr. Sutton, the better he will like you for it."

"Tonight, d'you think?" Jonas looked both alarmed and excited at the prospect.

"No time like the present." Sebastian gave his shoulder a friendly pat. "Go to it, man. Faint heart never won fair lady, as the proverb says."

"Yes . . . yes, you're right. I'll talk to him right now." Jonas headed back into the drawing room, where William had remained, trying not to nod off in the fire's warmth as the buzz of departing guests continued around him.

He looked up as Jonas coughed politely, standing nervously beside his chair. "Goodness me . . . is that the time?" he exclaimed as the mantel clock chimed midnight. "What kind of a time is that to seek one's bed?"

"I wonder, sir, if I might have just a moment of your time?" Jonas offered a tentative smile.

William frowned, but the sleep had vanished from his eyes, and they regarded the young man shrewdly. "Well, now," he said. " 'Tis a little late for business talk, Mr. Wedgwood. Come and see me tomorrow, eight o'clock, when I've finished my breakfast and my brain's at its sharpest."

Any other young man would quail at the prospect of such an early hour, but Jonas was bred in the same school as William Sutton and accustomed to being at work early in the day. "At eight o'clock, sir." He bowed and smiled. "Good night, sir."

"Good night, Jonas." William nodded at him, concealing his own smile. He was fairly certain what the young man had to say to him, and he was more than pleased about it. Marianne would not be, but, indulgent husband though he was for the most part, the battles he chose to fight with his wife he always won. If his little Abigail wanted Jonas Wedgwood, she should have him.

"Allow me to escort you home, Lady Serena." Sebastian took her cloak from the footman and draped it around her shoulders. "A chair has been summoned for you."

"Thank you, sir. I would welcome the company," she said, her eyes sparkling despite the studied formality of her tone. She took his arm out to the street and settled into the sedan chair.

"Stratton Street," Sebastian instructed the chairmen as they picked up the poles.

Serena raised an eyebrow but said nothing. They said not a word to each other on the short journey. But words were not necessary. The silence was charged with anticipation, with shared secrets, with old wounds that needed to be cauterized.

Outside the house, in the same silence, Sebastian handed Serena out of the chair, paid the men, and took her arm as he inserted his key in the lock. The hallway was in darkness, only a line of candlelight showing from beneath the parlor door.

Sebastian put his head around the door. Perry was gazing at a problem on a chess board, frowning in concentration. He looked up. "Ah, you back?"

"*We* are," his twin said.

"Ah." Perry nodded. "My respects to the lady."

Sebastian backed out and closed the door. "Come." He took Serena's hand and led her up to his bedchamber. He kicked the door shut behind them with the heel of his shoe and stood looking at her for a moment, before, with a tiny cry of exultation, he reached for her, lifting her against him, holding her up.

She laughed down at him. "Oh, are we playing strongman tonight?"

"Samson to your Delilah," he agreed, letting her slide

slowly down his body till her feet touched ground again.

"I promise I won't cut your hair," she murmured, smoothing her hand over the shining fair head before her fingers swiftly untied the velvet ribbon that held the shining queue at his nape.

"Oh, two can play at that game." He took the silver fillet from her hair and then the silver-headed pins, slowly, one at a time, dropping them onto the washstand. He lifted her hair free of the pads that formed the pompadour and then let the blue-black mass cascade over his hands, using his fingers to tease out the tangles in the silky curls.

She turned her head into his hand, her tongue darting to lick the salt skin of his palm. Sebastian caressed the column of her neck, bent his head to kiss her ear, his tongue tracing the intricate whorls, his teeth nibbling the lobe. They said nothing, their bodies expressing all that was necessary. After a moment, they moved apart, their eyes locked as they took off their clothes. Silently, he helped her with ribbons and laces, watched as she unfastened her garters and slid her stockings over her feet. Then naked they came together, her skin cool against his as they fell back together onto the bed.

And cool became heat, and smooth became slippery soft, and hunger became a desperate need to expiate, to heal, to renew. Until finally, they slipped apart to lie flank to flank, exhausted, replete, and restored.

Sebastian wasn't sure whether he had slept when

he became fully aware of his surroundings again. Serena was clamped to his side, one leg thrown across his thighs, her head pillowed in the hollow of his shoulder. Her breath was moist on his cooling skin, her heart beating rhythmically against his ribs. He tried to reach the coverlet to pull it over them without waking her, but she stirred as he moved.

"Don't go."

He kissed her forehead. "I'm not. But I fear you'll catch cold. The fire's almost out."

Slowly, she struggled up against the pillows, her hands crossing over her breasts. "What time is it?"

He swung off the bed, gathering up the coverlet and pulling it over her. "Near dawn." He went to the fire and threw fresh kindling onto the glowing embers. It caught quickly with a crackle and spurt of flame.

"I must go."

"Why?" He stood at the foot of the bed, his body caught by the light from the fire behind. "If, as you say, he can no longer harm you, why would you worry what time you returned?"

Serena leaned back against the pillows and closed her eyes. He was right. She had said she had her stepfather in hand, so what was to stop her doing what she wished, as long as she gave the general what he wanted in the salons?

Sebastian watched her. After a moment, her eyes opened. "Yes," she said. "You're quite right. But for as long as the charade has to continue, just until Abigail is safe, I would prefer not to antagonize him unnecessarily. Can you understand that?"

He sighed. "I suppose I can. I just wished to see what you would say. I'll escort you home in a few minutes, but first . . ." He hesitated, wondering if now was the time. Then he decided if it wasn't now, it never would be.

Chapter Seventeen

"What is it, Sebastian?" Serena frowned at him in puzzlement, wondering why he was standing so still and silent at the foot of the bed. "Why are you staring at me?"

"I didn't realize I was staring. I beg your pardon." He punched one fist into the palm of his other hand as if making up his mind. "Last night, I asked you a question, one you told me was absurd. Now I'm going to ask you again, and I need you to think before you answer. Will you marry me, Serena?"

She paled, her eyes growing huge in her heart-shaped face. Reflexively, she pulled the coverlet up to her chin. "Why would you persist in this, Sebastian? You know 'tis impossible."

"No, not only is it possible, 'tis absolutely the right and proper thing for us. I love you." He spoke steadily, his eyes never leaving her face. "I cannot live without you."

"Marriage to me would ruin you, my dear," she said with soft insistence. "I love you too much to let that happen. A Blackwater cannot wed a member of the demimonde, a fugitive from a river of unpaid debts, a gambler, a cheat . . . a poverty-stricken vagabond." She laughed, a short laugh full of bitterness. "Oh, once, before the general appeared on the scene, it could have been, but not now, my love. You must see that."

He came around to sit on the bed beside her, taking her hands in both of his, holding them tightly. "Will you let me explain to you why 'tis the perfect solution to everything?"

She looked at him, her eyes still huge in her pale countenance. "Must you prolong the agony, Sebastian? You know there is no answer."

For a moment, exasperation flared in the deep blue eyes. Then he shook his head once and said with calm deliberation, "Trust me, Serena. Sit quiet and hear me out before you say another word."

She owed him that, she thought, and even as she thought it, a tiny flicker of hope, a little flare of something remarkably like optimism, crept over her. Could Sebastian possibly have found a way through the maze? Could there be an answer that she just couldn't see? Her fingers fluttered in his hand, and his warm hold tightened. "I do trust you," she said. "I will listen."

He nodded, relief shining in his eyes. "The answer, my love, lies in my uncle's will."

Serena couldn't stop herself despite her promise. "What has that to do with us?" He looked at her in reproving silence, and she sighed. "I beg your pardon."

"So I should hope," he responded, but there was the hint of a smile in his eyes. And then, quietly, he explained Viscount Bradley's will. He explained how he had had his sudden epiphany when he saw his uncle's musings. He was careful to describe none of the details to Serena, merely gave her enough to understand the simple, glorious fact that if the viscount considered her fair game in the world of the demimonde, then he could not argue, despite her conventionally aristocratic breeding, that when she married his nephew, his nephew had not fulfilled the terms of the will.

Serena sat for a long time deep in thought. She was not squeamish about her own position vis-à-vis society, she had lost such delicate sensibilities long since, but her instinctive dislike of Viscount Bradley surged into a deep loathing. *How dare the man make such assumptions, treat me with such contumely?* "Did you hear about Lord Burford's proposal from your uncle?"

"Yes, but does it matter?"

She hesitated. It *did* matter, and yet her pragmatic self told her that it shouldn't. The only thing that really mattered was that, however despicable the means, the end could only bring happiness. Sebastian still held her hands between his, and she could feel his tension, his anxiety about her answer, radiating through his fingers. She looked up at the ceiling, watching the dancing shadows of firelight. "A little, I suppose, but not enough."

"Do you love me, Serena?" He released one of her

hands and used his own to catch her chin, turning her face towards him.

She could not deny it, not even if she wanted to. The truth shone in her eyes. She said simply, "I always have done, from the first moment I saw you."

"As I have you. *Marry* me."

And there was only one answer. "If we can disentangle this tangle, I will, with all my heart."

Sebastian felt a surge of such pure joy he could have danced on the table. He leaned forward, took her face between his hands, and kissed her. A long, slow kiss of final affirmation. "We can disentangle it," he murmured against her mouth. "I have a special license, and we can be wed whenever and wherever we like."

Serena could not respond to that for quite a while as he kissed her again, even more thoroughly than before, but finally, he moved his mouth from hers, trailed a kiss down the side of her neck, and then sat up, smiling at her with a look almost of wonder on his face.

She returned the smile with some of the same wonder. It did, indeed, seem as if they had wandered into a miraculous world where everything was golden. "How do we go about disentangling this? I cannot leave Pickering Place yet. And besides, what will we live on? Until you get your inheritance, that is. I don't imagine you wish to open a gambling hell, and that's about the only business I know."

"Oh, I don't know," he murmured. "I might quite fancy the disreputable life."

"Well, I, for one, have had enough of it," she responded. "So what alternatives do we have?"

He became serious again. "Until my uncle dies, I still have only five thousand pounds to my name." It was rather less than that now, he reflected, after the special license and the six-month lease for the cottage. He went on musingly, "Of course, if we moved to the country in the interim, we could live very cheaply, even grow our own food."

Serena began to laugh despite the gravity of the discussion. "Oh, dearest Seb, you don't know one end of a spade from the other. And you couldn't identify a carrot if it wasn't cooked and buttered on your plate."

"I'm not so feeble," he denied, but then his eyes began to dance with merriment as he saw the funny side. They would be married. What difference did it make what they lived on?

Serena, smiling, said, "I didn't say you were feeble, just not educated to till the soil and plant the corn." Then she became serious again. "But you said that your brothers, too, must satisfy the terms of the will if any of you are to inherit. Can you be sure that will happen?"

"Jasper is already married. You'll like Clarissa . . . Lady Blackwater. She's rather like you in many respects."

"Oh?" Serena's interest was piqued. "How?"

"Independent, determined to pursue her own course, definitely not one to love, honor, and obey with any enthusiasm," he said with a teasing smile.

Serena accepted that that particular quarrel was a

thing of the past and didn't respond to the comment. Instead, she asked, "What of Peregrine?"

"He'll do what's necessary. He knows there is no choice."

"So what do we do now?" she asked. "I won't leave Pickering Place until Abigail is out of the general's way."

Sebastian sighed. He hadn't really expected anything else, although he had half hoped. "As I said, I have a special license—"

"You were very confident, weren't you?" she interrupted, and then gave a little squeal as he reached for her, hauling her towards him across the bed. "I beg your pardon, I didn't mean to interrupt." She laughed up at him as she lay with her head on his lap.

For answer, he placed a finger firmly on her lips. "Keep quiet and listen. We will be married as soon as possible, wherever you wish. And afterwards, you may return to Pickering Place just until Abigail is out of the way. And believe me, Serena, that's not going to be very long. If something goes wrong with the Wedgwood proposal, then I will tell Sutton the whole truth and get him to whisk his daughter back to the safety of Stoke-on-Trent. And that, my love, is a promise."

There was no way she was going to allow that to happen, but Serena kept that to herself. "Very well," she said amenably.

Sebastian looked suspiciously down at her upturned face. "I do mean it, Serena."

"Yes, my dear, I know you do." She touched his mouth with her fingertip. "No need to look so stern."

He gave up. "So when d'you wish to be married, and where?"

Serena considered. "There seems little point in waiting," she mused. "Tomorrow, or rather today . . . is that too soon?"

"Oh, no," Sebastian murmured. "Not too soon at all. Where shall it be?"

Serena's eyes lit up. "In that little church in Knightsbridge. No one will know us there."

"Tomorrow in Knightsbridge it shall be." He lifted her so that she was sitting on his knee, her face level with his. "Will you mind if I bring my brothers as witnesses?"

She shook her head. "No, of course not. Besides, I'd like to meet the Earl of Blackwater and his countess. I'm interested to see if she truly does resemble me."

"Oh, trust me, you two will get on like a house on fire."

Jonas Wedgwood was banging the doorknocker of the house in Bruton Street five minutes before eight that morning. Morrison didn't seem in the least surprised to see this very early visitor.

"Mr. Sutton is at breakfast, sir. If you'd come this way." He escorted Jonas to a small room at the back of the house, where William was consuming his first breakfast; the second and less serious took place when the ladies eventually made an appearance.

He looked up from his veal cutlets as Jonas was announced. "Come in . . . come in . . . take a seat. What'll you have? These cutlets are very fine, but I can vouch for the deviled kidneys, unless you've a hankering for the black pudding and the oat cakes. Can't get those in London, but m'cook knows exactly how I like 'em. Try 'em, dear boy."

"Thank you, sir. I haven't had an oat cake for two months." Jonas helped himself liberally from the sideboard. "And blood pudding, too. Wonderful."

William nodded his approval. "These southern folk don't know good food . . . all this namby-pamby fricassee and coddled eggs. How's a man supposed to do a day's work on that?"

"How indeed, sir." Jonas sat at the table with a laden plate and nodded his thanks when a full tankard of ale was pushed towards him.

"So." William buttered a hunk of bread. "What was it you wished to talk about?"

Jonas choked on his oat cake. In the joys of such a familiar breakfast, he'd actually forgotten for a moment what had brought him there. He recovered quickly, took a swallow of ale, and stated, "I wish to offer for your daughter, sir."

William nodded. "Always did like a man who didn't beat about the bush," he said. "What does Abigail think of this?"

Jonas looked a little shocked. "I haven't approached her directly, sir. It wouldn't be proper before I spoke with you."

"Oh, stuff and nonsense. If a man likes a maid, he makes it clear, and if she likes him, she makes it clear back."

"I do think Miss Sutton . . . Abigail . . . returns my regard," Jonas said with some difficulty. "Nothing has been said exactly, but . . ."

William laughed and refilled his tankard. "Yes . . . yes. I think you're right. Well, you have my blessing, my friend. Whether you'll have Mrs. Sutton's is another matter. She's her heart set on a magnificent marriage for Abigail." He shrugged. "I'd have no objection if I thought the child wanted that, too, but I'm not so sure about that. I think she'll be more comfortable among her own kind."

"Oh, yes, sir, so do I," Jonas said with so much enthusiasm he blushed brick red. "I can give her everything, sir. Every comfort, her own carriage, a fine house, a harp—"

"Don't, I beg you." William lifted an arresting hand. "You'll regret a harp to your dying day. A pianoforte, maybe."

Jonas dropped his eyes to his plate, trying to conceal his amused agreement with his love's fond papa. "Whatever you say, sir."

"Well, I'll talk to Abigail and then to Mrs. Sutton, and we must hope for the best in that quarter." William returned his attention to his breakfast and his newspaper.

Jonas knew better than to renew a conversation that was clearly over. He finished his breakfast with enjoyment, rose, thanked his host, and made for the door.

"Come back this evening, Jonas. Take your pot luck with us," William instructed as the young man opened the door. "If you're going courting, best to start right."

"Yes, sir." Beaming, Jonas went into the hall and out into the chill but sunny morning, feeling as if all was right with the world.

William completed his own breakfast and went into the library to start on the day's business. At ten o'clock, he heard his wife's voice from the hall telling Morrison to serve breakfast, and a few minutes later, Abigail's light step sounded on the stairs a moment before she put her shining head around the library door.

"Good morning, Papa."

"Good morning, m'dear." He beamed at her. "Fresh as a daisy, pretty as a picture, as always."

Her blue eyes sparkled. "Mama said to tell you breakfast is served."

"I'll be along in a minute."

Abigail closed the door and went into the dining parlor, where Marianne was already seated in front of the teapot. "Is your father coming, Abigail?"

"In a minute." Abigail took her seat at the table and smiled her thanks as a maid set a plate of eggs in front of her. She glanced covertly at her mother, trying to gauge her mood. Marianne had said nothing to her daughter last night, apart from bidding her good night as usual, and Abigail was curious to know what her mother had thought of the evening.

"The dinner party went well, don't you think, Mama?" she ventured after a moment.

Marianne sipped her tea and buttered a finger of toast before saying, "On the whole, yes, I think I did."

Abigail knew her mother too well to let this stand. "But?" she said.

Marianne dipped her toast into her tea. "I'm sorry your father insisted on young Mr. Wedgwood's being invited. I felt quite sorry for the poor young man . . . a fish out of water. You could see how uncomfortable he felt among such Society folk."

"Oh, I didn't think he was uncomfortable at all, Mama." Abigail's eyes flashed a little. "He seemed to have plenty to talk about with the other guests, particularly hunting. They all seemed to pay him most particular attention, I thought."

"Hunting is not a suitable subject for a dinner table," Marianne declared, closing her lips tightly.

Abigail's eyes opened wide. "But Mama, 'twas Lady Serena who introduced the subject."

Her mother contented herself by attacking her toast with the butter knife, rather as if it were vermin that required extermination. Abigail continued with her eggs in silence until William's entrance broke the tension.

"Ah, good morning . . . good morning, my dears. You slept well, I trust, Mrs. Sutton."

"Not particularly well, Mr. Sutton," Marianne responded with a sniff.

William helped himself to bacon and tomatoes from the covered dish on the sideboard. "I'm sorry to hear that, my dear." He sat down and twinkled at Abigail. "So, puss, how would you like to be Lady Heyward, eh?"

Abigail paled. Her mother dropped the finger of toast she was dipping into her teacup.

"Yes, it seems that our little Abigail has caught herself a good husband quicker than we expected," her husband continued with a bland smile, forking bacon into his mouth. "Doesn't surprise me, though. Such a pretty, clever puss as she is. What d'you say to that, then, Mrs. Sutton?"

Marianne wiped her mouth delicately with a lace-edged napkin. "Has the general spoken to you, then, Mr. Sutton?"

"Yesterday. Asked my permission to address the girl." William glanced at Abigail with a sly smile. "I told him it was up to Abigail. So, how would you have me answer the general, puss?"

Abigail pushed aside her half-eaten plate of eggs. "I do not wish to marry General Heyward, Papa." Her eyes darted to her mother, who was beginning to turn an alarming shade of puce. "Forgive me, Mama, but I cannot like him. He's so . . . so *old*."

"Nonsense," Marianne declared. "I daresay he's not above five and forty. A man in his prime, vigorous, successful, a respectable member of Society."

"Now, don't badger the child, Mrs. Sutton. If she'll not have him, she'll not have him."

"She *will* have him." Marianne fixed her daughter with a gimlet eye. "You can't expect a chit of a girl to know what's best for her, Mr. Sutton. I tell you, she *will* have him."

"I will not." Abigail threw her napkin to the table, pushed back her chair, and ran from the room.

"Now, see what you've done, Mrs. Sutton," William said, not without a degree of satisfaction. His daughter's reaction had been all he had hoped.

"You would see our precious child waste away an old maid," Marianne cried. "Just because the child has taken a notion into her head that Sir George is too old for her, she'll wither on the vine . . . wither on the vine." She burst into noisy tears.

William sighed and continued placidly with his breakfast until the storm had abated somewhat. "Now . . . now, my dear. Nothing so dire is going to happen to Abigail. I already have another, most suitable offer in hand for her."

His wife's tears dried miraculously as a wonderful thought occurred to her. "Another . . . oh, could it be . . . oh, do not keep me in suspense, sir."

"I fancy you have a pretty good notion already, my dear."

Marianne could think of only one possibility. "Our daughter marrying into the family of an earl . . . oh, Mr. Sutton, what a wonderful thing!"

"Eh?" He blinked. "An earl, you say. Oh, I doubt Mr. Wedgwood has any earls in his family, ma'am."

"Mr. Wedgwood?" His wife stared at him. "That . . . that tradesman's son?"

"You seem to be forgetting, my dear, that your daughter is a tradesman's daughter," William pointed out drily. "If she's good enough for him, then I daresay he's good enough for her."

"Oh, but Mr. Sutton . . . *William* . . . you know my hopes. We came to London to give Abigail a Season, to give her the chance to make a fine match. She could have married Jonas Wedgwood in Stoke-on-Trent."

"And I daresay that's exactly where she will marry him, if she wishes." William sighed. "Come now, my dear. Look at the bright side. You'll have your daughter well married before she's eighteen. I daresay your friends will be green with envy. They don't have a daughter among them who can hold a candle to our little Abigail."

"But that's exactly the point," wailed Marianne. "Abigail is so lovely, she could make a stunning match, but you would throw her away on a *Wedgwood*."

"They are a fine family, ma'am. I'll not hear them traduced."

William's tone of voice was one his wife had heard rarely during their marriage, but it was one she understood. She subsided into her handkerchief.

"Well, we'll hear what Abigail has to say about it," William said, his tone now soothing. "She may dislike the idea, for all I know."

"I hope she has a better appreciation of her own merits than to agree to such a match. I have the headache. I shall go and lie on my bed." Marianne rose and swept from the room.

William drained his ale tankard and followed her. "Morrison, ask Miss Abigail to come to the library immediately." He wanted to tell his daughter himself, before Marianne could get her oar in.

Abigail had locked herself in her chamber and was pacing restlessly, tearing at her cambric handkerchief, when Morrison knocked on her door. "Your father wishes to see you in the library, Miss Sutton. Immediately, he said."

Abigail hesitated, but she didn't have the courage to disobey a summons from her father. He was a doting parent, always inclined to indulge his daughter, but there was no question about his being the master of the house. She unlocked the door and hurried past Morrison, glancing once at the closed door to her mother's chamber.

William was awaiting her in the library and smiled cheerfully as she came in. "There, now, puss, let's have no more tears. What a to-do about nothing."

" 'Tis not nothing, Papa, when you would force me into a loathsome marriage." She scrumpled the handkerchief tightly in her balled fist.

He shook his head. "Such a drama, child. No one will force you into anything. But I do have another offer for you to consider."

Abigail's heart jumped.

"Young Jonas Wedgwood called upon me this morning and asked me for permission to address you. What d'you say to that, puss?"

His daughter's expression told him all he needed to know, and he smiled with satisfaction.

"Oh, yes . . . yes, *please,* Papa," Abigail managed to say at last, clapping her hands like an excited child. "I do like him so very much."

"Good. Then that's settled."

Abigail looked suddenly doubtful. "But Mama . . ." she began hesitantly.

"Oh, you leave your mother to me, m'dear. She would never stand in the way of your happiness, Abigail, once she sees that's where it lies." He patted her shoulder, then kissed her brow. "Jonas is coming to take his pot luck with us this evening, so you go and buy yourself some new frippery. Look your best for him, and I'll persuade your mama to leave you two alone for a few minutes so that the young man can make his declaration to you himself."

"Yes, Papa." Abigail flung her arms around his neck and kissed him. "You are the *best* father anyone could ever wish for." She ran off, and he heard her calling to Morrison, "Have the barouche brought around in an hour, please, and tell Matty I will need her to accompany me shopping this morning."

William resumed his business, knowing it would be best to leave quiet reflection to do its work on his wife. His peace was short-lived, however. Half an hour later, Morrison announced General Sir George Heyward.

William grimaced, but he was never one to shirk an unpleasant duty. "Show him in, Morrison, and bring some of that sherry wine these London folk seem to like." He could at least offer the man a drink to soften the blow.

Heyward came in, rubbing his hands, beaming broadly, with every appearance of bonhomie. "Good morning, Sutton. And 'tis a fine bright one." He extended his hand with a little military bow.

William shook hands and bowed in turn. "Have a seat, sir." He gestured to a fireside chair. "Oh, here's Morrison. A glass of sherry, General?"

"With pleasure, Sutton." Still with his jovial smile, Heyward received the glass from the butler and settled back into his chair. He waited until Morrison had left before broaching the subject of his visit. "So, Sutton, have you discussed my offer with your dear lady and little Abigail?"

"I have." William looked pensively into his own glass. "Fact is, General, the child don't much fancy the idea."

Heyward's expression changed, lost all sign of conviviality. His eyes darkened, his jaw clenched. "Why's that, sir?"

"Got the odd notion you're too old for her," William said, still somewhat pensive.

"Nonsense . . . utter nonsense," his visitor blustered. "A man in his prime . . . I daresay I could beat any of these young bloods at whatever sport he might choose. Oh, I grant you, I've a deal more worldly experience than these youngsters who think the world belongs to them, but experience is no bad thing in a husband, Sutton."

William gave a light shrug. "Well, that's as may be, General. But the girl won't have you. Simple, but there it is."

The general's complexion became a dark, angry red, and his small eyes filled with fury. "If she were mine, she'd know better than to disobey her father."

"Oh, Abigail's biddable enough," William said mildly. "But I'm disinclined to compel her in such a matter. 'Tis her life, after all, and if her heart lies elsewhere, then that's the way it is."

"She has accepted another offer?" Heyward's voice was now very quiet, little more than a hiss.

"In a word, sir, yes." William stood up as his visitor sprang from his chair like a jack-in-the-box.

"You led me to believe there was no competition for the girl," the general accused, pointing a finger at his host.

William shook his head. "No, sir, I did not. At the time, I said I would put it to my daughter. Her answer you now know. I believe that closes the matter." He was angry himself now. In his opinion, the general was behaving like a cad. Any gentleman worthy of the title would have mastered his disappointment and gone on his way without a further word.

Heyward stood, red-faced and glaring, for a long moment, then spun on his heel and marched out. The front door slammed in his wake, making the house shake.

"Good riddance," William muttered, wondering what Marianne would say if she'd witnessed that display. Abigail was well out of it.

General Heyward stormed into the house on Pickering Place and slammed his way into the library. He filled a goblet with brandy and tossed it down, refilled it, and as his rage dropped from full boil to an angry simmer, he considered his situation. Marriage to the little Sutton had been his last chance to get a handle on things before they spun out of control. Burford's disappointment at not getting Serena into his bed had turned nasty, and his threats to call in the mortgages grew more persistent by the day. Heyward knew he could not meet the payments, even with a killing at the tables.

He opened the desk drawer and took out the accounts, sheets of parchment covered in Serena's neat columns of figures. Addition, subtraction, division—it was all there, and the conclusion was unmistakable. They were making small profits every night but nothing large enough to make a one-off dent in the debts. Serena had always stressed the need to build profits slowly, cautioning that if the bank started to win particularly heavily, then the gamers would become suspicious, and however addicted they were to faro, they wouldn't play where the odds were consistently so heavily against them. There were other gambling houses.

He needed one coup. One perfect coup that would banish his troubles once and for all. Abigail Sutton was that coup. It was simply a question of how to effect it. He took his brandy to the window and looked out at the bare trees. An idea slowly took shape; it would need a little refinement, but it would work. The chit was such a naïve little fool; she would fall into his hand like a ripe plum. His reflections were disturbed by a sharp rap on the door. It was a rap he recognized. Serena was never one for gentle taps.

"What is it?"

She came in. "I just wished to inform you that I am going to be out for the day. I will be back for this evening."

"And where are you going?"

"Oh, just visiting friends," she said vaguely. "No one you know. But I will be back in plenty of time for the evening."

He glared at her, wanting more than anything to assert himself but knowing that he couldn't. That Rubicon had been crossed. As long as Serena performed her allotted tasks in the gaming salons, he could demand nothing else from her. He needed her skills more than ever at present, and that knowledge, together with his helplessness, burned like acid. The time for his vengeance would come, however.

He contented himself with a curt "See that you are."

Serena nodded and stepped back, closing the door firmly, and her stepfather sat down at the desk, drew a sheet of parchment towards him, and sharpened a quill. An unpleasant little smile twitched his fleshy lips as he began to compose.

Chapter Eighteen

Serena felt a warm glow of satisfaction as she hurried out of the house. She had been right to tell Sebastian her stepfather's reign of terror was finished. She walked quickly to the corner and smiled when she saw the Blackwater coach standing a few yards away, the door open and Sebastian waiting on the pavement by the footstep. He looked every inch a bridegroom in a suit of midnight-blue silk, a waistcoat of silver brocade, a froth of Brussels lace at his throat and wrists, his shining fair hair caught at his nape with a silver clasp, silver buckles winking on his shoes.

He greeted her with a seductive smile, eased her up into the carriage with his hand beneath her elbow, and jumped in after her, pulling up the footstep and closing the door. The coach started forward at once. He leaned back, regarding her closely. "No difficulties?"

"None." She smiled. "I told you, love, I've drawn his teeth."

"I'll not rest easy until you're out of that hellhole," he stated.

She shrugged. "Once Jonas has made his move, I can make mine." She glanced around the dim space. "Did you decide not to bring your brothers and Lady Blackwater?"

"No, they'll meet us there. Perry will ride over, and Jasper will drive Clarissa in his curricle."

"What did they say?" She tried to conceal her curiosity by leaning back into the corner shadows, but in truth, she was both curious and a little anxious. She knew Peregrine had reservations about her. She had never met the earl but guessed that if he knew the history, he, too, would regard this union with less than complacence. And she had more than once sensed the closeness of the fraternal bond that bound the three Blackwater brothers. It would not do for her to be a splinter in that bond.

Sebastian smiled a little. Peregrine, incredulous at first, had listened to the neat scheme whereby his twin's love affair could be translated into the perfect, will-satisfying love match, and then he had laughed as the full beauty of the idea sank in. He had said only, "If you're sure this will make you happy, Seb, then I am happy for you both."

Jasper had been a little more reserved, listening in frowning silence to his brother's explanation before saying, "Lady Serena made you very unhappy once." Sebastian had simply said that Serena had had her reasons and they were good and sufficient. That was all in the past. Jasper had then given them both his blessing and promised that he and Clarissa would be at the wedding.

"They wished us both happy," Sebastian now told Serena with a tranquil smile.

She wasn't sure she was quite convinced but accepted the assurance anyway. She would judge for herself.

The journey to Knightsbridge passed quietly. After the night's passionate encounters, the urgency of their time together seemed to be less pressing; there was time to sit in reflective silence, time to smile, to touch hands, to make the occasional casual remark. And Serena wondered if marriage would be like this, a serene, companionable closeness. She thought with an inner smile that while that was pleasant, the calm would need to be punctuated by more than the occasional bouts of passion.

Sebastian was thinking much the same as he regarded her through half-closed lids. He wasn't sure which of the many facets of Serena he found the most exciting. She was so wonderfully passionate, whether in love or fury, but then, in the next breath, she could be as calm and rational as a philosopher. He adored her for her loyalty, her caring, even as it exasperated him when it interfered with his own plans. If it weren't for that aspect of her character, they would be on their way to Venice by now, married, certainly poor, although that he hoped would be temporary, but safe and happy. Instead of which, she still teetered on her tight rope, he still stood helplessly on the sidelines, while they waited for Serena's self-designated charge to escape her stepfather's greedy grasp.

"What are you thinking?"

At the soft question, he opened his eyes properly, saying vaguely, "Oh, a variety of things, but all of them about you."

"Won't you share them?"

He shook his head. "Oh, no, you might become conceited."

She laughed and leaned sideways to look out of the window. "We passed the Knightsbridge toll, so we must be nearly there."

They pulled up outside the little cottage and went inside, where they were greeted with warm surprise. "Why, Mr. Sullivan, you didn't tell me you was coming. I haven't prepared anything, but there's a chicken in the yard just about ready for eating. I'll have that in the pot in no time."

"First, Mistress Greene, we have to talk to the vicar," Sebastian said. "Where will I find him, do you know?"

Mistress Greene looked startled. "Why, at this time, he'll be in the vicarage, I'm thinking, sir. 'Tis hard by the church." She looked curiously between them. "Something special, is it?"

"Yes, Mistress Greene, a wedding." Sebastian couldn't conceal his delight. "And we shall have the chicken to furnish the wedding feast. Will it serve to feed five, d'you think?"

"Oh, my goodness, well, glory be." She clapped her hands in delight. "I loves a good wedding. I'll need more than one chicken, that's for sure, and I'll have to get young Jen to give me a hand, then. Now, ma'am, you'll be wantin' to refresh yourself afore going' to the church, I'll be bound. Come along abovestairs, and I'll bring up hot water and a nice glass of elderflower wine to soothe your nerves."

Serena thanked her with a smile. The last thing her nerves needed was soothing. She followed the landlady up to the bedchamber, where everything looked just as it had before—clean as a new pin, fresh and sweet, smelling of potpourri and the lavender strewn between the sheets.

Sebastian went off to the church, whose steeple showed above the thatched roofs of the cottages in the center of the village. He found the vicarage next door and was shown by an elderly lady into a study, where the Reverend Simon Boothby was dozing by his fireside.

"Vicar, a visitor," the lady said, her voice loud enough to qualify almost as a shout.

The dozing vicar started awake. "Oh, my goodness me." He fumbled for his glasses, which had slipped off the end of his nose. He set them straight and peered at Sebastian. "What can I do for you, sir?"

"Marry me, in a word, vicar." Sebastian handed him the special license.

"Oh, my goodness me," the vicar repeated, examining the paper. "Well, well, don't see many of these in my parish." He looked up at Sebastian, his gaze unexpectedly shrewd. "Where's the lady, may I ask?"

"Getting ready at Mistress Greene's house," Sebastian said. "I do assure you, vicar, the lady is more than of age, is very much in favor of our union, and is as eager as I to have the marriage performed."

The vicar heaved himself to his feet. "Well, if that's all so, then we may as well proceed. Did you bring witnesses?"

"My brothers should be here soon, sir."

"Good . . . good. You go on and fetch the good lady, then, while I fetch my cassock. I'll see you in church."

Sebastian bowed his way out and hurried back to the cottage. Serena was waiting for him at the front door. She had chosen to be married in a gown of russet velvet edged in silver lace, with a fur-trimmed cloak of rich cream velvet with a high collar of deep sable fur. Her black hair hung loose to her shoulders, and she looked somehow younger than he had seen her since their disastrous parting three years earlier. Certainly more carefree, he thought with a surge of pleasure. He took her hand, raised it to his lips. "The vicar awaits, my love."

"Then it would be impolite to keep him waiting any longer." She tucked her gloved hand into his elbow, and they walked the short distance to the church.

Jasper's curricle stood at the lych-gate, and he was in the act of handing his wife down as the bridal pair approached. He looked particularly elegant in a dark silk coat and breeches, a striped waistcoat, a diamond in the fall of Michelin lace at his throat, but he would cheerfully admit that his wife outdid him. Clarissa's gown of emerald-green damask embroidered with silver thread was a perfect complement to the titian hair falling from a high knot in a cascade of ringlets around her face. A velvet traveling cloak edged with silver fox hung open over the gown's wide panniers. Her shoes of green kid had scarlet heels.

Serena felt a warm glow. It seemed that the Earl of Blackwater and his bride, whether they approved of the marriage or not, were prepared to celebrate in style.

Jasper stepped forward as Sebastian and Serena came up to them. He bowed deeply, taking Serena's hand and bringing it to his lips. "Lady Serena, an honor, ma'am."

"My lord." She curtsied as deeply. "Thank you for being here."

Jasper straightened, but he kept her hand for a moment, looking closely at her. Then he said with a smile, "I wouldn't miss my little brother's nuptials for the world, Lady Serena. May I make you known to my wife?" He gestured to Clarissa, who stepped forward. "Lady Blackwater, Lady Serena Carmichael."

"Oh, enough formality," the countess declared, coming close to kiss Serena lightly on the cheek. "My name is Clarissa, and we are to be great friends, united in the same cause." Her jade eyes twinkled, and Serena couldn't help an answering chuckle.

"I hope so, Clarissa," she said.

"You are all before me," a cheerful voice called. "And I made sure I would arrive before Jasper and his curricle." Peregrine, on a bobtailed gray gelding, rode up to the lych-gate. He examined the little group with a nod of approval, declaring, "My, we are all very fine." He swung down from his horse and handed the reins to Jasper's groom, who was holding the curricle's pair. "I hope I do justice to you all." He was dressed in a suit of black velvet and gold brocade, and his fair hair was caught at the back of his neck with a black velvet ribbon.

"Rest assured you do justice to the occasion, my boy," Jasper responded in the mock-lofty tone of an elder brother.

Peregrine greeted his sister-in-law with a warm kiss, then bowed to Serena, kissing her hand. "Lady Serena, I wish you and my brother very happy."

It sounded sincere, and Serena could see nothing but sincerity in his eyes. She smiled. "Thank you, sir."

"Oh, we'll be done with formality soon enough," Perry said cheerfully. "I shall kiss you as my sister-in-law as soon as the business is done."

"Then I suggest we get on with it." Jasper waved a hand in the direction of the church door. He offered his arm to his wife.

The vicar was standing in front of the altar, prayer book in hand, as the little procession came up the aisle. He waited until they were gathered in a semicircle in front of the altar, the bride and groom in the center, before he began the service. Serena wondered for a moment if Sebastian had thought to bring a ring. Everything had been arranged in such haste it wouldn't be surprising if it had slipped his mind. It was on the tip of her tongue to interrupt the service to ask him, but the reverend gentleman was in full flood, and it seemed rude to disrupt his flow.

She needn't have worried, however. At the appropriate moment, Sebastian reached into an inside pocket of his silver brocade waistcoat and drew out a piece of lace. He unwrapped it to reveal a delicate circlet of seed pearls and amethysts. Serena gave him her hand, and he slipped the ring on her finger. It could almost have been made for her, she thought, smiling at its delicacy, its lack of ostentation. She looked at Sebastian, who raised an interrogative eyebrow, a half-smile on his lips. She nodded, and he seemed visibly to relax as he nodded in his turn.

The vicar pronounced them man and wife, they signed the register, Jasper and Peregrine signed their own names in the register, and it was done. Sebastian slipped a golden guinea into the vicar's palm as he shook hands, and they walked arm-in-arm, leading the little family procession into the bright wintry sunlight, blinking a little after the church's dimness.

Sebastian stopped under the lych-gate, turning to Serena, his eyes devouring her. "So, wife."

"So, husband." Serena chuckled. "You are looking very pleased with yourself."

"I'm *feeling* very pleased with myself." Sebastian gave a deep sigh of satisfaction. "At last, I have you, Serena. Finally, you belong to me."

A shadow passed across her eyes, then she dismissed

it with a quick shake of her head. She understood what he meant. "And I have you," she said softly.

He drew her tightly into his arms, his hands cupping her face as he kissed her eyelids, the tip of her nose, and then her mouth. It was a long, slow kiss of affirmation there in the open street, as heedless of the family audience as he was of curious eyes at cottage windows, and Serena felt as if nothing of importance had occurred in her life until that moment.

Jasper exchanged a glance with Peregrine, who nodded infinitesimally. Jasper nodded, too. It was good. When the bridal pair finally drew apart, Jasper said, "So do we return to town now? Or find some hostelry for a wedding feast?"

"Oh, 'tis all taken care of," Sebastian said. "Our landlady is preparing chickens."

"Landlady?" Peregrine raised an eyebrow.

Sebastian merely grinned. Jasper said, "Well, that's all to the good, since I had the foresight to put a case of some of Blackwater's finest burgundy into the curricle. My groom's watching over it now at that inn . . . the Bear and Ragged Staff, I believe."

"Then let us go."

The wedding feast was everything Serena thought it should be. The food was plain but plentiful and well cooked, the wine flowed, and the company was convivial. Within an hour, she was feeling as if she belonged in this family, and Sebastian had been quite right—she and Clarissa were two of a kind.

"Let us stay here tonight," Sebastian murmured as their guests finally took their leave. "There's no need for you to go back now . . . now or ever."

For a moment, Serena was tempted. How easy it would be to throw away the old life as if it had never existed. If she never went back to Pickering Place, it would all be over. Then she put temptation aside. Not yet. It would be cowardly to give in before she had completed her self-appointed task. She could never live with herself if she abandoned Abigail at this juncture.

"We have an hour before we must go," she said.

Sebastian sighed but said only, "Then let us put it to good use, wife of mine. 'Tis time to consummate this marriage."

"You understand what to do?" General Heyward regarded his visitor with a scowl.

The individual was a man of few words and contented himself with a nod as he continued to pick his teeth with the tip of his dagger. "Deliver the letter to Bruton Street." He patted the inside pocket of his waistcoat.

"And then what?" Heyward demanded, his frustration obvious.

The man shrugged. "I understand that if'n you pays me what we agree, 'alf now and 'alf on delivery, then I'll do the job just like you want. If that's not good enough for ye, then 'tis no skin off *my* nose."

General Heyward's nostrils flared as his temper rose,

but he knew from experience not to press the man, who had never failed him yet, despite his insolence and infuriating taciturnity. But if he took against a job or decided he wasn't being treated with suitable respect, he was perfectly capable of abandoning the business without a word.

"So, if'n you'll give me the ready, I'll be gettin' on wi' it, then." The man sheathed his dagger at his belt.

Heyward opened a billfold. "Twenty, we said."

The suggestion received a short, derisive laugh. "For a fast chaise an' all those changes on the road? Don't make me laugh. Fifty."

The general peeled off two bank notes and went to the desk to unlock a drawer. He withdrew a purse of sovereigns, counted out ten, and pushed them across the desk. His visitor slid them off and bit each one with a reflective air before dropping them into the pocket of his moleskin waistcoat. "Right, I'll be off, then."

"You'll let me know when you've delivered the letter?"

The question was not dignified by a response, and the man in the moleskin waistcoat left the library without a word of farewell. He was crossing the hall to the front door when Flanagan materialized from the shadows behind the staircase.

"Kitchen door," the butler said, gesturing behind him to the door to the back regions.

The man in the moleskin waistcoat gave him a look of contemptuous indifference and continued on his way to the front door, which opened as he reached it. He brushed past Serena as she came in and hurried off down the street.

Serena stood in the doorway for a moment, frowning. What was her stepfather up to now? She knew the visitor. He was always nameless, but she knew the general employed him to deal with the occasional young man who found it difficult to meet his gambling debts. One visit from the moleskin waistcoat was usually sufficient to ensure instant payment.

She shrugged and headed for the stairs. It was already past five o'clock, and she had to dress for the evening.

"Good evening, Lady Serena." Flanagan bowed. "Cook is rather put out. I wonder if you would see her for a few minutes."

"Yes, of course. What's the matter?"

"A problem with the fish, I understand, ma'am. Not as fresh as she would like."

"Oh, dear." Serena grimaced. The cook was of a somewhat temperamental nature and inclined to see disaster where none really existed. "I'll go to the kitchen now." Her idyllic day was well and truly over, it would seem. She touched her ring finger, smiling at the feel of the dainty circlet beneath her glove. She would have to take it off before she saw her stepfather, of course, but for the moment, whenever she touched it, the memories of the afternoon would become so wonderfully vivid she had difficulty keeping a smile from her lips.

She dealt with the kitchen crisis by suggesting that

the cook prepare chickens in elderflower sauce instead of the spoiled whitefish. "Either is lovely with the sauce," she offered in soothing accents, and was relieved to receive a rather dour nod in response. She hurried upstairs to dress, preparing herself for the evening's social obligations and mental gymnastics.

Chapter Nineteen

Jonas Wedgwood presented himself at the house on Bruton Street with a carefully chosen posy of hothouse winter roses for his hostess. He was nervous about his reception by the lady of the house but did his best to appear confident. He thought of Sebastian and tried to emulate that easy manner, the appearance of being totally comfortable in his skin. He knew his dress was impeccable. His coat of dark blue silk was perfectly complemented by his striped waistcoat of blue and silver damask. His knee breeches were dove-gray silk, his stockings plain white. In the froth of lace at his throat, a diamond winked, as good a gem, he thought, as any in Mrs. Sutton's jewel box. Tucked into an inside pocket of his coat was a small packet containing a delicately engraved silver locket that he thought was perfect for Abigail. In perfect taste, not too ostentatious, not in the least vulgar. No mother could object to her daughter's receiving such a gift from her betrothed.

Always assuming the betrothal would happen. But Jonas would not allow himself doubts on this score.

He knocked and was admitted by Morrison, who, it seemed to him, had a smile in his eye and a certain warmth in his voice as he took his hat, cane, and cloak and said, "The family is in the drawing room, sir."

"Thank you, Morrison." Jonas twitched at the wide skirt of his coat, fingered the lace at his throat, swallowed, and went manfully up the stairs in the butler's wake.

"Mr. Wedgwood, ma'am . . . sir."

Jonas stepped into the drawing room. Abigail was sitting on a sofa, an embroidery frame in her lap. She looked as enchanting as always in a gown of palest pink chiffon, with a lace fichu at her neck. Her hair was bound in bands of cherry-pink velvet ribbon, and she peeped up at him with a shy smile, rising to curtsy before sitting down again.

Mrs. Sutton did not rise from her chair. She regarded Jonas through a lorgnette, a new adjunct to her appearance, he reflected. If it was intended to intimidate, it would have succeeded but for Abigail's smile and William Sutton's hearty boom of greeting.

"Come in, m'boy, come in and welcome." He shook Jonas's hand vigorously, patting his shoulder. "Sit down . . . over there by Abigail. Plenty of room on that sofa, eh, puss?" He twinkled at his daughter, who blushed a little but moved her skirts closer against her to create more space.

Jonas smiled at Abigail before bowing to her mother and presenting his posy. "Ma'am, I hope you like roses."

Marianne received the gift with a stiff smile. For all her frustrated ambitions for her daughter, she was incapable of an overtly unkind response to such a charming gesture. "Thank you, Mr. Wedgwood. They're very pretty." She leaned sideways to ring a little handbell on the table and instructed the parlor maid, who appeared almost instantly, "Put these in water, Sally. They'll look very nice in the small cut-glass vase."

"So what'll you drink, Jonas?" William asked. "The ladies are curdling their insides with ratafia, but I daresay you'd like something stronger . . . a tankard of ale, perhaps?"

"No, Mr. Sutton, Mr. Wedgwood will drink sherry or madeira," his wife said quickly. "Ale is all very well for the morning but not before dinner."

William looked disappointed but said cheerfully enough, "So my lady has decreed. Which will it be, m'boy? Sherry or madeira?"

"Sherry, if you please, sir." Jonas took his place on the sofa beside Abigail, and she gave him a quick sidelong smile.

"When are you planning to return home, Mr. Wedgwood?" Marianne inquired, taking a genteel sip of ratafia. "Soon, I expect." She seemed to answer her own question.

Jonas looked a little startled. "I haven't made any plans as yet, ma'am."

"Surely your uncle requires your presence in his business?"

"I am conducting his business here in town at the moment, ma'am. He has given me several other commissions to execute."

"Oh . . . really?" Marianne sounded doubtful.

Jonas looked in appeal to Mr. Sutton, who declared, "Such an inquisition, Mrs. Sutton. 'Tis well and good that he's doing his uncle's business in London, if he's to go a-courting. Eh, puss?" He beamed at his daughter.

Abigail murmured something inaudible, but her eyes glowed as she glanced at Jonas. Marianne gave a tight smile but said nothing.

"Well, now, surely 'tis time for dinner," William stated into the awkward moment of silence. "Let us go down. Mrs. Sutton . . ." He offered his arm to his wife. "Young Jonas here can take Abigail down."

Marianne had little choice but to put a brave face on what was clearly now a fait accompli. Abigail was going to be Mrs. Jonas Wedgwood, and she might as well accept it. With acceptance came the first glimmer of pleasure as she thought of announcing to her fellow mothers of marriageable daughters that *her* daughter was to be the first among them . . . married before her eighteenth birthday and married to the scion of one of the most prominent and successful families in the Five Towns. She knew they would be green with envy. And of course, William would spare no expense on the wedding. It would be the most lavish affair seen in the Potteries in the last ten years. She permitted herself a small smile as she took her seat at the table and glanced at her glowing daughter. After all, when all was said and done, Abigail's happiness was really all that mattered.

William caught his wife's little private nod and was well satisfied. He knew his Marianne, and he'd known that she would see the light eventually. He could bid farewell to the peaceful routine he was accustomed to for the next few months. Life in the Sutton household would be a whirlwind of preparations, Marianne would be in and out of his business office with demands, suggestions, crises both real and imagined, but he would endure with a good grace if it would make his womenfolk happy. He nodded to himself and began to carve the sirloin of beef in front of him, serving his guest generously.

"Nothing like a good piece of beef, I always say." He passed the full plate to the footman, who placed it in front of Jonas. "You have some of that good Yorkshire pudding now, m'boy. Mrs. Sutton's cook knows exactly how to make it. And those roast potatoes are the best in the country, I'll wager. Need to feed you up if you're going to live through the next few months." He laughed and winked.

Abigail's shyness dissolved under her father's merry innuendos, and she began to chatter in her usual free and easy fashion. By the end of dinner, Jonas had lost his wariness and set out deliberately to charm his soon-to-be mother-in-law.

He succeeded so well that when William said, "I expect you two young people would like a little time to yourselves. We'll go up to the drawing room, eh, Mrs. Sutton?" Marianne merely nodded and rose to take her husband's arm. Jonas stood up, clutching his napkin, and bowed.

The door closed on them, and Abigail was once again mute with shyness. She played with the stem of her wine glass. Jonas coughed, pulled at the damask square between his hands, then sat down again. A second later, he jumped to his feet and blurted, "Miss Sutton . . . Abigail, would you do me the honor of becoming my wife?"

Abigail raised her downcast eyes from the tabletop and whispered, "Yes."

Jonas gave a great whoop of delight, seized her hands, and pulled her to her feet. "Yes, you will? Really . . . truly?"

She nodded. "Really . . . truly, I will, Jonas."

He danced her around the table, laughing with relief. "You have made me the happiest man in the world . . . the luckiest man in London." He caught her against him and impulsively kissed her.

"Jonas, you shouldn't," she murmured. "Not until we are wed." But she made no effort to escape his hold.

"Oh, no, I'm sure I shouldn't," he said, kissing her again. "But I can't help it, Abigail, my dearest Abigail. My love."

He began to dance with her again, swinging her off her feet in his exultation.

"Oh . . . I almost forgot . . . I have a present for you."

He released one hand and reached into his inner pocket. "I hope you like it." He placed the little packet in her free hand and watched anxiously as she freed her other hand and unwrapped the locket.

"Oh, 'tis lovely, Jonas. So pretty." She opened it up. "What should I put in it? Oh, a miniature of you . . . but that will take too long, and I want something *now.*" She frowned, then her expression cleared. "A lock of your hair." She darted to the sideboard and took up the little pair of grape scissors in the fruit bowl.

Jonas submitted to the loss of a dark strand but then took the scissors from her and cut one of her own guinea-gold curls. He twisted the two locks together and inserted them into the locket, closing it gently. "There now . . . a promise of a lifetime together." He turned her around and fastened the clasp at her nape.

Abigail stood on tiptoe to see her image in the mirror above the mantel. She lifted the locket and gazed at it in the mirror, her eyes shining. "Oh, 'tis exquisite, Jonas. Quite perfect."

"Made by a silversmith in High Holborn," he said with a touch of pride. "I'm told he is renowned through-out the city."

She smiled at him in the mirror. "How did you know of him?"

"Oh, someone told me," he answered vaguely with a careless wave of his hand. "Someone who knows about such matters."

"Oh . . . I wonder who." But to his relief, Abigail

didn't press him further. He was reluctant to tell her that Sebastian had given him the information, even as Sullivan told him with a wry smile that he would be hard pressed to afford the silversmith's work himself. It would be both inappropriate and vulgar to share that confidence with his beloved, Jonas felt.

"We should go back to Mama and Papa," she said, slowly dropping the locket back to nestle in the hollow of her throat. "Before Mama sends Morrison to fetch us."

"Yes . . . yes, of course." He had no desire to find himself on the wrong side of redoubtable Mama again. He hurried to the door, opening it wide, bowing as Abigail went past him with a little curtsy of acknowledgment and a mischievous smile that quite spoiled the decorum.

William was pacing restlessly in the drawing room. He wanted to retreat to his private sanctum with a glass of brandy and his pipe before seeking his usual early bed, but he couldn't leave his guest, and Marianne was showing signs of impatience at the lovers' prolonged absence. He sighed with relief as the door opened and the young people returned. One glance at their faces told him all he needed to know.

"So, 'tis settled, then . . . all right and tight," he declared, coming forward with hands outstretched. "Welcome to the family, dear boy." He enclosed Jonas's slender hands in his own giant paws. "You just make sure you make my little girl happy."

"Oh, I will, sir. Indeed, I will." Jonas was aware that his smile was probably somewhat fatuous. He turned to

Marianne, who was smiling, although with rather more restraint than her husband. "Ma'am, I will treasure Abigail," he said earnestly.

She nodded, and a small smile lurked at the corners of her mouth. "See that you do." She turned to her daughter, her sharp eyes missing nothing. "What is that around your neck, child?"

" 'Tis a locket, Mama. A present from Jonas . . . Mr. Wedgwood. Is it not the prettiest thing?" She leaned over so that her mother could inspect the piece.

Marianne nodded her approval. "Most appropriate, very pretty, indeed."

"We have twined two locks of hair together," Abigail confessed, blushing a little. "I shall wear them close to my heart."

Marianne looked a little askance but was willing to grant a degree of latitude to young love. "Well, that's as may be, child. But 'tis time you sought your bed after all this excitement. Bid Mr. Wedgwood good night. You may call upon us tomorrow morning, Mr. Wedgwood. I daresay Mr. Sutton has various matters of business to discuss with you, and then you may sit with Abigail for half an hour."

Abigail couldn't help a little moue of disappointment. "But Mama, I am not in the least sleepy. 'Tis still early."

" 'Tis past nine." Marianne set her needle firmly into her embroidery and laid the frame aside.

Abigail gave her father a pleading look, and he

laughed. "Oh, let the girl say good night to her betrothed, Mrs. Sutton. There can be no harm in a private
word of farewell." He winked at his wife. "I remember
that you and I shared a few private good nights during
our betrothal, eh, Mrs. Sutton?"

Marianne shot him a repressive look but couldn't
hide the sudden softness in her eyes.

William chuckled. "You may see him to the door,
puss. I'm sure your mother has no objection to that."

If she did have, Marianne was not about to articulate it.
William had spoken. "Just to the door, then," she agreed.

"Oh, thank you, Mama. You are the best mother."
Abigail flung her arms around her neck and kissed her
cheek. "And I promise we shall be most discreet."

"If I thought there was the slightest danger otherwise,
child, you would walk no further than the drawing-
room door with Mr. Wedgwood, betrothed or not,"
Marianne pronounced, but her eyes were still soft.

Jonas made his bows, agreed to present himself at
nine the following morning to discuss settlements with
Mr. Sutton, and followed Abigail downstairs to the hall.
She was dancing with exuberance, jumping off the last
two steps, laughing up at him.

"Oh, I do so wish you didn't have to leave, Jonas."

"But you know that I must." He smiled the smile that
he didn't think would ever leave him. It seemed to have
become a permanent fixture of his features. "But only
for a short while. Once we are wed . . ."

Her eyes narrowed, startling him with the sudden seductiveness of their expression. "Once we are wed, we shall never be apart," she stated, reaching for his hand.

Morrison watched indulgently from the shadows at the rear of the hall, moving forward to the front door only when the couple did. He unbolted the door, opening it onto the crisp, cool night air of late autumn. "Good night, sir."

Jonas stepped past him onto the top step. "Good night, Morrison."

Abigail darted out to stand beside him. "Oh, just close the door, Morrison . . . just for a minute. 'Tis too cold to leave it open."

The butler regarded her with a raised eyebrow, then said, "I'll pull it to just for a minute, Miss Abigail. You mustn't catch cold." He stepped back, allowing the door to close on the latch at his back.

Abigail chuckled, reaching to stand on tiptoe to circle Jonas's neck with her arms. "Good night . . . oh, I wish we didn't have to say it."

Jonas put his hands at her waist, lifting her slightly against him as he bent his head to kiss her mouth. After a long minute, he let her feet touch the step again and reluctantly moved his mouth from hers. He held her face for a moment, and she looked up at him, something lurking in her wide blue eyes that startled him for a moment. It was hunger, even passion. He was inexperienced in the ways of love himself, but the need he saw in Abigail's eyes matched the need that was now stirring his loins, setting his blood afire.

Hastily, he stepped away from her. "Go in, Abigail, 'tis cold." He kissed his fingertips to her as he hurried down the steps to the street. "Until tomorrow, my darling."

"Until tomorrow." She blew him a kiss and stood watching as he almost ran down the street. Even after he'd rounded the corner, she stayed on the step, her fingers touching her lips, where the warmth of his mouth still seemed to linger. At last, she turned slowly back to the door.

As she did so, a small voice spoke in a whisper behind her. "Miss Sutton? You Miss Sutton, miss?"

She turned and saw a small urchin on the bottom step holding out a slim package. "Gen'leman gi' me twopence to deliver this, miss. But only to Miss Sutton . . . you Miss Sutton, miss?"

Bewildered, Abigail nodded. "Yes . . . yes, I'm Miss Sutton, but I'm not expecting anything."

"This 'ere's fer you, miss." The lad thrust the package at her, and she took it automatically. She looked down at it. Her name was certainly there, written in a bold, decisive script. Above it, in much larger letters, was written: "TO BE READ ONLY IN PRIVATE."

Abigail was bewildered but also intrigued. There was something exciting about such a communication, about its method of delivery, the urgency that seemed to radiate from the sealed parchment. It had to be something from Jonas, some wicked love letter that he needed her to read in private. It was just like him to come up with such a romantic idea. He would know that her mother wouldn't allow her to receive a private correspondence, even from her betrothed. He could have written it earlier, brought it with him, and given it to the street urchin on the corner. These youngsters hung around on every corner and in every mews, looking for a way to earn a penny. But why hadn't he just given it to her as he left?

Perhaps in the heat of the moment, he'd forgotten he had it and only remembered as he'd got to the corner.

Abigail smiled and tucked the document into her bosom. She would bid her parents good night and seek the privacy of her bedchamber to read her love letter.

Serena was barely aware of the passing of time throughout the evening. She was lively and entertaining, as always, moving gracefully through the salons, playing her part at the tables, supervising the staff, keeping a watchful eye on the supper tables, but she was not really there, not in essence. Her body went through the motions, but her spirit, her self, was on some other plane altogether.

Her mind sang with thoughts of Sebastian, with the knowledge of their future, waiting to begin. Nothing here could touch her anymore, not even the malevolent eye of her stepfather, who seemed to be watching her every move. Vaguely, she wondered if he could tell that something definitive had happened to her, but then she dismissed the fancy. How could he? And even if he did, so what? He could do nothing to alter the fact. As soon as Jonas and Abigail were united, her part would be played, and she would be free.

She floated through the evening until the last player had gone, the doors bolted, the lamps sconced, and the night's takings locked away in the safe. Her stepfather bade her a curt good night as she passed him on her way to the stairs. He seemed restless, pent up in a way that she knew of old boded ill. He was planning something . . . usually that mood presaged a midnight flit. Had Burford finally pushed him to the limit?

A prickle of anxiety disturbed her tranquility. Sir George Heyward in extremis would be like a cornered bear. But until he revealed his hand, nothing could be done beyond what she was doing. She made her way to her own chamber. She had sent her maid to bed much earlier and now undressed, tossing her gown carelessly over the daybed, and climbed into bed, sinking deep into the feather mattress, hugging her thoughts and memories tightly as she slid into sleep.

She awoke early the next morning, filled with a wonderful sense of well-being, and lay savoring the moment of warm relaxation as her body gradually surfaced and her mind dwelled pleasantly on thoughts of the coming day. She had arranged to meet Sebastian in Bruton Street at eleven o'clock. It was a perfectly reasonable coincidence that they should both decide to visit the Suttons at the same time. Sebastian was going to call upon

Jonas on his way and try to persuade him to go with him. Nature and circumstance would do the rest.

Serena reached for the bell beside the bed and rang for Bridget, who hurried in with a tray of hot chocolate and bread and butter. "Good morning, Lady Serena. And 'tis a frosty one. Winter's comin' on apace." She set down the tray and drew back the curtains. Pale wintry sunshine filtered through a sparkling, frost-sprinkled window pane.

Serena sat up and drew the thick quilt up to her chin, sipping her hot chocolate while Bridget raked the embers and relit the fire in the hearth. Soon the comforting crackle of the logs made the room feel warmer, even though the tip of Serena's nose still felt chill.

"I'll wear the tawny velvet gown this morning, Bridget, with the heavy woolen petticoat and the brown damask underskirt. And I'll need the dark cloak with the silver fox lining and woolen stockings."

"You'll be goin' out, then, m'lady?"

"Yes, just a visit to friends. I won't need you to accompany me, but before I go, I'll talk with Cook about tonight's supper." She set down her cup and steeled herself before throwing the quilt aside. Bridget made haste to bring her a heavy wool dressing gown with a fur lining, and she huddled gratefully into its warmth. "I do not like winter," she declared. "The cold gets into your bones."

She and Sebastian had talked of traveling to Italy or the south of France for a while. It was cheaper to live there than in London, and it was warmer, even in midwinter. She let her mind dwell on the buttery sunshine of the Mediterranean, the rich colors of the bougainvillea on whitewashed walls, the warm red-tiled roofs, the heady scents of thyme and marjoram crushed underfoot in the silvery olive groves. For a moment, it was so real she could almost imagine she was there now, arm-in-arm with her husband.

Soon, she told herself. Soon it would be reality. And until then, she needed to keep her wits about her.

She was glad the general didn't make an appearance when she went downstairs. The library door was closed as she crossed the hall to the door leading to the kitchen regions, and she could hear the rise and fall of voices within. Vaguely, she wondered who might be calling upon her stepfather this early in the morning. She pushed through the green baize door and hurried down the passage to the kitchen at the rear.

The room was full of contained activity, as always, steam from bubbling cauldrons on the range, a cloud of flour as one of the cook's assistants threw it liberally onto the marble slab she was using for rolling pastry. Serena blinked to clear her vision. A scullery maid dodged past her with an armful of pots and pans. The cook was standing, arms akimbo, in the open kitchen door, loudly berating the butcher, who had arrived with the day's order of meat.

"I told you I wanted four calves' feet. How am I supposed to make calf's-foot jelly with only two?"

"All I got, missus." The butcher shrugged. "You want 'em or no?"

The cook sighed. "I'll manage. What else 'ave you got?"

"'Alf a dozen rabbits . . . beautiful they are. Shot last night up on the 'Eath." He held up a limp gray form by its ears. "Plump as can be."

The cook prodded the offering, peered into its glazed eyes, then nodded. "They'll do for a fricassee."

Serena stepped into the negotiations. "How about your splendid rabbit pies? We haven't had those in a while." Her tone was conciliatory, concealing her inner haste.

The cook nodded. "If you'd prefer, Lady Serena. 'Tis all one to me." She turned back to the butcher. "I'll take the six, and half a dozen capons if you have 'em."

"Could we just go over the supper menu, Cook?" Serena asked, still hiding her impatience to be gone from the steamy kitchen.

The woman stepped away from the kitchen door, wiping her hands on her apron. "Fishmonger hasn't been yet, m'lady, but if he's got oysters, I've a mind to make an oyster stew."

"Excellent." Serena stayed for a few more minutes and was turning to leave as Flanagan came into the kitchen.

"Ale and meat wanted in the library," he announced. "You there . . ." He clicked his fingers at a footman. "Take it through, and don't use the best tankard."

Serena raised her eyebrows. "Does General Heyward have a visitor, Flanagan?"

"Aye, Lady Serena, if you could call him such," Flanagan replied with a curl of his lip that spoke volumes.

"Anyone I know?"

"I doubt you'd want to know him, my lady. Nasty-looking specimen, if I may be so bold," the butler declared. "But he's been around once or twice, and he's up to no good, you mark my words."

Serena's eyebrows climbed higher. Flanagan never stood on ceremony with her—he'd known her since she was born and had served her father's family since he was a small boy in a page's knee breeches—but usually, he refrained from overt criticism of her stepfather and the doings in the house. She was fairly certain he stayed with the general to keep a watchful eye on her, and more than once, she'd found the knowledge of his presence enormously comforting. It seemed logical that if in Flanagan's opinion the general's visitor was up to no good, then so, too, in that same opinion was the general.

She touched his arm, drawing him slightly to one side of the kitchen. "Is it the man in the moleskin waistcoat?"

"Aye, Lady Serena."

She nodded, frowning in thought. "Would you take the tray in yourself, Flanagan? Find out whatever you can . . . see if you can pick anything up . . . hear anything. I know I shouldn't ask you to do this, but I just have a feeling . . ." She gave him a slightly guilty smile.

"That's all right, Lady Serena. Just leave it with me." He waved at the footman with his tray. "Give that to me, lad. I'll take it."

The footman looked surprised but relinquished his tray, and Flanagan followed Serena out of the kitchen, back to the hall. She hung back as he knocked once and entered the library, leaving the door slightly ajar. She couldn't see into the room properly, but she caught a glimpse of the moleskin waistcoat as he took the tankard of ale.

"That'll do, man. No need to hang around," the general snapped, and Flanagan with a bow, backed out into the hall. Again, he left the door slightly ajar, glancing over his shoulder at Serena.

She nodded and glided softly past him towards the front door. It was safer for Flanagan to listen than for her to risk being caught by her stepfather lurking in the shadows with her ear to the door. Flanagan would have a ready excuse; she would have none.

Chapter Twenty

Abigail lay awake through the night, tossing from one side of the bed to the other. The dreadful communication was thrust beneath her pillow—she could think of no other safe hiding place for it—but it seemed to her as the hours wore on that it had become as hard as a boulder, pressing through her usually soft feather pillows. It wasn't true. It couldn't possibly be true. And yet if it were untrue, how had the general found the incriminating document? It wasn't possible for her father, so upright, so well respected in his civic circles, to be involved in something so despicable. But the document had her father's seal. She knew it so well. It sat on his desk beside the jar of quills and the little knife he used to sharpen them. She had seen it adorn so many letters and receipts, seen it pressed into the wax that sealed the papers William sent out of the house to the various men of business with whom he dealt.

Perhaps she had misunderstood the letter. Perhaps her father was not saying what he seemed to be saying. But if that were the case, why would the general use it for such evil? He must be sure it was true. It had to be true. Even the writing was her father's.

She sat up, finally giving up all idea of sleep, and lit the candle beside her bed. She drew the document out from its hiding place and unfolded it. It filled her with such horror she felt as if the very paper itself was poisoned. She stared at the words. The document was addressed to one of her father's business partners, a man she knew well. He'd held her on his knee as a small child and always brought a big box of sugary fruit jellies when he came to dinner. He and William Sutton were the senior members of the Board of Guardians of the parish's Poor House and responsible for administering the funds allocated for Poor Relief in the parish.

Abigail had always been proud of the way her father worked so hard for the poor and sick of their community, a task for which he received no payment himself. He always stressed to her that people in their position had a moral and social obligation to assist those less fortunate. He would take her with him on his supervisory visits and always had a kind word for the inhabitants of the Poor House and a purse of coins which he dispensed liberally.

But if this document were true, then that had all been a façade. Her father and Howard Barrett had been misusing the Poor Relief, diverting it into their own pockets, cutting the food rations, supplying green wood and slag from the coal heaps for the fires, neither of which would burn adequately but cost almost nothing, skimping on the already sparse clothing allowance for the poor.

When they presented their accounts to the Board of Guardians, the paper expenditures in no way matched the reality. The letter Abigail held, from her father to Mr. Barrett, laid out a clear, step-by-step scheme to siphon off money from that allocated to food, coal, and clothing for those on Poor Relief.

It was impossible to believe, and yet the evidence was in front of her, incontrovertible. And if she didn't agree to elope with General Heyward, he would send the evidence to the Board of Guardians in Stoke-on-Trent, and her father would be ruined. His name would be anathema; no one would do business with him again. If she told her father, confronted him with the letter, then General Heyward would make public other evidence of William Sutton's corruption.

Believe me, Miss Sutton, what I still possess is much more damning than the letter you hold. If you fail to make the rendezvous, everything I have will be made public immediately.

Abigail shuddered as she reread the final sentence of General Heyward's accompanying letter. Even if *she* didn't believe his accusations, and she couldn't begin to believe such things of her father, other people would. So many people would recognize the handwriting and the seal, and without Abigail's absolute faith in her father's goodness, they would believe the evidence of their eyes.

What would happen if she took the letter to her father? He wouldn't be able to stop the general, not unless he killed him. And that didn't bear thinking of, quite apart from the fact that Abigail knew her father would be no match for General Sir George Heyward in a physical battle on or off a dueling field.

She thrust the papers under her pillow and lay back, closing her eyes against a dull throb behind her temples. She had no choice but to make the rendezvous. That would at least stop the general from making good on his threat. But she would *not* elope with him. Surely she would be able to escape during the journey? Even if she had to kill him herself, she'd find a way. Was he intending to go to Gretna Green? His letter didn't say, just told her that a closed carriage would await her on the corner of Berkeley Square at four o'clock that afternoon. She need not bring anything, as all her personal needs would be supplied.

She fell into a fitful doze just as the sky began to lighten but was wide awake when Matty brought in her hot chocolate several hours later.

Serena left Flanagan hovering in the hall around the open library door and stepped out into the cold morning. It was a little before eleven o'clock. She hurried to the corner and hailed a passing hackney. Ten minutes later, she stepped from the hackney outside the house on Bruton Street and waited, glancing along the street to the corner where Sebastian would appear, unless he was already in the house. After a few minutes, he came around the corner, raised his hand when he saw her, and came at a half-run towards her.

"There you are . . . good morning, my love." He caught her around the waist, swinging her off her feet.

"Sebastian," she protested, laughing but serious as well. "'Tis the middle of the road. We can't afford to be indiscreet . . . not here, not yet, at least."

He sobered, letting her find her feet again. "No, you're right, of course. But I've missed you so much, and I've thought of you every minute. Your face has been all I've seen since we parted. Such a lovely face . . ." He stroked her cheek with his finger, and she stepped back.

"Not here, love."

He sighed. "Why must you be right?"

She smiled. "I'm not always. Where's Jonas? I thought you were going to bring him."

"He wasn't there. His man said he had left the house early this morning. Whistling to himself, I gather."

Serena looked up at the house. "Perhaps he's here already. Who knows, maybe matters have moved on apace since the dinner party."

"Why don't we go and find out?" Sebastian lifted the knocker.

Morrison greeted them and escorted them upstairs to the parlor, where Marianne was sitting with Abigail. A pale and wan Abigail, Serena thought the minute she stepped into the room. Had something gone wrong? Jonas was not in the parlor, where she'd hoped he'd be.

"Lady Serena . . . Mr. Sullivan, how delightful of you to call," Marianne said. She cast Sebastian a rather wistful look before telling Morrison to bring refreshment and bidding her visitors take a seat.

"We come with belated thanks for your delightful dinner party the other night, ma'am," Sebastian said with his most charming smile. He, too, had noticed Abigail's unusually wan appearance and set himself to distract Mrs. Sutton while Serena probed the daughter.

Marianne confided, "Well, I do think our guests enjoyed it, Mr. Sullivan."

Serena sat beside Abigail on the sofa. "You look a little tired. Too much excitement?" she teased.

"No . . . not at all," Abigail denied. "That is, well, something has happened." A slight blush chased the pallor from her cheeks.

"Oh?" Serena leaned forward. "I'm all ears, my dear."

"Well, 'tis Mr. Wedgwood . . . he asked my father for my hand."

Serena smiled. "And did Mr. Sutton give it to him?"

Abigail looked up at her. "If I would have him."

Serena felt a first niggling of alarm. Surely Abigail hadn't turned Jonas down? "And will you?" she pressed, wondering why the girl was so hesitant about something that should have had her jumping over the moon.

"I said I would." It sounded to Serena more like a confession than a joyous affirmation.

"That's wonderful," she said warmly, taking Abigail's

hands in hers, noticing how cold they were as she leaned in to kiss her. "I wish you both very happy."

"Ah, Abigail has told you her news, I see, Lady Serena." Marianne gave a complacent little nod. "Yes, she is to become Mrs. Jonas Wedgwood. Mr. Sutton and Mr. Wedgwood are at this moment discussing settlements."

"Well, that's a cause for celebration," Sebastian declared. "Mr. Wedgwood is a very lucky man. But I think he knows that," he added with a smile.

"Will you be married in London?" Serena asked, still trying to puzzle out Abigail's less than joyous expression.

"No, I don't think so. It will be a considerable event in our County society," Marianne stated. "'Tis only right and proper that our friends and Mr. Sutton's business associates in Stoke-on-Trent are invited to share our joy."

A faint shudder seemed to pass through Abigail, and Serena became even more concerned. "You seem a little glum, Abigail, on such a joyful morning," she murmured. "You haven't quarreled with Jonas yet, have you?"

Abigail colored deeply and spoke in an agitated undertone, "No . . . no, of course not. How could I? He's the most wonderful person."

"Wedding nerves, then," Serena said with a placidity she didn't feel.

The arrival of William and Jonas put an end to the possibility of further probing. Jonas came instantly to Abigail, taking her hands and kissing them before saying with a hasty bow, "Oh, forgive me, Lady Serena. Good morning, ma'am."

"Good morning, Mr. Wedgwood." She smiled at him. "I understand congratulations are in order."

"Miss Sutton has agreed to make me the happiest man in the world," Jonas stated.

Abigail suddenly rose to her feet. "Please, I must ask you to forgive me . . . Mama, may I be excused? I have the headache . . . it pains me most dreadfully."

"Oh, my poor child . . . too much excitement, I'm sure. Go and lie down, and I will send Matty with lavender water and sal volatile. I thought you were looking a little peaky." Marianne got to her feet in a flurry of silk. "Lady Serena, Mr. Sullivan, please excuse me. I must take care of Abigail."

"Oh, my poor darling." Jonas looked stricken as his future mother-in-law hustled his bride-to-be out of the parlor.

"Oh, never you mind, young man. She'll be right as rain in no time. Mrs. Sutton is right . . . too much excitement. Women are susceptible to the megrims, as you'll discover for yourself." William sounded unperturbed by his daughter's sudden frailty.

"We must be going, Mr. Sutton." Serena stood up in her turn, glancing at Sebastian, who nodded. "Jonas, d'you care to walk with us?"

Jonas recollected himself. He knew Mr. Sutton was anxious to get back to his work, and he couldn't sit around the parlor on his own. "Yes . . . thank you, I would. As far as the square, at least."

William made no attempt to detain them, and when the front door had closed upon them, he returned to his library with something akin to relief.

"My poor darling," Jonas lamented again as they began to walk up the blustery street. "I wonder what could have overset her so suddenly. She was so happy last evening." He glanced over his shoulder, as if hoping to see his betrothed standing on the steps watching him out of sight, as she had done the previous evening.

"Women suffer from headaches, Jonas," Serena informed him plainly. "There's no need to take them too seriously. Offer sympathy and peace and quiet, and all will be well."

"Indeed, 'tis good advice," Sebastian said with a chuckle. "Lady Serena is an expert on all matters female."

Serena merely smiled, but the smile hid a degree of consternation. A headache would explain Abigail's listlessness and pallor, but she had the sense that something more was troubling the girl. She was usually so open and bubbly, never seemed to have a care in the world, and yet this morning, she had struck Serena as positively careworn.

Jonas left them in Berkeley Square, and Sebastian looked quizzically at his wife. "Shall we go home, madam wife?"

"To Stratton Street?"

"'Tis the only home we have at present."

Serena hesitated. There was nothing she wanted to do more, but reluctantly, she shook her head. "Not now. Something's going on with my stepfather, and I need to discover what." She saw the black cloud descend on his brow and said swiftly, "I've learned over the years, my love, that to keep one step ahead of him, I have to be forewarned as far as possible. If he's planning something, I have to be watching."

"Dear God, why can't the damn Suttons pack up their daughter and go back where they came from?" Sebastian muttered. "Abigail has a husband in the wings. What's to keep them here?"

"It only happened yesterday, Sebastian," Serena pointed out to him. "It takes time to pack up a household and move a hundred miles. Besides . . ." And then she let the sentence fade.

But Sebastian wasn't having any of it. "Besides what?"

"Oh, just that when the general's plans don't work out, he becomes unpredictable. If he thinks Abigail is going to slip away from him, there's no knowing what he'll do."

"What can he possibly do?" Sebastian exclaimed. "Abigail is as good as wedded and bedded."

"Not quite." She stepped back from him, regarding him gravely. "'Tis the endgame now, Sebastian. I've played it thus far, I must play it to the end. Otherwise, all the past sacrifices have been in vain."

He couldn't argue with that, much as he wished to. "Go, then. But you are not to make a move without informing me, is that understood, Serena?"

Serena understood how hard it was for him to let her go without him. She would have felt the same way herself if their positions were reversed. She said softly, "Husband, I promise."

He still didn't smile, but his eyes became less stern. "I trust you." He raised her gloved hand to his lips. "Send to me when we can meet again."

She nodded. Sebastian called over a chair and watched the chairmen trot off in the direction of Pickering Place. He wanted to throw something, run Heyward through with his sword, shoot a hole in his heart, snatch up Serena, and carry her as far from there as he could get. And he couldn't because she wouldn't let him.

⚬◈⚬

Serena's chair stopped outside the house, and she hurried up to the front door. Flanagan opened it at her knock. "A pleasant visit, Lady Serena?"

"Yes, thank you." She glanced significantly to the library door. It was firmly shut. She raised an interrogative eyebrow. "Did you hear anything?"

"Just some discussion about a postchaise, tolls, and changes of horses at posthouses. I inferred that the gentleman in question had been charged by Sir George to make arrangements for a considerable journey."

Serena frowned. Not another midnight flit, surely? "You couldn't gather where?"

Flanagan shook his head. "I'm afraid not, ma'am. Although there was some mention of Finchley Common, I'm sure."

"A journey to the north, then?" Serena mused. Maybe he thought to continue his pursuit of Miss Sutton into her own home territory. But that wasn't the general's style. He liked to be on his own turf. "Thank you, Flanagan. Let me know if you hear or remember anything else."

"Of course, Lady Serena."

"I'll be in my parlor." She made for the stairs, drawing off her gloves. The library door opened behind her.

"Ah, there you are. I need a word with you."

She turned, her foot on the bottom step, as her stepfather spoke. "Yes, sir?"

"In here." He turned back to the library.

Serena retraced her steps and entered the library. The general was standing in front of the fire, the usual brandy goblet in his hand. He said without preamble, "You'll have to run the house yourself for a few days. I am going away for a while."

Serena caught her breath, torn between a surge of pleasure at the prospect of his absence and an equally strong presentiment that this absence could only bode ill. "May I ask where to, sir?"

"No," he stated. "You may not. If you need to close

one of the salons, then do so. I don't expect to be gone above a week."

Postchaise, change of teams, tolls. A long journey to the north.

"When do you leave?" she asked, neither her voice nor her expression showing so much as a hint of surprise at his announcement.

"This afternoon." He sipped his brandy and shooed at her with the fingers of his free hand. "That's all. You may go."

She sketched a mock curtsy and retreated to the hall. Thoughtfully, she made her way upstairs to her parlor.

Abigail made her plans very carefully. Lying in her darkened bedchamber, a damp cloth soaked in lavender water on her brow, the bottle of smelling salts in her hand, she had moaned her desire to be left to sleep, and the hovering had finally ceased, and her mother and Matty had left her to herself.

It was close to one o'clock. She had to be at the rendezvous by four o'clock. If she left without leaving a note of explanation, her parents would be beside themselves. She couldn't let that happen.

They wouldn't worry, though, if she said she was spending the evening with Lady Serena, and then the evening could become the night without too much added explanation. Would Lady Serena agree to lie for her?

Abigail sat up, casting aside the lavender cloth from her forehead. She swung her legs off the bed and began to pace the chamber, frowning in thought. Could she trust Lady Serena? There was no one else. She wouldn't tell her the real reason, of course. And of course, she would be shocked at Abigail's lack of conduct in wanting to spend the night away from home, but she wouldn't betray her. The more Abigail thought about it, the more convinced she became that the older woman wouldn't betray her. Lady Serena was so sophisticated, so experienced in the ways of Society.

She sat down at her little walnut secretaire and wrote a hasty note, sealed and addressed it, and rang for Matty.

"Are you feelin' better, miss?" the maid asked as she came into the still dimly lit chamber.

"A little, thank you. But I need you to run an errand for me. Would you take this note to Lady Serena Carmichael in Pickering Place?"

Matty took the sealed note. "Right away, ma'am?"

"Yes, immediately. 'Tis urgent."

Matty dropped a curtsy and hurried away. Abigail lay down upon her bed again. Her head was beginning to ache in earnest.

Serena's reflections were disturbed by a footman with a tray. "Cook sent this up for you, m'lady. Thought you might like a little something since 'tis well past noon."

"Oh, thank you, Bill, and thank Cook for me." She

examined the contents of the tray, aware that she was actually quite hungry. A mushroom tart, bread, cheese, and a compote of apples and pears.

She took the tray and sat by the fire, her brain working overtime as she ate. It couldn't be a coincidence that Sir George was planning this sudden journey up north with fast horses. With frequent changes and no stops of his own, he could be in the Potteries by tomorrow morning. But what was he going to do up there? The Suttons were not leaving London just yet.

She set aside the tray, leaned back in her chair, and for a moment forgot Abigail and the general in the heady prospect of a week's freedom. She didn't really need to open the house in the evenings at all, although the general would notice the lack of receipts soon enough on his return. But by then, maybe she would be free and clear.

A knock at the door hauled her out of her pleasant trancelike reverie. Flanagan came in with a letter on a tray. "This just arrived, Lady Serena. The young person said it was urgent."

"Thank you, Flanagan." She took the letter, recognizing the writing. Abigail had written her one or two breathless little notes in the past. But there had been nothing urgent about those. She slit the wafer with her thumbnail and opened the sheet.

Dear Lady Serena, please don't think badly of me, but please . . . please . . . could you say that I came to see you at four o'clock and you invited me to spend the evening with you, and later please send a note to my mother saying that I am not feeling well and you feel it would be better if I spend the night with you? I know this is a lot to ask, but please *will you do this for me? 'Tis a matter of life and death. I will be everlastingly in your debt. Your grateful Abigail.*

Sweet heaven, Serena thought. She glanced up at the clock on the mantel; it was just after two. After a moment's reflection, she went to her secretaire and wrote a brief note to Abigail. *I won't fail you. S.* She rang for Flanagan and asked him to have it delivered immediately. "Oh, and summon me a hackney, will you?"

"At once, Lady Serena."

She put on her pelisse and hurried downstairs. The library door was still closed. Pulling on her gloves, she hurried to the street and climbed into the waiting hackney, telling the jarvey, "Stratton Street, please."

If Sebastian wasn't home, that would put the cat among the pigeons. She'd have to act on her own, and he would not like that one bit.

Chapter Twenty-one

Peregrine was on the point of leaving the house when the doorknocker sounded. He opened the door and regarded the visitor in vague surprise. Sebastian had confided to his brother that for reasons of her own, Serena wouldn't be moving under his roof for a few weeks. Perry had asked no questions. If Sebastian was content with the strange situation, then who was he to quibble? There was nothing ordinary about the marriage in the first place.

"Lady Serena Sullivan." He greeted her with a bow. "Come in. I'm afraid your husband is not here, but if you'd like to wait by the fire. . . ?" He moved to open the door to the parlor, then stopped, seeing the frown on Serena's face. "Is something the matter, Serena?"

"Yes, in a word," she said bluntly. "And the devil of if is that I promised Sebastian I wouldn't do anything without letting him know, but if he's not here, I'll have to, and he won't be happy about it."

Peregrine wrinkled his brow. "Can *I* help? We do sometimes substitute for each other."

She gave him a wan smile. "Thank you, but I don't think it will serve on this occasion. *Damn.*" She drummed her fingers on the pier table beside her. "I wonder how long he'll be."

"We could try to find him?" Perry suggested. "I could hazard a guess about where he might be."

Serena thought for only a moment before making up her mind. "Let's go." She turned back to the door.

"By all means," Peregrine said amiably. "I suggest we try Whites first. If he's not there someone may know where he is." He offered Serena his arm.

They walked briskly to Whites coffee house. "I'll just put my head around the door," Peregrine said, adding apologetically, "You can't really go in yourself."

"No, that would never do," Serena agreed drily. "I'll wait here."

"I'll only be a minute." Peregrine stepped into the noisy room, peering through the fog emanating as much from gentlemen's pipes as from the smoking fire. He could see no sign of his twin, but a trio of gentlemen gathered at one of the long trestle tables called a greeting.

Peregrine pushed through the crowd towards them. "Anyone seen Sebastian?"

"He was in a while ago," one of the men told him, "but I haven't seen him since."

"I think he said he was going to Albemarle Street for a bout with Maître Jerome," one of his companions offered. "Something about a new pass with the épée."

"My thanks. I'll try him there." Perry raised a hand

in farewell and threaded his way back outside, where Serena was pacing restlessly. "Albemarle Street," he said, offering his arm again.

"What's there?"

"Maître Albert's fencing salon. He has a new assistant who's a magician with the épée, I've heard. Apparently, Seb has gone for a lesson."

A lesson that might stand him in good stead, Serena reflected grimly. "What's the time, Perry?"

He looked at his fob watch on his waistcoat. "Close to three-thirty."

Serena set her lips and quickened her step. If Sebastian was not at the fencing salon, then she would have to act alone, but she hadn't any real idea what she could do alone. Maybe she would need to recruit Peregrine after all.

They reached Albemarle Street in ten minutes of swift walking. Peregrine held the door to Number 7 for her and followed her into the narrow hallway. He started immediately up the narrow flight of stairs, and Serena followed him. On the landing above, Peregrine opened the set of double doors, and Serena stepped into a long, mirror-lined room where two men in shirt sleeves and stockinged feet were fencing with foiled weapons.

Peregrine shushed her with an imperative hand just as she was about to speak, and she forced herself to wait as the tense exchange of passes continued, fascinated despite her anxiety at the skill of the two duelers. It seemed to her that Sebastian was every bit as accomplished as the maître. But then the other man slipped his foil under his opponent's, and Sebastian stepped back, raising his épée. "*Touché*, Maître. A masterly stroke."

He glanced towards the door, and his expression changed, his eyes darkening. "Serena . . . what is it?" He crossed the room. "What's happened . . . Perry?"

"I don't know," his twin said. "But your wife needed to see you urgently."

"We don't have much time, Sebastian."

"To do what?" he asked quietly.

"Rescue Abigail, of course. What else would be so urgent that I'd have to chase all over town looking for you?" She heard the snap in her own voice and sighed. "Forgive me, I'm so worried, and time's getting short."

"Give me a minute." Sebastian set aside his épée and sat down on the bench that ran the length of the salon to put on his boots, then reached for his coat. "Now, tell me what's going on."

"Well, it's all to do with the moleskin waistcoat," Serena began.

"You're talking in riddles," Sebastian responded, a snap in his own voice. "Just give me the facts, or whatever it is you know or suspect."

Serena nodded, accepting the rebuke as due. "There's a man who wears a moleskin waistcoat whom the general uses for his least savory errands." She gave a slightly bitter little laugh. "When you run a gambling house, there are quite a few of them."

The brothers said nothing.

"He only ever comes to the house when there's trouble in the offing. And he's been in the house twice. Once yesterday, and he was there in the library with the general this morning when I left. I asked Flanagan to listen to as much as he could of what was said. They talked of a postchaise, fast horses, frequent changes . . . a journey, it would seem."

"A reasonable conclusion," Sebastian agreed.

"Then he told me he was going away for a few days . . . and then I had this note from Abigail." She handed Sebastian the letter.

He read it, frowning. "So you think he's intending to abduct Abigail?"

"Not without her consent," Serena said. "Why else would she be planning to disappear and need me to lie for her? Doesn't that make sense?"

"Up to a point, but why in the world would Abigail agree to such a plan? For God's sake, she's just announced her engagement to Jonas Wedgwood."

"Blackmail," she said succinctly. " 'Tis a speciality of the general's."

Peregrine had no idea who Abigail was, but he understood blackmail. He glanced at his twin, who was rereading the letter in his hand. "Supposing you're right, where would they go?"

"Flanagan said he heard Finchley Common mentioned, which seems to imply they're going north . . . Gretna Green, perhaps?"

"We have a damsel in distress, it would seem," Perry

murmured. "Had we better launch a hue and cry?"

Sebastian tapped his mouth with his fingertips, thinking. "Finchley Common," he murmured. "And Abigail says she'll need you to lie for her from four o'clock this afternoon. How long for a chaise to reach Finchley Common, d'you think, Perry?"

His twin frowned. "An hour and a half, perhaps."

"Then we need to be in position by soon after five o'clock."

"Doable." Perry nodded.

"Position for *what*?" Serena demanded, feeling lost. She had sought help but perversely now felt as if she was being excluded.

"A hold-up." Sebastian's blue eyes were suddenly sparkling. For the first time, he could see his way to the end of this nightmare, to having his wife finally to himself.

"Oh." Serena's own eyes widened. "We stage a hold-up on the Common to rescue Abigail. What a clever idea."

"There's no *we* in this," Sebastian said calmly.

"Oh, yes, there is. Abigail needs a chaperone. You may do all the pistol-waving, make-believe robbery if you wish, but I need to be there to escort her back home, to maintain the fiction. The truth must not come out."

"Serena has a point there, Seb," Perry put in.

Sebastian didn't bother to argue. He said only, "As long as you promise not to get involved in anything with your stepfather, you may come."

"My thanks, husband." She dropped a mock curtsy, a flash in her eye, but he merely laughed and headed for the door, so she had no choice but to follow him meekly.

Outside, Sebastian consulted with Peregrine. "On horseback, we'll do the journey much faster than a coach and horses, particularly through town. I doubt it'll take us an hour. Do go to the mews and bring the mounts to the house. I'll fetch weapons."

"I'll fetch my horse and meet you at Stratton Street," Serena said. "Do you have masks? You can't be an unmasked highwayman."

"We've been to enough masked balls in our time to have quite a collection," Peregrine said. "Never fear, Serena, we will look the part, I promise."

"And so, I promise, will I. Believe me, I've made enough clandestine journeys in my time to know how to wear a disguise." She hurried away before either of them could say anything more.

Sebastian shook his head. "I wouldn't change one iota about her, but I don't think I'm in for a quiet life."

"I don't doubt it. I'll go to the mews."

Under the promise of action, all Serena's anxieties seemed to evaporate. As she ran up the steps to the front door, she noticed absently a strange horse tethered to the railings. Flanagan let her in, and she asked swiftly, "Has the general left yet?"

"Aye, m'lady . . . some twenty minutes past."

She nodded. "Would you send to the mews for my horse? I'll be down straightway."

"Yes, m'lady, but you have a visitor."

"A visitor?" She stopped with one foot on the bottom stair.

"A Mr. Wedgwood, he said, ma'am. He wanted to wait, so I showed him into your parlor."

This is going to complicate matters, Serena thought as she hurried up the stairs. She went into her parlor to find Jonas standing by the window, looking down into the street.

"This is an unexpected pleasure, Jonas," she said, closing the door at her back. "But I'm afraid 'tis not really convenient at present. I have an urgent engagement."

He turned towards her. "I understood Abigail was here with you. She wasn't with you when you came down the street. Where is she?"

Serena sighed. It wasn't four o'clock yet. Abigail's note must have been found earlier than she'd expected. "What made you think she was with me?" she temporized.

"She left a note for her mother. I went to see how she was doing half an hour ago, because of the headache, you understand, and was told that she'd recovered sufficiently to come and visit you. So where is she?" He sounded a little belligerent, and Serena couldn't really blame him. But how was she to get around this?

"I expect she's on her way," she offered.

"But you said you have an urgent engagement," he persisted. "Lady Serena, I know when people are not telling me the truth. Something's wrong, and I think you know what it is."

"Oh, to hell with it," Serena exclaimed, ignoring the momentary look of shock on Jonas's face. "Yes, something is wrong. But I have every hope that it will be put right without delay."

"Go on." He was rather pale, his face set, but she could see that he had himself well in hand.

She told him the whole story, watching his expression change from bewilderment to incredulity and finally to blazing anger.

"I'll kill him . . . forgive me, Lady Serena, I know he's your stepfather, but of all the despicable, vile vermin . . . my poor darling must be terrified. I will *kill* him."

"You'll be standing in quite a queue to do so," she said. "Is that your horse tethered outside?"

"Yes." He nodded.

"Then wait here. I'll only be a minute." She left him pacing and ran to her own chamber. She flung open the armoire, pulling out the leather breeches that she wore beneath her divided riding skirt. They strapped under her feet, inside her boots. Waistcoat and jacket and finally her black hooded cloak completed her costume change. She was halfway to the door again when she remembered. Masks . . . Jonas would need one, too. She took two domino masks from a drawer and flew back to the parlor.

"Here, Jonas. You'll need this if you're going to play highwayman." She thrust the mask at him.

He took it in bewilderment. "Highwayman?"

Serena explained Sebastian's plan, and his expression cleared. "A capital plan. There's not a moment to lose."

They rode fast to Stratton Street, where Sebastian and Peregrine were just mounting. Sebastian raised his eyebrows when he saw Jonas, and he looked a question at Serena.

"Jonas was waiting for me. Abigail's note must have been found earlier than she'd expected. Anyway, he's coming with us."

"The more the merrier," Peregrine said. "Do you have a firearm, Mr. Wedgwood?"

"Not on me."

Sebastian dismounted. "Just a moment." He disappeared into the house and came back with an elegant dueling pistol. He handed it up to Jonas. "It throws a little to the left, so watch for it."

Jonas thrust the weapon into his belt, and the little party set off. They rode in silence for the most part, threading their way through the busy city streets heading north. The traffic lessened as they left the hub of the town behind them and rode through the village of Hampstead and across the heath. There were few vehicles on the single road across the heath, and they paused at the Bull and Bush Inn, where coaches often stopped for refreshment. Sebastian went in and came out after a minute. "They say no coaches have been by in the last hour."

"So we must be ahead of them," Peregrine said, and they rode on, fast and in silence.

The weak November sun was dipping behind the

horizon when they reached the village of Finchley and the Common stretching just beyond it, bisected by a single narrow, rutted track.

As soon as Abigail had received Serena's succinct answer to her request, she struggled to compose her own note to her mother. It was almost impossible to explain why she hadn't asked her mother in person for permission to visit Lady Serena and even more so why she had gone unaccompanied to Pickering Place. She settled for a simple statement of facts, without explanation. Once this horror was over, they would know everything, anyway. A tear splashed on the paper, and she blotted it with her handkerchief. She had no idea how she was going to escape from the general, but there would surely be an opportunity. They would have to stop along the road; they couldn't journey all night without at least changing the horses. And they would need to rest and refresh themselves. There would be other people around. Maybe she could throw herself on someone's mercy. All was not lost yet.

She tucked the general's incriminating letter into the pocket of her pelisse, put her own letter on the dresser, where her mother or Matty would be sure to see it when they came in later to see if she was well enough to come down for dinner, then slipped quietly into the corridor outside her chamber. The house was very quiet. Mama was usually resting on her bed at this hour, before beginning her evening toilette. Her father would be dozing by the fire in the library, resting from the day's business. The kitchen was the only busy part of the house until the maids began to light the lamps, draw the curtains, make up the fires. Praying that Morrison was in his butler's pantry at this hour and not watching over the hall, she crept down the stairs on tiptoe, darted across the empty expanse of parquet, fumbled the door open, and stepped outside into the cold afternoon, closing the door softly behind her.

It was only half past three, but she had wanted to leave a few minutes in hand in case she was held up. She half ran up the street towards Berkeley Square, anxious to get out of sight of the house. She rounded the corner. There was no sign as yet of the promised coach. She crossed the road and let herself into the square garden through the gate in the railings. No one would remark her in there. She had made one circuit of the garden when a closed carriage lumbered into the square and came to a halt against the railings opposite Bruton Street. She left the garden and approached the carriage, her heart thudding, a nut of nausea in her throat. Two men were on the box, a coachman and a man carrying a blunderbuss across his knees. A postilion rode the nearside leader. As she reached the vehicle the door swung open.

"You are punctual, my dear. I like that in a wife." The general reached out a hand to help her inside. "Sit down, now, make yourself comfortable. We have a long journey ahead of us."

Abigail huddled into a corner as far from her tormentor as she could get. She said nothing, indeed, had sworn to herself that she would not speak one word to him, however long the journey took.

Heyward sat back against the squabs, regarding her though narrowed eyes. She was a pretty enough child, he supposed, but insipid and naïve. He felt no desire for her at all, not at all the way he had felt with his late wife. Ah, Serena's mother had been a real beauty, promising a sensuality that, to his dismay, he had eventually realized she didn't really possess. But in the early days, he'd been wild for her . . . couldn't get enough of her. It had paled, of course, as it always did. But this one was merely a means to an end. Once the marriage was consummated, he would have no interest in her body at all.

It grew dark as they passed out of the town and crossed Hampstead Heath. Abigail tried to close her eyes, to let the rhythm of the carriage lull her to sleep, but the road was too bumpy, and her mind was too busy, planning and discarding schemes for escape. How soon before they made the first change? It would be her first opportunity, and if it was still relatively close to London, so much the better. But she refused to ask.

The general seemed content to leave her with her silence. He took frequent pulls from a silver flask he kept in the pocket of his great coat and closed his eyes once or twice, but whenever she shifted in her seat, those eyes would open, and their gaze would be as sharp as ever.

They were traveling in near-complete darkness as

they left a little village and began to climb a hill. Abigail sat up to lift aside the leather curtain at the window, wondering if she could see anything that would help her identify where they were. It wasn't quite as dark as she'd feared. A half-moon swung in and out of light cloud cover, and every once in a while, the clouds would part to reveal a star-studded sky. The general took another swallow from his flask.

"Are you hungry, my dear?"

The sound of his voice made her skin crawl. She wondered whether if she said she was hungry, they would stop sooner. But she still was not ready to speak.

"If you are, you'll find a hamper beneath the seat," he said. "I do not intend to stop for food until we are well on our way to the Border."

So they were going to Gretna Green. Maybe there was something useful in the hamper. Abigail leaned down and pulled out the wicker container. She set it on the seat beside her and lifted the lid. There was a paring knife. Small, certainly, but it could inflict some damage. If he fell asleep properly, perhaps . . .

She took out a meat pie and retreated into her corner with it. There was no point starving herself. She held the curtain aside with one hand so that she could see outside; it gave her some sense of comfort.

The coach jolted over the top of the hill and picked up speed as the track straightened out. Through the window, Abigail could make out the shapes of bushes and tree branches waving in the sharpening evening breeze but no sign of habitation.

She had just finished her pie when a single shot was fired, followed almost immediately by the massive report of a blunderbuss. The horses reared, the carriage swayed, and for a moment, she thought it would overturn, but it righted itself as a voice said, "Look to your horses, man, before they get tangled in the traces."

The general was leaning out of the far window. "What the devil's going on?"

Swift as a flash, Abigail had tucked the paring knife into her sleeve. She sat forward on the bench.

The door on the general's side was opened, and a masked man stood with one foot on the step, a pistol in his hand. He regarded the passengers. Abigail knew those blue eyes, and they were sending her a clear message of reassurance. "Would you step down, sir?"

The general's hand went to his pocket, and in almost the same movement, the pistol was pressing into his throat, its owner leaning into the carriage, his eyes filled with loathing.

"I will fire this, make no mistake, sir."

Abigail watched, mesmerized. General Heyward seemed to shrink into himself, becoming a fraction of his size. Another figure appeared behind Sebastian, another pair of the same startling blue eyes, and for a moment, she wondered if she was mistaken after all. It wasn't Sebastian Sullivan who'd come to her rescue but someone just like him . . . or, rather, two of them.

"Does our friend require a little assistance?" the other masked man inquired. Even his voice was like Sebastian's, and Abigail belatedly remembered that two of the Sullivan brothers were twins.

"Oh, I think the gentleman will see the wisdom in cooperating," Sebastian said coolly, the pistol still pressed to Heyward's throat. "Ma'am, would you step out of the carriage through the other door?"

The door behind her opened, and she gazed in amazement at another man and then tumbled into his arms, murmuring, "Jonas, you came. 'Tis really you."

"Aye, love, 'tis really me." He cradled her against him. "Has he hurt you?"

She shook her head. "No . . . he hasn't touched me." She stepped away from him, looking around. A slender figure on horseback, masked like the others, held a pistol on the coachman, the guard, and the postilion as they struggled to calm the pitching horses. "Is that . . . ?"

"Lady Serena? Yes," Jonas said with a soft chuckle. "She will return with you to London, and no one will be any the wiser."

"Come now, sir. Which is it to be?" Sebastian spoke harshly. "If I have to shoot you as you sit, then so be it. But I had not thought you a coward."

At that, the general bellowed and lunged forward, grabbing the barrel of the pistol, forcing it to one side. He aimed a blow at Sebastian's chin. Sebastian ducked it neatly, letting Peregrine move in over his head, sending a fist into Heyward's jaw. The general stumbled and half fell from the carriage to land on his knees.

Sebastian stood over him, the pistol pointed. "I would prefer to kill you with my sword. Will you stand up, sir? I cannot shoot a man on the ground."

Heyward pushed himself to his feet. His normally rubicund countenance was gray in the pale moonlight. He brushed at the dust on the full skirts of his coat. "What is this? Who the devil are you?"

Sebastian laughed and cast aside his mask. "I might ask the same of you, sir. How is it that Miss Sutton is alone at night in a carriage with you heading for, I'm guessing, the Scottish Border?"

"Miss Sutton has agreed to be my wife." He spat dust.

"Oh, indeed. But in that case why is an elopement necessary?" Sebastian mused. "I am sure Mr. Sutton would have happily given his daughter's hand to you had she been willing."

"Perhaps General Heyward thought an elopement would be more romantic," Serena chimed in. It was over now. She had no more hostages to fortune, and she could finally show her stepfather every ounce of the contempt in which she held him.

Startled, he spun towards her, where she still sat her horse, guarding the men. *"You."* The one word cracked through the night quiet, filled with hatred.

"Yes, Sir George, me. You will not do to another woman what you did to my mother."

Sebastian had his hand on his sword, but he let Serena have her say. She needed it, and it would bring some healing balm to the wounds of the past. He took off his coat and handed it to Peregrine, who stood waiting.

The general seemed incapable of a response. He looked around the group of masked men and knew that he faced defeat.

"Draw your sword, General." Sebastian's blade flickered, sinuous and sudden in the pale silver light.

"No," Abigail gasped, the word caught in her throat.

"Don't trouble yourself, Abigail." It was Serena who spoke, but her eyes were on the men. "Sebastian is a fine swordsman."

Heyward shrugged out of his coat and let it fall to the ground. He drew his sword. Fair play had not been in his repertoire in his adult memory, but now he had no choice but to rely on his own naked skill. He had no backup plan, no trickery, no sleight of hand. Just the sword in his hand. And he knew he would be outplayed by the younger man.

Sebastian raised his sword in salute, and Heyward did the same, conscious of the throb of the bruise on his jaw. He lunged, too soon, too quickly for accuracy, and Sebastian easily turned the blade aside, dancing back, seeming to taunt the older man, to invite him to further assault.

Serena watched, aware that Peregrine was covering his brother. The general would not be allowed to win this, even if by some miracle he gained the upper hand. It was not exactly honorable, but it struck her as perfectly reasonable to use her stepfather's own tricks against him.

Heyward began to fight in good earnest, but every thrust was parried. Sebastian was playing with him. He had many opportunities for a counterthrust that would end it, and he sidestepped them all, watching as his opponent grew wearier by the minute, dashed the sweat from his brow, stumbled once or twice, and finally stumbled for a third time and gasped, "Finish it, God damn you."

Sebastian shook his head as he lunged, and his sword point cut into Heyward's shoulder. He dropped his point, stepping back as the general let his weapon fall to the ground, his hand pressed to the welling wound. "No, I've no wish for your blood on my head, Heyward. You'll not die of that scratch. See to him, would you, Peregrine?"

He loped over to where Serena still sat her horse. "'Tis done, sweet," he whispered, taking her hand.

She nodded. "And well done. I'll escort Abigail home now."

"I'll clean up here, and we'll meet at home."

"At home," she affirmed.

She dismounted, and for a moment, he held her tightly, before dropping a kiss on her brow. "Be off with you, then." All business again, he called to Jonas. "Help Abigail into the coach, Jonas. Serena will escort her home. We need you to help here."

"Of course." Jonas put his betrothed into the carriage. "I will come to Bruton Street tomorrow, my darling. You will be quite safe now with Lady Serena."

"Quite safe," Serena agreed, climbing into the carriage on the other side. "And while we journey, you had best tell me the whole story so that we may concoct a suitable tale for your parents."

Abigail shook her head vigorously. "No tale," she declared. "Only the truth. I will not keep this from Papa."

"Well, that is your prerogative," Serena said. "And in truth, my dear, I think 'tis the best possible course of action."

Chapter Twenty-two

By the time the carriage drew up outside the house on Bruton Street, Serena was in full possession of the facts.

"My father couldn't possibly have written such a letter," Abigail repeated passionately. "And he couldn't possibly have done those horrible things. But 'tis his writing, and the seal . . ." She shook her head in confusion. "I know 'tis his seal."

Serena reread the incriminating letter before handing it back to Abigail as the postilion opened the carriage door and let down the footstep. "Oh, I know how it was done," she said grimly. "Let us see what your father has to say." She stepped out and waited for Abigail to join her.

Abigail was pale but resolute as she banged the knocker on the front door. It was opened instantly by her father, who was dressed for the outside, a thick cloak around his shoulders. He looked at his daughter in astonishment. "Where have you been, child? I've just returned from Pickering Place to bring you home. Your mother would not countenance you spending the night away. But I was told that you had never arrived there and that Lady Serena had left the house with Jonas Wedgwood in the mid-afternoon. What does this mean?"

He waved the note Abigail had left. "How dare you leave the house without permission? Without even your maid? Your mother is in strong hysterics. As for you, Lady Serena . . ." He turned his attention to his daughter's companion. "What is your part in this? Aiding and abetting clandestine meetings between my daughter and Wedgwood? I had thought better of you."

"That isn't exactly what happened, sir," Serena said swiftly as soon as he paused for breath. "I believe you should listen to Abigail's explanation, Mr. Sutton, but not here . . . in the public hall," she added, conscious of the hidden eyes of servants.

William looked back to his daughter. She was very white, her eyes filled with tears. He turned on his heel and stalked to the library. They followed him, and Serena closed the door firmly.

"Well?" he demanded.

Abigail, in silence, handed him the general's letter to her and its accompanying letter from her father to Howard Barrett.

He looked down at them in his hand. "What *are* these?"

"Read them, Papa," she said in a hoarse whisper. *"Please."*

He frowned, then opened the papers. His expression changed from initial confusion to incandescent fury.

"What the devil . . ." He looked at Serena. "What d'you know of this . . . this *slander*? What's your part in it? You weasel your way into my house, into my family's confidence and affection, to do *this*?"

"No . . . no, Papa, Lady Serena rescued me from the general. She had nothing to do with this," Abigail exclaimed.

Serena shook her head. "Abigail speaks the truth, Mr. Sutton. I admit that I knew Sir George had set his sights on your daughter's fortune, but I was not abetting him, sir. I befriended Abigail in order to protect her from him."

"Why didn't you tell *me*?" he demanded, his fury unabated. "I would have put a stop to him."

Serena bit her lip. "I was overconfident, sir, I admit it. I had thought I could stop Sir George myself. I've forestalled other plans of his, and I thought I could do it this time."

"She saved me, Papa. She and Mr. Sullivan and his brother and Jonas. They held up the carriage, like highwaymen," Abigail said in a rush.

"Good God." William's rage was diminishing. *"Highwaymen?"*

"It seemed the only solution, sir," Serena said, sounding almost apologetic. "There really was no time to waste. We had to stop them before they got too far from London. Once we knew they were heading north . . ." She stopped, seeing comprehension mingled with his lingering wrath.

"Gretna Green." It was not a question.

"But apart from the short time she was alone with the general, and no one but us knows of that, Abigail has been with me, as she said in her note to you. Her reputation is unassailable."

He sighed deeply as his fear-fueled anger finally left him. His eyes were bemused as he looked again at the papers he held. "I did not write this, but 'tis my hand and my seal. How . . . how?" He looked at Serena. "How the *devil* did he manage this?"

"Oh, I can explain that," she said. "The general is a collector . . . a snapper up of unconsidered trifles, as Shakespeare put it. He picks up anything that he thinks might be turned to good use in some future situation."

She picked up Mr. Sutton's seal on the desk. "This, for instance. He collects seals, in particular. A simple imprint of the seal on a piece of wax is enough to make a duplicate. Any time he was in here or even in your study in the house in Brussels, he could have picked it up. If he was alone, so much the better. But if not, then an idle examination, a little sleight of hand, and he had the imprint."

William gazed at her in stupefaction. "And my handwriting?"

She shrugged. "The general is something of an artist when it comes to forgery. If he has a sample of your handwriting . . . and I assume you have sent him occasional communications?"

He nodded in grim silence.

"Then he would have no difficulty in imitating it. Maybe an expert might not be fooled, but experts are not his quarry. Usually, 'tis good enough to fool those he wishes to fool."

William shook his head as if dispelling cobwebs. "And your part in all this thievery and deception?"

"Unwilling," she said simply. "But I have ... I *had* ..." she corrected herself, "nowhere to go, no one to turn to, no resources except my own wits. I needed those to save myself." It was a simple but bitter statement of the truth, and William heard it as such.

"Where is the general now? He must be brought to justice."

Abigail spoke up for the first time. "Oh, Mr. Sullivan forced him to fight a duel on the Common, and he wounded him in the shoulder, Papa." She glanced a little shyly at Serena. "But I don't think he did so for my sake."

Serena smiled a little. "You don't do yourself enough credit, Abigail, but 'tis true that Mr. Sullivan ... my husband ... was exacting payment for more than the insult done you."

"Oh, wonderful. I knew it would happen," Abigail cried, clapping her hands in delight. "I knew you were made for each other all along. Have you been secretly married for months and months?"

"Not exactly," Serena responded.

"Well, you are to congratulated, Lady Serena," William said drily. "I assume that means that your stepfather no longer has any hold on you."

She nodded and said softly, "Yes, that's exactly what it means, sir."

"Well, what's to be done about him?" William asked. "If he's as slippery as you say, he'll find another victim soon enough."

"Not if he ends up in debtors' prison," she said quietly.

William's glance was sharply attentive. "How d'you mean?"

"The Earl of Burford holds the mortgages on Pickering Place. If he could be persuaded to call them in . . ." The plan lay clear in front of her, beautifully symmetrical and gloriously apposite. "No, better still. If he could be persuaded to sell them to you, sir, then you could call them in. If you act quickly, while the general is still laid up with his wounded shoulder, I'll wager odds every creditor he has will come out of the woodwork once he is dispossessed. An extended stay in the Marshalsea or the Fleet would be a fine vengeance, don't you think?"

William considered, and a slow smile spread across his countenance. "You are a devious woman, Lady Serena. But I own there is indeed a most satisfying correlation between crime and punishment. I shall visit Burford first thing in—"

A loud hammering on the front door interrupted him. "What the devil is it now?" He took a step to the library door when it was flung open. Sebastian stood on the threshold, his cheeks pink with the cold, his eyes glittering with purpose.

"I have come for my wife," he declared without preamble. "You were not at home, Serena."

"Mr. Sullivan, come in, come in." William extended his hands to the visitor. "Indeed, sir, I owe you a debt of gratitude that I cannot know how to repay."

"Not now, sir," Sebastian said firmly. "I am come for my wife. 'Tis past time she stopped looking after the interests of others and started giving her husband some time. Come, Serena." He reached for her hand and pulled her smartly towards him. "I am tired of not finding you where you belong."

"*Sebastian,*" Serena exclaimed as he pulled her to the door so fast her feet skipped across the carpet. " 'Tis discourteous not to make our farewells."

"Courtesy may go to the devil." He marched with her to the door. His horse stood at the railing outside, and without hesitation, he lifted Serena onto the saddle and mounted behind her. His arm went around her, holding her warmly against him. He nudged his horse into a brisk trot to Stratton Street.

Serena offered no further protest; indeed, she had none to make.

Outside the house, he lifted her down and hurried her into the house, calling for Bart to take his horse to the mews. The lad scampered out of the house, pulling on his jerkin. There was sudden quiet in the house.

Sebastian turned Serena slowly towards him, his blue gaze intent. He pushed up her chin with his gloved hand and spoke with soft determination, "'Tis over now, my love. Trust me. From now on, we are all and everything to each other. The bad times are finished. I am your sword and your shield."

Tears pricked, and Serena blinked hard. She caressed his cheek as she so loved to do. "I don't have much of a fencing arm, but I shoot straight."

He smiled, wiping the teardrop from her cheek with his fingertip. "All and everything to each other."

She nodded. "All and everything to each other."

Epilogue

The two young women sat on the wide window seat, their heads together as they spoke in low voices in the salon of Blackwater House on Upper Brook Street. When the door opened suddenly, they both looked up, two pairs of eyes turning to the door, one a deep purple, the other a soft jade, two heads, one titian, one black as a raven's wing.

"You didn't sit long over the port," Lady Blackwater observed with a smile.

"Sebastian was too anxious to get back to his bride," Jasper responded.

"That is certainly true, Clarissa." Sebastian looked for a long moment at his wife, relishing once again the words that set the fact in concrete. "But besides that, 'tis time we left to pay our duty visit to Uncle Bradley. He has yet to meet my wife."

"He's met faro's daughter before, however." Serena's tone was matter-of-fact, but the look she gave her husband was anything but. "He didn't frighten me then; he's not going to frighten me now."

"I still don't envy you the interview," Clarissa said with a shudder. "He's the most loathsome individual. I've never come across anyone as malicious as the viscount. He really seems to enjoy other people's discomfort."

"I'll come with you if you like," Peregrine offered. "A little leavening can do no harm."

"By all means," Sebastian agreed cordially. "I'll lay odds Serena's more than a match for the old reprobate, but there's always safety in numbers."

"Are you going, too, Jasper?"

The Earl of Blackwater considered his wife's question. "On the one hand, a united front and superiority in numbers might dilute the malevolence, but on the other, I have no desire to leave you for the evening, my love."

"I shall be perfectly content in the knowledge that I don't have to endure another moment in the viscount's company," Clarissa declared crisply. "Go with them, Jasper, and then you can come home and tell me how Serena beat the old man at his own game." She gave Serena a quick complicit smile.

Serena chuckled and got up from the window seat. "I'll bear in mind the need to provide you with some amusement, Clarissa."

"I'll send to the stables for the carriage. We might as well arrive in style." Jasper went out into the hall to give Crofton the instruction, and half an hour later, Serena and the three Sullivan brothers were ensconced in the traveling carriage, swaying through the London streets to Viscount Bradley's mansion on the Strand.

"So where's your stepfather now?" Jasper inquired. "I heard he lost the house in Pickering Place."

Serena nodded. Her plan had been successful down to the last iota. William Sutton had cheerfully bought the mortgages from the Earl of Burford for considerably more than they were worth. He'd called in the debt, had the general evicted, and just as she'd predicted, Sir George's creditors had swarmed over him. He had had no time for his usual midnight flit, and William, ably supported by the army of creditors, had had General Heyward committed to the Marshalsea for debt.

"As far as I know, the general is still housed in the Marshalsea."

"And likely to remain so for the foreseeable future," Sebastian put in with his own note of satisfaction. "Unless he can pay his debts, and that's notoriously difficult to do from the depths of debtors' prison. I doubt he'll see the light of day again."

"For which I am profoundly thankful," Serena said. "And Pickering Place is for sale to anyone who can come up with the price . . . Oh, are we here?" The carriage slowed to a stop.

Jasper looked out. "Yes, we're here. Let's hope the old man's in the mood for visitors." He swung open the door and stepped down, offering his hand to Serena. "Ma'am . . ."

"Thank you, my lord." She stepped down beside him. The formality was in jest. In the time since her marriage to their brother, Jasper and Peregrine had embraced Serena as one of their own, and as Sebastian had predicted, she and Clarissa had become fast friends, sharing, as they did, the bond of love for the men of the Blackwater family.

The viscount's factotum opened the door for them, giving Serena only a cursory glance. "My lord, gentlemen, madam . . . I will see if his lordship is receiving this evening. Would you care to wait in the antechamber?"

"As you wish, Louis." Jasper gestured to his companions, and they followed Louis's unhurried step upstairs.

"Who shall I say accompanies you, my lord?"

"Lady Serena Sullivan," Jasper replied placidly.

"My wife, Louis," Sebastian informed the man, just in case he'd missed the point.

Louis merely nodded, as if nothing could surprise him, and went through a pair of doors into the adjacent chamber.

Serena looked curiously around the anteroom. It was rather like a museum, she thought. Dark, ornate, filled with objets d'art that on a second glance revealed some very interesting quirks. "Eroticism?" she inquired a touch caustically.

"Oh, you don't know the half of it," Sebastian said. "Just be thankful he's unlikely now to show you his memoirs."

"Why unlikely *now*?" She peered at a statue of copulating nymphs.

Sebastian exchanged glances with his brothers. "I expect he'll come to the conclusion that they won't have the desired effect on you," he explained carefully. "Before our marriage, they might have done. Now there would be no satisfaction for him in your reaction."

"Later, you're going to have to explain that to me more fully," Serena said.

Louis came back to the antechamber. "His lordship will see you all for a few minutes, gentlemen."

They entered the bedchamber, Jasper in front. Despite the midwinter cold, it was overly hot, the fire in the grate burning fiercely, the window curtains drawn tight. The viscount sat in his armchair by the fire, wrapped in a fur robe, a fur lap robe across his knees, his feet on an ottoman. A glass of brandy was at his elbow. The black-clad figure of his amanuensis, Father Cosgrove, hovered in the shadows behind the armchair.

"Well, well. This is an unexpected pleasure. All three of my nephews, and Lady Serena to sweeten the pudding." The viscount sat up a little straighter as he raised his quizzing glass to examine his visitors. "So, nephew, this is the whore you've taken to wife, is it?"

"Lady Serena Carmichael did me the great honor of becoming my wife, sir," Sebastian said evenly.

"Great honor . . . don't give me that nonsense, boy." The viscount turned his glass on Serena. "She always did clean up well, I'll say that for her. How is she, then, Sullivan? Worth the price in bed? I always did wonder if I should have fought Burford for her."

Serena silenced Sebastian with a quick hand gesture before sweeping an elaborate curtsy. "You do me too much honor, sir. Did you really consider I was worth fighting for?"

He regarded her through suddenly narrowed eyes. "Were you?"

She shook her head. "I have never considered myself to be the spoils of victory, my lord. It required more than swordsmanship or a fat purse to win me. Your nephew had the right currency. Something I doubt you would ever even consider." Her tongue was tipped with poison, her voice hard. She felt as if with every word, she was demolishing her stepfather's memory and the memory of every degradation he had forced on her and on her mother.

Lord Bradley dropped his quizzing glass and turned his gaze on Sebastian. "So you consider you've satisfied the terms of the will with this travesty of a marriage?"

"Sir, as Serena has just reminded you, you considered my wife to be a whore, to be bought if you so chose. She is now Lady Serena, wife of the Honorable Sebastian Sullivan. No longer for sale. I do not see how those facts do not satisfy the terms of the will."

"Neither, my lord, do I," Jasper declared.

The viscount pursed his lips and then with a shrug let the issue go by default, as he knew he must. He had been outplayed somehow. But the raw facts were in his nephews' favor. Instead, he turned his attention to Peregrine, who stood a little back from the fireside. "And what about you, boy? There'll be no inheritance for any of you until you satisfy the terms."

Peregrine sketched a bow. "Oh, I believe I will do that, sir." His tone was nonchalant, but his blue eyes were clear and sharp. "If you can prolong your existence until you've finished your memoir, I do believe I will present you with *my* reclaimed soul in good time."

Jasper exchanged a glance with Sebastian, who pursed his lips in a soundless whistle. It was the first either of them had heard of a possible candidate, but when Peregrine dropped hints, they were to be taken seriously.

The viscount dismissed them with an irritable wave. "I have a mind to die before morning," he declared. "Cosgrove, you black crow, I'll write my own obituary now."

The priest went to the secretaire and sharpened his quill. "Whenever you're ready, my lord."

The four visitors took their leave without further courtesies, and the viscount, suddenly impatient, snapped, "Get out, Cosgrove. I don't need you."

The priest bowed and slipped silently from the room. The viscount stared into the fire, nursing his brandy goblet. There was a faraway look in his eyes as he thought back to the time when he, too, had had his life ahead of him, when he believed he could choose his own path, love whomever he pleased. Just as his nephews believed now. Those two young women they'd married . . . what were they, really? He had wanted vengeance for his own ruined life, but looking at Jasper and Sebastian, he could see only their happiness in their wives. And the women themselves, hopelessly in love, the pair of them. It would seem, as he tried to avenge himself upon the puritanical family that had so cruelly destroyed his own young love, that he had merely enabled his nephews to find for themselves their own love matches. Love matches that his fortune would support. Always assuming Peregrine came up to scratch before the Grim Reaper came for his uncle.

Viscount Bradley's thin lips curved in an ironic smile. He had learned long since the tricks that life could play upon the best-laid plans.

The carriage took Sebastian, Serena, and Peregrine to Stratton Street before returning Jasper to his wife. Peregrine turned into the parlor. "A nightcap?"

Serena shook her head and started up the stairs. "Not for me, thank you. Good night, Perry."

"Not for me, either." Sebastian moved to follow her.

"I'll bid you both good night, then." Peregrine went into the parlor, closing the door behind him.

There was an awkwardness in the living arrangement now, and once Sebastian and Serena reached their own bedchamber, Sebastian drew Serena close against him. "Thank God that's over."

"Yes," she agreed. "And for Perry's sake as much as my own, could we please go and find the sunshine?"

"Rome? Venice? Where would you like to go?"

She hesitated. "Venice . . . but first, I'd like to go back to Scotland, to the lake where we sailed close to my home."

He looked at her quizzically. "The Scottish Highlands in the middle of winter, love? I thought you wanted the sun."

"Yes, I do. But . . . but I need to find myself again first. I need to be who I was before the general came and took it all away." She touched his mouth with the tip of her little finger. "Before I can become . . . properly become . . . who I am now, I must find that part of me again. 'Tis the only way to lose the bad part. Do you understand, my love?"

"Oh, yes, my sweet, I understand." Sebastian held her tightly. "But you must also know that I love all that you have been and all that you are and all that you will be. I embrace *you*, my Serena, my love, for everything that you are." His kiss stopped her mouth, but her body gave him all the affirmation he needed.

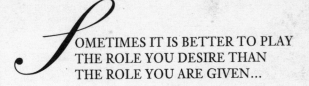
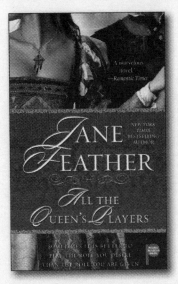

Fantasy.
Temptation.
Adventure.

Visit PocketAfterDark.com, an all-new website just for Urban Fantasy and Romance Readers!

- Exclusive access to the hottest urban fantasy and romance titles!

- Read and share reviews on the latest books!

- Live chats with your favorite romance authors!

- Vote in online polls!

www.PocketAfterDark.com

26119